MOUNTAIN VIEW
PUBLIC LIBRARY
Mountain View, CA

TOR BOOKS BY STEVEN GOULD

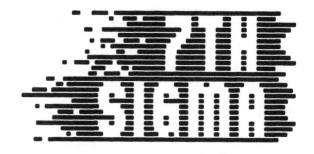

7TH SIGMA

steven gould

TOR®

A TOM DOHERTY ASSOCIATES BOOK
NEW YORK

This is a work of fiction. All of the characters, organizations, and events portrayed in this novel are either products of the author's imagination or are used fictitiously.

7TH SIGMA

Copyright © 2011 by Steven Gould

All rights reserved.

A Tor Book
Published by Tom Doherty Associates, LLC
175 Fifth Avenue
New York, NY 10010

www.tor-forge.com

Tor® is a registered trademark of Tom Doherty Associates, LLC.

Library of Congress Cataloging-in-Publication Data

Gould, Steven.
    7th sigma / Steven Gould.—1st ed.
       p. cm.
    "A Tom Doherty Associates book."
    ISBN   978-0-7653-7500-1
    1. Disasters—Fiction.   2. Survival skills—Fiction.
I. Title.   II. Title: Seventh sigma.
    PS3557.O8947A615 2011
    813'.54—dc22

                                      2011011566

It is the hardest thing in the world to frighten a mongoose, because he is eaten up from nose to tail with curiosity. The motto of all the mongoose family is "Run and find out"; and Rikki-tikki was a true mongoose.

—RUDYARD KIPLING, *The Jungle Book,*
Volume II, "Rikki-tikki-tavi"

In statistics, Sigma levels denote where a sample falls on the graph of Normal Distribution.

A Sigma level of one means an event will occur over 2/3 of the time.

A 6th Sigma is equivalent to 3.4 occurrences in one million (34 in ten million): 99.99966% odds against.

A 7th Sigma is equivalent to 1.9 occurrences in a hundred million (19 in a billion): 99.9999981% odds against.

He stopped; for there shuffled round the corner, from the roaring Motee Bazar, such a man as Kim, who thought he knew all castes, had never seen. He was nearly six feet high, dressed in fold upon fold of dingy stuff like horse-blanketing, and not one fold of it could Kim refer to any known trade or profession. At his belt hung a long open-work iron pencase and a wooden rosary such as holy men wear. On his head was a gigantic sort of tam-o'-shanter. His face was yellow and wrinkled, like that of Fook Shing, the Chinese bootmaker in the bazar. His eyes turned up at the corners and looked like little slits of onyx.

—RUDYARD KIPLING, *Kim*, Chapter 1

*when the student is ready,
a teacher will come*

High atop the Exodus Memorial in the plaza of Nuevo Santa Fe, Kimble paced back and forth, his hand raised to strike down the impudent. The Memorial had nothing to do with the early events of Judeo-Christian tradition, but there *were* several scriptural references on the ceramic tiles inset in the thick adobe wall, and young Orvel, whose father was the local LDS bishop, and young Martin, whose eldest brother was a deacon at the Church of Christ the Rock, argued from below that these affiliations entitled them to the place occupied by Kimble, an avowed apostate and *frequent* blasphemer. Alas, neither their spiritual superiority nor their physical efforts had dislodged the smaller boy from his perch.

"Let me *up*!" yelled Martin.

Kimble smiled kindly down at him. "Never while I breathe."

Martin stepped back to the side where Orvel was trying to form an alliance with César, an altar boy at *Nuestra Señora de Guadalupe*. César was bigger than any of them and might have turned the tide against Kimble, but César was having none of it. There was historical animosity. If Orvel and Martin had not previously sided against César in the affair of Mr. Romero's broken shop window (and borne false witness at that), César might have been more receptive to their appeal to Christian solidarity.

Rebuffed, Martin and Orvel steeled themselves for another attempt on the monument, a two-front assault from opposite ends of the wall. Unfortunately for them, Kimble was monkey quick, and a sudden flick of his hand toward Orvel's face sent that worthy sprawling in time for Kimble to turn and meet young Martin, pudgy and less fit, before he achieved the summit. A mild blow on Martin's grasping fingers sent him down into the dust of the plaza.

Their injuries were slight, but César's mocking laughter was like salt in a cut.

The Territorial Administrative Complex and the Territorial Rangers headquarters bordered the great square on two sides. The Commercial Galleria, a series of businesses clumped together around the main heliograph office, occupied the third side, and the fourth side held the sprawled booths of the city market, open every day but Sunday. Now, shortly after the end of siesta, people strolled the plaza and shopped.

As Kimble watched, a woman wearing goatskin boots, wide-bottomed gaucho pants, and a cotton smock walked out of the market and into the square. She was pulling a travois, a modern one, glass composite poles with a small wheel where they came together. A strap running between the two handles crossed her shoulders and helped support the modest, tarp-covered load. Though her short dark hair was peppered with gray, her face seemed young, or at least unlined.

"Gentlemen," she said, apparently addressing all four of them. "Would one of you be so kind as to tell me where the Land Registrar is?"

Orvel, still on his bottom in the dust of the square, didn't know, and he was mortified, convinced the woman had seen his ignominious descent. Martin, following his church's creed, was unwilling to talk to a woman not of his family. César didn't know but he said politely, "I would be glad to ask inside, ma'am."

"No need," said Kimble. "I know." He dropped lightly off the monument and rolled to absorb the impact, rising smoothly to his feet. He jerked his chin toward the fiberglass awnings of the Galleria. "If you'll walk this way?"

She fell into step with him, the trailing wheel of her travois squeaking slightly as it turned. "I would've thought it would be over there," she said, jerking her chin at the Administrative Complex.

Now that he was closer he could see that fine lines radiated from the corners of her eyes and her mouth. Not young, then, though not as old as the market manager, a veritable raisin of a man. " 'Twas. Both the Land

Office and the Census Department needed more records space. Census stayed and Land Office moved into an annex earlier this year."

"You know a lot about it. Does your mom work there? Or your dad?"

He shrugged. It was not his place, he felt, to inform against himself. The less said the better. He found that people filled in the gaps all by themselves with details that felt right to them. It wasn't his fault if they made assumptions. "I run errands. Sometimes it's messages. Sometimes it's guiding people to where they need to go." He waited for her next question but it was nothing like he expected.

"Where did you learn to roll like that?"

He blinked and looked sideways at her from the corner of his eye. "Pardon?"

"When you jumped off the monument. The forward roll."

Kimble opened his mouth to answer, but then shrugged again.

She sniffed. "As you like."

They entered one of the arched passageways back into the Galleria, past Bolton & Cable, specialty printers (ceramic type, of course); past Duran, importer of ready-made clothing and the hard plastic needles that fetched high prices over in the market; past the law firm of Mc-Kensie, Duncan and Lattimore, specialists in Native American, territorial, and immigration law. "Up there," said Kimble, pointing up a narrow stair to the second story and the sigil of the territorial government, the old

Zia of New Mexico rising above the Star on the Horizon of the old Arizona Flag.

The woman eyed the two flights and the tight landing and looked at her travois.

"I can watch it," Kimble offered.

She gave him a look, which made him add, "Really. No harm will come to it and it will be right here."

Again she considered him. "What payment would you want?"

He raised both hands palm up. "You decide." He smiled ingenuously. "No doubt you'll want to take into consideration how long I have to wait."

The woman snorted. "Your name?"

"Kimble."

"Is that your first name or last?"

He bowed as a player, one hand on his heart, "Yes."

She raised her eyebrows and then nodded. "I'm Ruth Monroe. See you in a bit, Kimble."

Her business took long enough to close the office—the great ceramic bell atop the Territorial Admin Complex had rung eight different quarters of the hour when, watching from below, Kimble saw one of the clerks escort Ruth to the landing outside the office. The clerk shook her hand and then took down the OPEN sign before vanishing back into the interior. As Ruth came down the stairs, perusing a piece of paper, Kimble heard the doors being barred from within.

"Well, Mr. Kimble, I am hungry. Can you recommend a reasonable eatery? I'm going south, toward the Rio Puerco, but I'd like to eat before I leave town."

Kimble's stomach rumbled at the thought, audible, almost echoing in the passageway.

"A meal for both of us," Ruth amended.

"There's Griegos—it's a taqueria by the south gate. The *cabrito* . . . this is a good time to go. Early enough—they run out."

They ate the goat tacos (whole-wheat tortillas, black beans, red onions, and *pico de gallo*) in the alley beside the taqueria, where Ruth could watch her travois. They were not alone. The alley had several diners as well as a few hopeful dogs. Ruth and Kimble were among the first, but as the alley filled, Ruth shifted the travois so that it leaned against the wall, handles down, wheel up, to clear more space. An older teen, not eating, took the opportunity to grab a spot by the wall on the other side of the travois from them.

A Jicarilla Apache couple sat against the opposite wall with their burritos. The woman was wearing a traditional deerskin dress with beaded trim. The man wore jeans converted for the territory—all metal removed. The rivets had been pulled and replaced with over-sewing and the zipper fly was now Velcro. His moccasins had thick rawhide soles and buckskin uppers.

The woman gestured at the travois. "I like your outfit," she said. "The wheel is a good notion."

"Thank you. It's worked pretty well as long as I grease it regularly."

"How far have you come with it?"

"I entered the territory at Needles."

The man seemed impressed. "That's almost five hundred miles. Walking the whole way?"

Ruth nodded. "Five weeks. Walk six days, rest one. I averaged fifteen miles a day."

"Any trouble?"

"What do you mean?"

"Bugs. Grass fires. Weather. *Ladrones.*"

Ruth glanced sideways at Kimble and he translated, "Thieves, bandits."

Ruth shrugged. "I'd been briefed on the bugs—I was careful. And it wasn't too dry—saw one grass fire far to the south. Wind was bad for a few days but fortunately it was at my back. I did have some trouble with la-*ladrones?* West of Montezuma Well. Two men wanted to take my outfit and, from what they said, rape me."

The woman's eyes grew large. "What happened?"

Ruth pursed her lips. "They decided not to." And then she surged to her feet and was standing over the teen who'd sat next to her travois. "They were clearly smarter than *you.*"

The teen looked up at her, eyes wide. "What?"

Ruth pointed at the lashing on her tarp. "You cut it. I saw the cord jerk when the tension released."

The boy gathered his feet underneath him. "I never touched your stupid rope."

Kimble watched with interest. If the boy had cut the cord what had he used? Was it still in his ha—

The boy slashed upward with a chunk of obsidian as he rose. Perhaps he meant to scare Ruth, to make her recoil, so he could bolt, but it didn't work out that way. Suddenly he was face down in the hard, baked dirt of the alley, his arm pinned to the ground by an absurdly small hand. The teen tried to move and yelped in considerable discomfort. Kimble saw Ruth's free hand take the back of the teen's hand and bend it, fingers toward the elbow. The teen's fingers spasmed, releasing the obsidian flake. Ruth released the hand but kept all her weight on the elbow.

Kimble was impressed. "Nice *ikkyo*!"

Ruth, without taking her weight off the teen's arm, looked at Kimble. "I *knew* you learned that roll in a dojo." She took up the flake of obsidian. The teen began to struggle again and she held the flake against his ear. "Feel that?" she asked.

The teen froze.

"I could just cut off your ear." She moved it down to his neck. "Or, since you attacked me with a lethal weapon, I'm sure the Rangers would understand a lethal response."

His voice, previously deep, broke, now high pitched. "I just needed some food, for my mother and sisters!"

"Kimble, check his pockets."

Kimble found a small roll of dollars and a handful of plastic territorial coins in the teen's pants and showed them to Ruth.

"Try another," she said to the facedown boy.

The teen didn't respond.

Ruth looked up. "Where would we find a policeman? It's not like we don't have witnesses."

The Jicarilla Apache had started to rise when the boy

surged up, but now he was back against the wall since he saw Ruth had things well in hand. He said, "There were Rangers at the city gate when we came in."

Kimble winced. The gate was only two hundred feet away. Conviction on charges of theft and assault could get the boy a trip outside where, at the very least, he'd be tagged, then jail time or community service. But it was the tag, a surgically implanted LoJack, that would keep him out of the territory. Not just because he could be tracked, but because the bugs would go for the EMF and metal like the chewy nougat center in a candy bar.

The teen spoke then. "No! All right, I did it! Take my money, just don't call the Rangers, I'm already on probation!"

The Apache woman said, "Maybe break his arm, too. The taking arm—his right." She said it seriously, but Kimble thought she didn't really mean it. The corners of her eyes were crinkling.

Kimble offered the money to Ruth but she said, "Just the coins. To replace the rope. Put the dollars back."

"What? He came at you with a blade!"

Ruth turned her gaze on Kimble.

"All right, all right." Kimble shoved the roll back in the teen's pocket. When he'd moved back, Ruth folded the teen's arm across his back and then leaned on it as she stood, keeping him pinned until she was all the way to her feet. She took a sliding step back, releasing him. He got up slowly, rubbing his arm.

Ruth held up the obsidian flake and said, "I'm also keeping this."

The teen turned suddenly and walked out of the alley, his steps quickening as he reached the open street. He took a sharp right, away from the city gate, and was gone.

A growling tussle broke out at Ruth's feet as two of the stray dogs fought over something.

"Crap," said Ruth. "I dropped my taco."

Kimble shook the coins together between his cupped hands.

"You can afford another."

"I'd like to talk to your parents," Ruth said.

She'd replaced and eaten her taco, knotted the cut rope, and now they were standing near the south gate.

Kimble's mouth went still. He could've told her one of the many fabrications he used on occasions like this, but he was reluctant. *My parents are working. They are out of town until next week. My father is on assignment with the Rangers. I'm only visiting today. We live near Grants.*

Ruth seemed to sense this. "I'm not going to inform on you. Runaway?"

He held out his hand and rocked it side to side. "My mother died when I was little. My father had heart trouble, uneven heartbeats, last year. He had to have a pacemaker—so he can't live in the territory."

"He left you here?"

"They airlifted him out. I was supposed to take a caravan north and join him in Denver."

"What happened?"

"I sold the travel voucher to someone who *wanted* to go."

She sat still, regarding him without speaking.

Finally, Kimble gave in. "My dad . . . he's not a nice man. Maybe when my mom was alive but not so much after. I hardly stayed at home when he *was* in the territory, not if I could help it. Not if he'd been working."

"Working?"

"If he worked he could afford liquor. When he wasn't drinking he was just grumpy. When he was—better not to be home."

"Where do you live now? The same place?"

"No. We lived in Golondrinas, but the Rangers there knew me too well. I joined a sheep drive here—dishwasher and orphan lamb care. I'm a useful citizen here."

"Yes," she said. "A guide."

"*And* messenger."

"But where do you live?"

"It depends on the season." He had a bedroll hidden in a roof garden near Eastgate. Everything else he owned was on his person. "In the winter there are shelters, but they preach at you something fierce."

"I would still think the authorities are looking for you. I mean, your father must've noticed when you didn't show up."

"Well, they're looking for Kim Creighton. I'm Kimble. The picture they have is three years old and I was so much pudgier then. I've been asked, you know, if I've seen myself around."

Ruth smiled briefly. "And had you?"

"Oh, yes. Traveling with a caravan headed into old Arizona. I was positive I'd seen the boy."

She swung her arm, backhanded, toward his face. There was no warning and, he thought, no reason, but she didn't connect. He moved his head back out of the way and took a back roll.

"Hey!" Kimble said, rising to his feet and eyeing her warily.

She smiled at him.

"Tell me about the dojo."

"Ohhhhhhh," he said, in a quiet voice. He squatted on his heels, still out of arm's reach. "That was back in Golondrinas. The kids' class was free if you did dojo chores. They taught karate and judo and aikido."

"The same teacher?"

"Oh, no. It was a cooperative. There were four different styles of karate. There were two judo instructors, but just one old guy who taught aikido."

"Old guy?" She stared at him. "Which classes did you take?"

"Aikido, of course."

"Of course? Is that what all the kids took?"

Kimble shook his head. "Oh, no. If they were the wrestling type, they liked judo. Otherwise, they all wanted to take karate. Punch, kick, punch, kick, and more kicking."

"So . . . why aikido?"

"They were the kids who weren't that interested in kicking and punching." Kimble looked down at the dirt. "I got enough of that at home. Besides, once I got the hang of getting off the line, aikido worked pretty well against the kickers and punchers."

Ruth was silent for a moment, then said. "I am building a dojo on the Rio Puerco."

"Oh. Really? You teach aikido?"

"For over twenty years now."

He raised his eyebrows. "So you already had a dojo. Why did you leave?"

She sighed. "Divorce. You know what that is?"

Kimble glared at her.

"Sorry, of course you do. My ex-husband and his new wife kept the dojo. I left. I left . . . everything. I'm starting over."

Kimble narrowed his eyes. She looked back at him, very still, like a rock, like a predator, like a statue.

"You'll need students," Kimble finally said. "You can't be a teacher without students. I mean, at least *one*."

She nodded. "Get your things."

"Yes, Ms. Monroe."

"Sensei," she said gently.

"Yes, Sensei."

walking to cold dog

"What should I do, Sensei?"

Ruth dropped the handles of the travois and said, "Ah, that is always the question, isn't it?"

It was their second day on the road, and they'd walked twenty miles since dawn. For Ruth, who'd walked 500 miles in the last six weeks, it was just another longish day, but Kimble's feet, his legs, his entire body hurt. Ruth had chosen a cluster of cottonwoods on the barest rivulet of a stream to camp.

"I could gather firewood."

"I'll bet you could."

"Sensei, just *tell* me!"

Ruth smiled. "Ah, I'm too lazy for that."

Kimble frowned, tired, cranky, and confused. "Right, then. I'll just go get some firewood."

When he returned with a respectable bundle of

deadfall branches, Ruth was setting up her foam-ceramic stove. The collapsible bucket was sitting beside the travois, empty.

Kimble looked at the bucket and then at Ruth. "Uh, Sensei, should I—"

She looked at him and raised her eyebrows.

"Never mind, Sensei." He took the bucket to the streamlet, finding a place where the water ran across a rock and dropped down a foot. He propped the bucket there, letting it fill slowly. When he brought the filled bucket back, she thanked him politely.

That night, before bed, she said, "The trouble with telling someone to do this and to do that is that once you've issued orders on that subject, they'll always expect you to do so. They lose initiative and you end up doing the thinking for two." She paused. When he did not say anything, she added, "If you do not understand, I will explain further."

He shook his head in the dark. "I understand, Sensei."

"Good. Now go brush your teeth."

He snorted, "But you just said—"

"Yes. What's the last thing I 'told' you?"

It had been the night before, their first on the road. "Don't drink water that hasn't been boiled, treated, or filtered. Not if you can help it. Not unless you're dying of thirst."

"Good. Now go brush your teeth."

In the middle of the morning it was Kimble who issued an order: "Down, Sensei!" He grabbed the wheel of the travois and jumped to the slight ditch on the high side of the road, where it tucked into the hillside, and crouched.

Ruth pulled the handles over and joined him, swiveling her head around, looking for the danger. "What are we—"

The first bug zoomed up the road, then another, and Ruth pulled herself into a ball beside the travois. Then they heard the yelling and pounding feet, and even more bugs buzzed through the air, about three feet off the ground. A figure rounded the bend, a man, and he was yelling, "Get it off! Get it off!" He was reaching behind him, one arm high, one arm low, trying to reach something on his back.

"Grab him!" Kimble said, issuing his second order.

Ruth snagged the man's feet, tripping him, and he slammed down hard. His yelling stopped as the breath left him. Kimble scrambled forward on all fours and together they pulled the man back to the ditch.

His back was covered in blood.

Kimble grabbed the man's t-shirt collar with both hands and ripped it down the back.

There was blood pouring out of a hole to the left of the man's spine, just below his shoulder blade. Ruth slapped her palm across it, pressing it to stop the bleeding, but Kimble said, "No. Gotta get the bug." He shoved her hand aside and reached his thumb and forefinger down into the hole.

The man screamed and thrashed. Kimble's finger and thumb were a good two inches below the skin. "Ah, ah, dammit! I felt it, but it's too deep."

The man yelled, then screamed and coughed. Blood fountained from his mouth, astonishingly red. His entire body convulsed once, twice, and then he went slack.

Ruth turned him on his back. "CPR!" She tilted his head back to clear his airway but his throat was full of blood. "Oh, God, oh God." She felt for a pulse on his neck. There was nothing.

"Look out, Sensei," Kimble said.

Ruth turned her head, looking around.

"Not out there. That bug is going to come out of him somewhere."

Ruth pulled her hands back, almost flinching away.

There was less blood when it came out of his chest, but the blind black snout of the june-bug-sized creature came right through the remnants of the shirt as if it weren't there. It crawled up and out, wet and red. It stood up high on its legs and spread its wings. It buzzed them and the blood splattered off in a pink mist. Then it lifted off and Ruth threw herself back as it passed over her and flew back the way it had come.

"Huh," said Kimble. He pointed at the shirt. The shape of the bug was outlined in droplets of blood, as if someone had spray-painted over the bug while it sat on the shirt. He looked at his own outstretched finger, then at both hands, covered in blood.

"Yuck."

They moved away from the body, still clinging to the bank of the road. There were other bugs in the air and the body was still in the ditch, a potent reminder of the need for caution. Ruth broke out her emergency reserve of water and a bar of soap and they scrubbed until it hurt.

"I wonder if he was traveling alone," Kimble said.

Ruth stared at him. "Are you all right?"

"Sure. I just touched the tail end before it dropped into the lung cavity. That's not the business end."

Ruth blinked. "I wasn't talking about your fingers. You ever see someone die before?"

"I did, yeah. My mom. Pneumonia. Saw bugs swarm a shepherd. Also a stabbing—a gang thing—back in the capital."

"Are you upset?"

Kimble shrugged. "Not right now. I get nightmares sometimes." He looked away. "What should we do with the body?"

Bodies, actually. After another half hour, the bugs settled down and Ruth and Kimble scouted ahead, leaving the travois in the ditch. The other man was lying in the middle of the road. He'd bled so much, the blood had eroded a path across the road's surface and into the ditch. Flies buzzed on the blood-soaked ground. Kimble counted five different bug holes in the man, including one in his forehead.

"Look," he pointed at a spot in the road a few yards away from the body.

"Those bugs?"

A dozen bugs clustered around a spot in the road. They were jostling each other as they all strove to reach something in the middle.

"Yeah. They're eating the broken one. The bug these guys stepped on."

"And started the swarm."

"And started the swarm." Kimble rubbed his upper right arm through the cloth of his shirt.

They covered the bodies using blankets from the men's own packs, which they had flung aside in the initial panic. According to Ruth's map, there was another village just two miles ahead. "We'll report it there," she said.

It was only a few houses clustered around a store and some surrounding farms. "You could've just buried them," said the storekeeper, examining the Oklahoma driver's licenses Ruth had brought from the bodies. "Driver's licenses. Ha! What they gonna drive?"

"What about their families? Won't they want the bodies?"

The storekeeper eyed Ruth. "New to the territory?"

Ruth nodded once. "Six weeks."

"We don't got no refrigeration. In winter you could get away with hauling bodies all the way to the border, but this time of the year you just want to get them into the ground as soon as possible."

He took Ruth's name and direction and said, "We'll get someone out there with a spade. You say they had stuff?"

"Backpacks. I put them in the bushes near where they lay."

The storekeeper brightened. "Good thought to hide them. It might be worth someone's while to go out and give them a Christian burial."

"Oh," said Kimble. "Is that what a Christian burial is? One with a profit?"

The storekeeper gave Kimble a dark look. "This isn't some vacation destination. They can't come into the territory without seeing that film. They had to sign the release before they were allowed in." He looked at Ruth. "They're still doing that, right?"

Ruth nodded. "Yes. At Needles, at least."

Kimble started to open his mouth again, but Ruth grabbed him by the collar and said good-bye.

Outside she said, "Why are you giving him such a hard time? Don't you want those bodies buried?"

Kimble ducked his head. "Sorry. It was that Christian thing. What about 'Christian duty'? They would preach something awful at the shelters. Some of them really meant it, but some of them would spout scripture then prey on the homeless girls. Let us 'prey,' " he said, holding his hands like claws.

She nodded. "I can see that. I don't care what people believe, myself. I care how they behave. Sometimes their beliefs are part of that, right? Let's make tracks."

THAT night they camped on the Rio Puerco, where the road crossed the river and merged with the River Road. A store and an inn were tucked above the bosque. Ruth talked to the clerk at the inn but shook her head at the prices. Several others had also found it too dear and were camped below in the bosque.

They found a spot to unroll their blankets and eat supper. As it got dark, they joined the group sitting around a campfire where the river had washed the sandy bank clean of foliage.

The Munn family, an Anglo couple with two kids, were headed for the capital to shop. Mr. Herbert was an older black man returning from the capital after a yearly physical. Honovi and Cha'risi were Hopi freighters, resting on the east–west run to Arizona. And there were Andrea and Samantha, two "sisters" who looked nothing alike and sat with their shoulders touching. The Reverend Torrance was a Baptist missionary from Alabama.

Kimble ended up telling about the two dead men from Oklahoma. Mr. Herbert raised his head. "I passed them, I think, while they were still alive, of course. They were walking, right? I was on my horse. They were headed south. Sad."

The Reverend Torrance bowed his head and clasped his hands together. "May God Almighty take them into his keeping and bring them into the glory of his presence."

Mrs. Munn said, "Amen."

Ruth said, "I've only been in the territory for six weeks, but it surprised me. Do you see that often?"

"Not as much, these days," said Mr. Herbert. "Not like it was during the Exodus."

Honovi, one of the Hopi freighters, shook his head. "No. Nothing like that. Most drove out, of course, in the first weeks, while the cars were still working. The Air Force dropped those leaflets after the power went."

Mr. Munn, father of the two kids, nodded. "I've got a whole stack of those on my bookshelf."

Mr. Herbert said, "Once the bugs started eating cars, though, that's when things got bad."

"Where'd you live?" Mr. Munn asked. "When it happened."

"I was outside, stationed at Fort Carson, First Battalion, 67th Armor. Hoo-ah." He smiled to himself. "It was Captain Herbert, then. We came south in all our mechanized glory and we destroyed bugs by the thousands. I will say this, we probably saved a lot of lives, 'cause the millions of bugs that came for us left the adjoining territory clear." The faint smile dropped off his face. "We lost over six hundred men and all our vehicles and weapons."

The other Hopi freighter, Cha'risi, said, "I was at the University of New Mexico then. I remember the helicopters falling out of the sky. The few that made it back went high quickly but it was a gamble. Sure, the bugs couldn't reach you but any bugs that had attached themselves lower down went for the electrical systems and it was a toss-up whether you'd lose an instrument or the engines. I got out into the west face of the Sandias. Took one of the trails. Eventually, the National Guard found me. The stripped down version of the guard. No weapons, no metal. They walked in supplied by air drops."

"Why'd they stop, Daddy?" asked Mr. Munn's daughter. "Why didn't they just eat all the metal in the world?"

Three people spoke at once.

"The barrier," said her father.

"The sunlight," said one of the sisters, Samantha.

"The army," said Honovi.

Then Mr. Herbert said, "Bullshit."

They all looked at him and he went on. "I've heard all of those but I've seen the barrier. The bugs don't go anywhere near it. And there's as much sunlight in southern Utah as in Arizona and New Mexico. Sure they seem to be solar-powered but they're not spreading everywhere there's good sun. And I was there, son. The army didn't stop them. We could destroy bugs, sure, but it just brought more. Once the bugs are on your own equipment, what are you gonna do? Shoot at your own tanks?"

He shook his head and knocked on his thigh, a hard rapping sound, knuckles on plastic. "My battalion's intelligence officer visited me in the hospital before my discharge. The bugs had stopped spreading over more territory. Even then they didn't know why the bugs stopped where they did."

The other sister, Andrea, asked, "I heard they came out of the lab, at Sandia. They were designed to clean up toxic and radioactive waste, but they got out of hand."

Mr. Munn said, "Heard something similar, but that it was from the labs up at Los Alamos. That the radioactivity caused their instruction set to mutate and we got the uncontrolled replication."

"I've heard all of those," said Mr. Herbert. "Also that it was from the Waste Isolation Pilot Plant down near Carlsbad or that the aliens seeded them at Roswell in 1947 and it took that long for them to grow." He shook his head. "I do know this—the original infestation spread from near Socorro. But that's all I know."

"New Mexico Tech?" said the other sister, Samantha. "The full name *is* the New Mexico Institute of Mining and Technology. That would make more sense. I mean, there's heavy metal pollution, but a lot of pollution is organic solvents that the bugs wouldn't touch. But if they'd been developed for mining—that would make sense."

Mr. Herbert shrugged. "There's no record of that kind of research. Some nano-technology stuff, sure, and robotics, but not like this."

Mrs. Munn said, "Well, there wouldn't be, would there? This would be big money stuff. You just turn your bugs loose on a deposit and they go mine it, making more bugs and more bugs and when they're done, they just fly back to you, to be melted down. Company or government that could do that wouldn't want his competitors to know. Then, when it went wrong, they covered it up, of course. Thousands died. Worse than Bhopal."

The Reverend Torrance said, "You're overlooking another possibility." His eyes shifted sideways to the "sisters" and back to the fire. "God, who created the world, who washed it in the flood, who burned Sodom and Gomorrah with fire, is visiting his wrath on our country *in particular* as we stray from the path of righteousness."

"God is certainly visiting a pestilence upon us in *you*," Kimble muttered, but only Ruth heard him and he shut his mouth at her glare.

Mr. Herbert shifted his artificial leg and stood. "The only thing worse than discussing politics with strangers is arguing religion. I'm turning in."

Andrea grinned at the Reverend Torrance. "I'm for bed, too." She looked back at Mrs. Munn. "Once you allege cover-ups and the machinations of the powerful, there's no proving anything. 'Evidence has been suppressed.' I will say this, though; we've been studying them for a couple of decades now and we're no closer to duplicating them."

Mrs. Munn said, "That you *know.*"

Andrea laughed. Mr. Herbert just shook his head and limped off into the night, followed soon after by everyone else but the family Munn, whose fire it was.

Later, after brushing his teeth *without* being told, Kimble asked Ruth, "What do *you* think?"

She shook her head. "Insufficient data. Don't think it's God punishing us. Seriously doubt Mrs. Munn's vast conspiracy." She turned back her bedroll and sat on it. "But after seeing that man die today . . . well, I'm imagining that times thirty thousand." She shook her head. "History. It has a distancing effect, doesn't it?"

Kimble stared off into the dark. Thirty thousand? All dead? He had a hard time imagining that many people in the entire world. He rubbed his fingers together, remembering the slippery blood. Thirty thousand riddled with bug holes.

"Yes, Sensei."

BUGS DON'T LIKE WATER

It took four days to reach the village of Perro Frio on a bend of the Rio Puerco. There was a more direct route, but bugs still worked the rusty remains of refineries, pre-bug communities, and railroad trestles, and Ruth and Kimble took the safe road, swinging wide. They arrived midday on Thursday, market day, when the population of the village increased fourfold. Though they had been taking turns pulling the travois, Kimble insisted on pulling it as they entered the village.

She bought fresh tomatoes and onions from one of the farmers using coin left over from the foiled thief.

"Passing through?" the man asked.

"No. I've come to homestead," explained Ruth.

"Near here?"

"Yes."

"You've already registered it? Then you must've taken one of those plots up on the east mesa. Mighty dry."

"Uh, no. It's on the river."

The farmer and his wife exchanged glances. "Everything near water is already being worked. Until you get about twenty miles downriver."

"According to the map, it's only a mile south of here."

"Oh, no, dear," said the farmer's wife. "Is it in the bend?"

Ruth took out her map and looked at it. "Yes. Did the registrar get it wrong? They said that land was unclaimed and took my fees. Is someone living there?"

"Bugs, dear. Lots of bugs."

Ruth's face froze. "Really? The clerk said it was unused. No building, no installations, no pipelines."

"They used to dump stuff there, before. Old cars and refrigerators and washing machines. Not legally. And it got worse when the bugs first came. People who stayed, trying to clear their land of metal, they dragged more stuff over there."

Ruth's face was still frozen as they left the market. Kimble said, "We should go look."

She turned to him. "Bugs are dangerous. Remember the men from Oklahoma?"

"So is water, Sensei. We still drink it. We've walked four days. You walked six weeks. What's twenty more minutes?"

She looked at him and took a deep breath, then let it out. "Very well."

———

THEY followed the old county road, now a mass of cracked and crumbling asphalt with stretches of sandy washes cutting across where there used to be metal culverts under the pavement. The worst of these had been filled with rock and packed down, as had the worst of the potholes. When they reached the section where the road bordered the homestead site, a former culvert, *not* filled-in, cut across the road, well washed out. Someone had painted on the old asphalt, DANGER: BUGS, and an arrow labeled DETOUR pointed to a new trail, mostly wagon ruts cutting through the brown grass, that swung wide to the east.

Ruth exchanged glances with Kimble. "Okay. Let's go see how bad this is."

Together they wrestled the travois down into the cut and then back up onto the asphalt on the other side.

There *were* bugs. They saw them almost immediately, mostly on the right—the western side of the road. The non-metallic detritus of appliances and old cars littered the ground. Here the plastic skirts of an automobile wheel well, here the plastic fins of a dryer tumbler, but there wasn't much actual metal left above ground. The bugs were digging, working chunks below the surface or simply sitting still in the sunlight, their silicon blue photovoltaic wings fully deployed, tracking the sun as it moved across the sky.

Kimble pointed past them. "I'm not really seeing many deeper in. It's like they dumped the stuff near the road."

"There's some," said Ruth, pointing. After a moment, though, she added, "Not as many as I would've expected."

They followed the old road down the entire property line, until they met the river, bending back. Here was another washed-out culvert and here the dirt-rut detour returned to the county road. Ruth said, "Let's take a look-see from the river side." They lowered the travois into the wash and carefully moved toward the river bluff, but there weren't any bugs in the wash itself. Those landing there by chance would be washed into the river and, unless substantial metal was uncovered, they wouldn't be drawn there purposefully.

The wash cut down to a layer of volcanic tuff as it neared the river and when they reached the edge there was a drop of about fifteen feet to the bosque.

Back before the bugs, the river had been drained for irrigation projects, taking it down to a mere stream most days, but the bugs had wreaked havoc on metal pipes and pumps and gate gears and reinforced concrete. There were still ditch projects that used the water, but nowhere near as much of the river's volume was diverted and, as a result, the Puerco flowed steadily most days and flooded on others, making the bosque below verdant.

There were a few bugs in the bosque but not as many as they'd seen near the old road. Cautiously, Ruth climbed up the side of the wash to the bluff top, well away from the road. "Huh." She stood.

"Can I come up?"

She crouched and extended her arm, then hauled Kimble up.

Once you got some fifty feet from the road, there was only one serious cluster of bugs intruding into the property, where an old path or driveway had let people dump their junk out of sight, but it was in the northern third of the land. As they cautiously walked back and forth, the area between the old road and the bluff's edge was clear of bugs.

Kimble and Ruth carefully approached the active cluster of bugs set in another shallow wash lined with vivid green grass and brush. "Looks like an old tractor, maybe."

Most of it was underground, so Kimble asked, "Why do you say that?"

She pointed at large chunks of black rubber. "Those were the tire lugs, for pushing the wheels through loose dirt. You don't see lugs that big on trucks or cars."

"If you say so." Kimble had been outside once, visiting relatives while his mother was still alive, but his memories of the trip had mostly been movies and cartoons played on a cousin's HD. Cars had also made an impression but the tires on them had been smooth.

"You'd think the tractor would be gone by now," Ruth said.

Bugs reproduced by binary fission, growing additional selves as they ate. One bug was two in three weeks, four in six, eight in nine, and so on. A year would see one bug become two hundred and sixty thousand if they could find the metal for unchecked growth, and it had been fifteen years since the bugs had appeared.

"Look," said Kimble. "There's water in the wash." He pointed at a trickle of water along the lower edge.

Bugs hated water. You could survive a swarm if you got into water fast enough.

"So there is. I didn't see any water running under the road, did you?"

Kimble frowned for a second. "Or through any of the cuts. No."

"If that ground is soaking wet, it would slow them down, wouldn't it?"

"It might," agreed Kimble.

They walked into the shallow wash closer to the bluff, where there were no bugs. Ruth dropped to her knees and dug her hand into the sand. The top four inches was dry, the next four inches was damp, and below that water seeped into the hole.

"That's a lot of water, for here, this high above the river."

They walked the perimeter again. The water didn't flow over the homestead boundaries but came out of a rock formation about fifty feet from the road. It flowed five feet down the limestone face and then into the shallow wash, which, without discussing it, they started calling the "wet" wash.

They made a fire back by the bluff and put water in the ceramic pot for tea.

"It would be easy to clear out the junk by the road," Ruth said as they waited for the water to boil. "The best thing would be to snag it with a rope and drag it out of the dirt and up onto the asphalt where the bugs can eat it proper."

"A very long rope," said Kimble.

"Why long?"

"You could catch a bug between something hard and the metal—accidentally pop it."

Ruth exhaled. "And they'd swarm, right?" She swallowed and Kimble knew she was remembering that moment on the road again.

Kimble pulled up his right sleeve and showed her three scars striping his upper arm. "It's not always fatal. But I wasn't that close."

"Okay. A very long rope," she conceded. "But what about the tractor? From the number of bugs there seems to be a lot more metal there. Maybe the engine block is sunk into the wash or the chassis or axles."

"Or all of those," agreed Kimble.

"There could even be a disc-harrow or a plow behind. I doubt we can pull it up with rope. I mean, not without a team of horses or oxen. If it weren't in the wash, we might try burying it, until it had enough dirt over it the bugs stopped sensing it. Maybe if we diverted the stream to keep the water away, we could bury it then without having it wash away."

"I don't think you need to keep water *away* from it," said Kimble. "Just the opposite."

Ruth looked at him with her head cocked to one side.

"What we need, Sensei, is a dam."

ONE of the reasons the wash was so shallow was because the same layer of volcanic tuff that floored the southern dry wash tilted up at an angle across the property. When they'd dug two feet down, twenty feet downstream from the tractor, they hit the rock layer.

"Good," said Ruth. "We'll have a solid base."

Her first inclination had been to buy some cement in

the village. But Kimble, doing their laundry in the river, turned up deep red clay in the bank and, while it resulted in a badly stained shirt, it saved them the cost of the cement. They used the travois to drag damp clay from the bank to the foot of the bluff where they lifted it up the cliff by rope a bucket at a time.

They trenched down to the bedrock and made the dam, bowed upstream, out of large rocks set in the clay. Though they'd left the stream edge of the wash unobstructed while building the remaining part, the subsurface water, now obstructed, increased the surface water from a slow trickle to a gushing flow. The sand was wet everywhere in the wash and puddles were forming in the low bits.

The bugs, almost as if irritated, lifted off frequently into the air, buzzing on their crystalline wings, as the water touched their six, eight, ten or, if it was right before budding off, twelve legs. They flew farther and farther from the buried tractor as the water crept higher, and more than once Ruth and Kimble had to retreat down the wash to avoid them.

Ruth and Kimble prepped carefully for the final bit of work. The dam or "Damn dam" as Kimble called it, was three feet high, a full two feet higher than the spot where the tractor block emerged from the wet sand. They had a stack of large rocks and a pile of clay set on the bank, and hollow reeds stuck in their belts in case they needed to retreat under the water.

"Ready?"

"Yes, Sensei."

They stuck clay on the rocks before shoving them down

into the gap, knowing that a large portion of it would be washed away, but they pushed more handfuls of clay into the gaps as they built. The water stopped dead and then perceptibly began to rise. They built above it, overbuilding, really, putting a thick layer of clay on the upstream side and then sticking a woven grass mat onto that, to reinforce it.

As the water rose, the buzzing from flying bugs increased, neared. The bugs were zooming back and forth, the midpoint of their flight always centering on the remains of the tractor, but, as the water rose higher, the extent of their flight increased. Twice Kimble ducked down into the water and once he flicked a bug out of Ruth's hair.

They smeared the last of the mud over the grass mat and hurried down the wash, then south along the bluff's edge. The bug activity was so great that even at their campsite, near the southern border of the homestead, the bugs buzzed angrily through the brush, clipping off leaves and branches.

"Fishing," said Ruth, and pulled out her package of Kevlar fishing hooks and nylon line. They moved down to the bosque and cut willow branches for poles and dug grubs. When they returned with their brown trout, the water was flowing over the lowest part of the dam and the tractor site was under two feet of water. Though a few bugs had settled to the ground on the banks of the new pond, the majority had settled back by the road, where there was still metal left to work.

———

THERE was no dojo by the first snowfall, but Ruth and Kimble had achieved a thick-walled, rammed-earth, adobe-plastered cottage, with three rooms and a bucket toilet in its own well-vented closet. A plastic water barrel perched on the live grass roof and a clay-lined, vertical-feed woodstove was built into the north wall. Its clay flue ran horizontally through the rammed earth before venting up and out, using the mass of the wall to store and release heat through the day.

They did practice, though, twice a day, over by the spring on a spot of grass where the dojo would eventually be. It was Kimble's responsibility to keep it watered and to find every sharp stick, hard rock, and goat-head sticker in the area. Most of these he found by looking and that was far better than the ones he discovered with his back, his knees, or his feet. He found out early, though, that if he pulled a rock from the earth, it was far better to re-place it with well packed dirt, than to leave the hole to catch his feet.

And he pulled so many goat-heads that he found himself spotting the tiny yellow flowers of the puncture vine in his dreams.

A great deal of Ruth's luggage had been freeze-dried foods, though she had a small set of territory-safe tools. She also had a great deal of cash, now stored in a hidden wall hollow of the new cottage. "Divorce—we split the dojo, we split the house." She shrugged. "There's much more in the bank, but the nearest branch is Nuevo Santa Fe."

She bought vegetables and eggs at the market. Cash

was hard to come by so she was always welcome. Most locals had to barter with each other. She was one of a small group of customers who, in the dead of winter, bought fresh greens from Covas, a farmer with a greenhouse. One day in March, Kimble and Ruth had just turned away from Covas' market stall when Sandy Williams staggered into their path and stopped. "Business must be good. What are your rates?"

Williams was a giant of a man with a full-beard and long, greasy hair that hung down his sheepskin coat in a thick braid.

Kimble had heard he was a spectacularly bad farmer whose wife had left him in the late fall. "He didn't get one single crop in," Masey Garcia, daughter of the district agricultural agent, told Kimble the month before. "He had some good tomatoes but he borrowed money on the strength of the crop and then drank it away when he should've been pickin' and dryin' them. Most rotted on the vine and that hailstorm in mid-September did for the rest."

Ruth frowned at Williams. "Excuse me? What do you mean?"

"Fine-lookin' woman like you, kept her figure, always has cash. I wonder how much you charge."

Kimble didn't understand but he saw Ruth blush and her jaw set. "Let's be *very* clear about what you are implying. Are you saying I'm a prostitute?"

Williams took a step forward and Kimble smelled alcohol on his breath. "That's sure a fancy way of sayin' it. I'd of said, 'whore.'" He leered at her. "With that cute tush of yours, I see why you're rakin' in the cash." Williams jerked his thumb at Kimble. "And I see you're a full-service establishment—sodomites, too?"

As his voice rose, conversations in the marketplace died and people froze, watching, mid-transaction, like some painted tableau: *Loudmouth in the market.*

Kimble's eyes narrowed and his stomach hurt. This was a little too familiar. He was shifting his weight, getting ready to move when Ruth shoved the shopping basket into his hands.

She drew herself up very straight, very still. "You have ten seconds to apologize," she said. Her voice, slightly raised, carried easily across the now quiet market.

Williams laughed. "Or *what*?" He gestured around. "There ain't a man around here that can take me, nor any group of th—"

Her slap turned his head around and he took a short step back to gain his balance.

"You little *whore*!" Williams drew one fist back and reached forward with the other, as if to clutch Ruth's jacket, but Ruth wasn't there.

He felt a hand take his collar from behind and another push down into the crook of his elbow, then he was spinning around and on his knees, facing the other direction, the hand on the collar shoving him down into the dirt. A voice whispered near his ear, "You should've apologized." With a roar, he surged back to his feet, shoving upward, but he encountered no resistance, just a smooth pull backward on his braided hair, and then an arm swept upward lifting his chin and arcing his body farther back.

There was a twist, and his entire lower body was neatly blocked out as he flew backward. He landed on the back of his head and shoulders in the packed dirt of the marketplace, his arms and legs folded awkwardly over, like a child's botched backward somersault.

Kimble felt the impact through the ground.

Williams fell sideways and thrashed his way onto all fours. He was shouting short forceful obscenities with great feeling. He jerked his way to his feet and staggered sideways into Covas' stall, knocking bushels of lettuce over. He clutched at the side of the stall for balance, as the obscenities continued like a fountain, becoming more complex and inventive as he regained his footing.

"*You whoring bitch!*" was the last and politest thing he said before he launched himself at Ruth, arms outstretched, trying to take her down by momentum alone.

Ruth feinted toward his face and dropped to her hands and knees, pivoting her hip into his knees. As he flew over her he got his hands out in front of him, but his face still smashed into the ground. When he rolled over, his nose was flowing like a bloody brook.

This time Ruth didn't wait for him to get up. She took one arm and used the elbow and shoulder like a crank, forcing him back onto his belly. Pinning his shoulder between her knees she took his pinky finger and cranked it (and the arm) toward the back of his head.

His response was less articulate than before, an animal grunt followed by a shriek.

"This," Ruth said, "is where you apologize."

"Sorry? You'll be sorry, you bitch—"

He shrieked again. Kimble, watching, saw that she was mostly extending the arm and putting pressure on the shoulder socket. The finger was just an extra.

"When I'm done with your arm I'm pretty sure you *won't* able to whip every man in this town. It's already clear you can't whip every *woman*." She applied a bit more pressure.

"*Jesus Christ, I'm sorry I fucking talked to you!*"

Covas, the greengrocer, nodded and said, "Well, that, at least, sounded sincere."

Ruth said quietly, "I'll start with the finger. Then the elbow. Then the shoulder." She gave him a sample.

"Ow! What do you want me to say?"

"Take back everything you said." Ruth twisted slightly at the waist.

"I take it back! I take it back! I didn't mean no harm!"

Ruth pinned his hand up between his shoulder blades and pushed on it while she stood. Before she let go, she said, "I'd just stay there for a while, if I were you." She released him and said, "Let's go home, Kimble."

When Kimble answered, he made sure it was loud enough to reach all the way across the marketplace.

"Yes, Sensei!"

Rotten Eggs

Sandy Williams' homestead was decent—not on the river, but on a major tributary creek—and he had a decent well, dug by him and lined with stone by his ex-wife. For all that he was a "farmer," his wife had done most of the agriculture—planting, weeding, and gathering. She had called on her husband only for the most arduous work—turning the soil in the spring and hauling water.

One of their neighbors, Ron Tingly, a shepherd with sheep and goats, said, "Most farms keep a dumb beast of burden—in their case, it's Sandy." But he did not say this where Williams could hear.

Now that Williams' wife was gone, there were only the chickens, three dozen, kept behind a coyote fence behind the house. There were only hens.

One hungover morning the last rooster had crowed one too many times. That night he'd had *coq au beer*, but it was badly burned. He was a lousy cook.

Now he ate eggs and bartered eggs in the market. He wouldn't be able to start a garden until mid-April. The village was at 7,000 feet and the heavy frosts could run into May. There'd been snow in June, once.

When the chickens laid well, he bought liquor, but this usually resulted in him forgetting to barter for feed. Underfed hens do not lay well.

When he was sitting at home, he spent a lot of time thinking about Ruth's money.

"SENSEI."

It was a bit after midday and Kimble had just returned from the village. He'd found, to his chagrin, that Ruth expected him to get an education, so he was spending his mornings at the half-day village school.

"There's soup."

"I saw Sandy Williams again."

Ruth had been cutting reeds, for basket making. Now she put down her flint knife and looked at Kimble. "On our land?"

"No, still that place on the other side of the road. He thinks he's hiding, but he really needs to wear something less bright or hide behind something that doesn't lose its leaves in the winter."

"Hmmm." She coiled the reeds she'd cut and put them in the sink to soak.

The sink was new, just a ceramic basin with a rubber

plug set in a rough wooden shelf. A plastic bucket stood on the floor below to catch the runoff. Ruth had plans to pipe water from the spring but, for now, and "in the best martial arts tradition," Kimble was hauling the water and gathering the wood.

Ruth dried her hands and reached over the window to where several wooden weapons lay across two dowels. She took down a *jyo*, a white-oak staff an inch in diameter and reaching from the ground to her armpit.

"Eat your soup!" she said, and left the cottage.

Kimble quickly filled his bowl, but instead of sitting by the coals of the stove, he went outside and climbed the ladder to the roof. Seated beside the gravity-feed water barrel, he ate as he watched Ruth make her way up to the road.

She came back fairly quickly.

"He was gone," she said. "I think he saw me coming."

They practiced *jyo* that afternoon, *tskui*—thrusting—and the appropriate blocks and counterstrikes. After an hour of this, she put aside her *jyo* and had him attack her with his staff, a process that always ended with her in possession of the *jyo* and him flying through the air. Fortunately, his ability to safely fall was far superior to that of Mr. Williams.

They switched and he practiced the same *jyo-dori* (staff taking) techniques with far less definite results.

"Never mind," said Ruth. "It will come."

On market day Ruth sent him off to school with the basket and some coin. "A dozen eggs, some kale from Mr.

Covas, and, if a shipment has come in at the store, some green tea."

When Kimble neared town, Sandy Williams stepped into the road, a straw-filled basket in each of his hands. "Good morning."

Kimble nodded politely, but kept walking.

Williams, with his longer legs, easily kept pace. "What's your hurry, boy?"

Kimble's thought was *none of your business*. He ameliorated that to a short, monosyllabic, "School."

"Buying eggs today? Give you a good deal."

"At the market, after."

"The deal won't hold, then." He pulled back the straw. The brown eggs in the straw were large and smooth. "Need a quick sale, half off for cash."

The eggs did look good and Kimble could use the savings to buy some bread, the only thing he regularly craved. Ruth served lots of grains, but usually in soups or porridge. She'd managed biscuits, cooked in a covered crock, and flat corn griddle cakes cooked on a heated stone, but nothing risen, nothing with a good crunchy crust.

He stopped walking. "Let me see one." He supposed Williams wanted the money to buy liquor, but that wasn't really his lookout.

Williams tilted the basket and reached awkwardly for an egg at the far end of the basket.

"Not that one," said Kimble. He pointed at an egg in the middle. "That one."

Williams looked annoyed. "Sure, kid. If you want. You drop it, though, you bought it."

Kimble accepted the proffered egg and formed a tube with his hands, the egg in one end, the other end pressed against one eye. When he faced the sun, the light shining through showed the bacterial ring, dark and prominent, and the air cell had expanded to half the volume of the egg.

He handed it back carefully. He certainly didn't want to drop it. He'd smelled rotten eggs before.

"Well?" said Williams.

"Too old. No thanks."

"You're crazy, boy. This is a good deal."

Kimble shook his head. "No, thank you." This time when he walked on, Williams didn't follow.

BY dint of superior comparison shopping, Kimble saved enough on the afternoon's egg purchase to buy a small loaf of multigrain bread. When he presented it, along with the tea and the kale, he saw Ruth's tongue dart out and touch her lips.

"How hard can it be to make an oven?"

It took a month, in their spare time. They made a traditional *horno*, the dome-shaped adobe oven of the southwest. They found that the soil down in the bosque, not too near the clay deposits, contained the right mixture of clay and sand. Chopping and shredding the straw without metal tools was one of the most labor-intensive parts. Their brick mold was made of finished outside lumber, a piece of two-by-four, drilled and pegged with dowels. They made the adobe bricks five inches wide and fourteen long, thick as the wood mold. They left a smooth wooden log in to form a small chimney, high and to the back, and the door was a three-inch-thick flat slab of limestone chipped to the rough outline of the arched doorway.

Rosemary Werito, a Dineh who lived west of town, consulted on the design and talked them through the first day of baking. She walked back and forth from the *horno* to the cottage, supervising Ruth with the dough preparation and Kimble as he fed the fire. "Too much," she said. When she returned fifteen minutes later, "too little." Kimble was burning mesquite roots and dried cow manure. When he wasn't building the fire, he was digging a nearby pit to safely dispose of the hot coals.

At the end of the day, Rosemary went home with two loaves of bread and some badly needed cash and Kimble proudly shelved five more loaves in insect-proof bags.

They only baked once a week, but this let them take a few loaves in on market day to offset the cost of the imported flour.

Sandy Williams did not see this as a sign of virtuous industry. He only saw it as proof of Ruth's additional *prosperity*. It galled him.

SCHOOL closed for three months in the summer. The cycle had turned. Long ago, children were not taught in the summer because their labor was critical to keep the farm going. That tradition survived into industrialization, but now, in the territory, tradition became necessity again.

They were gardening seriously, both near the stream

and down on the bosque. In addition, Ruth was using their red clay deposits to make storage crocks. As productive as the gardens were, the resulting food needed to be preserved. Now, every time they heated the *horno* for baking, there were pots in the back, being fired. The beans could be dried, of course, as were half of the tomatoes, but much of the food was canned in the crocks and sealed with wax.

Ruth now had ten students for the afternoon class, mostly classmates of Kimble's, but also a few adults who'd been there the day Ruth had put Sandy Williams in the dirt. They still practiced on the grass near the spring, but there were the beginnings of a structure. The boundaries of the practice area were now delimited by a rising course of adobe bricks and, in the wash below the dam, fiber-reinforced concrete roof beams were being cast in plastic-lined trenches in the sand.

One market day afternoon they returned to the cottage to find the door open and most of their belongings scattered about. A smoked chicken, recently purchased, was gone from the rafters, and the last two loaves from the previous week's baking were gone from the counter. But whoever had been there hadn't found the hidden wall hollow where Ruth kept her cash, or messed with the growing collection of crocks in the new root cellar.

There were tracks in the dust, a man's booted feet, larger than either of theirs.

"Williams," said Kimble.

"Maybe," said Ruth. "Whoever it was, I think we surprised him. He didn't go through all the baskets yet." She had Kimble stay home to pick up and trudged back into town to report it to Martha Mendez, the storekeeper who doubled as the county clerk, postmaster, and recorder.

The local law enforcement was volunteer and aimed more at transients and professional bandits. Disputes between locals were heard by the village council, which mostly depended on local quarrels working themselves out. For the worst things, messengers went twenty miles to the nearest Ranger barracks or one waited for the bimonthly visit of the territorial circuit judge.

"Did you see anyone?" asked Martha after hearing the details.

"Sandy Williams has been hanging around the edges of our property."

Martha made a face. Williams was the community's invisible elephant, the problem no one liked to talk about.

"Two loaves of bread and a chicken. Nothing else? No cash?"

"They didn't find where I keep it."

"I'll tell the boys." The boys were the council, grown men all. "Could be they'll go talk to Williams. Not promising anything."

Ruth snorted. "Well, I really just wanted it on the record and for you to spread the word. I'll be watching my place more carefully and I'll take care of it if I catch someone. Just suggesting others might want to keep an eye out, as well. You have any locks?"

She returned home with a Kevlar composite reproduction of an old mortise lock and enough epoxy to bond it in place on the inner face of the door. The door could be broken, but it would take time and effort. Their windows were small, head high, and double glazed. When they were swung open, Kimble could climb through them, but a large man couldn't.

The next time they both went to the market, they came back to find the kitchen window, inner and outer panes, broken. Just within the window, a crock with cooked beans and the last loaf of bread were missing from the counter.

"Now that's annoying," said Ruth.

Kimble was more than annoyed. He hefted the small clay crock of honey they'd just traded four loaves of bread for. "That was the *last*. I really wanted to try the honey on some bread."

Using some fine dark dust, Ruth checked the glass pieces for fingerprints, but the glass was still clear from the last cleaning. They did find some more boot prints though, in the threadbare yard.

"Looks the same," Ruth said.

Kimble pointed at the right heel. "It is. That crack is the same."

"Get some of that scrap cardboard and draw a full-sized picture. One you could hold up to a boot."

"Yes, Sensei."

There was one spare pane of glass stored in the cupboard beneath Ruth's bed and it was the work of a few minutes to place it in the frame. Summer was full on and there was no need of the second glazing until later in the year, but Ruth put it on her list anyway.

Kimble was comparing his drawing with the boot print.

"Not bad," Ruth said, looking over his shoulder. She tucked the drawing in her shoulder bag. "Fetch the dishpan, the one with the onions in it."

"And the onions?"

"Put them in the sink for now."

When he returned with the plastic tub, she carefully placed it over the boot print in the dust, then weighed it down with an adobe brick.

"Stay here," she told Kim. "I'm going to talk with Martha." She pointed two fingers at her own eyes.

Kimble bobbed his head. "Right, Sensei. I'll watch."

THOUGH Ruth had picked up the larger pieces there were still glass shards on the sill, counter, and floor, so Kimble gathered them all up. Goat-heads were bad enough—he had no desire to step on glass. It was a hot afternoon and stuffy in the cottage. He opened all the windows of the cottage, found a basket to put the onions in, and thought about the bread that was gone.

He deeply resented whoever stole the bread. Making more was really a six-hour job, between heating the *horno*, preparing the dough, and baking. In the summer, it was the sort of thing you began at dawn, before it got too hot.

There were many chores that could be done. They needed more clay from the riverbank for pottery, but he couldn't watch the cottage from there. Same problem with fishing or seining for crawdads. He could do laundry, but they'd done it two days before.

It was the worst time of day for it, but everything he needed to mix more adobe for bricks was already on site over by the dojo. He locked the cottage door, hung the hard, plastic key around his neck, and headed over there.

He stopped short.

There were two horses tied to the small cottonwood by the spring, one with a riding saddle and one with two filled canvas panniers on a pack saddle. The visible brand was the Bar Halo, a small ranch west of town belonging to the Kenney family. This wasn't too surprising. Ruth had let it be known that locals traveling her way were welcome to the spring's water, but he didn't see any of the Kenneys, or Orse, their hired hand. He heard distant movement and looked around the half-completed dojo wall.

Sandy Williams was in the garden, stealing tomatoes.

The kitchen garden was on the far (northern) side of the pond, handy to water, with a plastic mesh rabbit fence around it. Deer could jump (and had) right over the fence but they mostly watered down in the bosque. Also, the nearest neighbors' sheepdogs tended to keep the deer away from the top of the bluff.

Not very good at keeping people out, though.

"I'm seeing a couple of dozen Romas and a bunch of cherries in your basket," Kimble said loudly, from the other side of the pond.

Williams jerked around, a half-eaten tomato in his hand.

"Looking at your face and your coveralls, you've gone through another dozen, as well. That'll be six dollars. Then there's the matter of the broken window, the stolen crock of beans, and my loaf of bread."

Williams dropped the half-eaten tomato in the dirt prompting a cry from Kimble.

"Don't *waste*! What did you say to me when you tried to sell me those rotten eggs? 'You drop it, you bought it'?"

"Didn't have any choice, kid. Coyotes got my chickens last night. It was the last straw." Williams walked out of the garden gate. "Your house unlocked?"

"Sensei is going to beat the absolute crap out of you."

"We'll see about that. Anyway, I saw her head into the village just now. I'm done with this town—I'm gonna be long gone by the time she gets back. Just need a stake for the road and I know she's got it."

"The cottage is locked and even if you break in you'll never find it."

"So it *is* in the house," said Williams.

Crap.

Williams set the tomatoes down and stepped into the pond. "I'll bet *you* know where it is. I'll bet you even have a key."

Kimble's first impulse was to run hard and fast, back toward town. Even if Williams pursued him on horseback, there were places he could go no horse could follow.

But he doubted Williams would follow. Instead Kimble thought he'd kick in the door and ransack the cottage. Williams had done it once before, so he knew where *not* to look. He might find Ruth's savings this time.

Kimble circled to the left along the edge of the water. "You steal those horses? The council will ride after you for that. They'll send for the Rangers, too."

Unlike Ruth and Kimble, the Kenneys had lived in the town since before the Exodus. They were respected and well liked and stealing livestock was considerably more frowned on than just stealing food.

"Of course, if I were you I'd rather the Rangers caught me. The council might decide to go all Western on you, horse thief." It was an idle threat. Nobody had been hanged in Perro Frio, but it had happened elsewhere in the territory.

Williams, thigh high in the water, turned to track Kimble. "Shut up, you little faggot!"

Kimble began backing away from the pond's edge. "You know what's worse than a horse thief? A drunk and a horse thief!"

Williams surged forward through the water, and then stumbled. Kimble had moved sideways to put the old tractor between him and the man and Williams' toe caught it. Flailing his arms around for balance, Williams fell forward, sending a green tidal wave before him.

Kimble turned and ran back toward the horses, intending to at least let them go, scare them away, so they'd find their way home. He fumbled with the reins, but Williams had not used a slipknot and the horses, jerking away from Kimble's rush, had tightened the knots. Williams pounding feet grew closer and Kimble darted north, toward town, horses still tied.

The knots will slow him down, Kimble thought, but

Williams didn't even pause at the horses. Kimble was struggling through the brush, slowed by the mesquite thorns, but Williams seemed to plow right through, closing fast. *I'll never make the road*, Kimble thought, and cut left, toward the bluff top. He knew a spot with a ledge halfway down and a sloping face below where it was possible to descend the fifteen-foot drop into the bosque.

He felt fingers claw at his back and he swerved hard, then sprinted the last bit to the cliff top, opening the gap between them. Panting, he turned, knees bent, facing Williams.

If Kimble was panting, Williams was wheezing, his face beet red. Seeing Kimble stop, he slowed, managing a breathless, "Ha! Trapped yourself." William stepped closer, wide-stanced, ready to cut Kimble off if he tried to dart right or left. He gestured. "I see that string around your neck."

Kimble's top two buttons had come loose as he'd run through the brush and the end of the key was visible against his skin. He stood up straighter and tugged the string, so the key dangled. "This old thing?"

Williams lunged, arm darting forward like a striking snake.

Kimble stepped back off the edge of the bluff. As he dropped, he reached up and grabbed the sleeve of Williams' outstretched arm from beneath.

Kimble went down the cliff-face feet first, his toes scudding along the dirt and rock, his free hand dragging down the face, until he stopped hard, on the ledge. Williams arced overhead, a look of sudden shock and surprise on his face as he pitched forward. Kimble turned just in time to see him crash though the branches of a Russian olive tree, then slam into the ground below.

He didn't get up.

Kimble came down the last sloping bit of the bluff with a tumbling cloud of dirt and rocks. He approached Williams cautiously. There was a huge knot on the man's forehead and a bone was sticking out of his upper left arm. He was breathing, though, and the sluggish bleeding around the protruding bone didn't seem arterial.

A quarter of an hour later, Ruth came back, riding pillion behind Matt Kenney. With them rode Kenney's sons and half the village council, all on horseback and packed for an extended chase.

Kimble told them where the stolen horses were and led them around, the horse-friendly way, into the bosque where Williams lay.

"Too bad he didn't break his fool neck," said Matt Kenney. "What happened, boy?"

"He was chasing me. Wanted the key to the cottage. I knew there was a ledge there. He didn't."

"Serves him right. If he'd just ridden on by, we might never have caught him. Those were my best two horses. They can really *move*. Let that be a lesson to you, boys," he said to his own teenage sons. "Don't be greedy."

They found the missing bread and the crock of beans among Williams' belongings in the pack saddle panniers. While he was still unconscious, they extended his arm until the bone slipped back under the muscle and splinted it. He woke up before they finished rigging the horse litter and threw up all the tomatoes he'd eaten.

"There's justice," said Ruth. Later, after they'd taken him away, she said, "Now tell me what really happened."

He did.

"And was it wise to confront him while he was stealing the tomatoes?"

"They were *our* tomatoes, Sensei."

"Because a vehicle *should* stop at a crosswalk does not mean you should step out in front of a speeding truck. Be more careful in the future. Let him eat tomatoes . . . while you take his horses."

"Sensei!"

She gave him bread with honey. "Just be more careful."

"Yes, Sensei."

Kimble and the not-Dog

The monsoon season began well, the first two weeks of July, with a series of afternoon thunderstorms, but thereafter the clouds threatened but dropped their water on other watersheds. By the middle of August, the Puerco was down to a trickle, though many of the river's beaver dams still held good water. The grass and brush, green during the two weeks' rain, were now brown and dry again.

Concerned about fire, Ruth and Kimble cleared brush in a hundred-foot safety zone around the house and dojo. When filling the rooftop water barrel, Kimble hauled extra water for the grass on the live roof, to keep it from drying out.

The Village Council began inspecting chimneys, ordering the installation of ceramic spark grates on some, the removal of close trees in other places. They scheduled a time to tour Ruth's place.

Kimble exhibited a teen's outrage. "What business is it of theirs what happens on your land?"

"What direction is the wind blowing?"

It was a hot dry wind from the south, perhaps fifteen miles per hour.

The village was north of their place.

Kimble's righteous anger shriveled. "Oh."

When the council inspected Ruth's *horno* they said, "Nice that it's so close to the spring. You've got green stuff close around, but no baking on windy days, okay?"

Ruth had grown up in southern California and knew wildfires all her life. "Certainly. We only bake once a week as it is, but no—no baking on windy days."

The water level in people's wells began dropping. Ranchers who normally watered their livestock from catchment ponds began taking their livestock to the beaver ponds on the river. Ruth's closest neighbors began dropping by, with her permission, to get drinking water from the spring.

"My well's gone all silty," said Rooster Vigil, the sheep rancher across the road. "It's doing for my garden, but you have to let it settle to drink. Far quicker to come over here."

Rooster was walking his sheep down to the Puerco once a day, to water them at the clay-lined catchment where the spring runoff ran down the bluff. He'd floated the notion of having them water above, at the dojo pond, to avoid the roundabout route, but Ruth had pointed to her garden and said, "Sorry. I'm having enough trouble keeping deer and rabbits out."

"Sheep manure is good for growing."

"I wasn't even thinking about sheep poop. Make that 'Hell, no.'"

Rooster had laughed and left with his five-gallon jug of water.

After that it became a weekly chore for Kimble to collect sheep manure down by the catchment to add to their compost piles. "And it's low in phosphorous," Ruth told him.

"It still stinks."

Tempers rose as water levels in the beaver ponds fell. As livestock weakened, coyote predation increased on lambs and calves. Some ranchers became obsessed with finding coyote dens. Other ranchers just gathered their animals tightly at night and kept watch.

One morning, while Rooster Vigil was filling his water jug at the spring, he yawned widely, his jaw cracking.

Ruth, harvesting ripe tomatoes and snap peas frowned at him. "You all right, Rooster?" There were dark circles under the rancher's eyes.

Rooster shrugged. "Trey Cruz lost some lambs last night." The Cruz place was south of Rooster's. "I haven't, but I've been sitting up most nights."

"Ah."

Rooster looked Kimble over. "How old are you, boy?"

Kimble was working the zucchini patch, checking the stems for squash beetles. They were bad this summer. He looked up at Ruth, but when she didn't say anything, he said, "Thirteen."

"Huh. Small for your age. But then again, you did all right with Sandy Williams. How'd you like a job?"

"What sort of job?"

"Nighthawk. I fell asleep while on watch last night and I was lucky I didn't lose any. Ewes crying woke me up and I heard the bastards scramble off when I came up shouting. It'd just be a couple of weeks. The missus and me are building a coyote fence around the big pen. But we're not making any progress staying up all night."

"Margo all right?" Ruth asked.

Rooster grinned. "She's fine. I'm not letting her lift anything. She's just spinning the cord and lashing the uprights."

"When's she due?"

"Six weeks. But if I don't finish this fence, between the coyotes and the baby I'll *never* get a good night's rest."

"What's the pay?" Ruth asked.

Rooster gestured at the zucchini. "You got the squash bugs bad, yeah?"

Kimble shrugged. "Yeah. They're going to town on the cucumbers and the zukes."

Rooster spread his hands. "Chickens would take care of that. Eat up a bunch of your weeds, too. And there'd be eggs. I've got two dozen new chicks running around."

Kimble looked at Ruth.

"We'd have to build a coop. And *someone* would have to clean it."

Kimble laughed. "Someone. All right."

HE started that night, at sunset, after Rooster guided the sheep into the large pen, a circular, split-rail fenced enclosure, about one hundred feet across, with plastic mesh on the bottom to keep the lambs in. It was a quarter mile away from Rooster's adobe house.

"The sheep dung can get rank," commented Rooster. He handed a six-foot spear to Kimble, an oak shaft topped with a double-edged fiberglass spearhead. "Just in case, but this is your real defense." He led Kimble over the fence beside the gate where a hollow log lay across two split chunks of wood. "Thump it," he said, demonstrating with a broken ax handle leaning against the fence. When he brought it down hard, the resounding boom was impressive. "That should scare 'em off. I'm not gonna get out of bed for an occasional tap but if you need help—" He beat a fast-paced staccato tattoo on the log. "I'll come running but . . . you ever hear the story of the boy who cried wolf?"

Kimble laughed. "I'll do my best to make sure you can sleep."

That first night was the hardest. Nothing happened and his body was expecting sleep. He did *jyo* exercises with the spear and walked in circles around the inside and outside of the fence.

It got cold after midnight and since the air was still, he kept a small fire going in Rooster's clay *chimenea*. He used it to warm up, but he didn't sit down near it. The very thought was enough to make his head nod and his eyelids droop.

Rooster came out at dawn. "Any excitement?"

"Fighting sleep. That was hard."

"Get some rest during the day and it'll be easier."

The next night, Sensei sent some of her green tea with him and he brewed a cup every couple of hours. When the caffeine stopped working, his full bladder kicked in. Also, about two in the morning, the sheep awoke, bleated, and milled about.

He walked noisily around the fence, spear at the ready, but whatever was out there didn't show itself. He had no trouble keeping awake until Rooster came out at dawn.

That night, when he returned, Rooster said, "There were tracks, maybe six animals."

"Coyotes?"

"No. Coyotes tend to breeding pairs, not packs. Maybe a family group with half-grown cubs, but these were all large animals. I'm thinking dogs. Feral dogs."

"What about wolves? Don't they move in packs?"

The Mexican gray wolf and the timber wolf were increasing since the coming of the bugs.

"Just keep your eyes open."

Nothing disturbed the sheep that night or for the rest of the week. Each day, when Kimble showed up, the tightly spaced uprights of the coyote fence grew around the perimeter of the holding pen. As each section was completed, the Vigils transplanted prickly pear to the base of the fence, to discourage tunneling.

Kimble's patrol became smaller as he concentrated on the sections of fence that were still just horizontal rails.

One night, as he crouched before the *chimenea* feeding small chunks of wood to the fire, he heard a panicked bleating from the far end of the enclosure, squarely in the middle of the new coyote fence. Almost immediately he heard the sound of splintering wood followed by growling.

His eyes were still dazzled by the flames of the fire but the moon was quarter full and high. The entire flock surged toward him, pressed up against the fence. He heard a sheep scream.

He dashed to the hollow log and beat it hard, perhaps thirty taps in ten seconds, then pushed through the sheep toward the growling, holding the spear low, point out in front.

There were several dogs, at least five or six. Two of them were tearing at the screaming ewe. The others were barking and rushing the milling sheep. One other large dog was standing in the shadow of the fence, barely seen, but a hole, created by the splintering of four of the upright saplings, allowed moonlight to spill through the fence. Over the smell of sheep dung Kimble smelled wet dog and ozone, like after a lightning storm.

Kimble lunged, thrusting the spear like a *jyo* at the dog tearing at the ewe. The spear tip went in right behind its shoulder, twisting, hitting the lungs and heart. It dropped with a startled grunt.

Kimble pulled and thrust again, but the other dog jumped sideways. The spear tip scored across the dog's shoulder and it yelped and scrambled for the hole through the fence. The other dogs fled as well, though they ran around the flock toward the old rail fencing. Only the large dark dog, back by the fence, paused as the wounded dog wiggled through, then turned to follow, completely filling the hole torn in the fence.

Kimble skipped forward, thrusting again. There was a dull clanking sound as the tip struck and then moonlight flooded through the hole in the fence again. When he looked at the composite spearhead, he saw that it had snapped in half. He found the broken piece on the ground, sand-encrusted and bloody.

"I think you imagined hitting it. You probably got the fence," suggested Rooster, when he arrived a few moments later.

Kimble shrugged. He'd seen and felt the spear strike the animal's right flank solidly. Too solidly, apparently. However, he didn't argue.

Rooster was happy Kimble had killed the one dog and driven off the others. The screaming ewe had to be put down, but it could've been much worse. He was less happy about the broken section of new coyote fence. "How the hell did they break that?" he wondered, fingering the splintered ends. "Go home and get some rest but be back here midmorning. I'm getting together a few of the boys and we're gonna track that pack down. No point in building fence if they can do that."

WHEN Kimble recounted the night's events to Ruth, she said, "Well, glad you're all right. Get some sleep. I'll get you up in time." When she woke him, she was wearing her hat and walking boots, and when it was time for him to go, she handed him a *jyo*, took one herself, and walked along.

"I don't know, Rooster," said Barney Spinoza. "Not sure this is a trip for a woman, 'specially one who needs a stick to walk."

Shocked, Kimble turned to look at Ruth's reaction, but her eyes only crinkled.

Barney was new to the area and hadn't been around when Sandy Williams had his encounter with Ruth in the marketplace. Rooster just patted him on the shoulder and said, "Don't worry, Barney. It'll be all right."

Rooster had gotten Rosemary Werito's husband, Frank, to come, not just because he also ran sheep, but because he was a good tracker.

"You got one, all right," Frank said, as they headed out. "Lots of blood spoor." He'd brought a traditional bow. Rooster had a crossbow slung over his back and was carrying the same spear Kimble had used the night before, with a newly replaced spearhead. Barney carried a plastic rifle with a quiver of preloaded disposable cardboard barrels. Everyone brought water bottles.

The blood was the best indicator. It had been dry for so long the ground was sandy dust or baked hard. You could make out some vague tracks and sometimes claw scratches on baked dirt. It wasn't until the pack tracked through mud in the riverbed that they got anything clear.

"Yeah. Dogs. Seven, I'm thinking," said Werito, studying the tracks near the water.

"Well, we knew that," said Rooster. "There's a dead one back at my place."

"Didn't know if it was only dogs. They're headed downstream." He gestured south along the bosque. Barney and Rooster moved out, Ruth following. Kimble was standing by Frank, looking at the tracks, too. Frank pointed out the salient features. "Big dog. Medium dog. Fat dog."

"Fat dog? Why not another big dog?"

"Look here, where you can see how close its legs are together? Half the length of the others, but it's sinking into the same soil about as deep." He pointed at another set of footsteps. "That dog is big and heavy. See how far apart back and front paws are? See how deep the tracks—" Frank tilted his head to one side. "Huh."

"What?"

"It's the same track."

"Same dog, you mean?"

Werito licked his lips. "Well, I'm not that sure it *is* a dog."

"A wolf?"

"Uh, no." He stood up abruptly. He'd been carrying his bow unstrung but now he took a moment to string it. "Let's catch up," he said and started out briskly.

The blood spoor stopped with the blood's source.

"Huh," said Rooster. "I guess they turned on . . . no. What the hell did that?"

It was the medium-sized dog that Kimble had wounded. The pack had chewed on the body, but the head was lying in pieces.

Precise pieces.

It had been split bilaterally, like an anatomy illustration, right down between the ears, eyes, nostrils. One side was lying intact, the plane of the incision tilted toward the sky, displaying sinuses, throat, the top of the spine, and the brain split right down the corpus callosum. The other half had been sliced crosswise, in uniform half-inch sections perpendicular to the first cut and they were spread in order beside the other half. By contrast, the neck looked like it had been torn from the body.

Frank said something heartfelt in Dineh.

"You said it," agreed Ruth.

Frank opened his mouth to answer, then shut it again, studying the ground around the dead dog. "I guess I noticed something odd back when we found the tracks in the mud."

"Odder than *this*?" said Barney.

Frank said, "Pretty odd." He looked down at the precisely cut chunks of dog head. "But, no, maybe not this odd."

"What was it?" asked Rooster.

"One of the dogs has four right front feet." He knelt near the dog head but not facing it.

Rooster frowned. "I'm not getting you."

Frank pointed at the ground in front of him. "Look. That big dog stood right here? I've got good tracks of both front feet and one of its rear feet."

"Yeah."

"Every one of those tracks is the same. Look. See that little V-shape in the middle of that pad? Some sort of scarring, probably."

"Oh," said Ruth, kneeling down beside him. "That V-mark is in both the front prints." She shifted. "*And* the back paw print, also. That doesn't make any sense."

"It's worse than that. Look at the right-left symmetry. They're all right paws, the same right paw. In the mud, I saw all four feet. They were *all* the same."

"That's just dumb," said Barney. "Why would a dog have the same paw prints on every foot."

Rooster just pointed at the sliced chunks of dog head. "Why would a dog do this?" He looked closer, waving his hand to shoo off some of the gathering flies. "How could anybody? Haven't seen cuts this clean, especially through bone, since before the bugs came. Really good metal knives could do it. Maybe you could do this with a ceramic bone saw, but it would sure take a long time and it wouldn't look anywhere near as neat. I mean, the bone looks *polished*!"

Ruth had stopped looking at the ground and was scanning the bluff and the river. "Do you really want to chase . . . *this*?" Her gesture included both the tracks and the dissected head.

Rooster sucked his lips in and sat back on his haunches. He looked first at Frank, who shrugged slightly, then at Barney, who said, "I think someone's playing a prank on us. How could a dog do that?"

Frank looked amused. "Maybe it wasn't a dog. I don't see any other tracks. I suppose whatever did it could have flown in and then flown off."

"What do you think, Frank?" asked Rooster.

Frank shrugged again. "I must admit, I'm curious. We

had a weird crow last year, that flew wrong, but it was following the other birds around. I didn't get that close to it, but when it settled on a branch, the branch bent. I mean more than it should have. Not sure I want to fight this thing, but at the least I'd like to *see* it."

"Hell," said Barney, "no matter what it is, I'd rather fight it out here than back home while it's killing my goats."

Rooster nodded reluctantly. "There's some sense to that, too." He flipped his spear and shoved it into the ground, then unslung his crossbow, cocked, and loaded it. He pulled the spear from the ground and looked at it.

Kimble stepped forward. "I can carry it. Keep it ready."

"Uh." Rooster looked at Ruth. "Not sure if you're going on with us."

Kimble turned. Ruth was frowning at the dog parts. "Well, Sensei?"

"Not sure this is a good idea, but it would be better to know what's slinking around." She blew air out through her lips. "We'll go on for a while at least."

They followed the tracks through the bosque for another mile. Once, where the river had uncovered an old junk refrigerator, they had to wade across the river to avoid bugs, but the river was only ankle deep. Frank eyed the tracks. "The dogs didn't go around the bugs at all," Frank noted.

The tracks led them to a thicket of salt cedars at the base of the bluff at the edge of the bosque. The dirt cliff rose straight up behind the brush and Frank skirted around the edge of the cedars until he reached the other side. "The tracks go in there. They don't come out."

Rooster and Barney, who'd been standing right next to the brush, turned to face it and stepped back several paces.

"Well, I don't like the idea of going in there," said Ruth.

"Burn it," suggested Barney.

They just looked at him and he turned red.

"Oh. Grass fire."

"The bosque could burn all the way to the Jemez," Rooster said.

"Let's do it old school," said Ruth. "You guys cover the downstream half and Kimble and I will act as beaters. See if we can get them to come out on your side."

"Thought you didn't want to go in there," said Rooster.

"Hopefully we won't have to."

The three men positioned themselves about thirty feet away from the thicket in a semicircle that covered the downstream two-thirds. Frank put an arrow to his bow and stuck three others into the ground next to him, fletching up. On seeing this, Rooster did the same thing, only he dropped to one knee so he could brace his elbow on his forward leg and pull the shorter bolts from the ground. Barney took up a similar posture, but he just laid his replacement barrels on the ground beside him, double-checking the orientation.

While they were doing that, Ruth and Kimble gathered fist-sized river rocks and a couple of stout sticks.

"Want your spear?" Kimble asked Rooster.

"Uh, sure."

Kimble stuck it in the ground near Rooster's quarrels and trotted back around to Ruth.

"Ready?" asked Ruth.

"I guess," said Frank.

The other two men nodded.

Kimble banged a short stick against his *jyo*, loud as he could. Ruth began pitching the rocks into the underbrush, low, changing her aim slightly with each one. On her fourth shot, there was a yelp from the brush. She pitched more rocks in that general direction. Kimble moved closer to the salt brush, dropped his short stick, and began whaling on the bushes with the *jyo*. There was another yelp from inside the brush and then Kimble heard the crossbow twang, followed almost immediately by the discharge of one of Barney's barrels, then the more muted noise of Frank's bow twice in succession and yelps of pain.

"One pulled back in!" yelled Frank. "Watch it!"

Kimble, still flailing at the brush, didn't see the pit-bull cross dart out of the bush to his right and, teeth bared, lunge at his exposed heel.

"Look out!" shouted Ruth.

Kimble twisted away as he heard the warning, followed almost immediately by a solid "thunk." He saw Ruth's *jyo* pull back and the dog drop into the sand, suddenly limp.

He backed away from the brush. The dog's head was lopsided, a definite dent behind one eye.

"You can look at it later," Ruth said. "Keep your eyes open."

"Yes, Sensei. Thanks." He backed away from the edge of the brush, his *jyo* held for thrusting. They were all frozen, watching, waiting for more movement. When nothing else happened, Ruth called, "How many did you get?"

"Four."

"We got one, too," Ruth said.

"Oh," said Frank. "What with the dissected one, that leaves just one. The odd one."

Kimble took a step back.

"I'd like to get a look at that," said Rooster.

"Me, too," said Ruth. "But I don't want anyone hurt, to get that look."

Frank walked around toward Ruth and Kimble. "Give it a hole to run through," he suggested. "We can try some more rocks, too."

They moved the semicircle more to the upstream side, leaving a gap near the bluff, and Kimble gathered more rocks for everyone. Barney changed out his barrel and stood ready. "If anything has a chance of stopping it, it'll be the gun, right?"

Ruth said gently, "And what if it doesn't *like* being shot at?"

Barney retorted, "What if it doesn't like you pitchin' rocks at it? Besides, I'm sure the dog I shot didn't like it, but he didn't have much say, either."

Frank and Ruth exchanged glances and Frank shrugged.

They picked up rocks and threw in unison, starting at the near edge and shifting their area of concentration. They could hear the rocks rattling through the branches and striking the bluff and the ground and then a clanking sound.

Rooster froze. "Christ. I swear that sounds like metal."

"Couldn't be," said Barney. "Where are the bugs?"

Rooster looked uncertain. "It was about dead center. Everybody?"

This time there were several clanking hits followed by the rustling of underbrush and then a cracking sound as one of the taller salt cedars abruptly fell to one side.

"What's that smell?" asked Barney.

"Ozone," said Ruth.

"I see movement!" Barney said excitedly, pulling the gun higher. Everyone shifted over to where they could look past Barney toward the far end of the brush.

The dark dog took three deliberate steps out of the underbrush and its head swiveled toward them. It looked like a Doberman except there was no brown on it, just an oily black. Where there should have been eyes there were slightly darker patches. The ears were triangular— sharp, with impossibly straight edges.

Ruth said, "I don't think you should . . ."

Barney fired, and the ceramic projectile hit the creature squarely in the chest and splintered, flying off in fragments. The dog took one involuntary step backward and then steadied.

It crouched.

"Shit," said Frank. Barney scrambled to change barrels, fumbling.

The black dog turned and jumped up, twenty feet, to catch the top of the bluff with its forepaws and pull itself up over the edge, triggering a small landslide with its rear legs. On top it turned once more and looked back at them, then, with another spurt of dust and flying grass, it was gone.

THEY reported the incident to the council, but Ruth told Kimble later, "They didn't believe it. I doubt they'll pass it on to the Rangers."

Rooster replaced the saplings where the dogs had broken through his fence and finished the enclosure the next week. There were no more problems with the sheep and Kimble went home with a basket of chicks and half a sack of chicken feed. They built a rammed-earth coop with a removable roof and let the chicks have the run of the garden. As the chicks fledged out, the squash beetles ceased to be a problem.

A week later, a storm rolled in from the west and it rained for three straight days.

Kimble huddled inside the cottage. He'd spent enough time out in the weather during his time in the capital.

Ruth, on the other hand, stood outside the door and let the drops splash across her face. "The drought is over," she said.

"Yes, Sensei."

Kimble Goes to Town

Ruth woke one morning and couldn't breathe.

"I imagine it's allergies," she told Kimble, but she had him lead class that afternoon. The next day was worse and Kimble fetched Marisol Aragon, the Territorial Medical System nurse, from the village.

"It's asthma," Marisol said, measuring Ruth's lung capacity with a plastic flow meter. "Pretty bad, too."

Marisol gave Ruth prednisone pills to relieve the immediate symptoms but said, "This is short-term. I want you to go on an inhaled corticosteroid. That's a much safer long-term solution, but I don't have any here. I can get some from the capital, but it will take a month. Better if it was quicker, but it's a catch-22. Traveling would most likely aggravate the asthma."

"I can go," said Kimble. "If I rent a horse, I can be back in four days."

Marisol, not tall, but still a head higher than Kimble, eyed him dubiously, but Ruth nodded and said, "Go see if you can hire one of Mr. Kenney's mounts."

Matt Kenney greeted Kimble warmly but shook his head violently at the request. "Hire a horse? When I'd probably have two less without your help? I'll *lend* you Suze." He led Kimble to a small, brown quarter horse with a gray muzzle. "Both my boys started on Suze. They're on to bigger mounts now, but she'll go all day with someone your size. Fact is, she doesn't get the exercise she should, so a trip to the capital and back would be good for her."

"I don't feel right not paying," Kimble tried again.

"Use the money on feed and put her in a livery while you're there. We just epoxied new fiberglass shoes, but if there's a problem, see a farrier." He patted the horse on her flank. "One thing—she's a bear for holding her breath when you're tightening the cinch."

Kimble left the next day in the cool of the morning, reversing the route Ruth and he had walked to Perro Frio. He was an adequate horseman, having ridden his schoolmates' hacks around the village and on occasional school excursions, but even though he was in good shape, his muscles weren't used to an entire day of riding. Getting out of his bedroll the next morning required rolling over to all fours and struggling upright. The evening before, it had taken him over twenty minutes to get the cinch off, so he doubled the end back in a slipknot. He didn't knee Suze in the belly as Mr. Kenney had recommended, but he waited, watching her breathing, and tightened the strap again, and then again.

On this last one Suze whuffed, turned her head, and looked back at him reproachfully.

He'd made even better time than he'd thought. He reached Nuevo Santa Fe's south gate by noon, in time to stable Suze *and* get the *cabrito* tacos at Griegos.

Marisol had given him a script for the medicine and he only had to wait a half hour at the TMS pharmacy before receiving several disk-shaped inhalers, nasal sprays, and some pump-operated "rescue" inhalers. "These ones are tricky. Outside the territory they use pressurized ones, but they're metal." The pharmacist talked about their use and gave him a ream of instructions for Ruth to read.

Next he took an order and check to Retterson & Morales, building supplies. The dojo walls were as high as they were supposed to be and the concrete roof beams had been laid in place. "Our freighter will deliver the roof tiles before the end of September," they assured him.

He felt odd being back in the capital—the bustle seemed louder, more frenetic. The loiterers seemed scarier. He felt like it had changed on him, but he realized it was really he who'd changed.

He saw people he'd known slightly, who would have greeted him a year ago. Now they glanced at him and squinted, like his face was teasing their memories without effect. He was feeling sad about this when he ran square into César Castellanos.

"Kim-BULL. Where you been, man? I thought sure the Rangers dragged you off, but then they came around again last week, so I knew they didn't."

Kimble had been about to name his new home but stopped mid-word. "Perr—they've been asking for me? By name?"

"They were asking for Kim Creighton, but someone must've recognized you from the new photo 'cause now they're asking for Kimble, too."

"They have a new photo?"

"They've got the old one, but they also have one of those aged-by-computer ones. That one looks a *lot* more like you."

Kimble fought the urge to look around for Rangers. He took out the floppy cloth hat he'd been wearing while riding and put it on his head.

"So where *have* you been?"

He thought he could trust César but he didn't want Rangers showing up at Ruth's door. "Better you should be able to say, 'I don't know.' Right? I mean, why add one more thing you'd have to talk about at confession."

César laughed. "But you're all right? I mean, you look good. You're nowhere near as skinny as you were."

"I'm good. I've got a good place to live, good work, and good schooling. And I'd rather not be dragged back to my good-for-nothin' old man and ruin it."

They talked about mutual friends, acquaintances,

and enemies. César's voice was deeper and he informed Kimble that he was walking out with Jessica Potter from his parish.

"What's that on your lip?" Kimble kidded.

"That's my mustache." It wasn't a very definite mustache.

"That's a relief," said Kimble. "I was afraid it was a caterpillar. A very sick caterpillar."

"Well, Jessica likes it so you can just shove it up your—"

"Great seeing you."

Before talking to César he'd planned to leave the next morning but now Kimble moved through the mid-afternoon crowds to the stables, trying to exude casualness. He panicked a bit at Southgate, when he saw an entire troop of Rangers lined up through the gate, not mounted yet, but apparently headed out. Their saddle holsters all held the composite gyro rifles and they all had two-and-a-half-foot truncheons hanging from their belts. Kevlar helmets and vests were bundled behind their saddles. There was a squad of lancers, too, carrying eight-foot shafts.

Kimble swerved toward Griegos but several of the Rangers were in line there, too, picking up food.

He took a deep breath, resettled the saddlebags over his shoulder, and headed back to the gate. A family— mother, father, son, and two daughters with unmistakable resemblance to each other—were walking out of the gate, the son pushing a two-wheeled garden cart full of purchases. Kimble took two long strides and joined them, walking through the gate at their side, earning a hard look from the mother, who shifted her purse to her other arm.

The Rangers were watching the two teenage daughters. The oldest daughter was walking with the studied casualness of a young woman well aware of her beauty. The younger daughter, walking behind her sister, was exaggerating her sister's walk, and rolling her hips, and getting a laugh from several of the troops.

As the family passed the head of the double-column of horses, Kimble increased his pace again, pulling out in front and taking the turnoff for the livery stable.

"Thought you were going to be overnight?" the livery man said.

"Was." Kimble paid him for the afternoon and bought some extra feed for the road. "Got everything done quicker than I thought." As he was saddling Suze the same family arrived, redeeming a team of horses, a wagon, and two saddle horses.

While the father and son helped the livery man harness the horses, the younger daughter came over to look at Suze. "Nice horse—I love her neat little feet. Huh. Why do you put the slipknot on the cinch?"

"'Cause otherwise it takes ten minutes of hard work to get it off. She has a rib cage like an accordion, I swear." Kimble turned the horse and took her to the watering trough.

The girl looked at the now-exposed brand. "Bar-Halo. That's the Kenneys' Ranch. Did you buy this horse from the Kenneys?"

Kimble had to look up to meet the young woman's

eyes. "Didn't buy. Mr. Kenney loaned me Suze. I don't recognize you from around Perro Frio."

"Oh, we don't live that far south, but our family and theirs go way back. Daddy and Matt Kenney were roommates at Baylor University." She turned and called out. "Daddy, this boy knows the Kenneys." She turned back. "What's your name?"

He thought about the recent inquiries. "Kim Monroe," he said, using Ruth's last name like he did at the village school.

"I'm Sarah Costillo." She pointed. "Those are my parents; my sister, Parker; and my brother, Paco. Paco's the oldest. I'm the baby."

"Uh, fifteen?" Kimble guessed.

"Next month," she said.

Kimble nodded. "Thirteen, myself."

"You came all the way from Perro Frio by yourself?"

He shrugged. "My guardian is sick." He patted the saddle bags. "Needed to get some medicine from the TMS pharmacy."

Her mouth opened and then closed and she frowned.

He answered the unasked question, half-lying. "My parents died when I was small."

"Oh." She turned and looked at her own parents, her face thoughtful.

Mr. Costillo, the harnessing done, walked over and stuck out his hand. Sarah did the introductions.

"Seems to me, Matt told me about some stolen horses back in June and a neighbor boy who got them back. You wouldn't be him, would you?"

Kimble blushed. "I'm the neighbor, but I didn't do anything, really. The man who stole them knocked himself out and broke his arm chasing me down the riverbank. The posse caught up because of that."

"Traveling alone? You're starting out awful late, aren't you?"

Kimble explained about the medicine.

"Ride with us. Our ranch is only six hours down the trail. You can spend the night and get an early start."

Kimble started to refuse, but then he thought about the troop of Rangers. If he was traveling with the Costillos he was less likely to draw the Rangers' attention.

"Well, thanks. That would be nice."

Mr. Costillo nodded firmly. "Good. It's safer that way what with all these attacks."

"Attacks? There's been attacks? What kind of attacks?"

"Ha. I thought you probably didn't know about them, heading out alone like this. *Ladrones.* A group of eight or so men, the reports say. They've been robbing travelers west and south of the capital and they've hit a few farms and ranches, too. I brought word to the Rangers about a raid on one of our neighbors—they lost some horses and one of their hired hands was clubbed down."

Sarah added, "Broken collarbone."

"He was lucky," said Mr. Costillo. "Some of the travelers have been killed. You hadn't heard about this?"

"Not a word," said Kimble. "I'm sure Mr. Kenney would've warned me if he'd known. I seriously doubt that Sensei—my guardian—would've let me come."

"Well, it's all been in the last ten days. They'll hear about it soon enough."

"Eight men? Are you sure that you will be safe to travel?"

Mr. Costillo laughed. "We caravanned up with two other families, but we're going back with an entire troop of Rangers."

So, thought Kimble. *That's a big fail on the avoiding-the-Rangers thing.*

THE Costillos' saddle horses belonged to the older daughter, Parker, and the son, Paco. Kimble expected Mr. Costillo to take up the reins of the wagon, but it was Sarah who drove it down to the main road. Mr. Costillo sat in the back bench seat with a disposable four-barrel cardboard rifle. His wife took up some wool and a pair of wooden knitting needles, but Kimble noted a composite crossbow with a quiver full of ceramic-headed fiberglass bolts at her feet.

The troop, fully mounted, was waiting at the main road. As soon as Mr. Costillo's party appeared, the commanding officer issued a short command and pairs of scouts headed forward at the gallop, reducing the troop by half. The remainder split into two groups, one before the family and one after.

Kimble heard Parker say, "Great. Dust for supper."

Her brother Paco smiled and said, "A-gaaaaaain?"

Underway, the commanding officer looped back to the wagon and rode alongside. "Good afternoon, Rosalita,

Sarah, John." He gestured at Mr. Costillo's four-barrel. "What you packing, John? Slugs?"

"Bird gravel. Not terribly accurate but at twenty feet it makes an impression."

"Well, I hope you won't need it. If we do spot them, though, I might borrow your wagon and try a decoy with a few of my men."

Kimble, riding behind the wagon with Paco and Parker, saw the CO gesture back toward him. "You've got a new recruit, I see."

Mr. Costillo raised his voice, "Come on up here, Kim."

Kimble took a deep breath and touched his heels to Suze's side. He hoped the CO wasn't up on all the territorial circulars.

"This is Captain Bentham, Kim. Kim Monroe here lives down in Perro Frio. He's a neighbor of Matt Kenney. You remember Matt, right?"

"Of course." Bentham was of medium height and build. He had a beaky nose and prominent bushy eyebrows. "Though what I really remember is Patricia Kenney's biscuits and apple butter."

Mr. Costillo laughed. "I can understand that. Kim rode up to the capital to get some medicine. He didn't know about the bandits."

Kim nodded agreement. He didn't like the way Bentham was studying him. The man was smiling slightly but it didn't touch his eyes, still and unblinking.

Bentham responded to Mr. Costillo. "Yeah, well the news probably passed him going the other way."

Kimble hadn't thought about that. "They'll be worried."

"Concerned, certainly," Mr. Costillo said.

The adults kept talking and Kimble let Suze drop back. Bentham gave him one more intent look before turning back to Mr. and Mrs. Costillo.

Back beside Paco and Parker, Kimble asked, "You know the captain long?"

"Oh, yeah," said Paco. "Ten years, at least. I was eight when he used to stay with us as a new lieutenant. He was in the ethnographic survey then, counting heads and keeping people away from major infestations."

An hour later, as the sun neared the horizon, a single rider appeared, one of the scouts previously dispatched. Kimble didn't hear the scout's report to Captain Bentham but the CO promptly halted the column and rode back to the wagon. "Looks like we may have spotted them. There's a bunch camped overlooking the road in the next valley—seems the right number of horses. My boys are keeping an eye on them, hidden, but if they are the ones, we can ride the troops around to the east and close unobserved by coming up an arroyo. If you don't mind, I'd like to try to decoy them with your wagon."

"What about the girls?" asked Mr. Costillo.

"All of you would ride with me," said Captain Bentham. "Sergeant Pouri and two of his squad will take the wagon. They're gonna change into mufti. Sarah, Rosalita, and you would ride their horses."

"That's good for Sarah and Rosalita but it is *my* wagon. I'll drive it."

Kimble saw Mrs. Costillo turn her head sharply. So did Captain Bentham, who said, "Sorry, John. Against regs. If you'd rather I didn't use your wagon, I can understand."

Grumbling, Mr. Costillo gave in and Kimble saw Mrs. Costillo exhale deeply.

The three Rangers assigned as decoys changed clothes behind a screen of their fellows' horses. They concealed their ceramic gyro rifles, Kevlar helmets, and their billies on the floor beneath a blanket.

"Wearing your vests?" Captain Bentham asked.

The sergeant banged his knuckles against his chest and the hard rapping sound was audible across the road.

"Right, then. Give us a quarter-hour before you start out. I can get there quicker, but I want to take it slow and keep the dust down."

"Yes, sir. Starting now?"

Bentham looked over to where a soldier was adjusting the Kevlar stirrups on one of the Ranger saddles to fit Sarah Costillo's shorter legs. "Ready?"

The Ranger held up his thumb and went to his own horse.

Bentham nodded. "Starting now."

The sergeant said, "Ramirez," and the soldier sitting behind him on the wagon began counting quietly.

The mounted troop with the Costillos and Kimble swung off the road and made for a low spot in the next ridge, riding briskly. Once there, they slowed to a walk, crested the ridge, and dropped quickly into a sandy wash. Kimble looked, as they came through the notch in the ridge, but the hillside bulged out and blocked the road up the valley from view.

The wash led into the bottom of the valley where a creek wandered down out of the Jemez on its way to the Puerco. Bentham gave orders to water the horses and then don vests and helmets. A few minutes later they rode on down the wash. At one bend, the advance scout suddenly turned his horse back and held up his hand. Bentham and the scout dismounted and peered around corner of the wash's edge.

Bentham remounted and came back to the main body. "The road fords the creek around the next bend but we'd also be visible from the hillside where our suspects are camped. Patowski, get up there and let me know what's happening." He pointed and one of the smaller Rangers slung his rifle over his back, dismounted, and was boosted by two squad mates up the steep side of the wash and into a waist-high clump of greasewood. Kimble watched in fascination as the Ranger used his ceramic knife to cut three branches of the brush and tucked them through loops in his Kevlar vest so they stuck up around his head.

"I can see the wagon just coming over the ridge. Don't see any sign of our scouts. I see the smoke from the suspects' camp, but they're hidden by some cedars."

Bentham moved his horse over to the Costillos and Kimble. "When we go, I'll leave Patowski here. Please don't move out until you get an all clear from me or one of my men."

Patowski called down softly. "Something's happening, sir. The wagon is well down the hill and I saw motion through the trees. Thought I saw a saddle being slung over a horse."

Bentham turned to his troops. "D Squad draw your rifles—fire only if cleared by Sergeant Fernandez. All other squads—truncheons or staffs. Patowski, when we go, you stay put."

"They're on the move, sir," said Patowski. "Looks like they're going to intercept before the wagon reaches the ford."

"Good. The scouts should block them by the ridge. If they head back the way they came, the hills will slow them down. Let me know when they're within a hundred yards of the wagon."

The sergeants dressed up the two columns of troopers and Paco took the reins of Patowski's mount.

"They're closing on the wagon, sir."

Captain Bentham chopped his hand forward and the column moved out at a walk, but by the time they'd reached the bend they were trotting. Dust drifted back up the wash and Kimble held his bandanna over mouth and nose as an impromptu filter.

Patowski called out. "Ha! They've started to run but the scouts cut them off. Oh, shit! Dammit!" Patowski jumped to his feet. "Three of them broke for the ford. Gotta cut them off." Patowski disappeared, running. Almost immediately there was the shrill shriek of a gyro rocket being fired. Then another and the sickening sound of a horse screaming.

Kimble edged Suze back toward the steep wall of the wash. *If the bandits couldn't cross the ford, there was another route they could take.* "Maybe we should mo—" One horse and then another sprinted around the bend and pounded up the wash toward them. The riders weren't Rangers.

Mr. Costillo started to raise his four-barrel but his attention was split between the approaching horses and his family. "Get back!" he yelled, gesturing to the side of the wash. He spurred his horse out into the middle of the wash and raised the gun.

No. Let them by! thought Kimble. *What are you thinking!* Armored Rangers were obviously the appropriate tool, not someone without armor whose family was present.

"Hold up there!" Mr. Costillo yelled hoarsely.

Maybe Mr. Costillo thought they'd stop or at least turn and go back the way they'd come. He probably didn't expect them to fire first.

The lead rider lifted a multi-barrel disposable, like Mr. Costillo's, but when he fired each barrel in quick succession it was clear from the sharp reports that he was firing rifled ceramic slugs. Kimble ducked reflexively. From a galloping horse the bandit was more likely to hit someone by accident than deliberately, but Mr. Costillo was not so lucky. He clutched at his chest and tumbled backward over his horse's rump.

There were simultaneous cries of "Daddy!" and "John" from Mr. Costillo's daughters and wife. His son Paco spurred his horse so hard that it jumped out into the wash, colliding with the first rider's horse. Both Paco, the rider, and horses went down in a tangle of flailing limbs.

Mr. Costillo, on the ground, thrust his gun out in the direction of the trailing rider and fired.

Gravel buzzed through the air and the second horse screamed and jumped sideways. The rider stayed on for the first convulsive jump but a second buck shook him free. He cleared the saddle cleanly and landed in a crouch. He took one step toward the horse and it bolted away, blood streaming from several gravel wounds.

Paco and the rider he'd collided with were wrestling on the ground. For a moment, both were in far more danger from flailing hooves, but then their mounts heaved themselves upright and danced away from the struggling pair.

Kimble hesitated, but at the sight of the red spreading across Mr. Costillo's chest, he thumped Suze's side and steered her past the struggling pair to where Mr. Costillo lay and jumped down, dropping the reins on the ground.

He ripped Mr. Costillo's shirt open, sending buttons flying. He was expecting a hideous wound, the heart or lungs, but the slug had gone in high, just above the collarbone, and torn into the trapezius. The ceramic projectile was actually sticking half out of the back of Mr. Costillo's shoulder.

Mrs. Costillo said sharply, "Parker, go get the Ranger's medic!" Kimble heard pounding hooves and looked up and to see the eldest daughter's horse flying down the arroyo, swinging wide around the second bandit. Mrs. Costillo's knees thumped to the ground beside Kimble and she had a clean handkerchief in her hand, already folding it into a pad. Sarah was right behind her, doing exactly the same. "Pull that on through," Mrs. Costillo said, jerking her chin at the projectile. She was holding Mr. Costillo's shoulder up slightly, keeping it out of the dirt, while she pressed the makeshift bandage against the entry wound in front.

"Right," Kimble said. He felt faint, and a bit nauseated at the blood. He took a deep breath, and tried to grip the projectile, but his hands slipped off the bloody point. "Gimme," he said to Sarah, taking the handkerchief out of her hand. The slug popped right out once he used the cloth to grip it, but blood, staunched on the front, poured freely out the rear wound. He wadded the cloth up and pressed it against the back. Mrs. Costillo slipped her hand over his.

"Help Paco," she said, jerking her head back where the two men had been struggling.

By the time Kimble stood and turned, Paco had his opponent facedown in the sand and was using a rawhide piggin' string to secure the man's hands behind his back.

"You rope calves?" Kimble asked.

Paco grinned, an odd contrast, a flash of white teeth against bloody lips. He started to answer when Mrs. Costillo screamed.

It was the second rider, the one who'd been bucked off by his horse. He'd come up and grabbed Sarah from behind. He pulled her back toward the center of the wash, a ceramic knife held to her throat.

"Get me a horse!" he yelled. "Right now or I swear to

God I'll cut her throat!" The man's eyes were wide, showing lots of white. He kept glancing back toward the ford. "I mean it!" he shouted, giving Sarah a shake that startled a sob out of her.

The only horse still standing in the immediate vicinity was Suze, reins trailing. Paco's, the first rider's, Patowski's, and the other two borrowed Ranger mounts were fifty yards down the arroyo. The bandit's own gravel-stung horse had completely disappeared, having run back around the bend toward the ford.

Paco started to step forward, his face suddenly white, his hands balled into fists, but the bandit shouted, "You'll kill 'er! Get back! I mean it." He pointed the knife at Kimble. "You, kid. Get that horse and bring it here!" He brought the knife back to Sarah's throat by way of emphasis.

Sarah was blinking rapidly and her jaw was clenched, but she actually seemed calmer than her captor. She was holding her head very still.

"Do I gotta cut her? NOW!"

Kimble walked gingerly over to Suze, clucking his tongue, and took her reins. The little horse jerked her head suddenly, nostril flaring, but he had her firmly. "Shhhhhhhh." He moved his hand to stroke her nose and she jerked even more. He realized, *it's the smell of the blood on my hands.* His hands were also shaking.

"Get a move on, kid!"

Kimble led Suze over, holding the reins at their full length to keep the blood away from her head. *Nice and easy*, he told himself. The horse wasn't the only creature he wanted to avoid startling.

"Stop there! Hold her head."

The man had lost his hat, either in his earlier fall or during his initial encounter with the Rangers, but the impression of the hatband was still across his forehead. His shirt had greasy stains on the front, and even from two yards away, Kimble could smell stale sweat and wood smoke. The man's jeans were faded, but he had on fancy boots with composite spurs. He was so tan that at first Kimble thought he was Hispanic, but his upper forehead was practically pink.

Kimble couldn't take his eyes off the knife on Sarah's throat.

"Hold her head, dammit! On the other side!" The man backed Sarah up to Suze's shoulder and grabbed her hair and pulled it until she was arched back to the saddle. He pinched her hair between his hand and the pommel and jerked up onto the saddle. "Up!" he said to Sarah, pulling on her hair.

Sarah gasped and hopped involuntarily. The man dipped and snagged her belt, pulled her up and across his legs, turning her facedown, head on one side, legs on the other. "Reins!"

Kimble handed him the right rein, then stepped around to the left side to give him the other.

The man had his knife arm across Sarah's back. He took the rein from Kimble and said loudly, "You tell those Rangers that each time I see them, I'm cutting off an ear. When I run out of ears, they'll find her head, you got that?"

Kimble thought he was talking to Mrs. Costillo, but just in case, he nodded.

The man gathered the reins in his knife hand and grabbed the pommel to secure Sarah. As he sawed the reins around, Kimble dropped to his knee and darted his hand forward, grabbing the free end of the slipknot on the cinch strap. At the same time the man jabbed his spurs back into Suze's ribs.

Suze, unused to such treatment gave a tremendous leap forward, her left hip knocking Kimble over. He slapped and rolled, coming to his feet in time to see the saddle, Sarah, and her captor fly off Suze's back.

Sarah, facedown, came off best, landing on her feet and falling forward. The man landed on his back with the saddle on top of him. The white ceramic knife winked as it tumbled through the air.

Kimble took three strides and picked up the knife, keeping an eye on the man. The man was having trouble breathing, but he shoved the saddle off and was struggling to sit up when Sarah grabbed him by *his* hair and slammed him back down. She had a rock in the other hand. "*See how YOU like it*," she screamed, holding the rock up in the air.

Then her brother arrived and took over, turning the man facedown and pulling another piggin' rawhide thong from his back pocket. For good measure, he tied the man's hands to one of his ankles, arching the leg up behind.

Sarah kicked the man in the side and went back to her mother.

Kimble's hands stopped shaking, but his knees buckled and he dropped back to the ground. *She could've broken her neck and it would've been my fault. What was I thinking?*

Suze came up and prodded him with her nose. Keeping the bloody hands away from her head, he climbed to his feet and stroked her neck. Mrs. Costillo spared an arm to pull her daughter to her, running her free hand across her neck, to assure herself there'd been no cut.

Kimble slid up onto Suze's bare back. "Right, girl. Let's go get those other horses."

"SO, you want to tell me what happened?"

Captain Bentham and Kimble were riding alone, forty yards in front of the Costillos' wagon. A single squad rode behind the wagon. Bentham had sent the remainder of his troop back to Nuevo Santa Fe with the prisoners. He'd offered to send Mr. Costillo back with them, to the Territorial Medical Facility, but Mrs. Costillo, after consultation with the Rangers' medic, decided he would heal better in his own bed.

"Saddle came off. He shouldn't of spurred Suze." Kimble reached forward and patted the side of Suze's neck. "She's not used to that kind of treatment."

"The saddle came off? How did that happen? I mean, if the cinch had been loose, he couldn't have climbed up in the saddle like he did, could he? Or hauled Sarah up. The saddle would've just slid around." He glanced sideways at Kimble. "Mrs. Costillo and Paco saw you grab the cinch. Sarah told me you kept it in a slipknot."

Dammit. "Okay. Yeah, I untied it. I'm sorry."

Captain Bentham had been drawing breath to speak but shut his mouth abruptly, blinking. "Sorry? For what?"

"She could've broken her neck. He'd taken the knife off of her to grab the pommel but he could've stabbed her as they fell. He could've landed on his feet and we'd be back in the same hostage situation only he'd be even *more* desperate."

Kimble glanced at Bentham who was looking back, eyebrows raised.

"Thought about it, I see. How old are you?"

"Turned thirteen in February."

"That's right."

Kimble frowned. "Right? What do you mean? Oh, yeah, told Sarah."

"Did you? No, that's not how I knew, Mr. Creighton."

Kimble felt his stomach sink but he tried to brazen it out. "Pardon? Name's Monroe."

"So you say, Kim. I was going to give you a lecture about how dangerous your stunt was. But I'm also mad at Patowski. Not only did he leave his assigned post when he blocked them at the ford, but that's what drove them up the wash. And I'm furious with myself. I should've left an entire squad behind."

"Save some of that anger for Mr. Costillo. If he hadn't tried to stop them, they would've just ridden on by."

"Yeah, well he paid for that choice, didn't he?" Bentham looked sideways at him again, considering. "You've a clear way of looking at things. It worked out that you pulled the cinch. Sarah is okay and the rat bastard didn't get away. But I'm also glad you see it could've gone wrong."

"I just did it, though. Didn't think about all that other stuff until after. He was so afraid."

"You mean her, right? Sarah was so afraid?"

"Hell, no. She was angry, I could tell. But he looked like a cow in quicksand, the whites showing all around. He could've done *anything* in that state. And, dammit, Sensei's medicine was in those saddlebags!"

"Sensei. Is that who you live with?"

Kimble nodded.

"What does he teach?"

"*She. She's* a fifth dan in aikido. I'm her *uchideshi*." At Bentham's blank look he translated, "Inside student."

"You've been studying long?"

"A couple of years. Nine months with Monroe Sensei."

"Ah. So that's where the name comes from."

Kimble clamped his mouth shut.

"Let's leave it for now, Kimble. I'm not usually out in the field like this, you know. This was the result of a platoon leader being on sick leave. What I usually do is sit at a desk and read reports. I tag things and collect things and put things together. When I think I see a pattern, I go investigate or send someone to investigate."

Kimble licked his lips. "Where is this going?"

"I've seen the missing child fliers coming from outside. The territory is a favorite destination for runaways, at least until they find out how hard life is out here. I remember things. It's my talent, the aptitude that got me my job, so I remember the fliers from after your father was medevaced. I remember the occasional queries since, and then the recent version with the computer-aged photo. Pretty close, by the way." He took a deep breath. "But I also remember the domestic violence reports from Golondrinas stretching back four years from before your father was transported."

"Oh." Kimble remembered visits from the village deputies, but hadn't realized that they'd resulted in reports. He blinked his eyes rapidly for a moment. He thought about some of their neighbors. *Guess they weren't ignoring the yelling after all.*

"You've got to balance things, sometimes," said Bentham. "We could go have an administrative hearing at the capital, but because your father can't enter the territory, I'd have to transfer you up to Colorado. Your sick instructor would have to travel there, to make a case for custody. Other relatives could get involved. Sounds like a right mess."

"I'd run," Kimble said. "I swear it. I'm not going back to that man."

Bentham eyed him. "No hearing necessary if I never recognized you in the first place. Getting older, you know," he said in a confiding tone. "Memory isn't what it used to be."

"You'd do that?" Kimble said.

Bentham looked at him with dead eyes. "Pardon, Mr. Monroe? What on earth are you talking about?"

Kimble exhaled. "Nothing, Captain. Nothing at all."

"GOOD trip?" asked Ruth. She'd used the rescue inhaler first and her breathing had eased and her color was improving. "You made it without any difficulties?"

"Yes, Sensei."

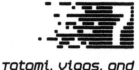

Tatami, vigas, and skinny-dipping

Fatigue is a symptom of asthma, one that often shows up before one feels the constricted breathing in the chest. A week after Ruth began taking the oral corticosteroids she had more energy than she had had in months.

As a result, Kimble was *exhausted*.

"Sensei, don't you think you should get some rest?"

"Shut up and keep weaving."

They were making *gozo* mats, the top layer for straw-core tatami. The layout of the dojo called for forty of them and they'd only completed one full tatami that Ruth had been satisfied with. When Kimble wasn't weaving the *gozo* or bundling wheat straw shafts for the tatami core, he was hauling Ruth's old travois up and down the bosque, cutting dried reeds for more mats, or running off to get straw from the local wheat and oat farmers.

They'd also taken delivery of the promised roofing tiles and had one third of the roof up, but were waiting for more *latillas* (lattice sticks that crossed over the *vigas*, the beams), before they could continue that backbreaking chore. But in the meanwhile, Ruth felt well enough to add an additional class every morning before the heat of the day took hold.

I should've let Captain Bentham take me back to Colorado. Bet I could've slept to a decent hour there.

In desperation he went to Marisol, the TMS nurse. "She's really overdoing it. I'm concerned for her health."

"I talked to her yesterday," Marisol said. "She looked good to me. Her lung function is really improved." She reached out and turned Kimble's head from one side to the other, looking in particular at his eyes. "You getting enough sleep?"

He pulled away. "*I'm* okay. It's her I'm worried about," said Kimble.

The nurse cleared her throat. "Ah. I see. Well, perhaps you're right. I'll speak to her."

The next day Ruth declared that she would take an afternoon nap.

"And what do you want me to do while you're asleep, Sensei?"

She looked at him and said, "Hmmm. There's the *latillas* for the dojo roof, the reeds for the tatami, the garden needs weeding, the compost pile needs turning, but what I really think the most important thing is . . . you should nap."

Two days later, returning from the bosque with more reeds, he overheard Ruth talking to Marisol by the spring. "You were right. I didn't have kids, myself, and it's been so long since I was a teenager."

"He's a good kid," said Marisol.

"He is."

Kimble blushed and crept back down the path. When he returned he let the bundled reeds rustle against the mesquite branches and dropped them noisily by the dojo walls.

The next time they went to town, Martha Mendez, the storekeeper/county clerk/postmaster had a letter for Ruth.

She sat down on the bench outside the store to read it.

Kimble could tell at a glance that it was from outside, laser-printed text on lightweight paper.

When Ruth was done reading it, she went back inside and penned a short response, paying for heliograph transmission. Perro Frio didn't have a heliograph tower but there was one ten miles north. The regular mail rider would drop it on his way and it would be transmitted from tower to tower to the edge of the territory, then e-mailed.

On their way back home Ruth said, "We will have a visitor sometime next week. She will stay for several days. You'll sleep in the *deshi* quarters, all right?" There was a set of student rooms on one side of the dojo. The one on the end was to be his and it was already roofed.

"Of course, Sensei. Might as well get moved in." He

was intensely curious about the visitor. Ruth said very little about her life before the territory.

"Who is coming?" he asked.

"Karen. My oldest student."

WHEN Karen came, she rode with a guide, three pack mules, and her own student, whose name, for all Kimble could see, might have been "trouble."

Kimble liked Karen at first sight. She was not as old as Ruth, but she had white streaks in her red hair and, like Ruth, the muscles in her arms were well defined. When Karen swung down off her horse she bowed immediately, but Ruth took two steps and pulled her into her arms. When they stepped apart, tears were running down both their faces.

Kimble stepped in and took the reins of Karen's horse, face averted. He'd never seen Ruth cry before.

"Here," said the other young woman, thrusting her reins at Kimble. He took them and bowed politely. She walked forward and bowed to Ruth without even looking at him.

Kimble shrugged and watched her walk. She was wearing tight pants and he'd reached an age where watching the opposite sex fascinated him. Her hair was blond but the roots were dark and she smelled of exotic deodorants and soaps.

Karen introduced the young woman to Ruth. "This is my student, Athena."

"Welcome. Are all these horses yours, Karen?"

Karen gestured to a weathered man still on horseback.

"Mr. Clemments is our guide—he brought us from Colorado. The horses are his. He's going to return in six days, if that works for you, Sensei."

"Unless you can stay longer, it works just fine."

"No, our flights out of Denver are set."

Mr. Clemments took the panniers off two of the pack mules. "I've kin near Isleta," he said. "I'll be back on Saturday." He loosened the girths on the two saddle horses and changed their bridles for halters before leading all the animals off.

"We brought extra provisions. I didn't decide to bring Athena until after I'd written."

"Not to worry. This is Kimble."

He bowed. Karen bowed back, though Athena only nodded.

"Give us a second to organize ourselves, all right?" She gestured to Kimble and stepped off to the side. Quietly she asked, "Would it be all right if we gave Athena your room? If I'd known, we could've finished another of the *deshi* rooms."

"Sure, Sensei. I can have my clothes out in a few minutes. The bedding was just changed."

Later he showed Athena the room, carrying her bags for her. She prodded the thin rolled-up futon and said, "It's better than the camping we did on the way here. Where's the bathroom? I could use a shower."

He showed her the composting toilet at the end of the hall. "Sorry the roof isn't up yet." He pointed at the two clay containers beside the seat. "You put sawdust in every time you go. If you defecate, add straw, too."

She wrinkled her nose up. "Don't you guys have flush toilets?"

"Seen 'em. Terrible waste of water."

"And the shower?"

"This time of year, we use water from the pond. When it gets cold, we heat water on the stove." He decided not to tell her about Sensei's plans for a solar-heated hot tub. "I'll be sleeping in the dojo proper if you need anything."

"What does that mean?" she said. "Why should I need anything?" She glared at him. "And why are you sleeping here? Why aren't you in your own room?"

He raised his eyebrows. "Let's just say that's not convenient right now."

He went back to the cottage to see if Ruth needed anything. She was sitting with Karen on the bench built into the wall and Karen was holding a long flat wooden box that Kimble recognized from the pack mules.

"So you were able to do it?"

"Yes, Sensei. They're still light but by increasing the density of the reinforcing fibers, we were able to come close. I did a test cutting with bundled straw and another with green bamboo. Very satisfactory."

"Let's see, then."

She slid the lid off and removed a sheet of packing foam. Beneath were three swords, *katana*, in black lacquered scabbards, and several extra blades. The blades were milky white.

"Why so many blades?" asked Ruth.

"I'm pleased with how strong they are. If you're really cutting properly, they'll slice through bone. But they're still not folded steel. I deliberately chopped at some bamboo—not slicing—and the blade snapped off near the hilt."

Ruth held the sword out, both hands on the hilt. "I've missed *iaido*. I thought I'd miss movies or the 'net or driving, but those haven't been a problem. I certainly missed certain *people*," Ruth said, smiling at Karen. "We've done what we could with *bokken* and *jyo*, but I was surprised how much I missed *iaido*."

Karen nodded. "I use your sword every week."

"*Your* sword. Good, it was made to be used, even if it is four hundred years old. It certainly wasn't made to be eaten by bugs out here."

That night Kimble slept on one of the new tatami in the corner of the dojo. He slept well but more than once he heard Athena tossing and groaning on the much softer futon. She was asleep when he got up at dawn. He could hear her snoring. He tiptoed out and started the morning chores.

The fuel in the kitchen stove had been prepared the night before. He lit it and put the clay water hob on as well as the porridge crock on the stove top. Then he hauled the water to the roof tank, fed and watered the chickens, and let them out of the coop into the garden. They were still too small to lay but they were fully fledged and did a good job on garden pests.

Ruth was up when he stuck his head in to check the porridge. She handed him two cups of tea. "For Athena," she said, indicating the second cup. "Breakfast thereafter."

He knocked on the frame of his bedroom. There was no response. "Athena!" he called.

He stuck his head in. She'd put the pillow over her head. He set the tea on the floor and said loudly, "Breakfast in ten minutes." He saw one of her hands twitch.

"I'm not sure if she's awake or not, Sensei," he said to Ruth when he came back to the cottage. Karen was sitting at the kitchen table while Ruth sliced bread.

"Did you use explosives?" Karen said. "Then she's not awake. Leave it to me."

She returned with Athena ten minutes later. Athena was blinking slowly and had a sour expression on her face. Ruth gave her porridge and bread. "More tea?" Athena's hands were empty. "Oh. We don't have that many cups, I'm afraid."

"I'll get it," Kimble said. The bedding was strewn across the room and, though empty, the cup was lying on its side. "Hmph," he said aloud.

He ran the cup back and gave it to Sensei without comment.

They held class in the dojo, on the hard adobe floor that would support the tatami when they were finished. He had changed in one of the roofless rooms and when he entered the practice area Sensei sent him back to put on his *hakama*. They tended to wear the dark blue, split-skirt for weapons classes and in the winter, when it was colder, but for most hot days even Ruth avoided them. But not today.

"*Bokken*," said Ruth, after warm-ups, taking her own oak sword from the rack by the *kamiza*.

They started with *suburi*, repeated cuts, dropping the center, bending the knees as the blade came down. Two hundred strokes along Kimble saw Athena wince, pause, and shift her grip. Shortly thereafter, Ruth stopped and had them do walking cuts, back and forth across the floor.

The floor had been smoothed to approximate flatness but it was rough. Athena stubbed her toes a couple of times, stumbling, flushing red when it happened.

Kimble had done his share of stubbing his toes over the past year when practice might be held on the grass, on the riverbank, or while walking down the road. It taught him to slide his feet cautiously, feeling for irregularities.

They went to partner practice then, cuts to the head with the attacker moving off the line and counterattacking. Ruth demonstrated the technique slowly, clearly, with Kimble as *uke*. She then bowed to Karen and they moved off to one side, to work together, leaving Kimble with Athena.

Athena lowered her sword, presenting her head by leaning forward. Kimble attacked at the same speed Ruth had been using and Athena blocked and struck, but her control wasn't tremendous. She cut down far enough to brain Kimble, but she was far enough off target that it brushed past his ear instead.

She glared at him, as if he'd moved or something, but he didn't even twitch. After three more repetitions, right and left, they switched sides. She attacked at full speed but he just did the technique, blocking as he slid off the line and striking back. His *bokken* stopped two inches from her forehead, dead on target.

Her attack was fast but it was nothing like Ruth's full-speed attacks. They practiced at full speed all the time.

"Should I speed up?" he asked, when it was his turn to attack again.

She said, "Certainly."

He had to pull his strike. Her block wasn't there in time and she hadn't gotten off the line. Next time he did it slower and she managed the combination, but her eyes narrowed.

"Relax," Ruth said, from across the room. "Your shoulders are raised—that means you're tightening up. No way you can respond fast enough like that."

"Yes, Sensei," said Athena. She blushed.

She never really managed to relax, not working with Kimble. He felt bad for her but he didn't know what to do about it. Ruth took them back to solo exercises a bit later and by the end of class, Athena had stopped blushing.

Though they were expecting a shipment of *latillas,* it hadn't shown up by midmorning. Ruth said, "Kimble, maybe you could check with Jason and then get some reeds on the way back?"

"Go with him and help," Karen said to Athena.

Athena stood up slowly. "Yes, Sensei."

They went by the road. Kimble carried the folded poles of Ruth's travois over his shoulder and a bag with obsidian chips and cord.

Jason Jones ran mules into the forests around Mt. Taylor, harvesting saplings and beams for the *vigas* and *latillas* of traditional roofs. They found him at his lumberyard near the edge of the village. "Sorry. We just got back last night. I've got the rest of your order but we still need to trim 'em up. Half tomorrow morning, I'd say, and the second half the next." His teenage sons, all older than Kimble and man high, came out of the yard as their father explained. Kimble smiled when he realized why they'd come forward and politely introduced Athena to them. "She's visiting," he said.

She smiled and shook their hands. On the way down to the bosque she seemed a bit more cheerful, so Kimble said, "Tall, those Jones boys."

"Hadn't noticed," she said.

"Well, they'll probably deliver the *latillas*, tomorrow, so you can notice then."

She snapped at him. "Why should I care?"

Kimble shrugged. *Can't win for losing.*

He gave her a choice of cutting the reeds or tying them into foot-thick bundles. She tried cutting but it became apparent that he'd cut more in two minutes demonstrating the technique than she had in fifteen. They switched.

When they headed back they had a respectable load on the travois. She insisted on pulling it, so he followed, lifting it over snags on the path out of the bosque until they were on the road. At the top she set it down and bent over, hands on her knees.

Kimble was surprised. It hadn't been that far.

"Let me take a turn," he said.

She straightened and looked at him angrily, but before

she spoke he pointed to where she'd been resting her hand against her pants legs. "Your hand is bleeding."

Athena turned her palm over. A blister had broken open, then bled. "Crap," she said. "Weapons class. How are your hands?"

He lied. "A little sore." Not a bit, actually. They did weapons almost every day, and even on Sunday, when there were no classes, he did two hundred cuts before breakfast. His hands were like leather.

She took a bandanna out of her pocket and wrapped it across her palm and when he took up the travois, she didn't say anything.

After lunch they sat in the dojo and worked on tatami. Ruth showed Karen and Athena how to use plastic needles to sew the bundles of straw for the inner core. Ruth herself packed them into the working frame and sewed them tightly together, while Kimble wove the thin reed *gozo* top coverings.

Ruth, concentrating on getting the thickness uniform across the frame, hummed absentmindedly. Karen's head came up and she began singing the words to the tune. Ruth didn't look up but after a moment she came in on the chorus, singing an alto harmony of surpassing sweetness.

They sang several other songs before Ruth called a halt for siesta.

They did evening class on the grass. "Just one more week," said Ruth. "If we could get some help on Saturday we'll have the roof finished. Possibly even the tatami."

They were up to ten outside students—villagers, farmers, or ranchers who came to evening class. Ruth had Karen teach. Karen started out using Athena as *uke*, but after Athena began flagging, she alternated between Kimble and Athena. The one time Kimble partnered with Athena she cranked hard on the pin and fast, a trick used to inflict more pain before an opponent tapped out.

When it was her turn, she slapped out even before he began the pin. He shook his head but didn't say anything. He watched carefully when she worked with the dojo's beginners, but apparently this treatment was for him alone. His wrists ached that night but he soaked them in the spring before turning in. Again, when he awoke in the night, he heard Athena toss and turn.

They had just finished morning practice when Jason's sons delivered the promised *latillas*. They showed a pronounced tendency to linger, asking Athena questions about aikido and outside, until Ruth said, "I'm sure Kimble could use some help putting those *latillas* up."

Toes were dug into the dirt of the yard. "Uh, Papa needs us back at the yard."

"Well, you could always come back for evening class. You could watch or even participate."

When they were gone and Athena was changing clothes, Karen said, "Yeah, well, she can get them in the door at our dojo, too. But they have to stay for their own reasons."

Kimble spent the day on the roof, lashing the *latillas* in place. Ruth and Karen continued work on the tatami. Athena was designated as general assistant. She fetched water, as needed, handed up bundles of the *latillas* to

Kimble, straw to Karen, reeds to Ruth. Kimble was exquisitely polite, thanking her each time she passed the *latillas* up. Athena was silent, ignoring his thanks or, at best, giving a short jerk of her head.

At one point he saw Karen watching the interaction, her eyes intent on Athena. When she saw Kimble looking back, she rolled her eyes exaggeratedly and smiled. Kimble's spirits lifted and he was surprised. He hadn't been aware his spirits were down, but the rest of the afternoon went smoother and he hummed as he worked.

That evening three of the four Jones boys observed class. They'd obviously come to talk to Athena, but they left with more sober expressions after watching her throw Kimble around. He slapped extra hard, making the falls seem harder than they were.

He was awakened in the middle of the night by a strange sound. Moving cautiously to the hallway by the *deshi* rooms, he realized it was muffled crying.

During morning class Athena had dark shadows under her eyes. Karen worked with her at half speed, concentrating on precision.

Ruth worked with Kimble at full speed, until it felt like it was raining oak.

The Jones boys delivered the final batch of *latillas*.

"We overordered," noted Kimble, comparing the bundles to the remaining unlatticed roof area.

"It'll make good coyote fencing. The chickens are getting bigger."

Two of the Jones brothers were still chatting up Athena but the youngest, the one who'd just left the village school, approached Ruth and asked if he could speak with her. Kimble left them. Later she smiled at Kimble and said, "New student. He did come to look at Athena. But it was you who impressed him."

"Me? I was just taking *ukemi*."

"He said if you could go through all that and still be standing today, it was something he'd like to learn."

He finished the *latillas* by the middle of the day and began gluing down waterproof felt with plastic roofing cement. He was hot and sticky by the time he finished.

"Going swimming before siesta, Sensei, if that's all right."

The three women had been working on tatami, perfecting their individual tasks so that production was speeding up. Athena, covered head to toe in bits of wheat straw and sweat, looked up. "Swimming?"

"Certainly, Kimble," Ruth said. "Do you mind if Athena goes along?" She turned to Athena. "It's just a beaver pond, but it's cold."

Kimble felt a sinking in his stomach but he said immediately, "Of course not, Sensei. She would be welcome."

"Does anybody have a swimsuit I could borrow?"

Kimble scratched his head. "Swimsuit?"

Ruth covered her mouth. Then she said, "You could wear shorts and a shirt if you want. Many just skinny-dip."

Kimble offered, "When I've been working as hard as today, I jump in with my clothes on, at first, but I rinse them and hang them out to dry while I finish swimming."

This did not seem to reassure Athena.

"And of course I won't look when you get in and out."

Muttering, "I'm going to regret this," she stood and flipped her wrist at him. "Go, go. Before I change my mind."

The beaver dam in question was downstream where a rocky gap in both sides had caught some logs during a flash flood. A family of beavers had filled in the gaps and the resulting pond was twenty yards across.

"Right *here*," Kimble said, pointing down at the water ten feet below, "it's about eight feet deep with a sandy bottom." He kicked off his sandals. "Just don't lock your legs." He jumped out into the air.

The water was icy and he bent his knees as he entered and didn't touch the bottom. As soon as he surfaced he kicked over to the beaver dam where his feet could touch the bottom and took several deep breaths. His skin was tingling all over.

Athena's splash hit him as he was pulling off his clothes. He looked over at the roiling water that marked her impact. She stayed under long enough to worry him, but then her head broke water and she slung her hair back so water flew up into the sunlight in a glittering arc.

She swam toward him but then stopped suddenly, treading water, as she realized that his bare shoulders were sticking out of the water. He ignored her and put his clothing up on the sticks of the beaver dam, draped in the sun. As soon as his shirt, shorts, and underwear were up he kicked back out into the deep center. "I'll go over to the shallows," he said, pointing at the upstream end of the pond where the water was only a few feet deep over sand and rock. "You want to rinse your stuff, feel free. I'll avert my eyes."

He didn't wait for an answer.

He cheated a little, glancing sideways enough to see her drape her clothes next to his. He saw her bare back and the swell of her buttocks and breathed out sharply between his teeth. The shallow water where he lay was a protected eddy in the sun, but he moved over to where the river flowed over a foot-high ledge before plunging into the pond. The water was much colder under the fall, uncomfortably so, but it had the effect he sought.

She joined him there, swimming a careful sidestroke. He sat cross-legged, on a mossy rock, the water lapping his chin. She swam up to the far side of a rock just sticking out of the water and draped her arms over it.

He tried to think pure, well unsexual, thoughts, but his mind wasn't cooperating. "The breast stroke" was taking on whole new meanings. In desperation he asked, "Why are you so angry all of the time?"

Her eyes went wide and she turned to look away. She bit her lip. He'd almost expected her to get angry again but she didn't. She looked vulnerable but he couldn't tell if the water in her eyes was from the river or another source.

"I don't know," she finally said. "It's not like I expected. Not at all. Out here I'm . . . nobody."

He blinked. "Nobody? You're a senior student of Karen Sensei, right? How long have you been studying?"

"Five years. I just tested for *nidan*. I asked her if I could be her *otomo* for this trip but it's been all *wrong*."

Ruth had told him stories of being *otomo*, baggage carrier, for a traveling instructor. It was more than just porter. The *otomo* took *ukemi* during instruction, took care of the instructor's laundry, meals, and general comfort.

"It must be different from when you're taking care of her at your dojo."

"I don't take care of her at the dojo."

Kimble stared. "Oh. There are other *uchideshis*?"

"Sensei doesn't have inside students. She doesn't live at the dojo. I do stuff for her but it's little stuff, like folding her *hakama* and making sure the dojo gets cleaned. Maybe organizing a seminar occasionally, though usually it's the more senior students."

"Where do you live, then? What do you do?"

"I have an apartment by the university. I'm a Ph.D. candidate in computer forensics. I teach some of the undergraduate computer labs."

He stared at her. He'd seen his cousin's computer once and had played a game on it (badly). That Athena was a master of this technology impressed him. "You must be very good at what you do."

She peered back at him, trying to decide if he was making fun of her. "I've already had job offers from three different federal agencies," she admitted. "One of them handles the IT for the territorial government."

"Is that why you came? To see what the territory is like?"

Athena looked away again. "That's what I told Sensei."

He nodded, but didn't say anything. He could tell she

wanted to talk about it, but he was afraid if he said anything, she'd withdraw again.

"She doesn't take me seriously," Athena finally said. "She . . . she thinks my aikido study is a phase."

"Why? Because you're in grad school, because you'll go to one of those jobs?"

"No. Because I've been inconsistent in my practice. I've been an on-again, off-again sort of student. Until this last year. Aikido is what got me through my dissertation without going insane."

"Has she said this to you? That you don't practice enough? That you're a lazy aikidoist?"

She looked down. "No."

"Didn't she just promote you?"

"Well, the *Shihan* did. I tested at summer camp."

"Did you ask to test?"

"During my dissertation? Are you nuts? Karen Sensei told me I was testing the week before."

Kimble wanted to reach out and hit her right between the eyes. "Excuse me, *Sempai*, but you're nuts in the head."

An annoyed expression flickered across her face, followed by a smile. "*Sempai*? Are you sure?"

"By every standard. You've been studying longer than I have, you outrank me, and you're ten years older than me. I am smarter, though, or at least I'm not being a total dork about some things, like *someone* is."

She splashed water in his face.

"Prepare to drown," he said.

The battle raged from one end of the pond to the

other, with great gouts of water, and more than one dunk-ing. A family of outraged ducks climbed out of the reeds and scolded them from the bank. She cried quarter first, out of breath.

"See?" she said. "It's been that way the entire trip. You don't give up so soon."

"Is that what's got your panties in a twist? Aren't you from Kansas City?"

"Yeah, so?"

"What's the altitude there, two thousand feet?"

"Not even. It's nine hundred feet."

"You're a git."

"If I weren't so out of breath I would drown you some more."

"As if. Why on earth do you think you're out of breath?"

She looked down again. "Well, it's obvious. I don't practice enough."

He yelled at her. "*We're at seven thousand feet! You don't have the red blood cells for this altitude!* No matter how hard you train, you won't get enough blood cells with-out waiting at least six weeks!"

She stared at him. "It doesn't seem to bother Karen Sensei."

"Karen Sensei is taking it easy. Karen Sensei is taking frequent breaks. Karen Sensei isn't trying to impress anyone. And unlike *some* people, Karen Sensei isn't a total dork!"

Breathless or not, she caught him and held him underwater. He struggled, but not very hard. It's not every day a naked woman lays hands on you. Again she had to give up to catch her breath but she got her revenge by dressing very slowly, in full view.

The walk back to the dojo was very uncomfortable for Kimble.

For the rest of the week, Athena stopped trying so hard, saying cheerfully, "Sorry, Sensei, need to catch my breath," when she needed to. Her shoulders dropped during weapons class and Kimble was able to work with her almost as fast as he worked with Ruth.

The evening before their departure, Ruth asked Athena to teach. She did basics, emphasizing footwork. Kimble took her *ukemi*, half expecting her to throw him very hard, but she did the techniques slowly, with precision, gently.

It was a good class and Kimble saw Karen and Ruth smiling at each other afterward.

The next morning Athena hugged him when he tried to bow farewell to her. To his surprise, so did Karen Sensei.

"Thanks," Karen said. "Thanks for your help with Athena."

"I didn't do anything," he mumbled.

"Sure," said Karen. "But that's not what she says. So thanks." She turned to Ruth and hugged her one more time. "I'll be back for the grand opening. I'll spread the word."

Ruth and Kimble watched until the last pack mule

went around the bend. Ruth gave Kimble a nod. "Right, then," she said, and smiled a smile of surpassing sweetness. "Chores."

Kimble sighed.

"Yes, Sensei."

The Peddler's Assistant

On the day they set the last tile in place on the dojo roof, Captain Bentham rode into the yard on a dusty brown horse, a lightly loaded sumpter mule following behind. Kimble, sealing the juncture of the roof and the chimney, did not recognize him at first for he was out of uniform and his broad-brimmed Panama hid his face. It wasn't until Ruth, talking to Captain Bentham in front of the cottage, pointed up at Kimble and the captain looked his way that Kimble recognized the beaky nose and the bushy eyebrows. He flashed back to their discussion on the road between the capital and the Costillos' ranch.

No hearing necessary if I never recognized you in the first place.

Kimble wondered if the captain had decided

to "recognize" him. He thought of his father, and his stomach suddenly began to hurt.

He finished pressing the ceramic flashing into the cement, then carefully made his way down the sloping roof and dropped easily onto the kitchen compost heap.

He looked at Captain Bentham warily. "How are you, Captain?"

Bentham dismounted. "I'm fine, thank you."

"Captain?" said Ruth.

"Rangers, Sensei," said Kimble.

"Oh. I guess you know him from when you lived in the capital?"

Bentham glanced sharply at Kimble. "No. We met last month, on the road. In the matter of the bandits."

Kimble squeezed his eyes shut. He had not yet mentioned the bandits. When he'd returned, Sensei was still having trouble with her asthma. He had mentioned traveling part of the way with friends of the Kenneys and overnighting at their ranch, but the bit with the *ladrones* and hostage and cinch strap he'd omitted.

Ruth looked sharply at Kimble. He started to open his mouth and she said, "Go clean up. That roofing cement is the nastiest stuff to get off. When you're done, water the captain's animals."

She smiled austerely at Captain Bentham. "Jeremy, was it? Come have some tea."

The cement *was* hard to remove. He used sand and soap and water, repeating the cycle many times. Then he took the horse and the mule to the spring, unsaddled them and, reluctant to go back to Ruth, rubbed them down with straw and tied them below the spring where they couldn't reach the garden but could reach the green tender grass.

When he'd delayed as much as possible, he came back to the cottage. Captain Bentham and Ruth were sitting on the stone bench before the cottage. He approached and sat *seiza*, on his knees. "I unsaddled your beasts and rubbed them down and put them on the green grass by the spring."

Bentham looked at him intently, but when he spoke he just said in a mild voice, "Thank you, Kim."

Ruth stared at Kimble. After a moment, she poured a cup of tea and gave it to him. "Your trip to the capital was a little more exciting than I realized. When was I going to hear about it?"

He gulped his tea. "When I first came back, you were still wheezing, Sensei. Marisol told me to avoid undue excitement."

"Oh, really?" Ruth's brows drew together like a gathering thunderstorm.

"That's my story and I'm sticking to it."

Ruth looked away and covered her mouth. Kimble could see her eyes crinkle. After a moment she turned back and said, "I'm glad to hear that the young lady wasn't injured. Jeremy tells me that her father has made a full recovery from his shoulder wound."

"Oh. *Excellent*," Kimble said. It had happened before he'd intervened, but guilt is a sticky thing, adhering to all manner of events, and it surprised Kimble how relieved he was.

She looked up at the sky. "I like to think that even wheezing as I was, I could've handled the story."

"Yes, Sensei. Sorry, Sensei." Kimble turned to Captain Bentham. "I meant what I said, on the trail. I won't go north."

Jeremy nodded. "And my answer, especially if you could see your way clear to helping me out, is still 'What are you talking about?'"

Kimble rocked back on his heels. "Oh."

Ruth looked puzzled again. "Okay, *now* what little detail did you leave out?" Her voice had hardened again.

Kimble licked his lips. "He knows who I am. About my father, about me being a runaway. When I was up at the capital they had a new flier with an age-adjusted picture."

"Oh," Ruth said in a surprisingly small voice. Her expression puzzled Kimble until he realized it was fear.

But she's not afraid of anything!

"Why *are* you here?" Kimble asked Bentham. "To check up on my story?"

Bentham sipped the last of his tea. "I checked up on your 'story' three weeks ago. I didn't have to leave the capital to do it.

"In my own building I found the transcript of the trial of a Mr. Samuel 'Sandy' Williams. One Kim Monroe led the posse to where Mr. Williams had fallen down a cliff and broken his arm." He tilted his head forward and looked at Kimble from under his bushy brows. "Very convenient, that. As convenient as a certain bandit falling off his horse." He cleared his throat. "Also crossing my desk was a report of outlier bug activity which came to me from your village council with a note doubting the veracity of the report, but listing the members of the group and stating that they are 'not known to drink excessively.' Last, I walked over to the Territorial Medical Service and read the monthly case summary for Perro Frio."

Ruth looked irritated. "Isn't that a violation of privacy?"

"The report is anonymized, but it lets the service track trends in epidemiology. All I really needed was a line that said 'one incidence of asthma, probably allergy induced; treated and prescriptions written for the central pharmacy.' "

Kimble didn't care about that. "What outlier bug activity?"

Ruth jerked her head. "The odd dog with the feral dog pack."

Bentham nodded.

"Bugs? That was bugs?"

"It seems to be related to the phenomenon known as 'bugs,' " said Bentham. "I gather such reports. That's all I'm allowed to say. Anyway, your story was verified a while ago. There were additional inquiries made as my agents passed through. Both of you are very well thought of locally."

"That's just creepy," said Ruth. "How long have you been in intelligence? Doesn't this blow your cover?"

He turned his hand palm up. "It's not, shall we say, a state secret. However, I would appreciate it if you didn't spread it around, either. A quid pro quo, if you like."

At Kimble's expression, Ruth said, "Latin: something for something. I take it he means we don't rat on him, he doesn't rat on you. The runaway posters and all."

Captain Bentham said, "The last thing I want is for Kim to get sent out of the territory. After all, I've come for his help."

IT was a small thing with no danger, at least that's what Captain Bentham said. "Just get to know some kids over in Parsons. There's some drug use and we want to find the supplier."

"You want him to narc for you," Ruth stated flatly.

"It's not the kids we're after. It's the supplier."

Ruth sent Kimble off to swim at the beaver pond. He heard voices raised before he reached the bluff's edge. When he returned to the cottage wet and clean, Ruth told Kimble, "It's up to you. If you do it, there's pay, but we don't need it. If you don't, that's all right, too. Captain Bentham won't rat on us, uh, on you."

On the ride east, Captain Bentham briefed Kimble a bit more thoroughly than he had Ruth.

In the territory there are several indigenous drugs: marijuana, which can be grown nearly anywhere, mescaline in peyote from the Chihuahuan desert in the southern part of the territory, psilocybin mushrooms grown by man and nature. But recently, Bentham told him, there was a growing problem with methamphetamine use. "And it's not coming from inside the territory."

"How can you tell?"

"While you could theoretically make it in the territory,

using only glassware and keeping your chemicals in glass carboys, it's usually a high-metal process. We watch the checkpoints, though, for that sort of thing. It's far easier for them to make it outside."

"Don't you watch the checkpoints for that, too?"

"Of course, and all the borders. But someone's still running it in. We want to know who and we want to know how."

He delivered Kimble to Lujan, a wiry man with a tall peddler's wagon drawn by two sandy mules.

"That's him?" Lujan said doubtfully.

"Yep," said Bentham.

"I was expecting someone . . . older."

Captain Bentham looked at Kimble and lifted his bushy eyebrows.

Kimble said, "That sure is a big wagon. Do you sell candy? Captain Bentham, can I have some money for some can-dee? Pleeeease? What kind of candy do you have, Mister?"

Bentham laughed. "Stop it, Kim."

Kim fell silent. He dropped off Captain Bentham's mule and untied his roll of belongings.

Captain Bentham touched his finger to his forehead, turned his horse and the mule, and rode off, heading north.

Lujan shrugged and said, "Put your stuff behind the seat. You're my assistant. Prices are chalked inside the compartment doors. You can read, can't you?"

Kimble nodded.

"Math? Enough to figure change?"

Kimble nodded again.

"You always this talkative?"

Kimble shook his head.

"All righty. Let's go."

Parsons was three times as big as Perro Frio. Divided by the Rio San Jose, it had cattle ranches to the south, Dineh shepherds and farmers to the north, and a two-year community college in town. There was also a Ranger barracks, but its troopers patrolled a six-hundred-square-mile area.

Lujan told him, "There's a two-man security force at the college and a sheriff with four deputies. The deputies are pretty rough—stay away from them."

Kimble was in town for three days. The evening of the third he and Lujan left, driving west out of town and, after dark, turning into a grove by the river. Captain Bentham was waiting, in uniform this time.

Bentham looked expectantly at Lujan. "Well?"

Lujan jerked his thumb at Kimble. "His work. His story."

Kimble glared at the peddler, but Lujan just looked back blandly. Bentham turned his attention to Kimble.

Kimble took a deep breath and began. "The regional operation is run by the chief deputy. The sheriff knows something is going on but he takes a cut to ignore it. All the other deputies are in on it. Local distribution is handled by the chief deputy's cousin, 'Dash' Dashefsky."

"How the—do you know where it's coming from?"

"It's Mexican meth, made in Chihuahua but air-dropped from a Texas-California overflight. They drop it at fifteen thousand feet with small drag chute. It's crystal meth. They don't care that it hits the ground hard. They're going for accuracy."

"Where? Where do they drop it?"

"At the south end of the Stevens Ranch, just short of the old refinery."

The refinery was an active bug site. It was avoided by day, but especially by night, when you could crush a bug accidentally in the dark.

"Night drop?"

"Just before dawn. Next one is Thursday morning, in three days."

"Are the Stevens involved? Any of their people?"

"Don't know. It's the biggest ranch in the area and they've lost cattle before. The deputies have blanket permission to sweep for rustlers. No one would think it odd."

"Anything else?"

"They've mostly been selling out of town, wholesale. But they figure they can make a bigger profit getting into retail. They're eyeing the college kids, figuring they can sell it as a 'study' aid. They plan on busting one of them for pot dealing and blackmailing him into dealing for them. That was Deputy Pritts' idea. He's a real asshole."

"How on earth did you learn this?"

"The idiots use their own product. Practically everyone I talked to said what assholes the deputies were. Aggressive. Some of them thought it was a *good* thing. That they were tough on the 'criminal element.'"

"You've seen meth users before?"

"Sure, in the capital. Street people do all sorts of drugs. I was on the street for over a year."

"Okay, so what about all those details? You heard that?"

"They have a clubhouse—the Deputies Den, they call it—a two-story building behind the town hall. The sheriff doesn't go there. The off-duty deputies practically live there, even the married ones." Kimble looked uncomfortable. "They have women there, too. You know how meth users get their thing on?"

Bentham nodded evenly. "Right. Hypersexuality. Where were you, Kimble?"

"On the roof."

Bentham closed his eyes. "On the roof."

"It was the best place to listen."

"Your teacher is going to kill me. I wanted you to look for kids, teenagers, who were using. Whoever sold them the drugs. We would've traced back from the users."

Kimble turned his hands palm up. "I looked. I hung out. I talked to rich kids and poor kids and two homeless kids. There's a little local weed and a lot of underage drinking, but no real stimulants. Then I found a fifteen-year-old girl coming off of crystal, down by the river, crying up a storm."

"From withdrawal?"

Kimble clamped his mouth shut and looked down at the ground. He started hyperventilating.

Bentham took a step forward, concerned.

Lujan spoke. "She'd been raped."

Kimble lifted his head and spat out, "It was Pritts. He

took her back to the clubhouse and got her high and went at her. He told her no one would believe her. That all the deputies would hang together." Kimble's face was almost completely unrecognizable, contorted with rage.

"Ah," said Bentham, stepping back again. "What's her name?"

"Francesca Cruz. Her father is a migrant worker, probably from Mexico. She's terrified of his reaction and terrified he'll be targeted or deported. That's just sick."

"Where is Ms. Cruz?"

Lujan said, "Outside of town, at the convent of the Sisters of Mercy. They run a shelter for battered women. *They* aren't going to talk to the deputies. In their experience, the deputies tended to side with abusive husbands. Also, one of their previous clients was the former Mrs. Pritts."

Bentham reached out and touched Kimble's shoulder. "The girl told you about the clubhouse?"

"What the hell do you think? Of course she told me!" Kimble's voice didn't rise at all but Bentham's head jerked back.

"What do you want, Kimble?"

"*I want it never to have happened!*"

Bentham nodded. "Right. Barring that?"

"I want to cut his balls off! I want to shove a cactus up his ass!" He took a deep breath and said in a quieter voice. "I want him to die."

Bentham nodded. "Understood. Then help me get him. The girl told you about the clubhouse. Next?"

Kimble stared off into the river bottom. "I went up at

dusk. There's a wisteria trellis on the back. The trellis is rotten and brittle but the vines are massive. Pritts and two others on the day shift got there about eleven. Pritts and one of the others started using—smoking rock, I think—and they began discussing the whole scheme. They talked about whether they'd have enough for the local market. Pritts said they'd have plenty after the Thursday drop. One of the others pointed out that the delivery could overshoot and hit the old refinery. Pritts said that hadn't happened since the second drop and there'd been thirty since then that went off without a hitch.

"Then the other one said, 'Except for the time the load took out one of the Stevens' steers.' They all laughed. They had a barbecue."

Bentham frowned. "Thursday morning."

"Yeah. An hour before dawn. They don't want anyone to see it drop but they want the light to look for it. Bugs."

"Which deputies go out to the drop?"

"All of them. They talked about a time they only sent two and they couldn't find the package. They were afraid a ranch hand would find it first. Now they all go, to do a fast wide sweep." He shook his head. "They talked a *lot*. Typical meth users."

Bentham nodded. "Talkative, yes, but also paranoid. It was dangerous!"

Kimble didn't deny it.

Bentham questioned him for another half hour, getting every detail. Finally he settled back on his heels. "Well, we'll watch them do the pickup and we'll watch them hand it over to Dashefsky. As he hands off to his distributors, we'll take them. Then we'll take Dashefsky and the deputies. I don't know if we can prosecute the rape, dammit. Maybe we can get one of them to plea deal, to rat him out, otherwise . . ." Bentham shrugged.

Lujan snorted, "Don't be so sure. The Sisters have SOEC kits and have been trained in their use."

Bentham said, "Oh, real-ly?" He smiled, but it was all teeth and it made Kimble cold to see it.

Kimble's anger had faded to depression. "What does that mean?"

Lujan explained. "Sexual Offense Evidence Collection kit. Means we have a good chance of getting him on the rape, too. We'll send it outside for DNA matching with a sample taken from Pritts."

"What kind of sample?"

"Usually a mouth swab. Why?"

Kimble shrugged. "The bigger the sample the better, right? I suggest you send a tissue sample. A large tissue sample." He gestured down.

"We can't cut parts off of him, Kimble," Captain Bentham said.

"That's a great pity."

SINCE Captain Bentham was coordinating his trap for the deputies and their associates, as well as liaising with the DEA to identify the outside-the-territory members of the chain, it was Lujan who delivered Kimble back to Perro Frio, dropping him on the road between the dojo and the village.

"Didn't know what to think," Lujan said, "when the

cap'n brought you in, but you done good, kid. Now I understand why he was so impressed."

Kimble's jaw dropped open. "He sure hides it well!"

Lujan shook his head. "I meant it. Work with you anytime." He turned his team north for the capital and Kimble walked south with his bedroll.

He arrived just as evening class began. He slipped back into his room, changed into practice clothes, and bowed in.

Later, Ruth asked him, "Did you eat?"

"A bit—dried fruit and jerky."

"I baked today. Come on."

She fed him bread and honey and tea. He was dreading her questions but she didn't ask any, cleaning the counter and then resuming work on a half-finished basket.

After a while he began talking. He told her about Pritts and the deputies and the rape of Francesca Cruz and the drug drops. He didn't tell her about hiding on the roof to eavesdrop.

When he'd stopped talking she put the finished basket aside and said, "Do you think you should have gone?"

He'd been wrestling with that all the way from Parsons. "Yes. Yes, I do."

"Pretty awful people," she said.

He nodded. "Yeah. Makes Sandy Williams look like a saint."

She grimaced. "Wouldn't go *that* far. I still have my doubts, but if it keeps any more girls from being assaulted—"

"Raped," said Kimble emphatically. "It's rape!"

She blinked then nodded. "Yes. Rape. No euphemisms, right?"

"I didn't want to know this. *I didn't want to*. Not so up close."

"Oh, Kimble." She exhaled. "I can't take it away. You can't un-know it."

"I used to think innocence was just not doing bad things. That it was just being innocent of wrongdoing. But it's not that simple, is it?"

"No," she said. "It's not. We all have to learn it at some point in our lives. It's never easy."

"Yes, Sensei."

Reiko, Reiko, Reiko

It was a different Kimble who came back to the two-room schoolhouse that September. He was quieter, burning through his math and science workbooks for the entire year before the end of October. Taken by surprise, Mrs. Sodaberg had to shoot an unscheduled order off to the capital for the next workbooks in the series. In the interim, she lent Kimble to Mrs. Sedaris to help with the elementary students in the other schoolroom.

One day, when the upper form was off on a field trip to the river bottom, Charlotte Ann Johnson fell in class and cut her forehead on the corner of a desk. Mrs. Sedaris left Kimble in charge as she hustled Charlotte to the village medical office so Marisol Aragon could glue the wound back together.

"You're not the boss of me."

"Excuse me?" said Kimble looking up from his novel.

Johnny Hennessey, a large boy who had failed to move out of elementary the year before, had gotten up from his desk and was glaring across the room at Kimble. It was not a secret that his problems were both academic *and* behavioral.

"Did you need some help with your math, Johnny?"

"You can't boss us around, you're not the teacher."

After Mrs. Sedaris and Charlotte Ann had left the schoolroom, the only thing he'd said was, "Do whatever Mrs. Sedaris assigned." Kimble raised his eyebrows and said, "Okay. I'm not the boss of you." He looked back down at his book. That would probably have been it, but several of the younger kids giggled.

Johnny glared around then said, "You're scared, aren't you. You're yellow." He took two steps up the aisle. "I knew that crap was phony about your martial arts stuff."

Kimble sighed and closed the book, his finger marking the space. "Johnny, you could be finishing your assignment. And so could everyone else, you know?"

"Yeah," said Pete Romero, a kid on the front row. "*Some* of us are ready to move to the upper form."

Pete was one of the smartest kids in the elementary room, but saying that when Johnny Hennessey, who outweighed Pete by fifty pounds, was standing right beside him was *not* smart.

Johnny dove at Pete, knocking over the desk and spilling both boys to the floor, Johnny on top. He raised a fist to smack Pete and suddenly the world changed.

Pete was no longer under him but off to one side, cradling a bruised elbow. Johnny could see that because his head was facing that way and *only* that way because his cheek was grinding into the floor and his arm and shoulder were positioned so that he couldn't look in any other direction. Or move. Not without a shooting pain from his wrist to his spine.

"Shhh," Kimble said. "You really shouldn't struggle. You could hurt yourself. Oh, damn. You made me lose my place."

By the time Mrs. Sedaris returned with Charlotte Ann, Johnny and Pete were back in their seats and, if not productive, at least quiet.

Later that week, Buck Hennessey came in to complain about upper form students being allowed to manhandle the elementary students. He glared around the schoolyard and demanded which of the assembled children was the brutal bully, Kim Monroe.

Kimble heard this and stepped forward, standing across from Johnny, who was a full head taller than him and fifty pounds heavier.

Mr. Hennessey complained a bit more but not quite so enthusiastically. Regretfully, Mrs. Sedaris sent Kimble back to the upper forms. Johnny Hennessey avoided Kimble in the schoolyard and Pete Romero started attending the kids classes at the dojo.

KAREN Sensei and Athena were the first to arrive for the dojo's grand opening, but they were by no means the last. They came two days early, this time renting horses and coming without a guide.

"We're quite the intrepid explorers," Athena said.

The horses, as prearranged, were boarded at the Kenney's ranch. Kimble gave up his room again, but this time to Athena *and* Karen. There were so many people coming that they expected to double up in each of the four deshi rooms, fill the practice area with sleeping bags, and overflow into some of the local students' homes.

Kimble's old bed in the cottage, the one Karen had used on her last visit, was reserved for Tamada *Shihan*. Kimble was cleaning the room in preparation when he overhead Karen and Ruth talking.

"He's actually coming?" Ruth said.

Karen answered emphatically, "Absolutely!"

"It's so *far*."

Karen nodded again. "He insisted. He said, 'If I can still walk up Mount Fuji every year, I can walk a few kilometers to Ruth-chan's new dojo.'"

"He hasn't been out of Japan since the opening of our old dojo."

Karen nodded. "True." She grinned wickedly. "I heard that Porter tried to get him to come for the twenty-fifth anniversary but Tamada refused."

Ruth blinked. "Real-ly."

Karen nodded. "Porter told me at summer camp, but he shrugged it off. Said it was a scheduling conflict. Tamada's dojo *cho* told me differently when I saw him in California. Tamada won't accept Porter's phone calls—he's 'unavailable' to Porter until further notice. He must be furious about the adultery."

Ruth shook her head. "Close as we were, Sensei wouldn't act that way because of mere adultery. It was Porter sleeping with his own student. *That*, to Sensei, would be unforgivable."

The rest of the guests had caravanned together, crossing into the territory at Aztec and taking four days to make it into Perro Frio on horseback and wagon. Tamada Sensei walked most of the way, carrying a bamboo walking stick, and, as the rest of the party's aches and pains increased, he leaned on it less and less. As their morning groans increased, his smile broadened and his step lightened and he led the way up to Ruth's cottage, the bamboo balanced jauntily over his shoulder.

Ruth ran forward and dropped to her knees before him. He bowed back and drew her to her feet, his face all folds and tears.

Kimble worked like a demon, fetching, carrying, serving, answering questions, and helping people unaccustomed to territory ways.

On the last day of the seminar, half of Perro Frio and a scattering from other nearby villages came to the opening ceremony and watched a demonstration of techniques by all the attending instructors. At the end, Ruth demonstrated *iaido*, drawing and cutting, with the milky white ceramic blade, then doing the same techniques again with wooden *bokken* as Kimble attacked with the same. When she was done, Tamada Sensei promoted her, on the spot, to *Rokudan*, sixth-degree black belt.

Kimble was sitting close and he heard him say to Ruth, "The instructor's quality is manifest in the student."

Ruth bowed very low and said, "My instructor is of the *highest* quality."

Tamada Sensei threw back his head and laughed. "I wasn't talking about *your* instructor!" He pointed at Kimble, "I was talking about *his!*" He started to turn and then said directly to Kimble, "What rank?"

Kimble was confused. "Excuse me, Sensei?"

"No rank, Sensei," said Ruth. "Just *keiko.*" Practice.

"*Keiko, keiko, keiko,*" said Tamada Sensei. "Good. Nonetheless, with your instructor's permission, you are promoted to *nidan.*"

Ruth bowed and Kimble followed her lead. "*Domo arigato gozaimashita,* Sensei."

After class ended Athena led several aikidoists over and surrounded him.

"What?" he said, wary.

"We normally do it at *shodan,* but you skipped that. Relax."

They made him lie back, supporting him with their arms, then, on the count of three, threw him as high as the rafters, so high, he had time to wonder if they were going to catch him.

They did.

As the audience trailed out of the dojo he saw a familiar set of shoulders in the crowd. He watched and saw the man glance back over his shoulder, revealing the beaky nose and bushy eyebrows. Captain Bentham saw

Kimble watching, touched his finger to his forehead, and walked on.

"Did I see Jeremy?" Ruth asked.

Kimble nodded.

"Too bad he didn't stay. It was nice of him to come."

"Yes, Sensei."

PART II

"When he comes to the Great Game he must go alone—alone, and at peril of his head. Then, if he spits, or sneezes, or sits down other than as the people do whom he watches, he may be slain. Why hinder him now? Remember how the Persians say: The jackal that lives in the wilds of Mazanderan can only be caught by the hounds of Mazanderan."

—RUDYARD KIPLING, *Kim*, Chapter 7

Lujan drove his peddler's wagon into the dojo yard and said, "Hey, kid. You want to buy some candy? I've got all sorts of different candy."

Ruth, standing beside Kimble, stiffened but Kimble put his hand on her arm. "It's Lujan," he said quietly. "The agent I worked with in Parsons."

She breathed out. "Ah. He's joking?"

"Yes. He's giving me back some of my own sass."

She turned back to Lujan. "Tea, Mr. Lujan?"

"Why thank you, Ms. Monroe. I'd take it kindly."

She turned back to the cottage. "See if he has some lamp oil. We're low."

Kimble invited Lujan to stay the night or for supper, but the man shook his head. "In a hurry.

Lamp oil? Take that plastic drum off the back. The whole thing. It's not opened yet and I'll travel faster for it."

"If you're in such a hurry, why'd you stop?"

"Pritts broke out of his own jail after the trial, the night before the troop arrived to transport him north to the federal pen in Colorado."

The blood drained from Kimble's face. "He got *away*?"

"Someone helped. The city appointed new deputies but one of them is missing. Oh, and two of them are dead."

"Pritts do it?"

"Or the missing deputy. Or both."

"Are you taking the word to the capital?"

Lujan tilted his head and looked at him.

Kimble said, "Right, heliograph. So what *is* your hurry?"

"Heading south. I've seen him close up and personal, like you. Possible he'll try for Mexico. I'm gonna haunt the crossings, hang with the Coyotes. The service will airdrop posters to the legitimate crossings but it'll take a couple of weeks to widely distribute his picture."

"You need me to go with you?" Kimble felt a fierce need to do something.

"Ha! Captain said you'd offer but he just wanted you to know so you could keep your eyes open around here. Period." Lujan leaned closer. "Ever since he saw the demo at your dojo's grand opening, I think he's a little scared of your teacher."

Distractedly, Kimble said, "Wise man."

Lujan stayed long enough to drink his tea. As he prepared to drive on he spotted the *horno*. "You bake? I've got two twenty-five-pound bags of flour. Would help with the weight."

He left them on the ground and drove off when Ruth stepped into the cottage to get her purse.

"He's in a terrible rush," Kimble said when she came back out. "I don't think he expected to be paid." He licked his lips, then told her about the jailbreak.

She eyed him intently. "You're furious."

Kimble blinked. "Oh. That's what that is." He knew he felt something, but until she named it he just knew that his vision had narrowed and his jaw ached from clenching his teeth.

"Yes, Sensei. Furious."

HE stayed late the next day at school, working through a tricky algebra proof with Mrs. Sodaberg. It was extra credit but he enjoyed figuring it out. Mrs. Sodaberg guided him lightly, mostly with questions, until it was solved.

He was taking the back path from the school toward the country road south when he heard voices and then a yell. "No! Johnny, stop it! NO!"

He followed the voices, bursting through the bushes into a small clearing. Two half-dressed figures, Johnny Hennessey and Luanne Tuscano, one of the younger upper-form students, struggled on a blanket. Johnny was shirtless and his pants were partway down. Luanne's dress top was down around her ribs, and her hem was up, and Johnnie was trying to pull her panties down past her knees.

Kimble took two long strides and kicked him in the side of the head.

"What the hell!" screamed Luanne. She was scrambling to cover her breasts while pulling her panties up.

Johnny fell over and lay unmoving.

"Why'd you do that? Are you insane?"

"He was raping you!"

"You killed him!"

For a dreadful instant, Kimble thought she might be right. He crouched over Johnny and checked the pulse at his throat. It beat steadily but his eyes were half open and the side of his head was swelling where Kimble had kicked him.

"Christ. Sit here with him. Make sure he doesn't swallow his tongue. I'm going after Miss Aragon."

When he returned with Mrs. Sodaberg and the nurse, Luanne was fully dressed. What's more, even though he was still unconscious, Johnny was also dressed and the blanket had disappeared.

Johnny woke up while they were carrying him into the village. He couldn't tell what day of the week it was or who was president. "Concussion," said Marisol.

"Not necessarily," muttered Mrs. Sodaberg.

Kimble had already told Mrs. Sodaberg and the nurse what had happened as he guided them back to the clearing. Luanne told a completely different story.

"Me and Johnny had been looking for butterflies for my science project when Kimble came out of the bush and kicked Johnny! You know its not the first time he's picked on him."

Mrs. Sodaberg and Marisol believed Kimble. "The blanket was stuffed behind a stand of cholla," said Marisol. "And she didn't get his fly buttoned straight."

Both Luanne's and Johnny's parents sided with their children and, as both fathers were on the school board, the school board did also.

Martha Mendez's husband, Carlos, was the village council member whose turn it was to be constable. He interviewed all three teens multiple times. At the end of it all, he refused to pursue charges of assault *or* rape.

"Your daughter's told me three different stories, now," he said when Mr. Tuscano protested. "Johnny doesn't remember, he says, and with a concussion, that's possible, but he also has given me different versions of what he was doing with Luanne. Every time I talked to Kimble, I got the same exact story. And isn't this your blanket?"

The school board suspended Kimble for a month.

"Thank God," Kimble said.

Mrs. Sodaberg brought several months' worth of course work out to the dojo and let Ruth know in no uncertain terms, what most of the village really thought. "He may be the apple of his parents' eye, but too many broken windows, black eyes, and stolen pies can be laid at Johnny's door. And he and Luanne may have thought they were discreet but it wasn't the first time they'd been caught making out."

When Mrs. Sodaberg had left, Ruth finally commented on the whole mess. "Now I *know* you had less dangerous techniques you could've used. Kicking him in the head? He wasn't Pritts, you know."

Kimble sighed. "Yeah, I know. Now." He kicked the base of the wall. "Luanne looks nothing like the Cruz girl, but it was Francesca's face I was seeing. Her voice I was hearing.

"Luanne and Johnny were probably fooling around and he wanted to go farther than she did. She was yelling for him to stop. Not really yelling for help."

"Did *she* say that?" Ruth asked mildly.

Kimble shrugged. "She was chasing butterflies, remember?"

Ruth said, "Could be she *was* yelling for help. She just didn't want to admit to her parents what she'd been doing. Her father is very religious."

"That's not how you put it after the school board protest."

There'd been an effort by a minority of the school board to introduce Bible studies into the school curriculum. At a well-attended public meeting, Ruth had spoken against the effort on a First Amendment basis. Kimble's teacher, Mrs. Sodaberg, had agreed. She also expressed the opinion that changing their status to a "religious school" would result in the Territorial School System cutting support for their school. The TSS currently supplied all study materials and over half of the teachers' salaries. In a narrow majority, the board had concluded, "Church matters for church. School matters for school." It could be read as a victory for Separation of Church and State but behind-the-scene reports said that what really killed it were arguments over whose specific doctrine would be taught.

"Didn't you call him a 'narrow-minded, fundamentalist bigot'?"

Ruth glared and said to Kimble, "You have a good memory but that's not always a virtue."

Kimble sighed. "It's not the month away from school that bothers me. It's going back."

OF the two-dozen chicks they'd gotten from Rooster Vigil back in August they had seventeen survivors. A roadrunner had taken two while they were still chicks and, more recently, a breeding pair of coyotes had carried off two fledglings one early morning. The last three casualties had been roosters and, while they got up early most mornings, Ruth liked to sleep in on Sunday. The roosters had been the centerpiece of a meal served during the dojo's grand opening.

Kimble wasn't sure whether the chickens thought of him as another chicken or even their mother but whenever he showed up, they all came running. They were nearly full-grown and a few had started clucking. Most, though, still peeped, but all knew that when Kimble showed up he often had feed or scraps or would turn over rocks in the garden to reveal bugs and grubs.

They liked melon rinds, cracked corn, and worms, but cockroaches were like crack cocaine to them.

For his part, Kimble loved sitting by the garden as the birds scratched and pecked. Every time he moved they would run over to see if he was reaching into a pocket for a treat or turning over rocks. Whenever he was upset, he would go sit with the chickens.

That's where Captain Bentham found Kimble two weeks after the incident.

"Tell me what happened."

"Did you catch Pritts?"

Bentham shook his head. He went to the short log they used as a bench and eyed the chicken poop decorating its surface. He rolled it ninety degrees and sat down.

Kimble told him about kicking Johnny in the head as well as what he'd learned the day before. He talked about Luanne's story and being suspended from school.

"And what should you have done?"

Kimble licked his lips. "Well, for starters, I could've just told him to stop."

Bentham nodded. "Yes, I suppose. You would've sacrificed the element of surprise, though."

"Yes, but there were lots of other things I could've done, too, without giving him a concussion."

Bentham pulled a scrap of bread from his belt pouch and began shredding it. The chickens flocked around him, pecking the bread from between his fingers. "Greedy beggars." He dusted the last of the crumbs into the dirt causing a small riot of pushing and pecking. "Learn anything?"

Kimble nodded. "Ask first before rendering aid?"

"Don't know about that. What if there'd been a weapon?"

"No, not in that circumstance."

"What else?"

"Sometimes things aren't black and white."

Bentham nodded. "You said a mouthful there. Any-

time there are humans involved, things can get tangled—
no, make that *always* get tangled. Maybe Johnny learned
something, too."

"That might be reaching," Kimble said.

Captain Bentham held out a piece of paper. "Here."

"What is it?"

"Court order."

Kimble's stomach hurt and he pulled his hands back.
"My dad?"

Bentham blinked. "Hell, no. Don't worry about that.
He gets wind of you I'll give you plenty of warning.

"Young as you are, a court order is necessary for you
to take the GED. Ruth wrote me. I've been talking to
your Mrs. Sodaberg. She says you'd pass it now but if you
prepped the next few months, you'd get top marks." He
pushed the paper forward again. "Take it, already."

Kimble took the heavy paper.

"This'll let you take the GED at the Territorial Complex. They give it once a month."

"I don't have to go back to school?"

"Well, not *that* school."

"What do you mean?"

Captain Bentham, he decided, had a very unsavory
laugh.

TWO months later Kimble borrowed the mare, Suze,
from the Kenneys and, with an overnight at the Castil-
los' ranch, rode into the capital to take the GED.

That was the least of it.

"I've made a deal with the captain," Ruth told him.

"He wants you to do his training things but you'll stay with *Thây* Hahn."

"Who or what is *Thây* Hahn when he is at home?"

"He is a priest of the Tiep Hien Order." At Kimble's blank look she added, "It's a form of Zen Buddhism."

"You want me to be a Buddhist?"

She shook her head. "No. I want you to sit. Meditate."

"I already do that, with you," Kimble said.

"Some," she said. "But we don't do much. I want you to sit with *Thây* Hahn in the morning before you go to Captain Bentham."

Kimble wondered if he'd have time to do the captain's training, too, if he was sitting in the morning with *Thây* Hahn. "I thought you'd never been to the capital before the time we met."

"Right. I knew *Thây* Hahn outside."

"This is because I kicked Johnny in the head, isn't it?"

Ruth nodded. "Among other things."

"What good is it going to do?"

"Ah. *That* is the question. Let me know what you find out."

HIMBLE took the GED the afternoon he arrived, going directly from the livery to the Territorial School System building where it was administered. He used less than half of the allowed seven hours. "The results will be mailed within two weeks," the examiner said.

Kimble thanked him, took his bag, and left.

Thây Hahn lived in a small house surrounded by a large garden in the northwest quadrant, close to the city wall. When Kimble knocked, a small girl, about nine years old, with enormous brown eyes and jet black hair, opened the door. "Hello," Kimble said.

She looked at him for a moment, taking in his bag and his height. "You're too young to be a new novice. You must be Kimble."

He nodded.

"Take off your shoes." She indicated a shoe shelf just inside the door. "We don't wear shoes in the house. *Ba* is at work. He'll be back in time for supper. I hope you like lentils."

"*Ba*?"

"Sorry—means Father."

"Your father is *Thây* Hahn?"

"Yes. I'm Thayet."

She led him to the back hallway and showed him the guest bed—a narrow bunk behind a sliding panel in the back hall—then the privy and the solar shower in back where the runoff helped water the garden.

Thây Hahn was short, Kimble's height exactly, and Kimble found himself automatically following dojo etiquette in his presence: bowing, sitting in *seiza*, and being exquisitely polite. This politeness was tested when Thayet woke him well before dawn.

"Time to sit," was all she said.

He used the privy and swallowed some water before joining them. They sat for four forty-five-minute sessions, stretching briefly between. They were finished by the time the city bells struck eight.

Great. Plenty of time for Captain Bentham's training.

The question now was, would he be able to stay awake through it?

"BAD night?" Communications Technical Sergeant Chinn didn't know who Kimble was. Captain Bentham had introduced him as "My Little Friend" with the capital letters clearly audible.

"The night was okay, just too short." Kimble was yawning a lot but the communications office had a ceramic biofuel burner and Kimble was on his third cup of strong tea. He was leaning on the table, resting his chin in the palm of his hand. "Please continue."

"Okay. Buried messages are best. They won't even try to break a code if they don't realize it's there. We like simple alert phrases for urgent communications so if you use any of these phrases in a letter or heliogram, it'll get noticed by our analysts. Just don't use them accidentally." He handed Kimble a thick slab of wood with a sheet of paper glued to it.

It was surprisingly heavy. "What's with the board?"

"Keeps it from wandering off. By the end of the week you'll know all those phrases by heart. You'll even be able to write them all down once you've left here, but don't."

Kimble was looking at the list. " 'Sick Leave'?"

"Right. 'Subject Lost.' They're all like that to aid memorization. Same initial letters, see? 'Got to Go.' "

Kimble ran his finger down the list. "Ah. 'Gone to Ground.' What does that mean?"

"Basically, you're in hiding. Probably because you're blown and the opposition is actively searching for you. You know 'blown'?"

"My cover is blown. Yeah, that I know."

"And 'cover' is?"

"Jeeze. What do you think I am, twelve or something?"

The tech sergeant laughed. "How old are you? You look twelve to me."

In a haughty tone, Kimble said, "That is on a need-to-know basis." In his normal voice he added, "But I did take the GED yesterday. 'Cover' is a covert identity. You know, Bruce Wayne, Clark Kent. If we get to pick, I want to be the millionaire playboy."

"Okay. You need any of these other terms explained, just sing out. In a bit, we'll cover fixed signals for ground to air communication. We'll also be working on the heliograph. How's your Morse code?"

Kimble buried his face in his arms and groaned.

KIMBLE went to bed almost immediately after supper. Thayet woke him again at four. "I hate you," he said.

She giggled and then sat like a rock through the sessions. At breakfast he commented about how well she sat to *Thây* Hahn.

"She sleeps," he said. "She's like one of those soldiers who can sleep in formation. I'd leave her in bed but she insists. She's very stubborn."

"Can I sleep through the meditation?"

"Better to stay in bed."

"I'm with you there."

Thây Hahn leaned forward. "Then why are you sitting?"

"I don't know why, yet. But I trust my sensei. I guess I'm sitting to find out why I'm sitting."

Thây Hahn nodded. "That will do. To start."

"OKAY, Little Friend," said Lieutenant Durant. "The guy with the red shirt coming out of the courthouse. Got him?"

Kimble nodded, though he kept his eyes on the subject. They were standing by the Exodus monument and Kimble half-expected to see his own younger self atop it, challenging all comers.

"When the bell rings four, report to me at Café del Mundo and tell me where he went and who he talked to. Remember. Covert. From the Old French by way of Old English. Past participle of *covrir*, meaning to cover. Not 'overt.' Discreet."

"Discreet. Yes, ma'am," Kimble said, and wandered diagonally across the plaza, pacing the man with the red shirt. He would much rather be watching the lieutenant. He'd had a crush on her from the moment Captain Bentham introduced them.

He glanced back for one more glimpse of her and saw his own tail, a corporal he'd last seen behind a desk in Lieutenant Durant's outer office. The man was now in mufti, a large straw hat shading his face.

Ha! Kimble spent five minutes losing the corporal and

then watched *both* of them, for the corporal was keeping track of the man in the red shirt, probably in hopes of reacquiring Kimble.

"Any difficulty?" Lieutenant Durant asked later when he met her at the Café del Mundo.

Kimble shrugged.

Lieutenant Durant frowned. "Did you lose your subject?"

"Ha." *Her corporal must've reported in.* "No, ma'am." Kimble listed the places the man in red had gone and the people he'd talked to.

The lieutenant looked at a piece of paper as he spoke, ticking through a list. Her eyebrows rose as Kimble went along. When Kimble stopped talking she said, "Anything else to report?"

"Your corporal ate chicken souvlaki at Petra's Greek Food. The bill was eight-fifty with a beer. Was he on duty? Should he be drinking? I always liked their dolmades. Looked like he fell asleep for a few minutes on the bench near the livestock end of the market. That could've been the beer. I really think that's a bad idea, the beer, though I must admit I was having a hard time not falling asleep myself, but that was because I was up at four."

"Stop," she said, laughing. "I'm never going to let him live this down. How'd you do it? Disguise?"

"If I tell you, he'll be harder to lose next time. Buy me a pastry?"

He really loved the way she laughed. "I promise not

to tell him, but I have to evaluate your methods. Now, by results, you're doing pretty darn good. How'd you do it?"

"Let's just say your corporal should look up occasionally."

She blinked. "Oh. Rooftops?"

"Yes, though I did stick my head in the back door of the restaurant while he was eating and talked to his waiter."

"Nice." She nodded thoughtfully. "What will you do when you can't use the rooftops?"

"Try me."

She laughed again. "Oh, we will. We will."

CAPTAIN Bentham took him on horseback out to the Territorial Academy. "I've seen you in action in your dojo and that's very impressive, but I'd like to see how you operate against non-aikidoists."

"What, you think it's just forms? That we're cooperating with each other when we practice?"

"Well, to a small extent, you do. Otherwise you'd kill each other, yes?"

Kimble conceded the point with a shrug.

"We've got some practical exams today for our Unarmed Combat and Prisoner Control Tactics class. I'm going to slip you in as a perp on some of the arrest scenarios."

"Aren't you afraid they'll hurt me?"

"Not worried about *you*. Just don't kick anybody in the head, okay?"

Nine out of the ten arresting cadets ended up facedown on the mat. The tenth, more aggressive than the others, sprained his shoulder when Kimble used the energy of the man's initial rush to project him along his way. They would have to fix the plaster on a wall, too.

On the ride back, Bentham kept chuckling.

"Not really fair, was it?" Kimble said. "I mean, slipping in a ringer."

"Maybe not. But it taught them a valuable lesson about appearances, didn't it?"

SITTING was getting easier. The first days had been struggles against sleep alternating with the cries of joints, random itches, and stiffness. Now Kimble struggled with vivid images and thoughts and occassional hallucinations.

The worst was Pritts standing beside Thayet's cushion, looking down and licking his lips. He'd yelled and fallen out of half-lotus.

Thây Hahn said, "Of course it is impossible to empty your mind. Things drift across your consciousness inevitably. What's important is that you don't attach to any of these thoughts. Let them go their way."

Kimble tried. It was hard to avoid thinking about Parsons and the deputies, or Johnny Hennessey, or even Sandy Williams. But mostly he thought about sex.

He tried not to, but he was nearly fourteen and the images and thoughts that went through his head were like forces of nature. He thought about Lieutenant Durant and that idiot girl Luanne, whose breasts he'd glimpsed the day he kicked Johnny in the head, but mostly he thought about Athena and the afternoon swimming naked in the beaver pond.

Without details, he confessed these thoughts to *Thây* Hahn while Thayet was out in the garden. The priest had nodded seriously. "Yes, of course you do."

"I *try* not to."

"You can't 'try' something without attaching to it. Don't try anything. Let them come and let them go. Just sit." He looked out the window at his daughter. "When I was your age there was the daughter of a fruit seller in Nha Trang who fired my loins. I sat and I sat, 'trying' to get her out of my mind, and while I could dismiss certain things—her clothing mostly—she stayed. Usually, when I think back on those sessions, I deeply regret the waste."

He winked at Kimble. "And sometimes I rejoice."

An out-of-uniform Lieutenant Durant took her "Little Friend" for a walk into the northeast part of town. Behind the temple of the Church of Latter-day Saints she indicated, with a shift of her eyes, a two-story house across the lane. "Know it?"

Kimble, taking his cue from her averted gaze, didn't even nod. "Madame Rosario's. When I left, it was the best in town—or at least the most expensive." It was easy for him not to look toward the bordello. The lieutenant was wearing a formfitting sundress and light sweater. *And I thought she looked good in uniform.*

Still walking ahead, casually, she said, "Hearsay? Or experience?"

"Of course hearsay. I was only eleven, after all. But

young men brag. They pay for someone in an alley and they don't say much, but they scrape together enough for Madame Rosario's and they strut around like kings."

"Well, it's still the top house. You've got to have the money or, in the case of our local marshal or our public health director, you need to be in a position to shut them down. No window shopping for *them*."

"Are they your targets?"

"No. Despite their patronage, or perhaps even because of it, Rosario's has got a much better record on the STD front. No underage sex workers, either."

Kimble froze, mid-step, and she said, "Relax! Keep walking. You're breaking character!"

He dropped his shoulders and stuck his hands in his pockets, and concentrated on his breathing.

Lieutenant Durant pointed at some of the stonework on the temple. "What was that about?" she said quietly.

"I did some work for the captain, in Parsons. There was a rape. A fifteen-year-old girl—I found her." He bent down and took off one of his sandals, pretending to dislodge a pebble.

Even the lieutenant had trouble appearing casual after he said that. "That meth ring. Heard about it." She took a deep breath. "As I said, underage sex workers are not the problem here, though I certainly couldn't vouch for all the houses in town."

They resumed their walk, swinging west on Avenida del Flores.

"Why the concern? Isn't this the marshal's jurisdiction?"

"Corruption in territorial government is our lookout." At his glance, she said, "Not the marshal, not the public health director. One of the governor's junior aides was seen here, a Mr. Franks. He's not a wealthy man. Happily married. Three kids. He wants to cat about town, that's his business, but where's he getting the money? Either he's peddling influence, which doesn't fit what we know about him, or someone else is paying for his time in the saddle."

"If he won't take money directly to influence the governor, it doesn't seem likely that he'd do it for the nookie."

"Hard to say. Everybody's different. But I'm more worried about what Mr. Franks would do to keep his wife from finding out. There could be photographs."

Digital and metal-cased cameras were impractical in the territory, attracting bugs as they did, but there were territory-safe cameras with plastic cases and light-sensitive emulsions.

"Ah. I see. So I'm following him?"

"Yeah. At least tonight. I've got a man in his office. Mr. Franks sent a message home saying he had a late meeting tonight. But there's nothing on his office calendar."

"So this is real. Not another of your tests?"

"Cross my heart and hope to die." She did not suit her actions to the words. "Let's go give you a look at Mr. Franks."

MR. FRANKS, a lanky redhead in a tropical-weight suit, left the Territorial Complex on the plaza side about a half hour after the rest of his staff. He ate tacos alone at one of the market stalls before taking the Avenida del Sol toward Northgate.

Kimble found himself falling into a meditative state, standing, sitting, and even walking, aware of Franks but not attaching.

Even from half a block away, Kimble could tell that Mr. Franks was nervous. He paused a lot. Once he ducked into a store when he spotted two women coming up the street and didn't come out again until they were well past. Yet his glance skipped right past Kimble.

He's avoiding people he knows.

At least twice, Franks paused on street corners and gazed westward. Lieutenant Durant had told Kimble, "He has a cottage near Westgate right across from his kids' school."

Kimble staggered suddenly. The street was shaking and the sound of a bell was swelling, blocking out all noise, yet people were strolling calmly by, as if nothing had happened. Kimble steadied himself against a garden wall.

Franks is conflicted. It had come out of the Zen state, unasked for, unlooked for, but it had pushed up out of his unconscious with volcanic force.

When Franks took the right that led toward Madame Rosario's, Kimble took the closest turn, sprinting down the middle of the street and then through an alley. He was catching his breath at the alley mouth when Franks came up the walk. The man was slowing with every step and glancing back to the west and Kimble knew his analysis was correct.

"Mr. Franks," Kimble said, "please come with me."

Franks took a step back, startled. "What? Did Sam send you? Who are you?"

Kimble said, "I'm a friend."

"I don't know you!"

"No, you don't know me. Life is full of friends we've never met." He gesture at the city in general. "I really do have your best interests at heart. For instance, I'd like to see you keep your job and not go to jail."

Franks' eyes widened. His voice raised in pitch, strident. "I don't know what you're talking about!"

Kimble wanted to slap him. "Fine. It's your marriage. Do you really want to go back to Madame Rosario's?"

He'd said it quietly but Franks' hand went out, toward Kimble's mouth, as if to cover it, to silence him, even though he was two yards away. Franks hissed, "How do you know about that?"

"That's not the question you should be asking. What I'd worry about is 'who else knows' and 'what are they going to ask you to do to keep them from talking to your wife?' "

PER orders, Kimble reported to Lieutenant Durant back at Café del Mundo. She was wearing reading glasses and had a thick volume open before her.

"Cervantes?" said Kimble. "In Spanish?"

"Yeah, the original seventeenth-century Spanish. It's more like modern Spanish than Elizabethan English is like modern English. What are you doing here?"

"Reporting."

"You found the contact? Already?"

"Samuel Peralta. He's an attorney who works for Richardson and Sons, Importers. They're seeking a change in the governor's import regulations, specifically the interdiction against some of the nastier insecticides."

Durant made a face. "We know Richardson and Sons."

"The first and only time Franks ended up at Rosario's, he was drinking with Peralta, who got him in there after four quick whiskeys. Franks thought they were going to another bar but he was up to his armpits in tits and ass before he knew it."

Durant said, "Now how the hell did you learn that?" The book shut with a thump. "You *talked* to him, didn't you?"

"Well, yeah. The question is, why didn't you guys?"

Durant glared at him. "You were told to follow him. Not blow your cover."

"He wasn't going to make the rendezvous. He was skittish from the start and getting more so the closer he got to Rosario's."

"But now we don't have Peralta. There's no evidence."

"You wouldn't have him even if they had met. Not until Peralta tried to cash in. Now you've got Franks on your side."

"We do?"

"He's expecting someone to call on him tomorrow morning. His office. I didn't say who. Didn't know if you'd want to talk to him or the captain or whoever, but he'll cooperate. He'll help you sting Peralta and testify."

"So he never went to Rosario's?"

"Not last night. After our little talk, he went home. I followed. He was playing with his kids in the front yard when I left." He scratched his head. "You might want to send someone to keep an eye out. Be a shame if Peralta got to him tonight."

Lieutenant Durant swore and threw down a territorial twenty-dollar bill. "Pay my bill." She tucked *El Ingenioso Hidalgo Don Quixote de la Mancha* under her arm and left, hips swinging.

Though Kimble thought he would regret it in the morning, he watched until she was out of sight.

AFTER supper Kimble told *Thây* Hahn that he would be leaving the next day after an eleven o'clock meeting with Bentham, and immediately regretted it.

"Eleven? Ah, good. We can sit for six hours." He laughed at Kimble's expression. "It will be my gift." Suddenly *Thây* Hahn reached out with both his hands and grasped Kimble's head. "What happened?"

Kimble blinked. "*Thây* Hahn, I may not tell what I do in the day."

Thây Hahn rapped him on top of the head. "Not that! I don't care what you were doing or who you were talking to. There was a moment when things came undone, yes? And when it came back together there was something more there."

Kimble's eyes went wide. "The street shook and a great bell rang and, yes, I realized something when it was done."

Thây Hahn released his head. "Were you meditating?"

Kimble licked his lips. "Not intentionally. I was watching some . . . thing and I was trying to relax, to observe without judgment, without—"

"Without attachment," said *Thây* Hahn, with certainty.

Kimble turned his hands palm up. "Perhaps."

"Have you done *công án* study? You may know it by the Japanese word, koan."

Kimble shook his head. "I've read about it. Sensei said she wasn't qualified. That it was enough to sit and breathe for now."

"Until it is time to stop breathing, it is always good to breathe. Take this, if you will: A man walks through the territory carrying his Buddha nature in a metal cup. The bugs come and eat the cup. Where is his Buddha nature?"

Kimble opened his mouth and *Thây* Hahn held up his hand. "Not now. Tomorrow, after you sit."

Kimble slept hard and deep and if he dreamed he did not remember. When Thayet came to waken him, he was sitting upright in bed. "Yes," he said first. "Time to sit."

They did six sitting and two walking meditations and he was shocked at how quickly it went.

"Do you have an answer for me?" *Thây* Hahn asked.

"Will you hit me with your sandal?"

"Do you want to be hit with my sandal? Doesn't your sensei hit you enough?"

"I don't know where his Buddha nature is, but it was never in the cup."

Thây Hahn put his hands together. "Travel safely."

"YOU don't follow orders very well," commented Captain Bentham.

Kimble felt his ears go hot. He hated blushing. He knew he had the criticism coming, but Lieutenant Durant was also in the room, and this morning he was feeling less certain about his actions of the night before.

"Any word on Pritts?"

"And you like to change the subject," Bentham said. "No. Nothing yet."

"Okay. Did you make contact with Franks? Is that working out?"

Lieutenant Durant started to speak but stopped herself. She looked sideways at Captain Bentham, who gave her a short nod. "Yes," she said. "I read him the riot act this morning in his office. He's talking and he'll cooperate. I strongly urged him to confess to his wife, too. If he ends up testifying in court, it could come out. Better if he opens that can of worms now."

Kimble nodded "I'm glad. During meditation this morning I had a panic attack. I was convinced they'd killed him during the night."

Bentham, for some reason, looked pleased at this confession. "Right. Something like that could've happened. Oddly enough, it could've happened if you'd said nothing and Franks had still skipped the rendezvous." He raised his bushy eyebrows. "You know, this reminds me of your incident back in Perro Frio."

This seemed unfair. "I didn't kick anybody in the head!"

Bentham laughed. "That's not what I was referring to. It was the other thing that you learned."

Kimble thought for a moment, recalling the conversation. "Sometimes things aren't black and white?"

"Exactly. Sometimes things aren't black and white and sometimes strictly following orders is the wrong thing to do." He pulled an envelope out of an inside pocket and handed it to Kimble.

"Not another court order?"

"No. It's your GED results. You averaged 765."

Kimble blinked. "Uh, is that good?"

"Out of 800. You needed to average 450 to pass. You're in the top five percent."

"Congratulations," said Lieutenant Durant, and she kissed him on the cheek.

For the second time that morning Kimble turned bright red.

Broken Glass

Ruth wanted a small greenhouse so that she could grow vegetables in the winter like Mr. Covas, so, one sunny day in late March, Kimble floated down the Rio Grande on a plywood deck over bundles of netted plastic soda bottles. Mr. Covas' cousin, Julio, accompanied him.

They'd entered the river between the rubble of Algodones and Bernalillo, moving across a bug-free stretch of the Santa Ana Pueblo. Julio's unmarried sister, Patrice, drove them and the disassembled raft by wagon.

"In a week, then, right?"

"*Seguro*," said Julio, "where the Puerco joins the Grande."

The river widened to a lake where the old 550 bridge had collapsed. Flood detritus, helped by beavers, had plugged gaps, but the bugs still mined the metal from the dry side, following the embedded metal reinforcing rods and wire mesh like the veins of ore they were. Occasionally they'd succeed too well and a part of the dam would collapse, but then the beavers would drop trees into the water and guide them across the gap.

The dry parts of the dam were covered by an iridescent mass of aluminum, steel, copper, and crystalline blue.

"I've never seen so many bugs," said Kimble.

Julio laughed. "Wait until you see downtown."

They slid the raft over the dam at its lowest point and ran down the tumble of rapids to the river below.

They spent their first night on a sandbar near Corales, cooking with driftwood. The sandbar was less than a foot above water level and before the sun had dropped over the horizon, they'd made sure it was clear of any bugs.

"This bar wasn't here when we came five years ago," Julio said. "The river's always changing."

In the morning, they waded across to the west bosque and cautiously moved up the banks toward old Corrales, but the bugs were too thick.

"It's the old steel erosion bars."

Kimble raised his eyebrows.

"They were girders welded into crosses, no, that's not right, more like axis, like in math? X, Y, and Z? They put these through the brush, near the old embankments, to catch stuff during the floods. It looked like those obstructions they put on the Normandy beaches to keep troops off. There was steel cable strung between them. I think that's why the bugs are still here."

"Perhaps metal debris, too?" suggested Kimble. "Washed into the river during heavy rains and piled up here."

"Could be."

They retreated to the raft and headed farther downstream. The dam and lake formed by the collapsed Alameda Bridge got them past the bugs. The lake had flooded the bosque, submerging the erosion control beams there. Julio and Kimble floated the raft up to the old recreation area, a green area where the most metal had been vinyl-covered steel park benches. They beached the raft and threaded their way past an old strip mall into the old residential areas.

Bugs make a mess of frame houses. They go for metal window frames and metal roofs first, but there's so much metal used: nails, anchors, galvanized wall plate and joist hangers, and even the chicken wire fastened to the siding to anchor the stucco. Sometimes the houses remain standing, a fragile honeycombed froth of a building, but more often they come down, collapsing onto their slabs or into their crawlspaces. The bugs take longer to mine out the reinforcing rods in the slabs and foundations.

But sometimes the collapse is slow and surprisingly gentle.

That's where they looked for the glass panes they needed.

It was sweaty work. They needed the best light to make

sure they didn't accidentally step on a bug, so they tended to work in the hottest part of the day, while the sun was high. They moved the debris cautiously, lest they uncover chunks of copper plumbing or conduit still being consumed by the bugs. They averaged a few panes of glass a house, doing better with vinyl-framed windows. If it was an old metal casement window, the edges of the glass tended to be uneven—not broken, but eaten where the bugs went right through the glass to get at the metal. Provided the pane had a large enough expanse of glass, they took these anyway.

They managed to pull several chunks of heavy glass from a bank, useless for window glazing because of its thickness, but almost as good as Jemez obsidian for flaking into cutting edges.

The second day, pushing aside some cinder block, Kimble uncovered a home security system. There was metal. But worse, an old sealed lead-acid battery shorted as he shifted the material above. The sudden surge in EMF was almost as bad as stomping a bug. He threw himself sideways, rolling across shards of glass and stucco and scrambled away as the sudden buzzing of descending bugs rose to a shriek.

He got down the bank without any bug burns but he was bleeding from several cuts.

Julio, walking back from taking a load of glass down to the bank, saw the incident from a safe distance. "Wow. You moved before I saw anything."

"Heard 'em," said Kimble.

Julio looked puzzled.

"That high-pitched sound they make. Like, oh, super high crickets."

"Huh. I don't hear that. I hear the buzzing when they fly."

Kimble shrugged.

Julio helped him clean out the cuts. "Young ears, I guess. You never used an MP3 player, I bet."

They had to abandon a small pile of their salvaged glass panes near *that* house.

Water flowed over the top of the Alameda dam and fell six feet straight down so they spent most of the next morning portaging glass around the dam. It would've taken half an hour if they could've stuck to the shoreline, but the bugs were there in droves and they had to go inland a bit to find a safe path.

This time of year, the water's source was snowmelt and it felt like it, but after hauling the raft and glass around, Kimble let himself fall full length into the shallows.

"We had good luck near Montaño, last time," said Julio.

The bridge at Montaño had not become a dam. The main span had fallen one section at a time and the first section had sunk deep into a sandy area of the riverbed, leaving most of it above water. This had allowed the bugs to eat it to rubble and floods had pushed the chunks downriver. The water rushed through the gap and down a set of rapids. They had no choice but to run it. Bugs heavily infested both banks along the old thoroughfare, so portaging the glass around was more dangerous than the river.

Though the run down the rapids took less than ten minutes, they spent half the day packing the glass between layers of dried reeds and lashing them securely to the middle of the raft. They caromed off rocks twice and Kimble stopped worrying about the glass and instead worried about the raft itself, but despite the shaking, they reached the still water below the rapids with both glass and craft intact.

The houses closest to the river in this part of the city had been large, with correspondingly large lots. The yards, once xeriscaped or green with grass, were now brush and weeds and young woods, fortunately threaded with game trails.

"The deer came back with a vengeance, and the coyotes, and the rabbits," said Julio. He set some snares in the rabbit runs. "But you really have to watch out for the dogs." Which is why they both carried spears.

They hit the jackpot working a street farther from the river than Julio had reached on his previous trip.

"Looks like it was a solarium."

On the south side of a large adobe house—almost a mansion—an exterior wall had been filled, ceiling to floor, with double-glazed windows, admitting light. The panes, two feet by three, had been set directly in the adobe. When the metal roof had been eaten, the rains had turned the exposed wall to mud, sloughing and sagging gently over the years. The glass had settled with the wall and was embedded now in loose dirt and rotting straw, overgrown with bindweed and goat-heads.

It took them less than half a day to pull more intact

panes than they could carry on the raft and, though they once had to drive off a pack of feral dogs by throwing rocks, the worst thing they had to contend with was the quarter-inch barbs of the puncture vine.

"I hate goat-heads!" Kimble repeated for the twentieth time.

Julio nodded in agreement.

They abandoned some of their previously salvaged glass in favor of the consistently sized panes from the solarium. When the cargo had been padded and packed, the water, previously a good six inches below the deck now lapped at the wood.

That night they ate rabbit on a sandbar near the old Rio Grande Nature Center. The weather had warmed and the mosquitoes were bad but they burned half-dried cattails and the smoke kept the gnats and mosquitoes away.

The next day they spent two hours getting the raft over the dam formed by the old Interstate Bridge. The water flowed over a large section and the problem wasn't rapids but water that was too shallow. They pulled and lifted and dragged until they made it down.

"And that should be that," said Julio. "The bridge at Cesar Chavez washed out completely, there's a nice gap at Rio Bravo and the highway bridge where 25 crossed back over. We might have to drag the raft over some shallows but there'll be no more rapids before the Puerco."

They were in the old South Valley when they heard the hail from the east shore. A shirtless man with sunburned face and shoulders stood in the tall grass. His pants were khaki with a small stripe down the side in brown.

Uniform? He thought he'd seen pants like that before.

"Can you give me a ride? Bugs cut us off."

On these lazy stretches they let the river do the work, using a pole to push the raft this way or that. Julio was slipping it into the water when Kimble said, "Wait. What does he mean, 'us'?"

Julio raised his eyebrows but he didn't push the raft any closer to shore. "How many of you are there?" he called out. "We're pretty low in the water."

The man crouched. "It's just two of us," he said. He let one hand reach down to something in the grass.

"We couldn't take two." He gestured at the driftwood caught among the salt cedars. "You could lash together a raft pretty quick, though. Couple of hours."

Another man stepped out from behind those very same salt cedars, a multi-barrel rifle dangling from one hand.

Kimble slammed his shoulder into Julio and they both tumbled off the raft into the icy water. It was mid-channel and the water was over their heads. Julio came up sputtering. "What the hell!" He grabbed the edge of the raft and started to pull himself out but Kimble grabbed his shoulders from behind.

"No! That's Pritts! He murdered two deputies back in Parsons breaking jail. He'll shoot you as soon as look at you." As if on cue, a ceramic slug slammed into the edge of the deck and shattered, sending fragments and splinters flying. The raft, jostled by their abrupt departure, was spinning in the current and they had rotated around to where it no longer shielded them.

Kimble saw the bare-chested man, now standing, another multi-barrel rifle in his hand. Pritts was pointing his rifle at the raft. If they'd all been loaded, he had three more barrels to fire. "Put into shore or the next one goes into your head!" he yelled across the water.

Kimble kicked sideways, turning the raft. Another shot hit the deck and they heard glass break. Julio, bleeding from a cut on his forehead, got the idea and they quickly positioned the raft and cargo between them and the men.

They were a good hundred feet out from Pritts and now directly abreast of their position. Kimble started kicking the raft farther away but Julio said, "Kick downstream. We go any farther toward the other bank and we'll be in the shallows again, where the current slows."

The current was moving as fast as a man could run and Kimble, peeking, saw Pritts and his companion doing just that, trying to keep up with them, but then they stopped, swearing, as a large cloud of bugs rose up around them. Kimble hadn't heard them step on one, but the two fugitives dropped their guns and dove sideways into the shallows.

The river curved away and the bend soon blocked their view of the shrinking figures. Chilled, Kimble pulled himself aboard and then helped Julio up over the edge.

"You've got a splinter in your forehead," Kimble said. They had an extra pole but the one Julio had dropped when Kimble pushed him into the water had floated down with them. They recovered it and then Kimble pulled the splinter out of Julio's scalp and staunched the bleeding. "Looks intact," he said, examining the splinter.

"How did you know about them? That guy?" Julio asked as Kimble bandaged his head.

"Pritts? Saw him once when I was working with a peddler over in Parsons. He was chief deputy. He ran a meth ring with the other deputies. Surely you heard about it?" There, all true, without saying anything about the Rangers or Captain Bentham.

"Oh. Yeah. Heard about that. Not sure I heard the name. Hadn't heard about the jailbreak."

"You should look at the posters at Martha's store more often." Another truth. Kimble grabbed the pole and started pushing the raft over toward the eastern shore.

"What are you doing?" Julio looked back upstream, as if expecting the two fugitives to show up any second.

"You all right? I mean, your head and all?"

"Yeah. So?"

"I'm going to keep tabs on them. You go on and meet Patrice, unload the glass, but then float on down to the Ranger Station near Isleta Pueblo. That'd be the quickest. Okay?"

"How am I supposed to get home from Isleta Pueblo?"

"Have Patrice come get you by road—without the glass. Go back for the glass after."

Julio was inclined to argue. "Ruth will kill me if I let you go back there. She thought this trip was dangerous enough with just the bugs."

The raft grounded in the shallows, out of the current, and Kimble grabbed his bedroll, backpack, and the food bag. "Patrice has more supplies, so I'm taking this."

"You can't go," Julio said sternly.

"It's okay, really."

"I mean it!" said Julio and reached out to take Kimble's arm.

Kimble put him down on the deck relatively gently, Julio's wrist locked painfully at ninety degrees to his arm. Julio tried to get up and quickly found the futility of that. "Sorry," Kimble said. Still holding the *nikkyo* grip, he stepped off the raft into the shallows, pushed Julio away to flop onto his back and, before Julio could get back up, shoved the raft out into the current.

Before Julio was standing, Kimble had vanished into the bosque.

Rapid Responses

Kimble's first thought was to head for higher ground, but the South Valley was named that for a reason, broad and flat. The old earthen levee was the highest ground and it had eroded badly over the years. He settled for a large cottonwood tree growing in one of the old irrigation ditches and used a strap from his backpack to shinny up the trunk to its lowest branch, fifteen feet off the ground.

He couldn't see them, but there was smoke from a fire drifting up near the river in or beyond a clump of Russian olive trees. Examining the ground between his tree and the fire, he saw lots of bugs. From the debris scattered around he realized this area had been junkyards, old auto salvage yards and light industrial.

He could always wade upriver, but he thought Pritts and his friend would be watching, looking for more river traffic. He headed due east, instead, threading up a dirt alley. After a while, he hit an old high-tension electrical right-of-way. The wires and their metal towers had been the first things to go, back when the bugs first showed up. Just as the shorted battery had called them up in Corrales, the high voltage EMF had drawn them from all corners.

Scraps of insulation wound through the weeds and coiled across the ground like shed snakeskins, but the metal had long ago walked or flown away in the bodies of robot bugs.

Kimble followed the path carefully, slowly. Watching out for bugs and for Pritts required two different observation behaviors. Failing at either would have disastrous consequences.

Sensei is going to kill me, he thought. *Or Captain Bentham will.* For some reason this cheered him up a little. *They can't* both *kill me, after all.*

He came to a spot where flooding had strewn debris from a sheet metal shop across the electrical right-of-way. The bugs weren't solid across the ground but they covered most of it. He rested in the shade for fifteen minutes then picked his way carefully through the stretch of feeding bugs. He was halfway across when he smelled ozone and something moved in the adjacent auto salvage yard.

Something big.

He froze and crouched. *Did I walk right up on them?* By his estimate, he was till several hundred yards away from the campfire smoke. He took two quick, stretching steps over patches of bugs until he came to a stand of head-high cedar brush that shielded him from whoever was moving in the next field. The base of the bushes was clear of bugs. He leaned forward and parted the cedar branches slowly, trying to see through, but it was too thick. All he succeeded in revealing was a hollow three feet off the ground formed by several branches. Loose feathers and broken eggshells showed that a chicken had nested there in the past. He stepped up into the hollow, sat on his rucksack, and leaned forward again, moving a branch down on the far side.

The thing moving in the yard was not human. It looked like a longhorn steer, including long horns and a swinging tail, but it was not a steer. It was oily black and the ears were perfectly circular. Below the horns there were no eyes, just patches of darker black. And the horns . . . well, the horns looked like lightly oxidized aluminum.

It was walking in a circle, head down, swinging its horns from side to side. If Kimble had seen an actual longhorn walking like that, he would've suspected a serious illness or perhaps jimsonweed (of which the Dineh say, "Eat a little, and go to sleep. Eat some more, and have a dream. Eat some more, and don't wake up.").

This not-steer's movement, though odd, seemed filled with purpose. The circle was getting smaller and smaller as the not-steer spiraled in. Finally it began slight movements forward and backward, little half steps. It stopped. In fact it froze, motionless for a few moments, then it took four precise steps forward and its tail lifted.

You're shittin' me!

The cow pie looked like many others, except for its color—black. The mixture of solid and liquid was just right, and in the twilight Kimble would've passed right by it without a second thought.

Well, he would have if it had stayed *still*.

At first Kimble thought it was shrinking, but after a moment he realized it was burrowing, instead, sinking into the earth. There was a haze around it as if vapors were being given off but it soon dropped completely below the surface. The steer—the not-steer, that is— turned in place until its head was back over the hole, for now it was definitely a hole. From his perch in the cedar, Kimble thought the opening was at least ten inches across. He could see eight inches down the opposite wall before the near edge cut it off and there were still steam-like vapors rising out of the opening.

The not-steer lowered its nose until it was a foot above the hole and froze. The silvery horns, at first nearly touch-ing the ground, rotated upward until they pointed straight at the sky.

Kimble rolled out of the tree without thinking, land-ing back in the clear space at the cedar's base. Then he heard the buzzing that followed the near ultrasonic sound of swarming bugs. Bugs had lifted into the air all around him, not unlike a swarm. Their passage through the air was not as urgent, but they were all headed his way.

He sunk down, hugging the ground as the bugs buzzed overhead, several bouncing through the cedar brush.

The old electrical right-of-way was temporarily empty and Kimble crawled sideways until he could see past the cedar. Like a miniature tornado, the bugs formed a descending funnel hanging down from the drifting cloud above, drawing tighter and tighter as they streamed down into the hole created by the not-steer.

That must be some deep hole.

A low-flying bug cut through a cedar branch, which dropped to the ground in front of him. Kimble scrambled north up the right-of-way. When he looked back over his shoulder, the not-steer had turned and was watching him.

HIS light shorts and shirt had dried by the time he passed the not-steer, but when Kimble came up on their campsite, he could tell that Pritts and his buddy were still cold, if not also wet. The fire Kimble had been using to spot their camp was a bonfire now, as they'd gotten some of the drift logs alight. Both men stood close to the flames, rotating slowly.

It was getting late and Kimble didn't want to step on a bug in the night. He found a hollow under some brush cedar overlooking the camp, and he edged in, inspecting carefully for bugs. He was shielded from view on all sides, though he could move a branch if he wanted to see them. He was close enough that an occasional word or phrase drifted over the distance, but most of what the men said was being drowned out by the snap and roar of the fire.

While there was still light, he dressed in warmer clothes, laid his bedroll out, and put his other things where he could reach them easily.

As the bonfire died down he could hear more of what the men said.

"If I have to go into the water one more time to avoid bugs, I'm just gonna let them eat me." It was the other deputy, the one who wasn't Pritts.

"We don't find some food, soon," said Pritts, "*I'll* eat you."

"Bet those two on the raft had some food."

"Yeah, well, we won't know now you scared 'em off, Ortiz."

"*I* scared them off? They didn't jump into the river until you showed your rifle."

"They were already leery. The older guy started asking questions before that. You were too eager."

"Sure I was."

The give and take sounded routine, almost like an old married couple. Pritts got up and threw a long branch of green cedar on the fire that went up with a bunch of crackling and popping, drowning out the next phase of their argument. Kimble just caught fragments.

The month before, they'd ridden in from the west, crossing over the lava of the Three Sisters, threading down through the Petroglyph National Monument. They'd lost Pritts' horse on the edge of Paseo de Volcan, when it had punched a leg down into the earth, probably where an old pipeline had been eaten down its length, leaving the earth above unsupported. Ortiz's horse they'd killed in the city, to eat.

They'd tried smoking most of the meat but at that time they'd still had some crystal meth. Pritts had done the last of the meth and, hopped up, put too much firewood under the smoking rack. The meat had burned instead of drying and there was a big fight about it when Ortiz returned from hunting. They had last eaten two days before, the remains of a doe Ortiz had shot the week before. They'd tried to hunt that morning but a surge in bugs had driven them back to the river's edge and, more than once, up to their necks in the water.

"Wish we had some rock," Ortiz said. "At least it would kill the hunger pains. But *someone* smoked it." The round of recriminations that followed proceeded like an ancient ritual, every part known by heart.

The plane came out of the north about the time the sun crested the Sandias, a four-engine turboprop aircraft traveling over the city at a bug-safe fifteen thousand feet. It was clear to Kimble that it wasn't just an overflight. The plane turned and made five passes, north to south, south to north, dropping in altitude and shifting eastward each time.

Looks like Julio got the word out.

After the last pass, six blue blossoms appeared high above the northeastern quadrant of the city and drifted with the wind, west, toward the river.

Whoa, Kimble thought. He thought it had just been a spotter flight. He hadn't expected them to send a unit of the Rapid Response Force.

Unfortunately, he wasn't the only one to see the parachutes open. Both Pritts and Ortiz were swearing, scrambling to get their bedrolls and gear together.

"You don't know they've come for *us*," Pritts was saying.

"Face it. Those guys on the raft reported us. I knew

you shouldn't have shot at them. They probably showed them your wanted poster down in Isleta."

The chutes were below the trees now. Kimble thought the RRF team was aiming to come down in the river, bug-safe, bug-free.

Pritts and Ortiz had planned ahead, apparently. There were no arguments over where to go. They had a small raft in the scrub near the river. It wasn't big enough to hold them, but it supported their saddlebags and bedrolls, a disturbingly large bundle of disposable rifle barrels, their rifles, and their hastily stripped clothing. They waded out into the river, swearing at the frigid water. They only had to swim ten feet, mid river, and then they were wading again. When they got over to the far shallows, they snatched up their belongings and shoved the raft away, then continued upriver, keeping to the water.

Kimble nodded. It was a smart move. The water hid their tracks and kept them away from bugs. It was also an unlikely direction for the fugitives to go, toward the city center, where the bugs would be worst. The Rangers would certainly have the camp's location. Julio would've pointed it out on a map and the information would've gone out by heliograph. Apparently all the way out of the territory. It was possible that even in the night the heat from their bonfire had been pinpointed by satellite.

Kimble waited until they two men had splashed around the next bend in the river before following. He had an unused plastic trash bag in his pack, reserved as rain-wear for a rare spring storm. It protected and floated his things across the river.

The water was *very* cold. He shuddered to think what it must be like for the two men, who hadn't eaten recently. Kimble's teeth were chattering as he dressed on the other side.

He went ashore, stepping past patches of bugs, and risked running along the top of the overgrown western levee. Twice the ground collapsed under him and he threw himself forward, remembering with vivid imagination the fate of the fugitives' first horse.

Maybe they'll eat me if I break my leg.

Once, the bugs became so thick he had to go back to the shallows, but he returned to the levee almost immediately. He could travel faster and more quietly than the men splashing through the shallows but he had only just caught sight of them when they turned up into the bosque a half a mile south of the wreckage of the Central Avenue Bridge.

It had been a mixed residential and industrial area, and it was thick with bugs. Pritts and Ortiz topped the levee and then dropped to the ground behind the crest, peering through the brush back at the river.

Kimble saw the Rangers, then, rounding the bend. They were in three inflatable kayaks, strung well apart. The man in the stern of each boat handled the double-bladed paddles. The men in the bows scanned the shorelines with binoculars, their gyro rifles in their laps.

The deep water was on the west side at this bend. They would pass very close to Pritts and Ortiz.

In Kimble's knife bag, a leather pouch where he kept a chunk of obsidian and a rounded river rock for chipping, he had a small piece of the thick bank window they'd gathered up in Corrales. He took it out and scrambled down to the riverbank.

It wasn't as good as a heliograph but he could tell, even from this far, that the Rangers saw his reflected sunlight. He'd practiced his Morse code for a half hour every day for the month after his training sessions with Communications Tech Sergeant Chinn, but not so much after that.

"AMBUSH WEST BANK." He hoped that was what he was sending. He wasn't that sure about "W." Was it dot-dot-dash or dot-dash-dash? He repeated three times and then water exploded next to him and the loud bang of the gunshot rolled back and forth between the riverbanks.

Pritts had seen him.

He jumped back into the brush. He kissed the chunk of glass, stowed it away, and snatched up his pack. He risked a look from the top of the levee. Two of the kayaks were putting into shore and the other had swung wide, both occupants training their rifles on the western bank. Ortiz and Pritts were both pounding up the crest of the levee toward Kimble.

Pritts saw Kimble and took another shot, but he was running and Kimble heard it tear through the cottonwood leaves high above him. Ortiz stopped running and, for an instant, Kimble thought he was going to give up, but instead he crouched and steadied his elbow on his knee. Kimble flung himself sideways, toward the river. A tremendous impact threw Kimble forward and he tumbled down the slope, his forward roll spoiled by his backpack. Still he came out of it standing, and then fell flat on his face.

He was dazed and he was having trouble breathing. There was something wet running down his ribs. He rolled over on his side and thought he heard his broken insides rattle together, then he realized it was Ruth's lightest ceramic cooking pan. He touched the wetness on his side and brought his fingers up. Water. From his plastic water bottle. He'd just been shot in the backpack.

He heard footsteps and looked up. Ortiz and Pritts stood atop the levee. Ortiz was looking back, toward the Rangers, and Pritts was staring down at Kimble. He raised his rifle. "Little shit," he said.

Blood fountained from Ortiz's shoulder, spraying across Pritts' face. Ortiz went down, clutching his shoulder, his rifle tumbling to the ground. Pritts' gun, halfway to his shoulder, went off as he jerked the trigger in surprise. The bullet tore into the ground in front of Kimble, stinging his face with gravel and fragments of ceramic slug.

A hissing gyro tore through the air near Pritts' head and he jerked sideways. He fired both of his remaining barrels back toward the Rangers, then dropped his gun and crouched, his hands scrambling for Ortiz's rifle. He found it, pivoted, and aimed it.

Kimble found himself looking straight into the barrel.

The south side of Pritts' head sprayed out, his eyes

went wide, and he dropped straight down, like a puppet whose strings had been cut.

"WE figured it out," said Sergeant Cletus Brown, commanding. "AMBUSH UEST BANK. You-est. Helped that I was sounding it out."

The squad member who doubled as med tech had finished gluing Ortiz shut. He had the shoulder immobilized and a bag of Lactated Ringer's Solution running I.V. Now the med tech was tweezing bits of gravel and ceramic slug from the cuts on Kimble's face.

"Thanks for the warning," continued Sergeant Brown. "They might have gotten me or Tumbo here—we were on point."

Kimble was holding very still but he said, carefully, "To be honest—OW!"

The med tech, Tumbo, held up a ceramic shard three-quarters of an inch long in his plastic forceps. "Oh, stop being a baby. It's not like it went into your eye or anything." He flipped it off to the side and muttered under his breath, "Though it could have."

Sergeant Brown whistled. "You can holler if you want to. Tumbo's a bit of sadist. You were saying?"

"To be honest, they were probably going to let you float right past. I think they were that rational, but they were both meth heads and they hadn't eaten in a couple of days. You might have been in more danger because of the rations you carried." Tumbo started smearing antibacterial ointment on the wounds. "Besides, you were here to get them, right?"

"If possible," said Brown.

"Huh?"

"Our mission was to get *you* out. If we could safely take Pritts and Ortiz, well and good, but the primary objective was to safely extract you. You aren't the illegitimate son of the governor, are you?"

Bentham, thought Kimble. He shrugged for the sergeant. "Pretty sure I'm not."

Sergeant Brown studied Kimble's face. "Well, you sure don't look like the governor." He jerked his thumb at Ortiz and the inert body beyond. "You're right. Going after those two is more our sort of thing. Rescue missions . . . well, we might go after government VIPs who get themselves in trouble. Do you have any idea why you had priority?"

Kimble shrugged. It wasn't yes and it wasn't no.

Sergeant Brown raised his eyebrows. "Well, I guess if they wanted us to know, they would've told us."

The plane hadn't left Albuquerque, it was just circling far enough that Kimble hadn't been aware of it. One of the team took a small heliograph out of his gear and flashed a message, acknowledged by a blinking laser on the belly of the plane. The plane dropped a cargo chute from an altitude of 10,000 feet (5,000 feet above the river) and a quarter mile east. It crossed the river and landed in the bosque on the west side, several hundred yards downstream.

Sergeant Brown watched it intently through his plastic and glass binoculars. "Uh, not seeing any swarming, so I think we're okay."

The cargo pack had body bags and a larger inflatable raft, suitable for transporting both the wounded Ortiz and the deceased Pritts. "If it'd just been run-of-the-mill bandits, we'd take prints and a photo, then bury the remains, but this guy stirred up so much shit, they wanted us to bring him in even if it was just pieces."

The Rapid Response Force team delivered Kimble to the junction of Rio Puerco and the Rio Grande. Before releasing him to Patrice and Julio, who were camped there, Sergeant Brown had Kimble identify them, checking their names against a printout from his pocket.

From his kayak, Brown said, "I'd say, 'see you around, kid,' but I'm hoping not."

"Thanks for the rescue."

"Thanks for the warning."

THEY could've made it back to Perro Frio by nightfall if it weren't for the cargo. As it was, they got in by noon the next day and finished unloading the dojo's share of the glass by early afternoon.

Over supper that night he told Ruth most of the story. He minimized the danger a bit, telling the truth about a bullet going into the backpack but implying that he hadn't been wearing it at the time. The cuts on his face he grouped with the cuts from the glass back when he'd short-circuited the battery in Corrales.

Ruth said, "I knew I shouldn't have let you go."

"We can replace the water bottle and the cooking pan."

Ruth rolled her eyes.

Kimble changed the subject. "Anything happen while I was gone?"

Ruth scratched her head and exhaled. After a moment she said, "Your old schoolmate Luanne Tuscano is pregnant. Her father is furious, alternating praying over her and shouting. Johnny Hennessey is denying any involvement and his father is backing him. The school board, in a vote of three to two, decided to reinstate you but Mrs. Sodaberg explained about your GED, so they amended it to an apology." She looked up from her basketwork at Kimble's astonished expression.

"In other words," Ruth added, "nothing much."

Kimble and Mrs. Petdicoris

Captain Bentham showed up a week after Kimble's return. He sat on a log while Kimble turned the compost bins.

"As Lieutenant Durant would say, the best agents should *ser invisible como fantasma*," Bentham said. "Like a ghost. The people they're reporting on never even notice them. You've really got to work on that."

"Well," commented Kimble, "I wasn't the one that sent the RRF after some random kid. Those boys were asking all sorts of questions."

Bentham dismissed that with a wave of his hand. "I'm not worried about those guys. The last thing I want is for Ortiz to start talking about this kid who works for the Rangers. I mean, yes, he's in the pen, but word gets around. Prisoners talk to family members."

"He saw me to shoot me in the back . . . pack, but then Sergeant Brown shot him. Doubt he was even conscious until after I left the RRF team. He never heard a name. Never even got a clear look at my face."

Bentham growled. "But that wasn't *your* doing!"

"What did you want? For me to let the team float into an ambush?" He saw Bentham grimace. "This isn't about what I did, is it? It's about what Sensei said."

"I told her what my orders were!"

"Right. And what was that about? How dare you put the capture of Pritts second to my 'rescue'? What the hell were you thinking? You know what the bastard did! Besides, how can I be *invisible* with you pulling *that* crap? Pritts was on the most-wanted list and you put rescuing me before that?"

Bentham looked away. "Well, yeah. In hindsight, not one of my best decisions."

Kimble blinked, surprised. He liked the man for admitting that.

"It's just she was furious with me after the mission in Parsons. I told her I'd do my best to keep you out of danger." Bentham shrugged. "She scares me a little."

Kimble laughed. "Well, she scares me a *lot*."

Bentham muttered. "If only anything *else* scared you."

Kimble sobered. "Oh, I'm getting there. I didn't tell Sensei I was wearing that backpack when Ortiz shot it."

"Well . . . *she* scares you, after all."

"After Ortiz, bullets scare me, too." Kimble raised his sleeve to reveal the bug scar on his deltoid. "Bugs scare me." He spread his arms. "But after seeing what people like Pritts do, the thing that scares me the most is *failure*. You know what I mean?"

The corners of Bentham's mouth pulled down. "I'm afraid I do. But that road is full of heartbreak. 'Cause you *will* fail. You can't stop all evil and sick acts. Most of the time we won't know about the bad guys until after the damage has been done. It's what they do that defines them. It's the screams of their victims that alert us."

"But we can keep them from doing it again. Pritts won't, that's for sure."

Bentham nodded. "Is it enough? 'Cause I guarantee for every one you help catch, others will get away. And too many of the ones you *do* catch will walk away scot-free."

Kimble recognized the voice of bitter experience. "So, do you think I should just do *nothing*?"

Bentham looked away and didn't say anything.

Kimble nodded. "Yeah, right. You were the one who recruited me. That's what they call it, right? In the spy biz?"

Bentham nodded.

"You recruit many?"

"Sure. Three dozen or so in the last ten years."

"How many have been underage, kids, like me?"

Bentham sighed. "In my whole career? Only one."

HIMBLE first met Mrs. Perdicaris at a stopover on the old trail between Zia Pueblo and Acoma. Bentham had sent him there to wait for a passenger caravan coming in from Needles.

"DEA has some information on the organization that was dropping the meth into Parsons. Seems they're sending in someone to meet with a potential new distributor. The DEA has ID'd the outside contact, but we have no idea who these territorial guys are . . . but the meeting is supposed to be there."

"Can't they just arrest the guy they know about?"

"Not right now. I *think* their info comes from an undercover agent and they can't act without compromising him. Anyway, it's the Territory I care about. They grab that guy and we won't see who's willing to do the dirty here. There are always suppliers for a ready market. So we need to find and destroy the local market."

Bentham gave Kimble a battered pair of binoculars. "Those are Zeiss optics—we only made them *look* beat up—so *you* treat them gently. The right-hand side is also a camera." He showed him how to use it. "You've got thirty-six shots." Then he gave him a printout photograph of the contact from the outside cartel.

"Careful with that. It's the last thing you want found."

It was three days walk from Perro Frio to the watering stop, but Bentham took him within five miles by horseback. "There were thunderstorms and flash floods around the Mogollon Rim so the caravan could be delayed. They're due in three days but it could be as much as a week. The potential distributor could be anyone but I'll vouch for Tomás, the spring keeper. If you run out of food, he sells supplies. There's a roll of cash in the bottom of your food sack."

The tanques at the old stopover were above the caravan route, up a rising sandstone ridge. When the tanques just caught rainwater, they dried out during parts of the year, but now they were supplemented by PVC piping running from a spring in the sandy ridge above.

Kimble was talking with Tomás when he saw Mrs. Perdicaris.

"Yeah, the tanques were used by Clovis-era peoples, too. We get anthropological field trips out here every summer."

Kimble heard the mule's braying first.

She was a light brown mule with a snowy nose and hocks, and must've had an encounter with bugs at one time, for one of her ears had a bug-size hole through it. She was grievously overladen, carrying roughly carved eight-foot beams, four on each side of her packsaddle. That would've been a respectable load for a short trip, but she also had a bedroll, saddlebags, and four sacks of cement lashed atop that. She was walking stiff-legged up the road, moving very slowly, being prodded up the last bit from behind by her driver, a limping angry man who whipped rhythmically at her rump with a yard-long, inch-thick stick.

The driver was not a tall man, but he was wide, both in his shoulders and his belly. The keeper, standing beside Kimble, took one look and said, "Christ, Heimie, you keep that up you'll kill that mule!"

Heimie glared at the keeper. "Would suit me!" He

pulled up his left pants leg. On the side of his calf an ooz-ing bruise, black and blue—and several other colors—stretched across swollen skin. "That bitch has kicked me for the last time!"

Under his breath the keeper muttered, "But who started it?"

Heimie drove the mule on toward the water trough, which was placed back from the tanques to keep the live-stock from fouling the water. Heimie stamped up to the treadle-operated pump that lifted the water from the tanques. He thrust down on the lever with his good leg, bracing himself against the trough until water splashed across the dry bottom of the trough. But he stopped pumping almost immediately.

The mule slurped at the water, chasing the dribbles across the bottom of the trough.

For a moment Kimble thought the man was being careful not to let the mule water too fast, but it looked like he was taking a perverse pleasure in watching the mule try to get the last bit of the water off the boards.

The keeper said, "Heimie!"

"What?" Heimie said belligerently.

"You don't water her, you'll never get back to your place. You want to carry that stuff yourself?"

"Damn your eyes. Mind your own business!"

The keeper turned and walked away in disgust. Kimble, deeply disturbed, followed him.

"Is that legal? Isn't that animal cruelty?"

The keeper looked at Kimble. "Sure it is. You want to take it up with him?"

"Tell the Rangers!"

"You think the Rangers care about some mule? They don't even interfere when bastards beat their wives and kids, much less their livestock!"

Kimble winced, remembering his own childhood. The Rangers hadn't saved him. It was the Territorial Medical Service that had taken his father out of his life. And that was for his father's sake, not his.

"It makes me sick," said the keeper. "That's a right pretty mule and deserves better."

Kimble turned back toward the trough. Heimie had limped over to the people pump, the one that drew water from a covered cistern that was filled from the spring above. He was letting the cold water pour over his bruised leg. Kimble walked over to the treadle pump and began working it hard. He got several inches of water into the trough before Heimie noticed.

"What the hell do you think you're doing?" Heimie yelled. He struggled to his feet with the aid of his stick.

"Oh," said Kimble, smiling. "Saw you were laid up. Thought I'd help. You want me to start unloading her?"

Heimie was taken aback by this apparent conviviality. He frowned. "Why would I want to do that? You know how heavy that crap is? It would only have to be reloaded."

"Oh. Sorry. Just saw that the mule was all in, and with that bum leg you'd probably want to rest before moving on."

"You see too damn much. Get the hell away from my mule!" He lifted his stick as if to hit Kimble.

Kimble raised his eyebrows and took a step away from the mule, but closer to Heimie. He stared up into his Heimie's eyes. "You're kidding, right?" The man out-weighed Kimble three to one.

Heimie lashed out at Kimble's side, just as he'd lashed at the mule's rump to drive it.

Kimble slid back a step and the tip of the stick missed him, cutting through the air a couple of inches away. "I'd think about that, if I were you," he said calmly.

Maybe Heimie wasn't used to people not being afraid of him. He jerked the stick high and this time aimed for Kimble's head, but Kimble skipped forward, inside the swing, and kicked Heimie in the calf, right on the mule's previous strike.

Heimie screamed and fell to the hard dirt, dropping the stick in his attempt to catch himself.

Kimble picked up the stick and stepped back. He raised it in the air experimentally and cut sharply through the air. "You hit your mule with this? I wonder how it feels?" He brought it hard down toward Heimie's face, but stopped short of his flinching head. "Tempting." He broke the stick over his knee and threw the pieces far out into the brush.

Heimie swore at Kimble. He rolled over and tried to get up, but his leg buckled under him.

"Looks like you're not walking anywhere for a while. How about I unload that mule." He didn't make it a question.

The mule did try to kick him as he unloaded her, but it was half-hearted and Kimble sidestepped it easily. He left the beams and cement stacked neatly off to the side where they wouldn't block the watering trough and tied the mule to a piñon where the runoff from the people pump had greened the grass. There he rubbed the mule down with tufts of dried grass and fed it an apple from his food bag. She didn't try to kick him once after that.

While Kimble tended to the mule, Heimie had scooted back into the shade of the cistern. Without comment, Kimble dropped the saddlebags and bedroll beside the man, keeping his distance.

Kimble was swearing at himself. *Invisible. You're supposed to be invisible!* He sighed heavily.

"You'd probably do a lot better with carrots than a stick," he said.

"Go fuck yourself," Heimie said.

KIMBLE walked up the ridge to the spring, and then higher, where he could see off to the west, where the caravan route cut across the lava flows of the *malpais*—the Bad Lands. The old freeway also cut through the lava flow north of the tanques, near old Grants, but it swarmed with bugs.

He sat in the shade of a piñon and tried to make out movement but there was no sign of the caravan. *Well, Bentham had said it could be another four days.* He took a nap by the spring before returning to the watering stop, trying to avoid any more conflict with Heimie. *Could Heimie be the drug contact?* If so, and if he distributed drugs like he managed his livestock, the drugs weren't going far. As nice as it would be to ID Heimie as the distributor, he doubted it was the case.

When he got back down to the tanques, the neat pile of building materials was still there but Heimie and the mule were gone.

"He had to hop on one leg, but he managed it," Tomás told him. "The mule tried to kick him several times, though, until he put a twitch on its lip. He said he'd be back for his materials and that you'd better be gone when he got here. What the hell did you do to him?"

"I watered his mule and unloaded it."

"And he *let* you?"

Kimble said vaguely, "I think his leg hurt."

Before sunset that evening, a group of Dineh drove in in four wagons, returning from a trade fair at the capital. They laughed with Tomás and traded some pottery for dry goods at his store.

About sunset, the clip-clop of hooves came up the path and Heimie's mule walked up to the watering trough and stood there. Heimie wasn't on her and the cinch strap was loose and the packsaddle hung under the mule's belly. Though she still wore her bridle, one rein was missing completely and the other was snapped off near the ground.

When Tomás walked up she shied away, showing her backside, one hind hoof lifting, and Tomás backed off. He circled around until the trough was between them, then pumped several gallons of water into the trough.

"She bucked him off, you figure?" asked Kimble.

"Looks like. Don't blame her, really," said Tomás. He

tried to reach the mule's bridle as she drank but jerked his hand back when her head shot forward and her teeth snapped together.

"Uh, kid? You want to see what you can do with her?"

Kimble went back to his food bag and returned with an apple, which he broke into small chunks. He didn't approach the mule but sat upwind on a stump. When she'd drunk her fill, the mule turned her head. Over the course of several minutes, she worked her way over to Kimble. He hand-fed her half the apple before he attempted removing the bridle. The composite bit was worn and jagged, and when he unbuckled the straps, she spat it out, glad to get rid of it.

Kimble put the rest of the apple on the stump and, while she ate it, he got the twisted cinch and saddle pad off. He went over to where the dry grass grew, to pull some tufts to rub the mule down, if she'd let him. He thought that once the apple was gone, she'd move off, but instead, she lipped up the last of it and followed him.

"Heading back to the path, girl?" Experimentally, he stepped off to the side, to give her room to pass, but she swerved toward him when he did. When he stopped, she walked right up to him and nudged his stomach with her nose.

Aren't you *the vicious beast*, he thought as he rubbed her down. *Ah, well, in the morning, you'll probably be gone.*

He woke the next morning with her standing next to his mosquito netting, pulling grass from the ground beside his bedroll.

When Tomás watched the mule follow Kimble up to

the store, he said, "I guess she's not so scary after all, are you girl?" He raised his hand to pat her neck and the mule's mouth jerked around and snapped like a striking snake. Tomás jerked his arm back and tripped over the porch step.

Kimble stepped between the store and the mule, concerned, and the mule turned back to the trough. As she drank, Kimble stroked her neck and she stood there, meek as a kitten, leaning into it.

Tomás picked himself up, rubbing his backside. "O-kay. Wonder how she'll react to Heimie when he gets back."

But Heimie didn't show up and, by noon, Tomás was frowning. "Hate to say it, but someone should go look for him. He could be lying out there with a broke back or something."

Kimble had just returned from one of his walks up the ridge. He knew the caravan wasn't anywhere close and, since the Dineh left that morning, there were no candidates around for him to evaluate as possible drug distributors. "Where was he going?"

"He's got a place due south of here, right next to his big brother's ranch. I got a lot more use for Linc, his older brother. Family man—certainly doesn't mistreat his livestock."

Is that what a family man is? "How far?"

"Ten miles, maybe."

"Huh. Why do you think the mule came back here, then?"

Tomás shrugged. "Well, the water here is especially

good. Most of the wells hereabouts are brackish. Linc has some pretty good rainwater cisterns but Heimie just has the one well. Reliable—doesn't dry up, but brackish, not like our sweet spring." He looked over at the mule's hindquarters. There were some raised welts and a little crusted blood left over from Heimie's rod. "And maybe she just didn't want to go home."

Kimble got detailed directions to Heimie's place and packed up some food, some parachute cord, a blanket, his first-aid kit, and refilled his half-gallon water jug. He didn't want to be gone overnight but he also didn't want to be stupid about travel in the territory.

He started walking down the trail and he heard noise behind him. It was the mule, braying. He turned and looked. She was stretching out her neck toward him but she was standing back by the watering trough. When he turned, she straightened and put her long ears up. He waved, and then walked on. More braying, getting more and more urgent.

"What?" he shouted. The mule danced in place, moving forward and back, reminding Kimble of nothing more than a child who really needs to go to the bathroom. He shrugged and walked on, doing his best to ignore the frantic braying.

When he reached the first bend, a gentle switchback to help wagons get up the hill, he heard hooves pounding down the road. He glanced back and saw her galloping after him.

His first fear, that she was going to attack him, calmed when she dropped back to a canter, then a trot as she neared him, but then she passed him and turned, block-ing the path.

He tried to walk around her and she sidestepped, swinging her shoulder across his path. He moved back the other way and she brayed at him. He stopped again and stroked her cheek, letting her shove at his other hand with her soft nose.

Still stroking her head he started walking. After a mo-ment she seemed to give up on the blocking and let him continue on his way, but she followed right behind him. "Not much water out here," he told her.

She snorted.

He thought about riding her but decided against it. He might be able to survive being bucked off better than Heimie, but so much of the landscape consisted of jagged lava or thorned branches that he didn't want to risk it.

Heimie was about four miles along the southern trail. He hadn't broken his back but had badly sprained his good leg by trying not to land on his injured one. He had his saddlebags and his water bottle and he'd rigged his bedroll for shade. He was not happy to see Kimble and he was even less happy to see "that god damned bitch of a mule."

"Well, glad to see you're alive," Kimble said. "Tomás thought you were lying out in the sun with a broken back."

"You telling me you came *looking* for me?"

"Well, when Molly came back, figured she threw you."

"Her name is Mrs. Perdicaris!"

"That's a mouthful. Who's responsible for that?"

"The original owner. She named her for some movie character. Why did you come after me? Revenge?"

"Revenge? I don't need revenge. Maybe Mrs. Perdicaris wants revenge." He patted the mule's neck. "As I said, it wasn't my idea."

"Well, if you thought to loot the body, I don't have five bucks to my name."

Kimble grinned. "Well, *that* wasn't my idea either. Guess I just have a soft spot for dumb animals. You want to try and ride her again? Doubt you're walkin'."

The suggestion was not popular, so he rigged a sledge of lashed cholla skeletons and deadwood, padded with Heimie's blankets. Kimble's rolled blanket became a strap across Mrs. Perdicaris' chest with lines of parachute cord running back to the sledge and held up with more line running over her withers and her back. The sledge lines were doubled for strength. He would've liked to triple it but this would've put Heimie perilously close to Mrs. Perdicaris' rear hooves.

Kimble didn't know who was more uncomfortable. Heimie swore at every bump.

Mrs. Perdicaris kept her ears pointed back and rolled her eyes a lot but as long as Kimble stayed at her side and fed her occasional chunks of apple, she kept pulling. They reached Heimie's brother's adobe ranch house an hour and a half later.

Kimble tried to leave the mule there. After Kimble had removed the jury-rigged harness, she walked calmly into a large, chest-high paddock of split rails where a half-full water trough stood. Linc, Heimie's brother, closed the gate while she was drinking.

Kimble let Linc's wife refill his water bottle, reclaimed

his blanket and cord, and accepted the family's thanks—if not Heimie's—for his efforts. He refused an offer of food and a bed for the night.

As he walked away from the ranch house, Mrs. Perdicaris began braying more and more urgently from the paddock.

"Sorry, girl," he muttered.

There was a cracking noise and he turned in time to see the top rail of a fence flying up into the air. The door to the ranch house opened and people came out onto the porch. He saw the mule's rear hooves flash once, then again, followed by another crack of breaking wood. The next lower rail broke in half and the splintered ends fell outward, onto the packed earth, hanging down from their lashings on the uprights. Then he heard hoof beats and Mrs. Perdicaris came flying over the low spot in the fence.

Nice form.

Mrs. Perdicaris darted past two adults and one child who, to their credit, were not trying to catch the mule. They were trying to get out of her way. The mule galloped hard until she was out of the ranch-house yard, then she dropped back to a trot and came on toward Kimble, her tail flying like a flag and her ears held up high.

Kimble sighed and petted the mule. "You really ought to go back. You belong to Heimie." *Yeah, Heimie who beats her.* He walked back toward the ranch yard, Mrs. Perdicaris followed at his side, bouncing like a big puppy. But as they approached the group on the porch, she snorted and shied back.

Kimble paused for a moment, hanging back with the

mule. He dug down into the food bag and found an apple for her. At the same time he took a covert look at just how big the bundle of emergency cash was that Bentham had left him.

"HEIMIE sold her?"

"He was going to lose her anyway. She wouldn't stay. Kicked her way out of Linc's biggest paddock and kept following me out of the yard."

Heimie had demanded $2,000, "For a premium broke mule. She was born and trained at Mercy Mules. I paid three thousand for her." Kimble had asked if Heimie didn't mean "broken" as in *ruined* with all the beating and overwork. Then he asked Heimie to demonstrate the broken-to-saddle bit. Heimie wasn't really in any shape to ride her and his brother, Linc, refused. In fact, Linc refused to let his kids or wife anywhere near the mule. Heimie's next offer was an even thousand and Kimble had started to leave. Trouble was, so had Mrs. Perdicaris. Kimble finally settled for two-fifty, "If you throw in the saddle pad."

Kimble showed the bill of sale to Tomás. "Mrs. Perdicaris has seen the last of Heimie."

A MOUNTED courier running messages north to the heliograph in Parsons brought word that the eastbound caravan would make it in the next day. They'd had trouble with flash floods and then bugs, as an old mining installation had eroded, washing metal tailings across the caravan route. They'd had to detour south.

Meanwhile, the westbound caravan had arrived and would stay two nights before heading on. This was a regular rest stop in both directions, but the schedule was normally set to avoid hitting the tanques with both caravans at once. Tomás took some soundings and decided it would be all right, especially if they got some of the late summer thunderstorms.

Kimble didn't think the westbound caravan would carry his target. The meeting had been set for the tanques according to the DEA. *But one thing is sure. The east and westbound caravans would've passed each other at* some *point.*

Meanwhile, two ranch families, three different peddlers, and a freight outfit with two six-team wagons had all hit the tanques that afternoon and planned to stay at least the night.

After evaluating all the travelers, his money was on one or more of the peddlers, though he hadn't ruled out the freighters. He couldn't see the ranch families, traveling with young children, as the drug-dealing type. After playing with some of the kids and fetching water for some of their mothers, his conviction was strengthened.

Mrs. Perdicaris continued to follow Kimble, though she shied away from other livestock and would threaten grown men who came too close. She didn't seem to mind the kids or women, though.

For the last three days he'd put Mrs. P's saddle pad on and cinched it in place. The day before, he'd added his bag and bedroll, tied behind. Mrs. Perdicaris had twitched a bit, but when Kimble made no attempt to climb aboard, she would still thrust her head at his hands and pockets, and if not tied, she would follow him around, even once having to be shoved back out of Tomás' store when Kimble was buying oats for her.

Now, whenever she came up to him, he put his weight on the pad, leaning into it. She just twitched her ears and leaned back. She was with him when he spotted the caravan. They were still at least ten miles out. Kimble patted the side of Mrs. P's neck.

"Well, let's go."

Kimble figured they could wander slowly down to the tanques and find an unobtrusive spot by the store from which to watch the arriving group. He turned away from the ridge's cliff edge and saw Mrs. P's ears stand up and swivel back up the ridge, not toward the tanques.

After a moment, Kimble heard hoofbeats, horses at a walk, more than one.

What the hell are they doing up there?

Tomás had told him the ridge kept rising for about three miles then dropped off precipitously, a good four hundred feet above the surrounding countryside. There was a good view, but you couldn't get down, at least not on horseback.

He took a few steps over toward a hollow between three piñons and Mrs. P followed. Three horsemen trotted down the wide trail near the middle of the ridge, not the rocky back-and-forth trail at the cliff's edge. A loaded packhorse on a long lead followed.

Kimble heard Mrs. P draw a deep breath and her lips went back to bray. He stabbed his hand into his front pocket and found a few oats and held them out. The bray died, stillborn, as she lipped the oats from his hand. In the time it took her to verify his hand was completely empty and to nudge his pockets, the three horsemen had moved on.

"Huh." So his pool of potential distributors had just gone up. He walked over to the trail. The path was sand and rock, mostly, but where the piñon mulch had accumulated there were some decent prints. The horses were shod, epoxied composites probably, but the packhorse was wearing trail boots.

If they'd been camped up at the high end of the ridge, they could've seen the caravan even sooner than Kimble had. *What have they been doing for water?*

The spring several hundred yards above the tanques was in a rocky outcropping, hard to get to on horseback, but fifty yards up the ridge, Kimble found several days worth of horse droppings and several circular imprints where a bucket had rested. The hoofprints matched, including the booted feet of the packhorse.

He looked around. The clearing where the horses had been watered was sandy, with patches of piñon mast and, unlike other parts of the ridge, the spiky cholla and prickly pear was absent. He put his arm over Mrs. Perdicaris' back and pulled himself up.

If he was going to be thrown, this was as good a place as any.

Mrs. P whiffed and took several steps sideways, then stopped still. Kimble leaned forward, careful to keep his head off to one side. He'd once been whacked in the face by the tossed head of a fractious horse—only once. He draped himself across her withers and stretched out his hand to where he could rub her poll. He felt some of the tension drop out of Mrs. P's back as he rubbed the muscles.

After a few moments, he sat back up and rested his hands on his thighs. He leaned back, about to swing his right leg over her withers and slide off her left side but, before he raised his leg, Mrs. P began backing up. He stopped leaning and she stopped. Kimble blinked. "Mrs. P! Are you kidding me?"

He squeezed in with his right knee and she turned calmly to her left. "You were trained!" He leaned forward and Mrs. P walked forward. She wasn't even wearing a hackamore, much less a bit and bridle, but on leg aids alone, he steered her down the ridge and up to the cluster of mixed piñons and maples above the tanques.

HE beat the caravan in, but the three saddle horses and the packhorses were watering at the trough when he came in.

At the store he asked Tomás, "Who are they?"

Tomás shrugged. "Those are the Jonas brothers. Lee, Bob, and Terry. Been through before. They live up on the Jemez. Near the springs. Terry has the worst teeth I've ever seen."

Kimble had a hard time keeping his face still. He asked for another bag of oats.

"You'll spoil that mule."

"You thought Heimie treated her bad and you think

I'm babying her. Make up your mind!" As if it were an afterthought he said, "By the way, I was up on the ridge. Caravan is coming in."

Tomás swore. "Figures. You want these oats for free, and some cash as well?"

"What do I have to do?"

"Get on the pump when the caravan gets in and keep the water coming. After, help muck out. There'll be thirty to forty horses tonight and twice that tomorrow."

"That's a lot of horse apples. How much cash?"

"Well, since you're so nice to that mule, I'll be generous."

HE took his pictures of the Jonas brothers before the caravan came in, using the binoculars from fifty yards, up by his bedroll. He used Mrs. Perdicaris as a shield, peering over her neck. He took three full-face exposures of each of them, convinced he'd found his distributors.

It was the teeth. They all had bad teeth, stained, with discolored gums, but the thinnest and youngest, Terry, had clear gaps where the enamel was rotted away. Bad teeth weren't uncommon in the territory, where you had to travel outside for dental work or deal with manual work done with ceramic tools in broad daylight by traveling clinicians, but this looked to Kimble like a classic case of meth mouth.

Meth users aren't too good about brushing, but they also get dry mouth from the drug and tend to grind their teeth during the first rush, cracking the enamel. Kimble had seen several when he lived in the capital. Terry's thinness was another mark against him. Meth is a serious appetite suppressant.

Yes, his money was on the brothers.

The trough was eight feet long and, with crowding, could water five or six animals at once. Kimble pumped it full as soon as the brothers led their animals away. He could hear the caravan by the time he finished. He took the plastic manure fork and policed the yard, throwing the few piles into Tomás' fiberglass wheelbarrow. He kept his head down but he was watching just the same.

The freighters, on seeing the size of the incoming caravan, grabbed their teams and watered them briefly. By the time the tail end of the caravan was in, they'd hitched up their wagons and packed their camps. Kimble raised his eyebrows at one of them, who shrugged and said, "Too crowded. We'll make some trail while it's still light." They pulled out without attempting to talk to the newly arrived passengers, who were walking stiffly around the yard.

The peddlers reacted as they had with the westbound caravan, opening their wagon cupboards and displaying their wares. They were smiling, talking to the passengers.

But they weren't talking, as far as Kimble could tell, to the outside contact. He'd spotted the man before he'd dismounted, though the large cowboy hat and sunglasses had thrown him for a moment. Bentham's picture showed the man bareheaded, wearing a suit. But it was him, one Charles "Chuck" Hohner, though Bentham had said he could easily be traveling under a different name.

Hohner had limped to the nearest shade, off to the

side of Tomás' store, and taken off his hat. He was looking around the yard casually, wiping his forehead with
a bandanna.

Lee, the eldest Jonas brother, walked over to the store,
swinging wide to pass a couple of yards away from
Hohner. He didn't turn his head but, as he went by, he
said something. Kimble saw Hohner's eyes flick toward
the man and then back away.

Kimble pumped more water as the caravan guides
brought up the next set of horses. As he finished, he saw
Hohner put his hat back on and wander into the store.
Kimble grabbed the rake, scooped up a fresh pile of horse
manure, and crossed the yard to the barrow parked at
the corner of the store.

He dumped his forkload into the barrow and paused
by the side window. Through the nylon screen he saw
Tomás step back into his stockroom for something. Lee
Jonas said something then, and Hohner shook his head
and said, out of the side of his mouth, "No! After dark."
Then he turned abruptly and left the store.

Kimble was satisfied. He would've ridden away then
and there if he hadn't promised to help Tomás.

He filled and emptied three wheelbarrow loads, running down the road to the manure pile, and helped the
guides with their horses. The passengers weren't expected
to curry or feed their mounts. The guides and grooms
did that but, from what he overheard, they were shorthanded because there were more passengers than usual.

"Hey, kid. Wanna make some money?"

Kimble fed and curried fifteen horses before dark.

Mrs. Perdicaris protested and threatened the tired horses, but when Kimble tied her within sight, but out of kicking distance, *and* spilled a bait of oats on the ground, she stopped being a pest.

Just upwind from the picket line of horses, in the camping space recently vacated by the freighters, a large passenger with Polynesian features set up a tent for Hohner, then began cooking a meal for them both.

Huh, guess he travels with a servant.

Two horses later, one of the guides walked past quietly. The Polynesian turned suddenly when the guide scuffed his foot and stepped between the guide and Hohner. His hand dropped into a large cargo pocket on the right leg of his pants. When he saw it was the guide he turned the movement into a stretch, then bent back down to his cooking.

Guess Hohner travels with a bodyguard.

Kimble was kneeling, cleaning out the hoofs of a bay mare, when he saw one of the peddlers approach Hohner holding a burlap bag in one hand. The man held up two apples in his other hand. "Apples? Best in the territory?"

"No, thanks," said Hohner.

Then the peddler lowered his voice and said something else. Hohner shook his hand side to side, below his waist. "No. After dark!"

Oh, crap. I'm going to have to take more pictures.

WHEN Bentham rode into the tanques two days later, Kimble was asleep on his bedroll. The sound of hoofbeats, braying, and swearing brought him awake.

"Oh, sorry." He called Mrs. Perdicaris off, distracting her with an apple before tying her to a tree. Except for the two of them and Tomás, the tanques were once again deserted. The westbound caravan, which had left three hours before, had also been shorthanded. Between mucking out, pumping in, and rubbing down, he was exhausted. On the other hand, he'd replaced most of the contingency cash he'd used to buy Mrs. P.

Kimble gave Captain Bentham the binoculars.

"If I haven't screwed up, the pictures that matter are the first fifteen. Three exposures each of Lee, Bob, and Terry Jonas of Jemez Springs. Three exposures of Perry Brochert, a peddler based out of Los Crucitos. And three exposures of Mateo Encino, another peddler based out of the Raton checkpoint."

"All of them matter?"

"Yeah, but it was three separate contacts. The Jonas brothers and those two peddlers. He waved off all three attempts to contact him in the afternoon. The meetings were held after dark. I'd say they're setting up three different distributors with different territories."

"You're sure?"

"Well, I didn't get close enough to eavesdrop, but I'm pretty sure."

"You followed orders?"

Kimble was hurt. "Don't sound so surprised. Jeeze."

"What's with the mule?"

"That's Mrs. Perdicaris. She . . . uh . . . well, she's with me. Oh, there's three shots of her in the camera, too. Can I get prints?"

PART III

"*But cannot the Government protect?*"

"*We of the Game are beyond protection. If we die, we die. Our names are blotted from the book. That is all.*"

—RUDYARD KIPLING, *Kim,* Chapter 11

Half-healed scars

Kimble's first thought when he heard the feet pounding down the path from the compound was *They're coming for me!* But then his breathing calmed and the sudden thud, thud of his heartbeat subsided as he remembered that *they* wouldn't be coming for anybody, not for a long time.

His second thought was *It's too damn hot to be running.* He'd picked this time of day to pull weeds in the bean patch because it meant the sun was low enough that the cottonwoods growing by the Rio Puerco shaded the field. But it was still too hot to be running.

He straightened as "young" Martha, one of the *uchideshi*, reached the field.

"Who's dead?" he asked.

Martha stopped in the shade and bent over,

hands on her knees. "No one, *Sempai*," she gasped. She was a redhead and her face was flushed from the run in the heat. "But Tommy wishes he was. Mrs. Perdicaris kicked him over the paddock fence."

Kimble pinched the bridge of his nose and squeezed his eyes shut.

"And *what* was Tommy doing in Mrs. Perdicaris' paddock? No. Never mind. I don't want to know." He pulled off the leather gloves he wore. Most of the weeds were purple nightshade or tumbleweed and both had pointy bits. He picked up his plastic water flask. "How bad is it?"

"Sensei thinks it's a greenstick break of the right radius. And he's got the most amazing bruises on the back of his thighs. I didn't see him get kicked but I did see him land."

He took a sip and handed the flask to Martha. "Did he roll?" Tommy was also an *uchideshi*. His ability to take a fall was normally pretty good.

"Tried." She smiled as she accepted the flask, then took a gulp of the water. "Came down on the edge of the cistern."

He winced. "How mad is Sensei?"

"She's furious! She said if Tommy had broken the cistern . . . well, you know."

"Now, Martha, it's not as if I didn't tell *everyone* several times to keep out of the paddock—"

"Oh, Sensei's not mad at *you*. She's mad at Tommy."

"Ah." He frowned. "Does Sensei need my help to set the arm, or something?"

"Oh, no. It's that man from the Territorial Rangers.

The one with the great nose and the bushy eyebrows? He rode in during the flailin' and the wailin'."

Kimble felt his face tighten. Martha licked her lips and took a sudden step back. "Uh, he talked to Sensei for a half hour on the veranda and"—Martha looked around reflexively—"and she *shouted* at him. And ten minutes later, she sent me down to get you."

Kimble shook his head, as if to throw water off, trying to return his face to neutral. "Why'd you step back, just then?"

Martha opened her mouth and shut it. "It was like you were going to hit me, *Sempai*. Never saw you like that, even on the mat—even when you *were* trying to hit me."

"Sorry." He felt funny with her calling him *sempai*. She was a year older than he was, but he'd been training with Sensei for years and Martha had come to be an *uchideshi*, an inside student, only five months before, in late spring, while Kimble was gone. When he came back, two months ago, she'd helped with the nursing, during those first two weeks in bed.

Kimble took a deep breath. "Better run back and be handy for Sensei. I'll be along directly."

HE could've run back easily enough. He'd been back on the mat for a full month and the wounds were scarring up nicely, but he wasn't going to run for Major Bentham.

He stopped at the paddock. Mrs. Perdicaris walked up and stuck her head over the top rail. When he was close enough, she shoved at him with her nose, not feeling a bit of shame at kicking Tommy.

"Mrs. Perdicaris, you are a lot of trouble."

He found a lump of sugar in his pocket and let her lip it off his palm, then went between the rough wooden rails of the paddock and ran his fingers down each of her legs, looking for signs of strain. "That Tommy is pretty hefty, girl. You oughta think twice before kicking him. You could hurt yourself."

She brayed lightly and nuzzled at his waist. He turned the pocket out, showing her it was empty, so Mrs. Perdicaris contented herself with letting him rub her poll while she shed copious amounts of mule hair across his shirt.

After a moment he sighed and climbed back through the rails, but didn't go to Sensei's cottage yet. Instead, he ducked into the men's dormitory behind the dojo, washed his face and hands, and put on a clean shirt.

He found Sensei and the major sitting across from each other on the stone benches under the twisted grape vines that wrapped the ramada on the north side of the cottage. They both turned their heads as he came through the gate in the coyote fence. Sensei kept her seat while Major Bentham stood. He held out his hand, but Kimble bowed to Sensei before taking it.

"Good to see you, Kimble," Bentham said.

It's not mutual, he thought. "Major." He turned back to Sensei. "How's Tommy?"

"Brain damaged!" Sensei snorted. "But that wasn't the result of his accident—it was the cause! His backside is really hurtin' right now, but by tomorrow it's going to be far worse. He'll live."

Kimble exhaled sharply. "Not if I get ahold of him. Why was he in there?"

"Hormones."

He opened his mouth and Sensei shook her head slightly, then tilted it toward the open kitchen window. Someone was rattling about the kitchen.

Later, then. "May I get you tea, Sensei?"

She gestured to the bench beside her. "Sit. Martha's on it."

He dropped down onto the bench. He thought it was deliberate, her gesture. Normally he would've sat *seiza*, on his knees, a respectful distance away, but this put them both facing Bentham, a united front.

"I was just reminding Jeremy that the last time I lent you to him, you came back broken. And I didn't even have a damage deposit." Her voice was light but she wasn't smiling.

Kimble almost lifted a hand to his right shoulder, where the whip had bitten deepest, but managed to keep both hands in his lap. *And unclenched.* He thought that was something.

Major Bentham sighed. "Now who's objectifying people? And was it really my fault? I seem to remember giving some pretty specific instructions."

"Too bad you didn't share those instructions with all involved," Kimble said. He was surprised at how mild his own voice sounded.

Bentham's voice was not so mild. "And if they had killed you, what would've happened to the rest of those girls?"

Now Kimble's voice did rise. "You want someone who follows orders like a robot, send a robot." He looked up at the grape leaves and nearly added *Oh, yeah, you can't.*

Sensei put her hand on Kimble's knee and he subsided. "So, if Kim did such a bad job, why are you back here, Jeremy?"

"*I* didn't say he did a bad job. I said he didn't follow instructions and, as a result, he got hurt."

Kimble looked down at the fieldstone pavers set in sand under his feet. There was justice in Bentham's position. He had mulled it over for weeks but his conclusion remained the same. Despite the bad dreams, he wouldn't have acted any differently.

"I need—" Bentham shut his mouth abruptly as Martha backed through the nylon-screen door with the tea tray. She set it on the end of Bentham's bench and he shifted to the other end to make more room. Martha knelt on the pavers to pour three cups.

As soon as she was done, Ruth said, "Thanks, Martha. Leave the tray. Unsaddle the major's horse and put him in the spare stall, then sweep and mop the guest *casita* and make the bed."

Martha started to open her mouth but Ruth just stared steadily at her. The girl bobbed her head and left.

Once she was well outside the fence, Kimble said, "I think she was going to point out that we just cleaned the *casita.*"

"Well, yes," Ruth said, "but did you notice how quietly she made the tea?"

"Yes." He'd thought she'd been listening, too.

"She's already too interested. Poor Tommy."

"Tommy?" It hit him. "He was showing off? Trying to impress Martha?"

"Well, duh. He's been trying to get her attention since spring without success. Then you came back on a stretcher and she only has eyes for you. He took it personally."

Kimble felt himself blushing. "I've been very careful not to encourage her. Tommy's not a bad guy. He's just—well."

"Stupid?" Ruth suggested. She was like that. She had probably said the same thing directly to Tommy many times.

"He needs to learn things the hard way."

"The learning part remains to be proven."

Major Bentham cleared his throat. "This is just fascinating. Really."

Ruth sipped her tea without comment.

"Does our deal still stand?" Bentham asked.

Ruth looked sideways at Kimble. Bentham wasn't the only person Ruth had shouted at in recent days. She knew his answer before he gave it.

"Yes," he said. "For another year, as agreed." *Unless you get me killed before then.*

Bentham let out a breath that Kimble hadn't realized he'd been holding. "Okay. I need to find out what's going on in the Pecos River basin south of Ft. Sumner."

"Really?" Kimble said. "But you have a post there. A full platoon at the barracks in Pecosito."

"Yes. In uniforms and everything. They've been asking

questions but they're not getting anywhere. I sent in Lujan, undercover, but they smoked him pretty quick. He had to be taken outside for surgery."

Kimble had worked with Lujan several times, mostly in the Valle Grande west of where Los Alamos used to be. "He gonna be all right?"

"I don't know yet. He took a gyro in the spleen."

"Your own troops shot him?"

Bentham shook his head. "No. All ammo and weapons accounted for, thank you very much."

"Shit."

The only military firearms in the territory were rocket rifles—smoothbore composite tubes that used chemical strikers to fire off self-stabilizing ceramic rockets. They were high-tech precision instruments of destruction and had to be made outside the steel curtain with full-metal tech. They were brought in by the feds and only for the Territorial Rangers.

It was the best part of a bad situation. Wasn't like there weren't other guns. Plastic rifles with disposable preloaded cardboard barrels. For small game, elastic slingshots were popular. For deer and elk there were bows and crossbows made in territory of horn and wood laminates or, on the other side of the steel curtain, fiber composites. You just had to give up on metal.

Traditionalists liked obsidian and flint arrowheads. Scavengers liked glass. Or you could buy fluted ceramic heads made beyond the curtain.

But nobody but the feds was supposed to have the multi-shot gyro rifles.

"Is that why he was there in the first place? Were there other shootings?"

Bentham nodded slightly, just the barest movement of his chin.

"Gun runners," Kimble finally said. "Isn't that supposed to be impossible?"

The major's nod was more definite this time.

CLASS was traditionally held when the sun touched the western horizon. This time of year that meant the northern flank of Mt. Taylor, forty miles off, at about eight o'clock. The idea behind the timing was to get things cool enough but still have natural light in the dojo till the end of class.

There were fifteen students who lived in the village and there were an equal number from other farms along the Rio Puerco. Besides aikido, Ruth taught *jyo*, the short staff, a very practical weapon for the territory—good for herding, driving off feral dogs, and walking up steep hills.

She used Kimble as *uke* as she demonstrated, throwing him or pinning him as required. The dojo floor was ultra-traditional woven tatami, but the reeds came from the Rio Puerco and were not as soft as one might like, especially when he rolled across his right shoulder. He didn't let the pain touch his face and tried to keep up.

He sometimes thought that if he'd made more noise, they wouldn't have gone on as long. Instead, he'd passed out under the whip, without screaming or yelling once.

The students all knew he was leaving again—though

they didn't know what he did during his occasional absences—so there was a lot of scrambling, especially among the higher ranks, to work with him. He groaned inwardly. The problem with being the senior student was that everyone wanted to test themselves against you. He ended the class out of breath and soaked in sweat, and with an extra bruise on his back where he'd tried to protect one of the recent wounds and had banged over hard instead of rolling smoothly.

He left the shower room, still wet, a towel wrapped around his waist, his folded *hakama* under one arm and his sweaty *gi* held at arm's length. Martha was outside, wearing a cotton kimono and carrying an oil lamp, but she didn't have a towel so he knew she wasn't waiting for the shower.

"Sensei want something?"

She shook her head and said quietly, "I've warmed the massage oil."

He blinked. He could hear Tommy groaning in the men's wing of the dormitory and a pack of coyotes was serenading the moon up on the ridge.

He lowered his voice even lower than hers had been. "And what would Sensei say?"

There were rules, especially for instructors, which he was. It wasn't impossible, but you had to talk it over with Sensei and sometimes it meant one of the parties had to stop training at the dojo if they wanted the relationship. It was meant to avoid abuses of power.

"I talked to her," Martha said. "I'm back to school in the fall." Martha's parents lived in New Madrid, east of the Sandias, but Martha went to UC Berkeley, outside. She'd started aikido there with one of Ruth's old instructors during her freshman year. "And you're going away tomorrow and won't be back before I leave. Sensei says it's up to you."

"Oh." He'd had romances away from the dojo. His missions for Bentham had given him opportunities. Once, he'd used one of those opportunities to further a mission, and the bad taste of *that* experience still lingered. "Was she just talking about the massage?"

"Well . . ." It was hard to tell in the lamplight but he thought Martha was blushing. "She asked if I had condoms."

MARTHA took her time, working from the balls of his feet to the very ends of his jaw muscles, where they anchored to the skull above his ears. She was afraid that she'd hurt the newly scarred wounds, though it was not the first time she'd seen them.

"The oil and your hands are really helping," he assured her.

"Sensei told me not to ask when you first came back. But it had to be a whip, a bullwhip, right?" Her hands could tell, when he reacted—not to her touch, but to the memory. "Sorry. Shhhh. Relax. I'm sorry."

He breathed deep and let her hands persuade his muscles to unclench. "It's all right. Hard to avoid developing a conditioned response to something like that."

"What do you do for that man, the Territorial Ranger?"

"This is the part that Sensei was talking about."

"Oh—the don't ask part?"

"I'm short. And without the beard I look younger than I am. But even when I *was* younger I did undercover work for the major. I still do. You need to not talk about it, all right?"

"What do you get out of it?"

"The Rangers have a scholarship at their disposal, outside. A choice of Stanford or M.I.T or Cal Tech or Rice."

"Oh. I guess that's worth it. If not for Grandfather, I wouldn't be attending Berkeley."

She unwrapped the obi and let her kimono slither to the floor. Later, after the touching became mutual, then urgent, then leisurely again, he told her about it.

"The People of the Book were a nasty fundamentalist sect down toward White Sands. There were reports of civil-rights abuses, big time, but no one would testify. I came in as a book peddler's assistant, which was a *big* mistake. They were happy to buy Bibles and they allowed the Farmer's Almanac, though they were iffy about it, but I gave a book on reproductive health to a newly married girl. And I *mean* girl.

"They had this nasty thing going where the elders were each other's in-laws. As in fathers-in-law and sons-in-law. They'd keep their wives pregnant until they died in childbirth, then marry one of their fellow elder's children—thirteen- or fourteen-year-old girls—and start the whole thing over.

"When they found the book in Sarah's possession they put her in the public stocks and whipped her until she miscarried. The Bible is supposed to do for everything, you see. We got her out and away, but they came after us hard and I decoyed them out into the gypsum sands while my partner got her into Gordo."

Kimble pushed his face into the crook of Martha's neck and inhaled deep. "They caught me. I hurt some of them but they took me back and put me in the stocks."

"And they whipped you."

"Well, they wanted to know where I'd hid her. Beware the anger of 'righteous' men. It was . . ." He broke off and licked his lips. "Anyway, they left me there, no water, no food, no shade."

"Did your partner send the Rangers?"

"Oh, yeah. But it took a while. Three days. It was overcast and he didn't have enough sunlight to signal the heliograph station. Once he did reach them, they dropped a Rapid Response Team followed up by mounted Rangers two days later."

It was Martha's turn to tense up, but he slid his hand down her back and hip. "Wonder you didn't die!"

He nodded into her neck. "True. Would've, but there was this kid. He'd sneak out in the middle of the night and bring me water. Never really saw his face. But he kept me alive long enough. I wasn't in any condition, after, to find him. Hope he's all right."

"Did they arrest them?"

"The Elders? Oh, yes. Statutory rape. Child abuse and criminal sexual penetration. Marriage laws in the territory are the same as the old Arizona/New Mexico statutes. Fifteen with a court order. Sixteen or seventeen with parental consent. Eighteen or older fine. Thirteen and fourteen—child abuse. There was also manslaughter. There'd been other deaths due to 'punishment,' and once the Elders were in custody, people were willing to testify.

"I'm told they put a social works station in there and they have a permanently detached squad of Rangers. But the thing that will really turn things around is a new library and mandatory reading competency."

"Didn't they have local law?"

"That would be Elder Povoni, county sheriff. Now a guest of a federal penitentiary in Colorado."

"Oh."

He turned the topic back to her. He was skin to skin with a beautiful girl and there were better things to talk about or not talk about. He already knew she was studying cultural anthropology. "What are your plans for after you graduate?"

"Territorial Studies—the palilithic zone."

The Territory—New Mexico, Arizona, southern Nevada and Utah and northern Chihuahua and Sonora. The place where the metal eaters live.

"Palilithic? Is that what they're calling it now? If Neolithic is new stone, what is *pali*?"

"Anew. Afresh. Again."

"Stoned again."

She giggled and this led to other things.

HE rose in the dark, while it was coolest.

By the time he'd hitched Mrs. Perdicaris to the cart,

filled his water barrels, and got his traveling gear loaded, the sky was half light and Mt. Taylor stood out against the western horizon like some sleeping giant's shoulder, shrugged up out of the covers.

He'd left Martha deep asleep, but there was a lamp in Ruth's kitchen. When he pulled the cart through the gate in the coyote fence, she came out and handed him something hot wrapped in a dishcloth. "For the road."

"Yes, Sensei. Thanks."

"Martha come to you last night?"

He felt his face go red. "She said she talked to you."

"She did. Just wanted to know what I would be dealing with, today. I like her. She's very straightforward—honest with herself. If she'd been disappointed, well—I would probably work her pretty hard to take her mind off things."

"She may still have been disappointed, Sensei."

"How much sleep did you get?"

"Damn little."

She snorted. "Well, then."

"Yes, Sensei."

Ruth pointed two fingers at her eyes. He nodded and she turned and walked away.

Mrs. Perdicaris headed out at a trot.

By late morning they'd gone fifteen miles and he was looking for a place to sleep through the heat of the day. They were on the river road, following the Rio Puerco down to where it flowed into the Rio Grande, so it wasn't as if he didn't have water, but he was still crossing the Jornada del Muerto. Better to sit out the heat.

Besides, he'd meant it when he said he didn't get much sleep the night before and he was barely keeping his eyes open, despite Sensei's gesture. That's what it meant. Keep aware. Keep alert.

When a few rocks and dirt clods rolled out of the brush on the low hillside and onto the road ahead, he dropped the reins on the seat beside him and rolled sideways off of the cart. Mrs. Perdicaris walked on and as the cart passed him he snaked his *jyo* out of the back, then climbed up the hill using a series of deep-set boulders, quiet as he could. It wasn't completely noise-free but the rumble of the cartwheels and the clop-clop of the mule's hooves were louder.

The crest of the hill was fringed with cedar, more bushes than trees, and some green tumbleweed, grown waist high in the summer thunderstorms. He reached the top just in time to see a man step out into the open with a fiberglass crossbow and yell, "Hold it right there!"

The man was looking down at the cart. Mrs. Perdicaris, at his shout, tossed her head, snorted, and walked on.

Kimble took a long stride forward and swung the *jyo* up, striking the crossbow string from below. It popped out of the catch and the quarrel fired over the road, a good twenty feet above Mrs. Perdicaris.

The man turned, eyes wide, and jerked the crossbow up like he intended to swing it at Kimble, but Kimble had stepped back after discharging the shot, holding the *jyo* low at his side.

The man was big, maybe six and a half feet tall, and muscled like a body builder—not like someone who worked on a farm, but like someone who spent a lot of time in a gym. He was the prettiest man Kimble had ever seen, like a movie star.

"That's not very friendly," Kimble commented.

The surprise wore off and the man calmed as he took in Kimble's height and size. Kimble was over a foot shorter and a good hundred pounds lighter. "Huh. Just a kid. Sorry about this, but my need is great." He dropped the crossbow onto a tumbleweed and lunged forward, raising his fist.

Kimble took another step back and brought the *jyo* around. It smacked into the man's ankle just before his foot touched the ground and the man went down hard. He tried to catch himself with his arms but it didn't keep him from pitching head over heels down the rocky hillside.

It was clear to Kimble that the man didn't know how to fall.

Kimble gave a sharp whistle and Mrs. Perdicaris stopped, maybe fifty feet down the road, but his attention was on Mr. Big and Tall.

The man wasn't moving.

Kimble picked up a rock and threw it hard, smashing it into the road a couple of feet from the man's head. Gravel and sand scattered but the man didn't move a bit.

Great.

He found where the man had been waiting, apparently for a while. There were six small apple cores eaten down to seeds and stems next to a burlap sack that contained a t-shirt, a couple of wrinkled apples, and half a roll of toilet paper. Beside the bag were a torn and frayed wool blanket and two more ceramic-headed crossbow quarrels.

The breeze shifted and Kimble smelled shit. Down the other side of the hill he found where the man had been going. He hadn't even bothered to kick dirt over his feces. The flies were buzzing all around and it was clear he'd had the squirts.

Someone has been drinking untreated water.

Kimble covered the feces with dirt, gathered up the man's meager belongings, and went on down the hill.

He was breathing, at least. Kimble ground his knuckle across the man's sternum, a trick he'd learned from a Ranger paramedic, but Mr. Big and Tall didn't flinch a bit. Well and truly unresponsive.

There was a goose egg of a lump over his right ear and a bit of blood had seeped through the hair. Kimble thumbed his eyelids back one at a time. The pupils looked normal and they responded to the bright sky, but Kimble didn't like his color. He was pasty under his tan. He hadn't looked like that before he'd fallen.

He'd hit any number of rocks on his way down the hill and Kimble was concerned for his spine. He fetched Mrs. P and the cart back and took off the cart seat, a padded board that covered the tool compartment at the front of the cart box. After he eased it under the man, he duct-taped him to it, a strip across his forehead and some generous strips across his chest to immobilize his head and neck.

Kimble unhitched Mrs. P and tilted the cart shafts

up, bringing the back of the box down to the road. Of course everything slid down, but Kimble moved most of his stuff to one side and eased the man in over the tailgate, then tilted the cart back up and rehitched Mrs. P. The man's legs were hanging over the back, but Kimble didn't bother to adjust him—he just wanted to get them out of the sun.

He walked Mrs. P another hundred yards along the road, to where it sank back down to the level of the river, then turned into the bosque and the shade of some Russian olive trees. Kimble unhitched Mrs. P and took off her harness, too. She walked off toward the river for a drink, then had herself a nice roll in the sand.

Kimble soaked a cloth with water and put it on the lump on Mr. Big-n-Heavy's head. He had a chemical ice pack in the first aid kit but he didn't feel the man deserved it. The cloth cooled down pretty good, though—evaporation in the dry air.

The man was wearing outside stuff, manufactured clothing from overseas, but the jeans had been retroed for the territory. The metal rivets at the corners of the pocket had been pulled out and oversewn to replace the reinforcement, and the zipper and slide had been replaced with Velcro and the metal snaps with plastic. His shirt was one of those long-sleeved sunscreen affairs, with the collar that rolled up high over the neck and vents for cooling, and he wore hiking boots with Velcro closures.

But his pockets were empty, no ID, no money—neither cash nor territorial script.

He also stank. He reminded Kimble of himself after three days in the stocks. Well, maybe not quite as bad— the man had been able to take his pants down when he needed to go.

Kimble tried to get a little water into him but it either ran out the side of his mouth or he inhaled it, so he left well enough alone.

There'd clearly been a thunderstorm upriver; the Puerco was up from its usual trickle to a steady flow. Kimble took a quick dip, rinsed out his pants and shirt and spread his bedroll for a nap.

He awoke to great swearing.

The man had gotten up but the way he was taped to the seat board, he was staggering around like Frankenstein's monster, his upper body stiff.

"Whoa there, fella," Kimble said. "Settle down—you'll do yourself an injury!"

The man swiveled around at the waist to look at Kimble. He was patting at the duct tape running across his shirt. "Who the hell are you?"

Trauma-induced amnesia? Then Kimble realized he was only wearing his boxers and probably looked a bit different. "We met on the hillside," he said. "You had a crossbow, I had a stick? You fell down the hill?"

"Oh." Then, "Oh, shit!" He dropped to his knees and threw up.

"Okay, then," Kimble said. He let the man get on with his retching and fetched the water bottle. Then, on reflection, added a cup. (He wasn't going to let the man drink out of the same bottle—Kimble didn't have any idea what germs he was carrying.)

The man was on all fours and weaving a little. Kimble held the cup to the man's lips and let him rinse out his mouth, then took hold of the board and eased him back against the trunk of one of the Russian olive trees. He put a bit more water in the bottom of the cup and the man swallowed it abruptly. "More?" the man asked.

"Sure, just slowly, okay? Unless you want to vomit it up again."

This time Kimble gave him a full cup, watched for a second to make sure he was just sipping, then went and found a patch of goat-heads and picked one of the bigger spiky seed heads. The man had finished the water by the time Kimble got back and, while he was still pale, he didn't look as green as he had a minute before.

"Want that board off?"

The man tried to nod, but of course that didn't work. "Yeah."

"I'm going to look for nerve damage, all right?"

"Look? What do you mean? How can you look for nerve damage?"

Kimble poked him in the back of the hand with the goat-head.

"Ow!"

"Good." Kimble moved the sticker toward his other hand and the man jerked it back. "Well, you have motor control." He jabbed him in the thigh.

"Stop that!"

The man tried to get up again but the board caught on a low branch and shoved him down again. Kimble used the interval to try his other leg. "Ow! Nerve damage, my ass. You're just trying to get even!"

Kimble grinned broadly. "Any numbness?" he asked. "In your toes? In your fingers?"

"No! Get that thing away from me!"

Kimble went back to the wagon and got his knife block, a core of glassy Jemez obsidian, and his knocker, an oblong fist-sized chunk of river-smoothed granite. He knelt down and chipped off an obsidian flake about two inches in diameter, a quarter-inch thick at one edge and tapering to razor sharp nothingness on the other edge.

"Hold still, I mean it." The whites of the man's eyes showed as he tried to track the blade as Kimble moved it close to the man's ear. Kimble cut the tape off on both sides of the man's head and then on both sides of his chest, but he let him peel it off his face and shirt.

"Ow!"

As soon as the man had sat up and moved away from Kimble, Kimble took the seat board and stripped off the remnants of tape, then put it back in place on the cart. Kimble's clothes were not quite dry, but he put them on anyway. The damp cloth felt good in the heat.

Kimble let the man drink more water. While he was doing that he commented, "You're not a very good highwayman, Mr. Big and Tall."

"Don't call me that. Name's Pierce." He put his hand to his head and glared at Kimble. "I'm not a highwayman, either."

"Well, you had me fooled, Mr. Pierce. Pointing a cross-bow at someone could get you dead around here."

"I was robbed," he said. "Twice. Had my horse stolen. Then someone else took all my food and luggage while I was, uh, away from my campsite."

"Away? What does that mean, away?"

He blushed. "There was this farm girl . . ."

"Let me guess. She wanted a place more private, more secluded. When you got back, your stuff was gone."

Pierce scowled and looked away.

"And there was a lot of kissing but you didn't get to first base."

"Someone called her name and she said it was her husband. She put her top back on and ran for it."

"Second base, then." Kimble tried not to laugh. "It probably *was* her husband. Or her boyfriend. And he had your stuff before he yelled for her."

Kimble whistled and Mrs. Perdicaris came trotting in from the riverbank where she'd been cropping green grass. He grabbed the burlap bag with Pierce's stuff out of the back of the cart and dropped the crossbow on it. The three quarrels he held in his fist. "I'll drop these beside the road after a bit. Don't want to tempt you." He set the quarrels on the cart seat. "Here." He set a two-liter plastic bottle of water on the burlap sack. "This is good well water. You wanna keep away from the river water unless you boil it."

He pulled the cart back around and went over to the tree where he'd hung Mrs. P's harness. He was keeping his eye on Pierce because he didn't want him going for the quarrels. He didn't think Pierce would be stupid enough to go for Mrs. P.

He was wrong.

She wasn't even looking at him but Kimble could see her ears were tracking Pierce and when Pierce stood and took a step toward her, the ears went back. Kimble opened his mouth to warn him, but Pierce took two quick steps forward and leapt, trying to get up on her back. Mrs. P bucked, a twisting sideways thing that slammed her hindquarters into him in mid-leap, like a rugby check. Pierce flew back at least eight feet before his feet touched and he fell backward, tumbling over and over.

It would not have met the standards for a back roll at the dojo. For one thing, he didn't end up back on his feet. And he was all corners, not smooth like a ball. Corners bang into the ground. Elbows, shoulders, hips, knees, head.

He groaned much too loudly to be dead, so Kimble didn't check on him until Mrs. P was harnessed and they were pulling out of the grove. Kimble looked down at him from the seat of the cart. Pierce had gone from lying to sitting and he was holding on to his elbow like it really hurt. He tried to glare up at Kimble but he was having trouble meeting Kimble's eyes.

"Try washing yourself and your clothes in the river—get rid of some of the stink. Don't drink the river water unless you boil it. And the *next* person who comes along, you might just consider asking for help. Tell them you've been robbed. You might be surprised." Kimble waited a beat and felt his eyes narrow. "But if you try this takin' shit with some of the people who ride this road, you're gonna be dead. Or worse."

"Go fuck yourself," Pierce said.

Kimble thought about the previous night and smiled again. "Have a nice day, Mr. Pierce." He clucked his tongue and Mrs. P headed out at a trot.

Bugs in the Arroyo

Kimble crossed the Rio Grande north where the Puerco joined it, upstream from an old county road bridge. It was concrete rubble, of course, all the steel eaten out of it by the bugs, but the debris formed a dam that spread the river wide and shallow. The water reached Mrs. Perdicaris' stomach but didn't quite make it to the bottom of the cart.

Safely on the other side, Kimble topped off Mrs. P's water barrels and spent the afternoon in cool, moist industry up to his waist in the river cutting *tule*—cattail—bulrush, and common reed until the cart was stacked high with tightly bound bundles. He also collected a pound of male cattail pollen for pancakes as well as a salad's worth of young shoots.

He spent the evening boiling river water to top off his supply of drinking water. He was headed east, over the hump of the south end of the Manzanos. There were some streams and seasonal water but you couldn't count on any of it and they would be crossing the alkali flats.

This close to the river, the mosquitoes were vicious, but burning dried cattail in the fire produced a dense smoke that kept them off. Kimble didn't try to sleep there, though. The moon, three-quarters full, had risen by then, and Mrs. P pulled the cart an hour east until the green bosque, bathed in moist air and mosquitoes, had been replaced by brown grass hillsides stirred by a bone-dry southern breeze.

He put Mrs. P on a halter with a long light lead she could easily break. It was a reminder more than an actual constraint and she did break it when a pack of feral dogs approached the camp during the night.

Kimble took hold of his *jyo* and stood with his back against the cart wheel while they circled. After Mrs. P broke her lead they charged her, barking madly, to stampede her, get her running in the dark where she might break a leg or at least tire enough for them to take her down.

Mrs. P turned away, as if she was going to run, and then kicked the pack leader, connecting with both rear hooves. The dog flew ten feet into the air and didn't stir after landing. More kicks connected with other dogs, sending them tumbling away, yelping in distress.

Kimble popped one of the dogs on its shoulder with the tip of his *jyo*, as it swung by, knocking it over, but the rest of the pack fled, more in fear of Mrs. P than of Kim.

Kimble slept late, until the sun crested the Manzanos, but Mrs. P had spent the time profitably, getting a good feed of dry grass.

TWO days after leaving the Rio Grande, on the downslope east of the Manzanos, they pulled over the lip of a hill and found an argument in progress.

Mrs. Perdicaris heard them first, her ears twitching forward well before the top of the hill, but Kimble was not surprised. The trail they were following had become more of a road, well-defined wheel ruts with fresh tracks and fresh horse manure just beginning to dry.

Mrs. P was driving herself—Kimble had looped the reins over the brake lever while he was weaving a wide-brimmed hat from green cattails—and she slowed as she approached the cluster of vehicles just over the hill.

There were five carts similar to Kimble's, high-wheeled boxes with composite wheels and axles. Three were horse-drawn, one mule-drawn, and one cart had lowered shafts and a crossbar so it could be pulled by hand, like a Mormon cart. Three freight wagons with six-horse teams stood in a row with a cluster of saddle horses in front of them.

Kimble took Mrs. Perdicaris off the edge of the road to where a tough patch of dry buffalo grass was doing all right in the shade of some low mesquite bushes. He pulled off her bridle so she could crop grass and said, "Pull up a chair, Mrs. P."

The road dipped sharply into a cut running down into a broad arroyo running down from the mountains. That's where the cluster of people stood, crouched, or sat.

"—dehydration is really the issue."

"Maybe we could throw a canteen?"

"Hell no. You crush a bug they'll swarm her for sure. Us, too."

Kimble looked out beyond them and saw that the arroyo glittered gray and copper and silver and crystalline blue. Out in the middle, on a large chunk of limestone, a small figure sat cross-legged and still.

"Oh," he said aloud.

Several people turned and saw him.

"Afternoon," Kimble said.

They looked at him blankly. A big man wearing a teamsters' emblem on his vest suddenly swore loudly. "Who's watchin' the wagons? Marty, Richard! Get your lazy asses up there! Unhitch the teams and let 'em have a little water."

A short, dark man in orange and maroon Buddhist robes turned around and Kimble blinked. It was *Thây* Hahn, the Buddhist priest from the capital. Kimble shaded his eyes and looked harder at the figure out on the boulder. "Shit! Is that Thayet?" It was. True to form she wasn't just sitting cross-legged, she was in full lotus.

Thayet was Hahn's twelve-year-old daughter.

"Kimble?"

Kimble bowed, his hands together. "*Thây* Hahn. What happened?"

Hahn stopped counting on his rosary and bowed

back, his face calm. "There was a storm up in the Manzanos that sent a flash flood. It happened before we reached the arroyo but the water was still high when we reached here so we waited, filling our water barrels."

"All of you?"

"Ah, no, Mr. Graham's teamsters arrived only an hour ago. Some of the others came yesterday. At first it was just the Joffrey family's two carts and us—we've been traveling the same road since we met near Isleta. The water was down to a trickle on the far edge and the sand was starting to dry so Mr. Joffrey took an empty cart across to test the footing."

A man with male pattern baldness was standing a bit farther down the road. He turned. He held a cloth hat and was twisting it back and forth in his hands though the sun fell full upon his head. "I ran over a damn bug."

Kimble squeezed his eyes shut for a moment.

"Was Thayet in your cart?"

The balding man shook his head. "Hell no. I heard that pop. It's like nothing else, right? Once you've heard one and seen what happens you know forever. I whipped up the horse and we bolted forward, but the damn thing sank up to its axle in some quicksand and I panicked. The bugs were already in the air and I just jumped up and ran for it."

"Let me guess," Kimble said. "Thayet went for the horse."

Hahn nodded. "Just so. She got him unhitched and tried to ride him out but he bucked her off when a bug burned him."

Mr. Joffrey added, "*He* made it out. Stupid was grazing on the far ridge at sunset."

"Sunset? How long has Thayet been out there?"

Hahn's fingers clicked through his rosary automatically. It was not unlike Mr. Joffrey's twisting hat. "The storm was two days ago. She's been on that rock for two nights."

Dehydration indeed.

Kimble looked over the wash. The cart was in pieces, riddled with bug holes, perhaps halfway across the wash. There were a couple of boulders also sticking above the moving sea of copper and steel but none of the bugs sat on them. "Iron rich sands?"

"I believe so," said Hahn. "There were dark streaks."

Not enough to attract the bugs in the first place but enough to keep them here once they swarmed.

A woman with a toddler asleep in her lap was sitting in the small bit of shade at the edge of the cut. "Isn't there something that can be done?"

One of the teamsters muttered, "Here we go again."

Mr. Joffrey turned, anguish twisting across his face like the hat in his hands. "If it would just rain again . . ."

Bugs hated water. They'd abandon the arroyo while water covered it. Of course, it was the water that probably uncovered a piece of refined metal to attract that first bug, the one run over by the cart.

The first rain was unlikely enough this time of year. No counting on a second storm.

"This won't do," Kimble said. "Anybody have a shovel?"

"What, you gonna tunnel to her?" the teamster boss,

Graham, said. "That's limestone under that sand. Might as well build a bridge above, as long as that would take."

"Lend me a shovel and I'll go get her."

Graham, a big man going gray, stared at Kimble, slight, young. Kimble had even depilated that morning so he looked his youngest. "Stupid to send one fool kid after another."

"You want to just sit here and let her die of thirst?"

"All I see is two dead kids instead of one and a shovel rotten with bug holes. No gain in that."

"I die out there, you can have my mule and cart and all its contents. That's a pretty good trade for a fiberglass shovel."

Hahn was listening to the conversation intently and Kimble saw him open his mouth, as if to argue on with Graham, but Kimble shook his head. The priest knew of his association with Major Bentham. He'd even passed messages to and from the Rangers for Kimble. Kimble didn't want him blowing his cover to convince someone to lend a shovel.

Graham said, "I've got kids myself. The only thing worse than losing one is losing two. Forget it." There was something in his voice that made Kimble think this wasn't just theoretical knowledge.

Kimble shrugged. "Right. How about you, Mr. Joffrey?"

Mr. Joffrey was looking at his wife. The hat was twisted tighter than ever.

She was biting her lower lip. Her arms tightened around the toddler in her lap and he awoke, complaining. She shushed him, kissing his head, and he settled again. She looked up at her husband and gave him a short nod.

"Right," he said. He stared down at the hat in his hand and then touched his sunburned bald spot. "Ow. What a fool thing!" He settled the hat on his head and started up the hill.

Kimble turned to follow him. "Now just wait a minute!" said Graham and started to walk up the hill after them.

Hahn stepped in the big man's way and held up his hand. "Your choice is inaction. I understand that. But she is not *your* child."

Hahn was a good two feet shorter than the teamster but something made that man pull up short.

Kimble kept walking. At the cart, he took a water bottle, his first-aid kit, and some dried apples and walnuts, and put them in a shoulder bag. Joffrey took a rough composite shovel out of his remaining cart and handed it to Kimble. "It's seen better days."

The edge of the fiberglass blade was worn and cracked but the handle was all right. "It's perfect," Kimble said.

"Be careful, right?"

Kimble nodded. He started to walk away but at the last minute stepped back to his cart and took the wide-brimmed green cattail hat with him.

He didn't walk back down into the cut. Thayet was far closer to the other side and he saw no point in traveling through more bugs than he had to. Besides, this would save arguing with the teamster.

A quarter mile upstream, where the edges of the arroyo were higher and steeper, a slab of limestone shelved across the bed, probably forming a waterfall when the water ran, but now it was a broken swath of rock with only a little of the iron-rich sands pooling between raised boulders. Kimble slid down the side of the arroyo in a cloud of dirt, dust, and pebbles and picked his way across the arroyo, boulder to boulder. He had to cut steps into the far side with the shovel to make it back to the top.

He came down the road cut on the far side and studied the space between him and Thayet's rock.

Bugs don't really care about people. As far as they're concerned, humans are just a slightly thicker manifestation of air.

Bugs care about three things, near as Kimble could figure. They loved metal. That's what they're after, what they're made of, what they ate to turn into even more bugs.

You don't want to have an artificial joint in the territory. Ditto for metal fillings.

Much as they love metal, though, they crave electromagnetic radiation even more. This means they love radio signals and, really, any of the humming frequencies caused by current flowing through conductors.

Forget computers, radios, cell phones, generators, and—remember fillings and crowns?—well, a pacemaker, an imbedded insulin pump, a vagal stimulator brings them quicker.

But there is one thing that brings them even faster than all of those, that makes them *swarm*.

A broken bug is to the territory what blood is to a shark pool. They come in numbers, they come fast, and they come with their coal-black nano snouts ready to eat through anything.

Kimble used the shovel like a spatula, easing it under the bugs, under the sand itself, and lifting. The minute it was up, he stepped there, into the moist sand temporarily free of bugs.

He sprinkled the shovelful of sand and bugs off to the side, gently, only inches above the others. Some rattled, some spread their silicon-blue photovoltaic wings from under their metal carapaces and buzzed off to land elsewhere, and some just fell to the ground and kept working on the bit of iron they'd separated from the surrounding sand.

Kimble took it very slow. He'd seen bugs sufficiently disturbed that a whole cloud of them rose up without the usual requirement of one getting broken—not quite a swarm, but sufficient to badly scar the horse that had stirred 'em up.

More than once one of the bugs buzzed to a landing on Kimble's clothing. He scraped them carefully off with the blade of the shovel and they'd drop or fly off.

When he was fifteen feet or so from Thayet's boulder he spoke. "Hey, lazy girl, you gonna sit there all day?"

She blinked and turned her head. She did not look good. Her lips were cracked and crusted with blood. Her nose was peeling and there was a hole in her pants above one knee that was brown with crusted blood. "Go away," she said, and closed her eyes again.

Kimble blinked. *Ah.* "Thayet, I'm not a hallucination."

"Yes you are. Kim is hundreds of miles from here."

He laughed. For some reason that made her open her eyes again. "If you can convince me you won't drop it, I have water."

She shook herself, then slapped her cheek. She looked back across the arroyo to where her father and the crowd watched. Kimble hadn't been looking at them. They were all standing, many of them with their hands raised as if they could reach out and snatch both of them to safety. Graham, the teamsters' boss, even had one hand raised to his mouth.

"Kim?" She looked back at him.

"Yes, Thayet." Kimble shifted another shovelful of bugs and sand, moved forward another pace. He stopped again, to let the bugs settle. "Here, catch."

He took the hat and threw it like a Frisbee. She clutched it weakly to her, eyes widening.

"Does that feel like a hallucination?"

She rubbed it between her fingers. "No."

"Put it on, silly."

She did and sighed audibly when the rim shaded the sun from her face.

"Ready for the water?"

"Give me a moment. I'm numb from the waist down."

"Well, you better do something about that." Kimble's legs had gone to sleep before during meditation but he was afraid her experience was really more like the time he'd been locked in the stocks by the People of the Book.

She had to use her arms to uncross her legs. She pushed them out, extended and leaned back.

Kimble took another shovelful, another step.

Thayet screamed as the sensation began returning to her legs. There was a sympathetic shout from the crowd across the arroyo. They probably thought a bug was boring through her, but Kimble saw Hahn talking, his hands raised, explaining about the legs.

Thayet gritted her teeth, then began methodically massaging her legs. "Aaaagghhh." After a few moments she said, "Water?"

"Sip first, right? You drink too much you'll throw it right up." He swung the bag by its handle, underhand and she caught it neatly.

She was careful, rinsing her mouth before swallowing. She managed half a liter in small gulps before he got the rest of the way to her boulder.

"Scoot over," he said, sitting beside her. "Whew, I'm bushed." It wasn't the effort, but the tension.

They sat there for another half hour. Thayet tried some dried apple and a few walnuts and another half-liter of water and Kimble bandaged the bug score on her right thigh. Finally, he helped her stand and encouraged her to take a few steps side to side atop the rock.

They went back the way he'd come, one shovelful at a time, with her hands on his waist. She stepped into his vacated footprints before the bugs filled them. The bugs crawled around their ankles and once one took a shortcut through the leather of Kimble's moccasin and the skin of his ankle, leaving a bloody dribble across the sand.

He cursed a blue streak but he kept his steps and the shovel steady.

When they made it back to the edge of the bugs, where the cut dropped into the sand of the arroyo, they staggered up the road several yards. As they collapsed there was a ragged cheer from across the arroyo.

Thayet bandaged his ankle and then drank more water. "You want some?"

"No, girl. That's your water. Until you're peeing frequently, copiously, and clearly."

"You're gross."

"Yes, Little Dove."

THEY found the Joffreys' errant horse, Stupid, near the road, its lead reins tangled in a patch of prickly pear, and Thayet refused to move another step until Kimble had gotten its halter and harness off. Its mouth was a mess after two days of chewing around the composite bit. Kimble settled both the horse and Thayet a good quarter mile up the road in the shade of a rock outcropping.

Back at the lip of the arroyo, across from the teamster boss, he shouted, "You ready?"

"Yeah," the teamster yelled back. "We got them back over the hill. Your mule didn't want to go. Josh was reaching for her bridle and she came *that* close to biting off his arm. You could hear the teeth come together clear down the hill. But Hahn, here, he bribed her with a bucket of oats and she followed him down."

"She's a lot of trouble. Okay, give me five minutes."

What he had in mind wouldn't take as long as the

painstaking slog across the arroyo to get Thayet, but it was probably as dangerous.

While one might be able to take the carts and saddle horses cross-country downstream to where the walls of the arroyo were less steep, the freight wagons would have to detour thirty miles to a crossing they could handle.

Unless they could clear this crossing of bugs.

The spot he chose was a half mile downstream where the walls of the arroyo had been undercut by the recent flooding but a three-foot stratum of limestone kept the rim above solid. There was more limestone below, with shallow pockets that had caught some of the iron-bearing sands and, while the bugs were nowhere near as thick as at the crossing, there were some grazing for ferrous bits.

He found the first thing he needed about fifty yards back, a place where water running between two rocks had dug a channel, perhaps two feet deep, two feet wide. He used the shovel and made it deeper, but he kept his eyes open as he dug.

The last thing he wanted to do was uncover an old metal fence post.

The second thing he needed he found closer to the arroyo, a big chunk of limestone about the size of a large watermelon. It was sunk in the dirt, but he cleared an edge and levered it out with the shovel. Its top and bottom were flat, so it didn't roll worth beans. He might have carried it a few yards, but instead he just flopped it over and over, thud, thud, thud, all the way to the rim. Then he shifted it sideways a bit and tested his choice by dropping a very small pebble over the edge. Nope. Another pebble, a foot to the right, was dead on target so he shifted the boulder, took a deep breath, and shoved.

He was running before it hit, but he still heard multiple "pops." One would've been sufficient. He could hear the bugs in the air, a harsh cicada buzzing with ultrasonic overtones. It was mostly from upstream but he still had to dodge a few that arose from the brush in front of him. He dropped into the hole and several buzzed overhead, more than he'd expected. Maybe there was some old barbwire in the neighborhood.

After five minutes his heart had stopped pounding and his breathing had slowed and he was back to boredom. He stuck to the plan, though. Bugs could keep coming for a while and it was better to be cautious.

He'd intended to meditate but he fell asleep instead.

The teamster boss' voice woke him, yelling at the top of his lungs, yelling his name from about ten feet away, worry and fear in his voice.

Kimble shuddered awake, his heart pounding, the sick sound of a bullwhip crack fading back into the dreamscape.

What on earth has happened now?

Kimble stood up and his head cleared the rocks. The teamster wasn't looking his way and when Kimble spoke the teamster boss almost fell over.

"Jesus, Mary, and Joseph! We thought you were dead!"

Oops. "How long have I been asleep?"

The man opened his mouth, shut it, opened it again, then just shook his head and marched back toward the crossing. "He's all right!" he yelled back toward the road.

They were all out there, the Joffreys, the teamsters, and the others, spread out across the desert, looking for Kimble. He picked up Joffrey's shovel and waved it overhead. Kimble started back toward the edge of arroyo, to take a look down at the impact site, but the bugs were thick on the ground before he reached the rim, their wings extended and held flat to the sun, so he veered away. He could only imagine what they were like in the arroyo below.

Back at the crossing they'd already brought the stock and vehicles across and when Kimble glanced down the cut into the wash it was just sand, clear of bugs.

Mrs. Perdicaris snorted and walked to meet him. Mrs. Joffrey, with a large smile on her face, handed him a cold apple empanada. When Kimble thanked her for it, she lunged at him and it was all he could do not to throw her in the dirt before he realized she just wanted to hug him. When she let go her eyes were wet. When Kimble gave Joffrey his shovel back, the man nodded gravely and said, "I'll keep this handy. I see it still has plenty of use in it."

Thayet was lying in the shade under their handcart, a jug of water to hand. Kimble approved. "You pee yet?"

She shook her head.

"Drink more water."

Dancing in the Dark

Kimble put Thayet up in his cart and Joffrey un-
lashed the crossbar on the Hahns' cart so they
could hitch Stupid to it.

"What kind of name is that?" Kimble had
asked.

"Sarcasm," said Joffrey. "Damn thing can open
any latch ever made. I couldn't tell you the number of times we found him in the kitchen garden
as a colt. Mrs. Joffrey kept saying, 'You get that
stupid horse out of my garden!' It stuck. He was
almost horsemeat before he got grown but he really turned into a good all-round workhorse.
Saddle, cart, plow. You name it."

Thây Hahn wouldn't ride in the cart, but he
led the hitched horse, walking, his fingers counting through the beads on his rosary, all the way

to the edge of the alkali flats. The area below the Manzanos is a closed basin and the flats were where the water ended up (if it didn't evaporate before getting down there).

The village of Three Bean Salad sat on two springs and one of the more reliable streams running down into the basin. Beans, as you might imagine from the village name, were the largest local crop—mostly pinto. *Las Tres Hermanas*—the Three Sisters—was a restaurant and hotel below the village on the last bit of raised ground before the flats began. In the summer, when the winds gusted from the south, there was little shelter from the stinging dust storms, but it was sited around a good spring that flowed year-round.

The Hahns and the Joffreys and Kimble paid a small fee to camp on the edge of the inn's cherry grove and draw water. The teamsters paid more for rooms and stabling and an active night watchman for their wagons.

Mrs. Joffrey wondered at the expense. "You'd think they'd want to save their money!"

Twelve-year-old Thayet laughed. "They want their visitors more."

Mrs. Joffrey had offered to fix dinner for all of them, and while Kimble had accepted immediately, the Hahns were vegetarians. Thayet shared the cook fire, though, to prepare their brown rice and lentils while her father meditated back in the grove.

"What on earth are you talking about, child?" Mrs. Joffrey asked.

"The bed girls. The hotel has a deal with them. They

don't go to the campsites and, in return, the hotel cuts them in on a bit of the room cost."

Mrs. Joffrey blushed. "Bed girls?"

Thayet added, "Sex workers. You know, women who—"

Kimble tried not to laugh. "She understands, Thayet."

Mrs. Joffrey turned away, busying herself with the stew she was cooking—the one she'd just checked.

Kimble turned back to Thayet. "Why are you here, Little Dove? Away from the capital?"

"*Ba* is officiating at the opening of the new buildings at the Pecosito Zen Center. We came down last fall for the groundbreaking. We stopped here then, and I saw the bed girls going from room to room and asked *Ba*. He said they are heavily yoked to the wheel."

Kimble shook his head minutely as Mrs. Joffrey's bustling became more pronounced. "Tell me about the Zen Center, Little Dove."

"You don't want to hear what else *Ba* told me about the bed girls?" She glanced aside toward Mrs. Joffrey and grinned.

"Little Imp, I will beat you. Your *ba* will let me."

She laughed. "Very well. The monastery is below the bluff but above the high flood, on the shared irrigation canal. They have several fields of good bottomland and a high-volume solar still." Suddenly she frowned and the cheerfulness of her earlier mood left. She poked the ground with her finger.

"What?"

"The still. Someone threw rocks from up on the bluff and broke the glass panels. And they threw shit."

Kimble's eyes grew wide. "They messed with their water? Their *drinking* water?"

This was vandalism by any standard but in the water-poor areas of the territory this was more extreme than a mere misdemeanor. In some of the smaller communities people had been killed for such an offense and their killers acquitted of wrongdoing.

Thayet nodded. "Several times."

"Is there any dispute about the water rights?"

"Not exactly. The rancher who donated the site deeded the water rights, too. It's complicated."

Kimble raised his eyebrows.

"Ask *Ba*."

After supper Kimble brewed a large pot of peppermint tea and offered it around. He slipped Thayet a large lump of sugar for hers with a whispered, "Brush your teeth well." The sky was clear, awash with stars, and the temperature dropped, making the group move closer to the fire and cup their tea in both hands.

When they were settled, he asked *Thây* Hahn why the land situation at the Zen Center was "complicated."

"Complicated?" He considered his teacup. "It is awash with suffering, like all life, with desire and the desires of attainment." He held his right hand before his chest, forefinger extended skyward. His posture, always straight, became somehow even more erect and grounded.

"Attend," he intoned. "A rancher named Ronson left

his ranch, split into quarters, to his three children and *Roshi* Mallory."

Kimble found himself sitting up. "Are questions permitted, *Thây?*" Thayet, on the other side of the fire, rolled her eyes at Kimble's respectful tone.

Hahn smiled. "Merit may be gained through seeking knowledge."

"Was Ronson a Buddhist?"

"Oh, no. He was, in his words, an indifferent Methodist. But the *Roshi* was the caregiver for his wife's passing."

"Doctor?"

Hahn shook his head. "Hospice care. She had colon cancer that metastasized throughout her abdomen. They caught it much too late, though they made the trip outside, to M.D. Anderson in Houston. They offered massive chemotherapy but they gave it less than a five percent chance. She'd been through one round already and wanted to die at home, without the nausea. It took two months."

"Oh."

"*Roshi* Mallory also sat with Ronson for the month after his stroke, until he died. The two sons maintained the will was changed then, when Mr. Ronson was *non compos mentis* and challenged its validity.

"The court found that the final version of the will had been witnessed several years earlier, right after his wife's funeral, by a county magistrate and their own sister, Ronson's daughter. The brothers appealed the ruling at the district level and then above. The Territorial Court awarded damages as well as court costs to *Roshi* Mallory, this last time, and they held the brothers and their lawyer were in violation of Rule Eleven of the Federal Rules—the part where they must perform due diligence to ascertain the factual basis of their case. They almost held the lawyer in contempt but, in the end, they just severely cautioned him never to come before their bench with any case so lacking in merit."

"Sounds like you were there."

Hahn smiled. "Oh, yes. Mallory stayed with us for the appellate hearing—the court is five blocks from the temple. Mostly I meditated, but I was there to support *Roshi* Mallory. I learned far more than I ever wanted to know about the laws of inheritance. The ACLU lawyer was very good about explaining things."

"Wait a minute—why was the ACLU involved? You've left something out, I think."

Hahn frowned and looked up for a moment. "Oh, yes. There was the religious intolerance part. The Church of the New Paradise hired the law firm for the challenge and the appeals."

Kimble mouth formed a silent, "Ah." The Territorial Church of the New Paradise was part of the Prosperity Gospel movement. Believe and you shall receive wealth here on earth. The leaders certainly received. One of the ways of expressing your "belief" was by giving heavily to the church. The movement was big outside the territory, too, where they were responsible for some of the mall-size churches you found all over.

They weren't so big in the territory, though they were

growing. You couldn't support the same concentrations of people without metal-based tech. No cars, no mass transit, meant no giant churches. The message itself wasn't unattractive and certainly found its willing recipients. Who wouldn't like to become wealthy just by believing, especially when you were breaking your back trying to farm a drought-ridden patch of desert?

"I take it one or both brothers belong to the congregation?"

"Both, I believe," said *Thây* Hahn.

Pecosito was a largish town for the territory, perhaps four thousand people, straddling the Pecos south of the ruins of Ft. Sumner. "How big is the church there? Congregation-wise?"

Hahn shook his head. "I don't know. There are many churches there."

"My brother belongs to Church of Christ in Pecosito," volunteered Mrs. Joffrey. "He said they've got about three hundred members."

"Is that where you're headed?"

She nodded. "We were farming but we were struggling because of last year's dry spell. Then while Michael was plowing, he uncovered an old pipeline that ran across our place. The bugs moved in big time before we could cover it up and that was that. My brother in Pecosito recently expanded his fish farm and needs the help." She poked the fire a bit. "That's the plan, anyway."

There was a burst of laughter from the direction of the inn, several voices, male and female, mixed.

Thayet said, "And the drinking has begun."

Thây Hahn sighed and shook his head. "Prepare for bed, child."

"Yes, *Ba*."

LATER, in the night, Kimble awoke, chilled, and sat up to reach for his second blanket. The moon had risen and he saw that Thayet's bedroll, near the fireplace, was empty. He listened carefully. He could hear the horses and Mrs. Perdicaris stirring at the makeshift corral, the slight wind through the trees, and the occasional pop and crack from the dying fire, but the most obvious noise was some raucous singing from the direction of the hotel.

He waited. If she'd just got up to pee she would be back shortly, but when five minutes passed, he sighed, pulled on his moccasins, and crawled out from under the cart. A breeze tugged at his shirt and he shivered. He reached back under the cart and took one of the blankets and draped it, shawl-like, over his shoulders.

He moved slowly through the grove, pausing to listen. A group of the teamsters had gathered in a puddle of lamplight outside one of the long rows of rooms with their "guests." Dress was apparently optional. A woman, wearing nothing but one of the teamster's hats, was dancing before the porch while the others sang and cheered her on.

She was easy to look at, but it wasn't why he was there. He settled down by a tree, in deep moon shadow, but instead of looking at the lamplight, he watched the grove.

There she was. A silhouette, perched in one of the trees, was visible against the moonlit sky. From the porch, the figure would be lost in the bulk of the grove's crowns. He thought about getting her attention, a thrown stone perhaps, but it was just as likely to get her noticed.

He glanced back toward the dancer. She was winding up her dance by twining around her client. The singing had stopped and the couples were moving back to their rooms in pairs and, in one case, a trio.

Thayet's branch broke with a sudden and loud "crack," and she fell down onto the ground with a startled cry. She scrambled to her feet and ran back through the grove, but there was a sudden burst of drunken interest from the hotel and four men headed back into the trees.

That's torn it, thought Kimble.

Shrouded in his blanket up against a tree, he was practically invisible. As two of the teamsters ran past, he stuck out his foot. The first one tripped and the second one fell over his fallen compatriot. Kimble jumped to his feet and ran off to the west, parallel to the hotel, scuffing his feet deliberately and snagging tree branches with outstretched hands to make lots of noise.

The two who'd fallen and the two lagging took the bait. One of them was a sprinter, with better night sight than the others, and he was well ahead of his fellows, just a few yards behind Kimble. Kimble slowed, letting him close, then, when the man's reaching arms brushed his blanket, he turned and dropped to his knees. The man tried to jump over, but he was too close, and Kimble snagged one of his legs as he went over.

He was already up and running before the man came crashing down, so he didn't see it, but it *sounded* very impressive, involving branches, a flailing impact, and lots of loud swearing.

Kimble led the trailing three men down toward the alkali flats but, before he reached it, he ducked behind a young tree, its branches still low to the ground, and edged quietly up against the trunk. He pulled the blanket up, like a cloak, over his head, and watched them run stumbling past.

He just sat there and tracked them by the sounds they made. They went all the way to the start of the flats, even splashing into the runoff from the hotel's springs, before they gave up. He heard them stumble back toward their rooms after a while, congratulating themselves on scaring off the intruder.

He shook his head and wondered what on earth they'd been thinking.

If you're going to drink, don't think. If you're going to think, don't drink.

Thayet was in her bedroll when Kimble walked softly back to the cart, still and quiet, as if she'd never left. He didn't know if Thayet had trouble getting back to sleep, but the memory of the naked woman dancing in the lamplight mixed with the memories of his night with Martha and it took him a long time to fall asleep.

"I DON'T know what you're talking about," Thayet said.

"Then maybe you should wear long sleeves. You scratched yourself on your forearm when you fell out of the cherry tree."

"You saw that?"

Kimble was grumpy. To cross the worst of the alkali flats while it was still cool, the entire group—the Hahns, the Joffreys, and the teamsters—had all risen well before dawn, watered the stock, and headed out at the first hint of predawn gray. He glanced ahead at the long line of teamsters' wagons.

But at least I'm not hung over.

"I led them down to the flats. Otherwise you would have had this conversation with your father and a bunch of drunk teamsters last night. I *hope* they would've taken you to your father. They were pretty drunk."

"Stupid cherry tree," said Thayet.

"Oh, *blame* the tree. I suppose you just happened to wake up and decide to climb trees, and you just happened to pick the one over by that wing of the hotel."

She grinned, unrepentant. "I was curious." She looked sideways at Kimble. "Are you mad about the guy who got hurt?"

One of the teamsters had been working one-handed. He'd badly sprained a wrist when he tripped over something in the dark.

Kimble snorted. "I'm not really going to spend too much sympathy on someone who thinks it's a good idea to go running around in the dark while intoxicated. Though it wouldn't have happened if someone *else* hadn't been climbing trees, trying to see a little skin."

"A *little*? Did you *see* that girl dancin'?" She lowered her voice, "And some of those guys weren't wearing much either."

Kimble cleared his throat and tried not to think about his own sleepless thoughts. "You're a little pervert."

"Don't be ridiculous. I just have healthy curiosity. It's perfectly normal for someone of my age."

"Perfectly normal. Your father wouldn't mind at all. So I can tell him about it, right?"

She glared at him.

He laughed. "Okay. I won't tell him, but you take the reins. I'm going to climb in back and catch up on some of the sleep I missed last night."

They cleared the flats in the early afternoon and started climbing up to the high plains between the Monzanos and the Pecos watershed. They spent the worst of the afternoon heat under a stand of cottonwoods lining a dry creek bed.

"Wouldn't normally stop so long," said Graham, "but my guys really tied one on last night." He laughed. He certainly didn't look like he'd spent the night in dissipation. "You'd think that drinkin' and . . ." he glanced sideways at Mrs. Joffrey, "uh, other stuff would be enough, but they also had to go haring through the night after lord knows what."

"Snipe hunt," suggested Mr. Joffrey.

"Close enough," Graham agreed. "Probably some village kids pokin' and peekin'. Might as well be snipe—they certainly didn't catch any."

Kimble was showing Thayet how to make hampers using split willow for the stakes and green cattail for the weavers. He'd done the hard part, the spokes on the bottom transitioning to the upright staves, and now she was building the sides.

Thayet had been listening raptly to the teamster and Mr. Joffrey, and now she opened her mouth to say something. Kimble darted his hand out and rapped the back of her hand with his knuckles. "Tighter. Snug it up before you start the next row."

She blinked and stared at him, startled, rubbing the back of her hand.

Kimble scratched his upper lip and, while she was watching, drew the fingertip sideways across his lips and then scratched his cheek.

She bent her head back down and concentrated on threading the cattail through the willow stake.

Later, when they were back in the cart and couldn't be overheard, Thayet asked, "Why'd you do that? Keep me from talking to Mr. Joffrey."

"What were you going to say?"

"If you didn't know, why'd you hit me!"

"'Cause you were going to talk about the noise the teamsters made last night, weren't you?"

Thayet's mouth opened but she didn't say anything at first. She shifted the hamper she was working on in her lap. "Maybe."

Kimble tilted his head and looked at her.

"Okay! Something like that."

Kimble looked back at Mrs. P and clucked again, to keep her moving. He was sitting on the reins and weaving a square box basket, all of cattails, a good size for organizing shelves. He'd made six of them in the last two hours.

"A partial truth is almost as bad as an outright lie. You start by letting them know you were awake and it's not much of a leap from there to the thought that you might've gotten up. That you could've been the one his teamsters were chasing around the cherry grove last night." He reached back into the bucket of soaking reeds and snaked out another weaver. "Open your mouth and you either have to tell the truth, part of the truth, or an outright lie. Keep your mouth shut and you don't have to worry about any of those."

Thayet said, "I wasn't going to lie. I know that trap. Easier to remember the truth. Less confusing."

Kimble nodded. "Very good."

"But you're saying even the truth is a problem."

"Ah, Little Dove, not if you don't care what others know. If you lead a completely transparent life. Your father, for example, can always tell the truth. But if your life includes spying on others—"

"Like yours?"

Kimble laughed. "I was talking about *your* life."

"*I* don't spy for the territorial government," Thayet said. Kimble gave Thayet a look and she added hastily, "Not that I know *anyone* who spies for the territorial government!"

"I'm glad that's clear." He clucked again. "Less is more. It's always easier to make mistakes with your mouth open than with it closed."

They camped on a distant tributary of the Pecos, where feral cats in heat serenaded them in the night until a coyote pack moved in and ended the romance. There was much yowling and hissing.

Thayet listened to the distant byplay. When it was over, she asked, "What do you think happened?"

Her father shrugged. "The wheel turns. The cats may have made it into the cottonwoods. Or the coyotes may have eaten."

"Cat tastes like rabbit. It'll take two more days to get to Pecosito," Graham said, "but it's downhill from here."

Baskets, Posole, and Water Under the Bridge

When Kimble arrived at the Zen Center with *Thây* Hahn and Thayet, he took the offered guest room gladly. But two days later, after he had talked with *Roshi* Mallory, he asked permission to camp on the bluff above.

"You would normally be welcome to do so," he said, "but I'm not sure it is safe. We've had some trouble with vandals—"

"*Thây* Hahn told me about the vandals and your solar still. When was the last time you had trouble?"

"Just last week. Rocks were thrown, but we've devised an awning to stretch across the glass, to protect it. We don't put it up until after dark. Otherwise they might throw bigger rocks, or something to tear or burn the awning. Anyway, the rocks were deflected. They didn't throw feces this time—perhaps because they didn't hear the glass break." He shook his head. "In any case, you can see why it is unsafe."

Kimble smiled. "Perhaps, but I'm thinking that if someone *were* up there, they wouldn't come. A deterrent of sorts. Have you set watch before?"

"Yes."

"And did they come while you were watching?"

He sighed. "They did not. But we put several people on the bluff at once. You are alone."

"You haven't met my mule."

Roshi Mallory was still reluctant, but after he talked with *Thây* Hahn, he said, "All right. Please be careful."

To drive his cart there he had a choice of going upriver a mile or downstream two miles to Pecosito proper. He chose upstream, working back on a county road until he came to the section marker that delimited the corner of the property. According to *Roshi* Mallory, the property to the north belonged to the daughter of the late rancher. The property to the south belonged to an unrelated rancher and the brothers' property was directly across the river. "Ms. Peterson, the daughter of Mr. Ronson of honored memory, grazes her sheep on the land above. She pays us in wool, which we spin and weave. If you see her shepherds, just tell them I sent you, right?"

He didn't see them, but he could tell they'd been there by the patches of cropped grass and dried sheep dung.

He camped well back from the bluff's edge in a sandy wash four feet lower than the surrounding grass. It led to a steep gully that cut down to the river bottom. The path down the bluff could be navigated by a man, and possibly by a mule, but not the cart. A hundred yards south of the cut was where the bluff directly overlooked the Zen Center and its glass solar still.

The vegetation there was tall grass, but Kimble found places where hooves had cut the roots, and there was a pile of rocks sitting on top of yellowed grass. Clearly they'd been brought there within the last month. He pitched these rocks over the edge of the bluff where they fell to the ground behind the monk's vegetable garden. *If they want to throw more rocks, let them bring more.*

THERE were fourteen theaters in Pecosito, with a local repertory performing in about half. The others featured touring companies, often running live productions of popular TV shows or movies from beyond the curtain. Kimble was partial to musicals, himself.

He'd been tempted to buy a ticket for a show but it wouldn't have been in character. He sat to the left of the entrance, instead, during a matinee performance, offering his wares. Some were the baskets he and Thayet had made on the trip, but the only thing that was really moving were the relatively simple hand-fans he'd cobbled up just that morning as he'd walked into town. He'd meant to sell them for next to nothing, but the day was unseasonably still and hot and the regulars knew it would be stifling inside so they were paying half a territorial dollar each.

The smarter theatergoers had brought their own fans,

all kinds, from silk-and-wood, to plastic windups powered by twisted rubber bands. But some had not and Kimble had a pocket full of hard plastic coins as a result.

Even though the customers were all inside, he continued to weave more fans. He owed ten of them to the concessions manager for allowing him to park in front of the theater. The man had made it clear that he'd prefer Kimble in front of the theater instead of the usual panhandlers. A town deputy also came by and started to roust Kimble, but the concessionaire had warned Kimble about the going rate. He remained, unmolested, but a dollar poorer.

He was almost done weaving the fans when a group of five Rangers came up the street, obviously off duty, for while they wore their fractal pixel desert camo fatigues, they didn't have their rifles and they certainly weren't in any sort of formal formation. Two of them were officers and the other three noncoms. They glanced at the theater marquee and one of the sergeants said, "Hey, that's the next episode of *Blood and Laughter*." He looked down at Kimble. "What time does it start?"

The town drummer had beat the third quarter of the hour a little earlier so he could say, "Matinee started twenty minutes ago, I believe, but of course, there's an evening show, and it won't be quite so hot."

"Damn. We're on duty later." He looked back up at the marquee. "Oh, well, it plays until next week."

The younger of the two officers, a lieutenant, casually said, "Do you barter for your baskets? I have some precious stones."

Kimble's hand stilled upon the fan he was weaving, and then he said, "Do I look like a man who buys precious stones?"

"Even a very poor man can buy a turquoise or posole," said the officer quietly, picking up one of Kim's square baskets. The cloth name label over his left breast pocket read, "Hodges."

"Let me see the posole," Kim asked.

Hodges stood, laughing, dropping the basket back on the steps. "Who's for a beer?"

"Maxine's?" said the captain.

The Rangers headed down the street in a group, but when they were halfway down the block, Hodges waved his fellows on and came back. "About the posole—it was cooked by a woman and that could be against your customs."

"There is no custom where men go to," and here Kimble paused before finishing, "look for posole."

"Right. Should we go somewhere?"

Kimble smiled broadly, ingratiatingly, the picture of someone trying to make a sale, but his voice showed his irritation. "Hell, no. After dark at the New Bridge. Moonrise."

"Moonrise? When is that?"

"Don't get out much? Tonight it's about two hours after sunset."

Hodges said, "I don't see why we can't talk now."

Kimble smiled again but his teeth ground together. "Buy a basket and get away from me."

Hodges looked a bit offended, but he picked one of

Kimble's square shelf baskets, haggled loudly about the price, then left.

Kimble settled back onto the steps and resumed his fan weaving.

Traffic was light but there were windows in all the facing buildings. What the hell had Hodges been thinking?

While it didn't have the commercials that padded the original broadcast out to an hour, set changes and a comedic or musical spot at the beginning and end filled out the full sixty minutes. This was especially important when the episode ended with a cliffhanger, to ease the audience's frustration.

Kimble returned to his baskets and managed to sell one of the larger hampers to a matron headed back to her house.

"Give it a good soaking every four months and it will last years," he said. As she counted the coins into his hand, he asked politely, "How was the show?"

"This was a good one! Of course, I see every episode, but I think I'll see this one again. I had to go outside for a medical procedure last year and I indulged in a positive orgy of HD watching—I saw *all* the back episodes." She headed off with her basket.

He stacked his remaining baskets for transport before he delivered the promised fans to the concessionaire.

"Good-oh," the woman said. She examined the fans critically, testing the flex and stiffness. "Nice work. You can have the same deal any matinee showing. Evening shows, double. We have packed houses so it's worth it."

"I'll think on it," Kimble said.

His baskets, stacked and tied together, made a large cluster, nearly four feet in diameter, but easily carried on his shoulders. As he started down the street, a man leaning against a wall across the street straightened and wandered in the same direction.

After the second turn, Kimble was sure of the tail. *Lieutenant Durant would not be impressed.*

Kimble went to the central plaza. It wasn't a regular market day and the stalls were mostly empty, but there was a middle-aged woman selling some early apples as well as bags of dried ones from last season. Her display consisted of burlap-lined, plastic five-gallon buckets, the contents of which she replenished from woven bags of recycled plastic in the typical ugly dark gray. She sat in front of the bags, but behind the buckets, on an overturned bucket, playing the main theme to Bach's third Brandenburg on a ten-hole ocarina.

Kimble stopped in front of her and lowered his collection of baskets to the ground, using the motion to get a better look at his tail. The man looked like a ranch hand—his boots were better suited to riding than walking. Worn jeans, denim shirt, white-blond hair sticking out of a straw cowboy hat. He had the local paper, all four pages, and was pretending to read it.

Most of what Kimble had left were the rectangular pantry baskets, though he also had three thigh-high hampers, one of which had been converted into a fish trap by the addition of a conical entrance tapering down to sharp-pointed split bamboo stakes.

The apple seller eyed him but didn't stop playing her

ocarina, so Kimble took one of his smaller rectangular pantry baskets and arranged three different kinds of apples within—green Granny Smith, dark-red Macintosh, and Yellow Golden Delicious.

The apple seller came to the end of the movement and said, "Pretty enough. Making up a gift basket? For a friend or are you a reseller?"

Kimble squatted back on his heels. "Sell you all these baskets, except the fish trap, for three bags of dried apples."

The woman eyed the baskets. "What's the catch?" It was ridiculously cheap. "You steal them?"

"Made every one with these hands." He held them up so she could see the calluses. "Cut the reeds myself from the Rio Grande bosque traveling here."

She turned her hand palm-up, conceding that he hadn't stolen them. "Why you so anxious to sell then?"

"Well, if it helps you move your apples better, perhaps you'll buy more later. Then you'll know what they're worth. Next sale, cash."

The woman picked up the filled basket, examining how much the bottom and sides distended under load. She picked up an empty one and flexed it. "Still green. They gonna fall apart when they dry out?"

"Not if you soak 'em every four months or so. And if you don't soak it, just throw it in the compost pile and get another." Without pointing, he asked, "That guy reading the paper over there?" He flicked his eyes sideways. "The one holding up the wall? Seen him somewhere."

The woman glanced over, then back at the basket. "That's Steve Bickle. You could've seen him in church, maybe. He's the handyman over at the Church of the New Paradise. You go there?"

"No," Kimble said neutrally. "Do you?"

"No!" That was almost vehement. "Not much of a churchgoer, but when I do, it's Mass at San Juan's."

"Isn't New Paradise one of those Prosperity Gospel outfits? Rewards on this earth and all that?"

She nodded. "That's it—pray and it will be given to you."

She flexed the basket again, her lips pursed. It was a decent basket. Kimble had tucked all the ends cleanly and the corners were neat and square. "Okay. Check back next week and we'll see how they've sold. While we're harvesting I'm here for the full market on Wednesday. Monday and Friday, too."

She started to hand him the dried apples and he held up his hand. "Can I send someone for the apples? Not going home right now."

"Okay. Who?"

"Don't know yet. They'll say they've come for basket boy's apples. Will that work?"

"Three bags, right? For basket boy. You sure I'm trustworthy?"

He shrugged. "One way to find out. Trust is like that." He put the fish trap under his arm, and, with a smile and a nod, left the market square, walking briskly.

STEVE Bickle passed Kimble off to another man a few blocks north of the market, a bearded Hispanic on horseback who moseyed after Kimble despite several changes in direction. Closer to the western edge of town, Bickle showed up again, also on horseback, with an attractive young woman riding pillion behind him, but as soon as Bickle saw Kimble, he dropped back around the corner. The next time he saw the man he was riding alone.

The woman showed up in his path five minutes later, leaning against a boundary wall as if she'd been there all morning. But her chest was rising and falling rapidly, like someone who had just finished sprinting.

Kimble nodded as he drew abreast of her. She flashed a brilliant smile and said, "I don't think I've seen you around. Are you new in town?"

Kimble smiled back and said, "*Perdone me, Señorita. Yo no hablo Inglés. Qué lastima. Tu eres muy atractiva.*" She opened her mouth and shut it again. Kimble blew her a kiss and kept walking.

He continued west, threading through the narrow streets as the more commercial parts of town turned to residential—big lots with small houses and large gardens. A system of irrigation ditches backed the lots and Kimble crossed the bridge over the main supply ditch, an eight-foot-wide waterway lined with reeds. He paused, perched on the wooden side rails, to watch a mother duck with seven ducklings splashing in the water where the edge of the bridge supports broke the force of the current.

Bickle and his companion turned their horses to the edge of a lot where the grass was growing thick and let their horses munch.

They're about as subtle as hailstones. He didn't want to

lead them back to the monastery. He preferred keeping his base secure. *Unless they followed you* from *the Zen Center?* He reviewed the morning's walk in, but he was sure he'd been clear all the way into town. No, they had picked him up at the theater and he was very much afraid they'd been watching Hodges.

Then there was the story *Thây* Hahn had told him about the Church's lawsuit against the Center, as well as the vandalism of their solar still. *Let's just keep them away.*

Kimble heard the geese before he saw them. A group of twenty white geese, herded by a border collie and a teenage girl with hiked-up skirts and the top three buttons of her blouse undone, came around the bend from the west, looking like an illustration from a book of fairy tales. At the bridge, there was a revolt as several of the geese broke for the irrigation ditch and the dog cut them off with some sharp barking.

His followers could've arranged another attempt in this short a time, but he really doubted they could've managed the geese this quickly.

He smiled at her. "Heading home or out?"

She cut off a goose headed for the bank with the stout stick she held. "Home. We've been weeding a grove."

"Pretty heavy stick for the geese, isn't it?"

"For the geese, yes. For feral dogs? Not quite heavy enough. About perfect for the neighborhood dogs, though."

Her look invited further inquiry, but Kimble sighed and resisted asking where she lived or what was she doing later. The girl opened her mouth to say something else but the geese were threatening to break out again and she moved on, chivying them over the bridge without additional revolts.

The horses Bickle and his companion rode did not like the geese and they danced as the honking mass went by. The riders, watching the goose girl instead of paying attention to their mounts, took a while to settle them.

When they finally stopped watching her progress down the road, Kimble was gone.

THE New Bridge was smaller than the old highway bridge several miles upstream. It didn't span river bluff to river bluff; it was down in the bottoms and *most* years it was above the highest flood mark. It was poured concrete, reinforced with composite fibers and rods, and it had been modeled outside using the latest computer drafting and modeling systems, then built on site using the oldest methods—human and animal muscle.

Kimble waited on the east side of the bridge, just off the road, concealed in a stand of sagebrush. The traffic was light, a lot of off-duty Rangers headed into town from the barracks, ranchers and farmers returning home after business in town, ranch hands headed into town for some form of debauchery.

It was well past twilight and, of course, the glow of the moon was visible on the eastern horizon. Some people carried glass-globed oil lamps and some walked in greenish pools of chem-stick light, but most let their eyes adjust and followed the lighter swath of the roadway. If there was one good thing to say about the bugs it was that they'd really cut down on light pollution. The glorious span of the Milky Way provided enough light to avoid walking off the road.

The first sliver of quarter moon was above the horizon when Lieutenant Hodges approached. He was using a service-issue reflector-focused chemlight, which made Kimble both glad and profoundly irritated. The plus was he had no trouble identifying Hodges from the other traffic. The negative was that neither would anyone else.

His first words as Hodges drew abreast were, "Keep looking straight ahead."

Despite this, Hodges started to swing the light to the side, but he checked himself and swung it back onto the road.

"Tie your shoe."

Hodges crouched, setting down his light so it shown on his boots, and untied one of his laces.

Kimble closed his eyes, to protect his night vision. "When you're done, kill your light and walk on. When you get to the bridge, leave the road and go down the bank. I'll meet you under the first arch."

"What if someone's there?"

Kimble nodded to himself in the dark. At least Hodges was thinking a bit.

"I checked. No drunks, no trolls. If I'm not there by the time the moon is above the bank, continue into town. Go now."

Hodges retied his shoe and, as he stood, clipped the dark cover over his lamp lens. Kimble heard him walk on down the road, his steps tentative at first but gaining confidence as he continued. Kimble hoped he wouldn't break his neck getting down the bank.

The tag was only a minute behind, a person Kimble had heard earlier, but whose footsteps had sped up as soon as Hodges had shielded the light. Kimble got a clear profile against the night sky as the figure walked past and the moonlight had increased enough that he caught a glimpse of straw hat and white-blond hair.

Kimble followed him long enough to see him continue across the bridge. Kimble spent a few minutes in the moon shadow of the railing, waiting to see if the man doubled back. When he didn't return, Kimble worked his way down to the deep shadow under the bridge.

Hodges was at the far edge, looking up at the sky. The burbling of the river as it tumbled across scattered rocks covered the noise of Kimble's approach. He stopped far enough away to avoid getting hit by mistake and said, "Evening."

Hodges jumped and spun, his hands up. "Jesus!" he said. "You nearly got yourself whacked."

Kimble didn't correct him. "Come on down by the water."

Kimble found a rock to sit on and waited for Hodges to pick his way down. Since Hodges had been staring at the moonlit sky, it took some time. *I swear if he opens his light I'm going to throw him in the river.*

When Hodges got close enough, Kimble asked, "Did you assign someone to cover your back tonight?"

Hodges stumbled on a rock and crouched to catch himself.

"What?" Hodges was still feeling around, trying to find his footing.

"Just sit there. That's close enough. Someone was following you. Did you assign someone to do that?"

Hodges didn't say anything for a moment, then, finally, "You must be mistaken."

"Not hardly."

"You're just a kid. What on earth are they thinking, sending a kid?"

Kimble thought about hitting him. He knew right where Hodges was and the Ranger probably wouldn't even see it coming. "How long have you been in intelligence?"

Hodges didn't answer.

"Did you assign someone to be your perimeter shield?"

Again, Hodges didn't answer.

Kimble kept his ears open. He didn't think Hodges was setting him up, but he was ready to move at the first sign of betrayal—probably into the river, though his afternoon float down the irrigation ditch had given him his fill of water. "You're the signal officer, aren't you?"

"That's classified."

Kimble counted to ten in Japanese. "Were you Lujan's contact?"

"Uh, yes."

Oh, shit.

"I'm leaving first. Count to a hundred before you follow."

"I'm supposed to brief you . . ."

"No. We won't be talking again."

"What? Nonsense. You were sent to assist in my investigation!"

Who trained you? "Message for Control: Delta Uniform. Got that?"

"Delta Uniform? That's it?"

"Send it as soon as you can. Don't forget to count to a hundred." Kimble walked into the deeper shadow under the bridge. When the bank rose and he was on the relatively smooth dried mud, he sprinted up. The moon was well clear of the horizon now and the road was a bright ribbon after the darkness under the bridge. He ignored it and took to the brush on the north side of the road.

A few minutes later he watched as Hodges climbed the bank and began trudging back to the barracks.

There was more traffic over the next hour, including several Rangers returning from town, but he didn't see Bickle among them.

Finally Kimble gave up. He went north along the riverbank and, well outside of town, waded across to reach the Zen Center and climbed up the steep path to his campsite.

messages

Thayet picked up the apples in town and also took a message to the Qwest Heliograph office the next day. It read:

> TERRITORIAL MEDICAL CLAIMS ADMIN
> OFFICE NUEVO SANTA FE STOP LEFT
> TOWN WITHOUT RESOLVING TREAT-
> MENT CLAIM 322355 STOP THREE TWO
> TWO THREE FIVE FIVE STOP PLEASE
> INFORM OUTCOME PECOSITO HELIO
> WILL CALL STOP DU OHARA

The message was converted into Morse blinks of reflected sunshine and passed from station to station before being translated back to paper in the territorial capital. The claims clerk who took delivery of the message pulled the folder for claim 322355 to see what was what. It was empty except for a scrawled note: "This claim on Director's desk. Route all correspondence to the Director."

When the heliograph arrived on that worthy's desk, she waited until the clerk had left, sealed it in an envelope and had her secretary run it across the street to a Sergeant Ruiz at the Territorial Rangers Headquarters Building.

Sergeant Ruiz raised his voice, as sergeants are prone to do, and the word "Orderly!" echoed down the hall. By the time the private on duty had arrived from the ready room, Sergeant Ruiz had written a name on the envelope. He handed it to the orderly and said, "Double-time, Major Bentham, Department 17."

Major Bentham was sitting in the analysts' bullpen, talking over border issues with the two men who ran the Mexican desk, when the note came to him.

"Oh, crap. Excuse me, gentlemen. I've got a problem over on the Pecos." He stepped away and stopped three desks down at the Eastern New Mexico desk. "Who the hell is the local Intel at the Sixteenth Barracks?"

The woman behind the desk, Captain Spitzer, frowned. "Oh, no. What has Hodges done now? I just got a Delta Uniform from your boy, LF, through him."

Bentham dropped the heliogram to Medical Claims on her desk. "Me, too."

Captain Spitzer looked at the message. "I'm unfamiliar with this code."

"Right. It's a last resort. You wouldn't see it unless

there was something wrong with normal channels. The only thing it really means is 'communicate directly via will-call messages into the Pecosito heliograph office.'" Bentham stabbed a forefinger at the signature, DU OHARA. "O'Hara is one of the code designations for LF, and the initials of the signatory are for any code groups—there's the Delta Uniform again."

"I guess Little Friend means it. It wasn't just Hodges screwing up . . . again."

"Didn't we get rid of Hodges? I thought we were going to shove him off onto supply."

Captain Spitzer shook her head. "You couldn't, remember? The governor? That little chat? Hodges' grandmother?"

Bentham covered his eyes with one hand and sighed heavily. "I'm supposed to be the one with the good memory."

Spitzer said, "Well, I'd want to put that out of my head, too."

"So why did we put Hodges in Pecosito?"

"Until the gun smuggling thing came up it was the quietest post in the entire territory. The bugs start to fade out there except for some isolated industrial infestations. I mean, the worst thing about the area is the religious intolerance."

"Well, he's screwed this up, apparently. Do we have anyone local, outside of the Rangers?"

"Not covert, no. That's why we wanted Little Friend. And Lujan before him."

"Okay. Please tell me we've got someone above Hodges

we can trust? And I don't mean just with the right security rating. I mean someone with his head on straight."

She pulled a file from the shelf behind her and flipped it open. "Well," she said, "the CO is Colonel Q."

"What? Quincy Anson? I thought he was still over at the academy."

"No. Reassigned three months ago. The brass outside decided they could do the training more efficiently with modern technology and he, uh, declined to live outside."

"I hadn't heard that."

She shrugged. "And you didn't hear it from me. They clamped a lid on it."

Major Bentham stared at her. "Why?"

"Don't know. Don't care. Until they start producing crappy Rangers, that is. They're still giving territorial residents preference in the recruiting process so at least they haven't screwed things up too far."

He shook his head. "But it does mean that Colonel Q is in the right place. *Muy bien.* Set up a secure call, won't you?"

"THEY said it was the need for modern educational methods—virtual sims, e-books—but I had it from my sources: Too many of the currently serving officers were my students. I think they even threw around that old Soviet phrase, 'cult of personality.' "

Bugs love electromagnetic radiation, but there are work-arounds. To get to the headquarters communication bunker, Bentham started in the basement and climbed down a ladder, then walked through a winding concrete-stabilized tunnel to a deep pocket in the earth, well underground. The equipment was powered by batteries and these were routinely charged by privates peddling on flywheel generators, all down here with tons of dirt between the EMF and any possible passing bugs. The signals left the buried room as packets of light, in glass bundles, fiber optics running straight up to the roof and then up a Dacron rope to a tethered communications balloon over fifteen thousand feet above sea level. There, solar-charged batteries powered a satellite uplink set, passing signals in both directions.

Bugs don't like thin air. Not because they breathe, but because they have wings. Smallish wings. And when the air gets too thin, the bugs don't rise any higher. It's why you can fly aircraft over the territory—just don't dip below ten-thousand feet. To maintain a margin of error, the legal limit is fifteen thousand.

There are balloons tethered over all significant territorial government installations, including most Ranger barracks.

Bentham took a breath of stale air and shuddered. Ranger communication officers really need to be comfortable in closed spaces.

"Well, I hate to say it, Colonel, but I'm glad you're available. May not be as good for the academy but it's sure good for me."

"Tell me what this Delta Uniform is. You've mentioned it three times and I still don't know what it means."

"Director unreliable. It refers to the field director— the person directing the operations of a covert field agent. In this case it means Hodges."

"I thought Hodges passed you that message."

"Yes. There are certain codes reserved for field agents so they can communicate things through their directors without the director knowing what it means. But Hodges did send it, so I suspect incompetence, not malfeasance."

"Well, I'll be honest with you. When I reviewed the staff files after taking over here, I was *not* impressed with Hodges' previous evaluations. I mean, seriously, why is he still doing secure work?"

Bentham cleared his throat. "I tried to transfer him into supply, but there were complications."

"Supply didn't want him?" Supply was chronically understaffed. Moving supplies with metal-free technology is not easy work. The common wisdom was that they would take *anyone.*

"His grandmother is chair of the Governor's Citizen Advisory Council. I got a visit from the man. He even put on the uniform."

"Oh, Christ," said Colonel Anson. "I thought he only wore that for academy graduations."

The governor was titular commander-in-chief of the Territorial Rangers, but everyone—the officer corps, the territorial administration, and even the governor's own staff—tried to keep him as far away as possible from the working Rangers.

"I don't know the basis of LF's Delta Uniform, so I can't speculate, but I really need to know what's going on."

Colonel Anson cleared his throat. "I suppose I can get him in here so you can talk directly, but not exactly secretly."

"No. It's asking a lot, but I'd like you to take over as his director in the field. At least until we know why he doesn't trust Hodges. You'd have to meet covertly, away from your installation."

"Humph. Secret handshakes and recognition codes? Don't you think I'm a little old for that?"

Bentham laughed. "Identity won't be a problem. You know the boy."

"I do?"

"LF is Kimble Monroe."

"Kim? The kid you lent us for the unarmed combat evaluations?"

"Right."

"Oh, very good. There were some punctured egos *that* day. I had to stop watching. I was going to bust a gut trying not to laugh at the poor bastards."

"So you remember what he looks like?"

"Pretty much. As of two years ago, anyway."

"No major changes. Maybe an inch or two of growth, but, if anything, thinner."

"Right."

"Is he still as, uh, proficient?"

"He lives in the dojo when he isn't on assignment, but

it's his judgment I value. And I try not to use him that often."

"Too young?"

"Too valuable. I don't want him overexposed."

"Well, put me in the loop, Jeremy. I'll do what I can."

A night at the theater

Kimble spent the afternoon weeding the Zen Center's bean field. It was oddly relaxing and gave him a chance to catch up with Thayet, who was helping, sort of, in that she was doing more talking than weeding. That was all right—Kimble pulled enough weeds for three.

She had been achieving merit, she told him, by sitting with the hospice residents, fetching water, and singing softly to a woman who wanted the same song sung over and over and over.

"And I learned a joke involving broccoli and a word I'm not supposed to say."

He took supper with the monks, watered Mrs. Perdicaris at the river, then led her in a scramble up the cut to his campsite while there was still light. He put her on a long tether on good grass and set out his bedroll in a hollow of the wash.

He was lying on his back watching the stars come out when Mrs. P made a snorting sound and turned abruptly. Kimble sat up and listened. He didn't hear anything at first, but after a bit he heard the horses—two of them, he thought—approaching from the west.

He crouched and stood slowly until his head was over the edge of the wash. The sun had set, but the western horizon was still light and he saw the riders silhouetted against it. They were headed for the edge of the bluff above the Zen Center.

They dismounted well back from the edge and, from the sound, tied their reins to a scrub mesquite, then walked off toward the edge.

Kimble heard Mrs. P whuff deep in her chest, getting ready to talk to the horses, and he clucked his tongue softly, to get her attention, then rolled up over the edge and went to her head, automatically checking his pants for sugar, but he wasn't wearing his pants, just boxers. He unhooked her from the tether and rubbed her poll vigorously.

"Lee, where did you leave those rocks?"

They were whispering but the voices easily carried across the grass.

"Hell, they were right there. Remember, you put them straight back from that notch in the cliff top."

There was the scratch of a match being lit. "You can see where they were. Someone moved 'em."

"Shit. Well, there's some back by the road, unless you want to climb halfway down the cliff."

"No. They'd hear that. Deacon Dave said not to be seen."

"Why don't we just throw the bag of shit?"

"'Cause it might not break the glass. You know? It doesn't do much good if it just splatters all over the top. They can just rinse it off."

Kimble had heard enough. He jumped on Mrs. P's back and, steering with leg aids alone, walked her over toward their horses. They didn't hear the mule at first, but as she neared the horses they whinnied and the two men heard.

"What's that?"

"Something's at the horses!"

Kimble leaned across and pulled the reins off the bush. He kicked heels to Mrs. P's side and took off at a gallop, leading the horses back to the road.

He could hear shouting over the pounding hooves but couldn't quite make out what they were saying. At the county road, he headed south, toward town. He dropped back to a trot. He could hear the men behind, still running. He smiled. When he got to the Socorro road and started to bear left toward town, the horses tugged on his reins and tried to stay on the county road.

"Huh," he said. They'd long ago outdistanced the men on foot. "Whoa. Hold up there." He dismounted and, lighting a match, he examined the horses and their markings until he was sure he'd recognize them in the future. Then he removed their bits and bridles and hung them safely on the saddle horns.

"Get!" he said, slapping them lightly on their butts.

They didn't need to be told twice. As before, they moved off across the main road, continuing south along the county road. They were picking up speed, like "horses headed for the barn," so Kimble jumped back on Mrs. P and followed them.

They turned through a wooden gate arch a few hundred yards down the road. The sign said, "Robinson Ranch" and showed their brand, a Bar-R, capital R with a line underneath.

Kimble turned Mrs. P around and went back to the crossroads, where he found a stand of trash elms to hide in. The moon was coming up and casting long thin shadows across the ground when two men came limping up the road. Even with the moon up, it was hard to see their faces, but Kimble remembered their voices.

"I'll kill the sonofabitch if it's the last thing I do."

"Yeah. You've said that. Which sonofabitch is that?"

"Well, it's gotta be one of the heathens at the center, right?"

"You've said that, too. What if it's not? What if it's the Metal Man?"

"Shut up."

"Why? Don't you believe in the Metal Man?"

"DON'T SAY HIS NAME!"

"Huh?"

"Don't say his name. Especially at night! You know, just shut up, period."

Like their horses, the two men walked across the Socorro road and went in the direction of the Bar-R Ranch.

Kimble waited another few minutes and then, when

he could hear them no more, turned Mrs. P around and went back to bed.

THE next morning, two days after his under-the-bridge meeting with Hodges, Kimble rode Mrs. Perdicaris west from the Zen Center, and, using the county roads to swing wide, entered Pecosito from the west about mid-morning, when the traffic was heaviest.

Even if he didn't know where the heliograph office was, he couldn't have missed it. The five-story tower was the tallest structure in town. He left Mrs. P in the alleyway behind the heliograph office and stepped in.

There were three clerks working the counter and a few people waiting in line. The delivery boys sat on benches in a small room off to the side, though two of their number turned a crank, powering the vertical conveyor with hanging boxes that entered the ceiling on one side of the room, ran across two large pulley wheels, and rose back through the ceiling, carrying messages to and from the top of the tower where the Morse operators worked.

"Will-call for O'Hara," Kimble said.

The clerk looked at a series of cubby holes with message slips and said, "Sorry. Don't have anything. . . ."

"Here it is—DU O'Hara?" said the clerk at the back of the room emptying the boxes on the conveyor. "Just came down."

He passed the slip forward. "Right. Long one. That must've cost a pretty penny." He entered the message number in his register. "Sign right *there*, please."

Kimble scrawled *O'Hara* on the line. He took a quick

glance at the message and nodded. It was ostensibly about a series of medical procedures and their cost, the portion covered by the TMS, and the copayments.

Code. He folded it away and put it in an inner pocket. "Thanks." He stepped out the door into the street and turned sharply to the right.

Steve Bickle was riding down the street and it was clear from the way he straightened in the saddle and turned his head that he'd seen Kimble.

Amateurs.

Kimble passed the alley entrance where Mrs. P waited, walked briskly to the corner and, once he turned it, sprinted to where a gap between two stores led back to the alley. There was a chest-high wall but he was over it and gone before Bickle reached the corner.

He mounted Mrs. P and, back beside the helio office, looked out the alley entrance. Bickle had gone on around the corner. He turned Mrs. P in the opposite direction and trotted away, turning off the main road as soon as he could. He twisted through the smaller residential roads until he was back by the main irrigation ditch where it flowed back into the Pecos south of town.

Here, under a willow on riverbank, he took Mrs. P's hackamore off, pulled a worn, thin leather-bound edition of *Departmental Ditties* from his saddlebag and, while the mule cropped weeds, decoded the heliogram.

Well, he thought, surprised. *Colonel Q.*

KIMBLE returned to town after dark, wearing his good clothes, dark suit, and a dark red shirt with a mandarin collar, and low boots. He wore his hair slicked down and large, dark-framed glasses with slightly tinted lens. By the time he got to town he was wearing a blister on his left heel.

Damn boots.

The suit was good in the shadows, but when he hit the oil-lamp-lit main road, the beggars came out. "Young sir, could you spare a bit for food. My children are hungry, my wife needs a doctor." Kimble had passed by many of these people during the day, and they'd assessed his patched clothing and worn moccasins and let him walk on. But now they blocked his way and tugged at his sleeves.

His money was in a hidden pocket in his jacket, so he wasn't worried much, but as he neared the theater district, he felt a hand dip into his side jacket pocket and he took the wrist and turned quickly away, sinking. The man came stumbling around and Kimble turned again, taking the man's fingers back over his own forearm hard. The man tumbled over in an awkward flop and Kimble swiveled again, forcing the man face down, his knee locking the arm.

The beggars around him backed away. Kimble took a good look at the man's face and laughed. It was Pierce, his would-be hijacker from back on the Puerco. He tried to struggle and Kimble leaned into the pin.

"You'll break it!"

"No," Kimble said quietly. "First the shoulder socket will tear. You won't be able to use the arm without surgery and serious rehab. Not for feeding yourself, picking your nose, and definitely not picking any pockets. I thought you learned your lesson back on the Puerco, Pierce."

There was a stirring up the street and Kimble saw the beggars fading away as a city deputy pushed through a forming crowd. Kimble dropped the arm and stooped suddenly, lifting Pierce to his feet.

The deputy pulled a billy club from a loop on his belt. "What's going on here?"

Pierce's eyes widened as he saw the deputy and he glanced sideways at Kimble, then at the street, looking for a way out.

Without taking his hand off Pierce's arm, Kimble started brushing the dust off Pierce's shirt. "You all right there, friend?" He turned toward the deputy as if just seeing him. "I'm afraid I wasn't looking where I was going and I bumped this poor man clean off his feet."

The deputy raised his eyebrows. "You sure? This man's a thief. Had him up before the magistrate just yesterday for suspicion. It could've been a setup, a distraction for one of his pals."

Kimble made a show of patting his pockets. "Nothing missing. Besides, I came up behind him and accidentally tangled his feet. Not like *he* targeted *me*." Kimble leaned forward and sniffed. "Doesn't smell like he's been drinking." Though Pierce could sure use a bath. "Really, Officer, just me being clumsy." He let go of Pierce's arm. "Isn't that right, friend?"

"I guess," said Pierce. "I mean, I was walking across the road and the next thing I know I'm all sprawled in the dirt. He helped me up."

The deputy laughed and said to the pickpocket, "Maybe you should check *your* pockets." He stepped back and said louder, "Nothing to see here. Get along with you." He was staring at the more ragged beggars as he spoke and tapping the billy club meaningfully against the palm of his hand.

Kimble let go of Pierce's arm. "You're sure you're okay, there?"

"I'm, uh, fine." Pierce was staring at him with a perplexed expression on his face. "See you later?"

He still *doesn't recognize me.* It was the suit and glasses.

Kimble gave him a big smile and said, "You can be sure of it."

HE bought a ticket to the last showing of *Blood and Laughter:* "Episode 56." There were plays and shows running he would have rather watched, but he wasn't planning to *watch* the show. As soon as the houselights were shaded and the stage lights came up, he left his aisle seat before the audience's eyes adjusted to the dark. He slipped up the stairway to the balcony and entered the third private box without knocking.

It was a four-seat box. Colonel Q and a hooded person were sitting in the front two seats. The back two were empty. The person in the hood jerked when the door opened but Kimble heard the colonel say, "Eyes front. You're watching the show."

Kimble dropped to the floor and crawled forward, sitting with his back to the solid balcony balustrade, facing Colonel Q. The man in the hood was Hodges.

Christ!

Before he said anything, the colonel said quietly, "Sorry, Hodges is a fuckup, but he knows more about this situation than I do. I can give you a précis, but if you have questions, I thought it better if you got the answers directly."

Kimble sat still. "Do you think you were followed?"

"No. We left the fort in my wife's buggy. Hodges wore her hooded cape. I stationed my aide-de-camp in town and we looped a couple of blocks. He signaled all clear the second and third time around. Also, I'm not an idiot."

Kimble grinned. "No, sir, you're not." He left unsaid who he thought *was*.

"Our first hint of the problem," the colonel said, "was an inquiry from a rancher in Texas, searching for his missing son. Roberto Mendez, the son, was headed for Pecosito with three wagons of territory-safe water-filtration units. It was his own venture. He'd borrowed the money from his parents. His drivers were school-mates, fresh out of high school. They were going to leverage the investment for a year to pay for college."

"Were all the boys missing?"

The colonel gestured at Hodges, who answered, "Yes. They hadn't been heard from for three weeks when the family started asking. We have a record of them going through access control at Andrews, and they were remembered at two different water holes. But then nothing." He was speaking quietly, but he was hunched slightly and his eyes darted sideways to the colonel as he talked.

"Satellite archives?"

"They looked, but there's too many wagons in the territory. And three is a pretty common number. It was a dry spell, too, but our patrol didn't find any sign of them leaving the road. Those filters don't weigh much, but they piled them high."

"Unless the tracks were hidden," Kimble added.

The colonel spoke. "That's one possibility. The real problem is that while the boys weren't heard from, some of those water filters did show up—at two different stores *here* in town."

"Other peddlers *do* carry water filters."

The colonel said simply, "Serial numbers."

"Ah. And what do the vendors say?"

The colonel gestured to Hodges again, who said, "They bought them from an itinerant peddler and he is long gone."

"Fell off the back of a truck, no doubt. You believe them?"

"Hard to say. They're established vendors. Upstanding citizens and all."

"Still no sign of the boys, though?"

"None. We considered they were just avoiding paying back the money, using this to get away from home, but one of them was engaged to be married. They were top of their class—not exactly the kind of boys you'd expect to rip off the parents who backed them."

"How about the wagons—anything special about them?"

The colonel glanced at Hodges again.

"Yes and no," Hodges said. "They were boat-tight Conestogas—a little fancy, but common enough around here—but the father said the sides of the wagons had been marked with his ranch's brand, both sides, right behind the driver's box. Melted in good, then filled with contrasting paint."

"What brand?"

"Rocking sunrise."

"I'm not picturing it. Semicircle below, the rocker, right?"

"Yes. Joined by smaller half-circle above with three rays at ten, twelve, and two o'clock."

Obviously you couldn't use a metal branding iron in the territory, but the marks were still used, whether applied with a ceramic "iron" or indelible dye writ large and renewed annually. Wire fencing was another casualty of the infestation, so open range grazing was common. Some form of tagging was necessary.

"You've looked, obviously."

"Yes. We have a territorial alert out."

"And for the boys, of course," added the colonel.

"Of course."

"It's not just that one time, though, right?"

"Right. There've been three others," said Hodges.

The colonel added, "That we know about."

Hodges flinched. "Yes, sir." He took a deep breath. "A party that was headed for the capital left from Midland-Odessa last month. We tracked them on the same route that Mendez took and further, to one more asequia where the keeper remembered them. But then nothing. Two of the women and one of the men were doctors going for a tour with the TMS. One of them was an internist who was bringing experimental diagnostic packs—metal-free biotech for blood work. The Medical Service launched that inquiry. We haven't seen any of the medical gear re-sold, but a coat ended up at a local flea market."

"Identified how?"

"A laundry mark. You only saw the writing if you pulled the hood out of its pocket."

"How many people?"

"Six adults."

"Vehicles?"

"Three horse-drawn FlyWeight buggies and a U-Haul wagon and team. No—no sign of them."

"Were those the 'three' you were talking about?"

The colonel answered. "I wish. I meant three other *incidents*. The other two were both single peddlers hitting their suppliers at access control and then heading back out. We haven't seen any of their stuff show up, but they disappeared in roughly the same area. The most recent one happened *after* Lujan was airlifted out."

"Okay. Let's talk about Lujan."

"Lujan was following the merchandise. He was looking at the two merchants who had the water filters and the flea market vendor who was selling the coat. He'd been here a week and really had nothing to report, yet, but he said he'd been developing sources."

"Have you heard his status?"

"He's fine. They had to remove his spleen and he'll have to be careful about infections. No more unpasteurized milk and all that. Your boss says he really hadn't made any progress with the merchants."

"And the sources?"

"Some street vendors and beggars. Sort of a Baker Street Irregulars, I gather," the colonel said.

Hodges looked puzzled at the reference, and Kimble said, "People he could use for low-level surveillance, messages, etc." It took a conscious effort not to scream *Sherlock Holmes, you illiterate idiot.* "Where was he shot? And I don't mean the spleen."

The colonel gestured to Hodges, who answered, "We were supposed to meet south of the barracks at our regular rendezvous. There's a small seep coming out of a rocky outcropping overlooking the river valley where the farm road bends to the east. When I got there, Lujan's horse was cropping grass, but there was fresh blood on the saddle and down the side. I'm not much of a tracker but the blood trail was clear. He was only a hundred yards away. I got him back to the barracks. The unit medic put him on IV fluids, glued him shut, and prepped him for airlift."

Badly injured casualties were sky-hooked off the ground in padded capsules connected to balloon-lifted lines stretching above the bugosphere. Special aircraft hooked them and reeled them in, getting them to the outside trauma centers within an hour of pickup.

If you were important enough. Lujan was an undercover Ranger.

Ordinary people would've had to take their chances with a local surgeon using glass scalpels and composite needles. No X-rays. No CAT scans. Minimal lab work.

Respiration and heartbeat monitored the old-fashioned way. That is, if they were anywhere near a local doctor.

"Did Lujan give Control any names?"

"Yes, but considering he was shot sometime after that, shouldn't they be avoided?"

The colonel and Kimble both stared at Hodges, whose eyes widened. "You think *I* blew his cover."

"Why not? You blew mine." But then Kimble shook his head. "I don't know that. It was probably the airlift that connected them to you in the first place. My money is on the merchants. Not that they shot him but that they probably talked to whoever supplied them with the filters. But rest assured, I'm not interested in being a target. Still, I want those names and anything else he had." Kimble stopped talking as the dialog from the stage stopped for a scene change. When the crowd began laughing a few minutes into the next scene, he asked, "Tell me why it wasn't a Ranger that shot Lujan."

Colonel Anson handled this one. "Didn't say it wasn't a Ranger. What we know is that it wasn't Ranger-issued ammo."

"But it was a gyro?"

"Oh, yeah. Same kind of ammo. But they're tagged, every one, and this serial number came out of a batch supposedly used at the factory test range."

"Where's that?"

"Geneseo, Illinois. Nowhere near the territory, if that's what you were wondering. The feds are checking that end."

"And the rifle?"

"That part's trickier. The rifles are really just graphite tubes with stocks and sights. The high-tech side is the self-stabilizing rockets. There's no rifling to mark the projectile. The friction tag is pulled by the firing mechanism and stays with the rifle and, even if we recovered it, the mark left by the mechanism is generic."

"Is this the only time you've detected unauthorized gyros in the territory?"

"So far. The bomb sniffers at access control have the rocket fuel's chemical fingerprint. There have been smuggling attempts before, and accidental carries—Rangers on leave with ammo in a uniform pocket—but this is the only one we know about." Colonel Anson sighed. "I'm wondering what we'll find, though, if we locate the missing parties."

The episode below ended to applause. One of the ingénues came out and sang a song for the closing act, accompanied by a nylon-strung guitar and a gut bass.

"Names from Lujan?"

Hodges gave Kimble a sheet of paper.

"Right. Let's limit further communication to message drops for now. There's a loose brick at knee level to the right of this theater's stage door. There's a little hollow behind it and I plugged the space below with mud to keep any messages from falling down into the wall. The brick has a spot of dried paint on the face at one end. If the spot is closer to the stage door, there's a message. If away—nothing. You leave a message, put the brick back in with the spot toward the door. You remove a message, leave it away. If I leave a message there will also be a piece of grass stuck in the cracks. That way you won't be checking your own messages. Got it?"

The colonel answered, "Sure. Toward the door and a piece of grass, 'Ding—we've got mail!' Toward the door and no grass—it's for you."

"Hodges is being watched, so he stays away. Better if you can get someone in mufti to carry the messages, but be sure of them, okay? Rangers on the whole aren't used to hiding things from normal citizens. They're not the *enemy* after all. They drink with them, they buy from them, and they sure as hell try to sleep with them, so pick someone who can keep his mouth shut." Kimble stopped talking abruptly and blushed. "Sorry, sir. Forgot who I was talking to."

The colonel laughed softly.

Kimble continued. "There are no windows in the alley and you can get out at either end. Anything else? I want to leave in the first rush."

Hodges said, "What code? For the messages?"

Reluctantly Kimble said, "Book code. You'll find a sealed envelope on your codes shelf—it's labeled L F underscore D D. Go ahead and open it."

Hodges repeated it. "Authorization?"

"All the world." Kimble repeated it slowly, making sure that Hodges was getting it. Colonel Quincy nodded, as well, so Kimble thought it would be all right.

He touched his palms together to the colonel, then crept out of the box and sat on the stairs. When the first wave started out of the seats below, he merged into the crowd, walking as if he belonged to a family group. He left them two blocks later, turning off into one of the unlit residential streets.

Five minutes later he was outside of town.

stolen wagons and bible verses

Kimble found Pierce in the shantytown south of Pecosito, sleeping under a length of plastic roofing material supported by two sticks and a cinder block. His mattress was scraps of cardboard and his blanket was knotted together burlap sacking. A spare shirt was draped over his face to keep the mosquitoes away.

"Wake up, Sleeping Beauty. I'll buy you breakfast."

Pierce thrashed out, startled, and knocked out one of the supports of his lean-to, dropping the roof onto him.

"It's not the first time," he said later. He'd washed his head and torso in the river, put on his cleanest shirt, and now they were walking to town.

"That your lean-to fell over?"

"Two days ago it was the deputies and vigilantes from town, riding through like the Cossacks riding through Anatevka. Bastards. I mean, it's out of city limits. They have no right."

"What did you do outside, Pierce?"

Pierce peered at him sideways. "This and that."

"White collar?"

Pierce drew himself up. "If you must know, I was a financial advisor."

"Ah."

"What do you mean, 'Ah'?"

"Just that you didn't deal with the law much. Other than the one time, of course."

Pierce's eyes looked haunted. "What do you mean?"

Kimble shrugged. "You're not in the territory for your *health*."

Pierce shook his head angrily.

"I could talk to the Rangers about it," Kimble said. "I still have your fingerprints on that cup you used." This was a gross prevarication. He'd washed it several times since their encounter. "I'm thinkin' . . . embezzlement."

"*Shut up!*" Pierce stared around. They were on the river road and the only other person in sight was a man on horseback several hundred yards away.

"Hit a nerve, did I? Didn't think it was anything violent."

"What do you want, dammit!"

"Got a job for you. Easy work. Not illegal. Give you a chance to buy some clean clothes, maybe get a job and stop sleeping in the dirt."

Pierce calmed down. Kimble heard his stomach rumble.

"Why don't we discuss it over *breakfast?*"

PIERCE had been in Pecosito only a little longer than Kimble, having snagged a ride with a ranch family traveling south to the Soccoro area, then freighters traveling east through Pecosito on their way to the Clovis territorial access point. He'd spent that brief time, though, among the kind of people that Kimble was looking for.

Pierce already knew two of the people on the list. Kimble wrote down the names of the others and what particulars Lujan had recorded. "Begs at the theaters evenings" or "turns tricks behind the Dog and Trumpet" or, in one case, "Catholic Aid."

"Just identify as many as you can. Try not to be obvious about it, okay? If anyone asks, say you're collecting hard luck stories for an article." He caught Pierce's eye. "Don't talk about me. You do, I'll turn you in to the Rangers."

"You don't have anything on me!"

"Assault with a deadly weapon, remember? What happened to that crossbow, by the way?"

Pierce glared at him for a moment before saying, "I traded it for a meal."

Kimble raised his eyebrows. "Really? Wouldn't it have been more cost effective to keep it and hunt?"

"Look, it's pathetic, I know it, but you don't have to rub it in. I lost all the quarrels and I never hit a single animal. And I broke the string."

Kimble raised his eyebrows. "And I shall call you . . . animal lover. Have you considered a career in middle management?"

"He had me follow Deacon Rappaport."

Alvarez was a part-time day laborer, mostly garden work and pumping the used sludge and slurry out of people's biogas tanks. He was fastidiously clean. Pierce had brought Kimble to Alvarez behind the Pecos Hotel's stables, introduced him, and then vanished, with cash, toward the nearest pub.

Kimble raised his eyebrows. "Deacon? Which church?"

"New Paradise. He runs the Public Action Committee."

"What does the Public Action Committee do?"

"They're assholes."

Kimble raised his eyebrows.

"They're into 'civic improvement.' That is, they rip through the shantytown every week or so. They beat up drunks. They chase migrant workers out of town 'cause they prefer to steer any daywork toward their newest members. 'Believe and thou shall prosper.'"

"Rappaport's first name wouldn't be David, would it?"

Alvarez looked surprised. "*Verdad*. You know him?"

Kimble shook his head. The men he'd interrupted at night above the Zen Center had mentioned a Deacon Dave.

"So, did you follow him around town?"

"No. I was doing some work for the widow who lives

next to the Rappaport place. The peddler wanted me to follow the Deacon if he left on horseback. I only did it the once. They almost caught me."

"They?"

"It was some of his 'pack.' That's what they called themselves—Public Action Committee, P.A.C. It was the top guys: Steve Bickle, the Ronson brothers, and Pudge Moorecock. They went out with draft horses, harnessed for wagon work, though they didn't take a wagon with them."

The Ronson brothers could be the ranchers who'd disputed their father's will over the Zen Center. The last name Alvarez mentioned also tickled a memory. "What does Moorecock do?"

"He's got the Pecosito Hardware and Feed."

That was it! One of the stores selling the stolen water filters.

"If I'd known how far they were going, I don't know that I would've done it. They went all the way out to the Pits."

"What are the Pits?"

"Where the old PeCo Refinery is. They had a lot of underground tanks and pipes, so the bugs ate down. Lotsa bugs. Strange animals, too. It's bad out there 'cause you never know when you're standing on solid ground or just thin crust over a deep hole. When I saw them turn off the main road, I holed up in a gulley and waited.

"Two hours later they drove back through and this time they *had* a wagon. I don't know what they did with it, 'cause my horse neighed as they went by and I had to run for it. Luckily it was near dark, by then, and I lost them."

"What did the peddler say when you told him?"

"I didn't. Never saw him after that. Kept expecting him to show up. He still owes me half—that guy said you'd make good."

"So this was three weeks ago?"

Alvarez thought about it. "Uh, yeah. Three weeks tomorrow."

Lujan had never shown up because he'd been shot the same day and sky-hooked out of the territory the following morning.

"I'll stand good for the peddler."

In general, it was a bad thing to travel at night in the territory. Not only did the roads leave a lot to be desired, but it was hard to tell when a random bug might end up in your path. And the other bugs needed no light to swarm on a crushed comrade.

But at least bugs were not acting with malice. Their motives, if you wanted to call them that, were straightforward: defense first, electromagnetic radiation second, eating metals third, absorb sunlight last.

Men's motives are rarely so obvious, even to themselves, but Kimble knew enough, now, to prefer the bugs.

He spent the afternoon encoding a message for Major Bentham. In the dusk he slipped into town and left it in the cavity in the theater wall. Before it was full dark, he was riding Mrs. Perdicaris southeast on the main road toward Andrews, Texas.

He was particularly interested in Alvarez's information about the Pits after finding out it was in this direction. All of the disappearances had happened on the route from Andrews.

The moon came up after eleven and he pushed Mrs. P up to a gentle canter, hoping that if he did crush a bug, he'd gallop past the site before the worst of the swarm got there.

He found the turnoff about three in the morning, two thin wheel ruts paralleling the old asphalt turnoff, but he wasn't willing to go any farther toward a known bug infestation without full daylight. He found a clump of cottonwoods in a dry gully and slept. When a noise in the grass awoke him, the stars were fading and the eastern sky was light. He lay still, listening. Without lifting his head he could see Mrs. P standing over by one of the cottonwoods, dozing. The noise had come from the tall prairie grass, to the south, away from the road. He heard it again: steps, not human. *Cattle?*

He opened his bedroll and pulled his moccasins on. He'd left his *jyo* lying beside him. He took it with him to the edge of the cottonwoods.

A mule stood out in the grass, its head down as if it were grazing, but the head was still. *Asleep?* He blew through his lips, imitating a horse's snort, and the ears swiveled toward him.

He felt his stomach clench like it was full of ice. "You're kidding me!" He said it aloud, and the black mule lifted its head fully and looked at him without eyes.

"Not-dog and not-steer. Now a not-mule?"

Just like the previous creatures, the not-mule had darker patches of black where the eyes should be and its skin was oily black, but the hooves were the color of old bronze, right down to green corrosion streaks. Even more disturbing, to Kimble, the not-mule had two holes in its right ear. One in the middle and one at the edge.

Just like Mrs. Perdicaris.

Kimble stepped back several paces. He kept imagining the high-pitched shrilling of an incoming swarm. He rolled up his bedroll and lashed it to his pack. He whistled to Mrs. P. He heard hoofbeats but she didn't come and she wasn't where she'd been dozing. He slung his pack, lifted Mrs. P's saddle pad, and walked back to the edge of the cottonwoods.

Mrs. Perdicaris and the not-mule were trotting across the grass, turning back and forth. The not-mule was moving beside Mrs. P, matching her step for step. Kimble shook his head hard. It was like double vision, the not-mule a solid shadow of Mrs. P. At one point Mrs. Perdicaris pivoted, putting her rear hooves toward the not-mule, and kicked out. The not-mule would've been struck, if it hadn't duplicated the maneuver exactly. Mrs. P's hooves flashed over the not-mule's lowered head, which dropped as the not-mule also kicked out with both rear legs.

"Come *here* Mrs. Perdicaris!" He whistled as loudly as he could, for emphasis.

Mrs. P flicked her ears at Kimble and came trotting. As did the not-mule. The ozone smell he remembered from the not-dog and from the not-steer was stronger. Mrs. P stopped with her nose up against his stomach.

The not-mule stopped a yard off to the side, in the same posture. Kimble could've stretched his left arm out and touched it.

Mrs. P shoved him with her nose. He smiled nervously. "Okay, girl." He dug out a sugar cube and fed it to her, wondering if the not-mule would demand its share, but it just stood there, its head turned toward Kimble and Mrs. P, watching.

Kimble stepped around to Mrs. P's left side, away from the not-mule, took a deep breath, and saddled her, keeping his movements small and careful.

Is this what happened to the travelers? Was it bugs?

He fingered the bug scars on his right arm. He wanted to run screaming, but he was also fascinated. *Like a bird staring at a snake?* He put on Mrs. P's hackamore.

The not-mule stretched out its nose, touching briefly the stirrup strap of Mrs. P's saddle, then backed up. It took a few sideways steps and stopped where it could see Kimble adjusting the Velcro closure straps on the hackamore.

Slowly, smoothly, Kimble pulled himself up onto Mrs. P's back. The not-mule stretched its neck straight up in a posture that raised the hair on Kimble's neck. He nudged Mrs. P with his right knee and she turned away. He looked back at the not-mule, half expecting it to follow, but it stood there, its neck and head still raised unnaturally high, and watched him ride away.

THERE was a thin trickle of smoke rising up from a stand of cedars near the Pits. Someone was either having breakfast or keeping their coffee warm. The clump of trees was on a slight rise and overlooked the old road and the new trail. Just beyond, the gaping holes that were the Pits began, two of them straddling the new trail. The old road terminated in one of them. Kimble didn't see any other movement, but the rims of the pits glittered in the early sunlight—photovoltaic crystalline blue, copper, and aluminum silver.

He changed Mrs. P back to her halter and left her, loosely tied, down in a draw where a pool of brackish water was left over from the last rain. He didn't try to bypass the stand of cedars. It was the first thing he wanted to see.

It took him forty-five minutes to work his way close, staying low, crawling through the grass.

There were two guards, but they weren't terribly vigilant. One was reading a Bible and the other one was playing solitaire. A canvas tarp strung between two trees formed a shelter and, dead center beneath it, between two bedrolls, Kimble saw two gyro rifles, indistinguishable from those carried by the Territorial Rangers.

As Kimble watched, the Bible-reader got up, went to the edge of the cedars, and walked around the grove, staring out at the horizon. Kimble dropped his head flat and stayed still in the dry, brown grass. The guard passed thirty feet away but didn't see Kimble. When the guard completed the circuit, Kimble saw him go back to his Bible.

There were no mounts at the camp, no saddles or other tack visible, though Kimble could see where horses had been tied, churning up the dirt and dropping manure.

He wondered how often they were relieved. It was hard to tell from where he lay, but the manure looked old, dried out and breaking up.

He drank some water and waited. After another ten minutes the Bible-reader said something to the solitaire player and that man put his cards down and did a similar circuit of the trees. It made sense. You could see five miles back down the trail. If Kimble hadn't diverted to the draw, earlier, they would easily have seen him before he got near their post.

If he hadn't seen their fire. He wouldn't have seen that, if they'd used drier wood. He looked around. The grove was pretty bare of deadwood. *They've stripped it clean. They're burning green branches.* They'd occupied the grove for quite some time.

Kimble didn't have to ask himself what Major Bentham would want him to do now. Get out. Get out and ride for Colonel Quincy. But Kimble wanted to know what was in the Pits.

It's not like it was with Lujan, he thought. *The last report I sent will lead them straight here.* He waited for the next patrol circuit and, as soon as the Bible-reader had seated himself on his stump, Kimble crawled away from the trees and ran downhill, fast as he could go, heading for the Pits.

He tried counting seconds, taking a break at what he thought was eight minutes after the last patrol. He sat beside a low sagebrush, looking back at the cedars. After a bit, he saw one of the guards make the circuit. When he'd disappeared, Kimble ran on.

He had no choice but to follow the trail. Bugs were thick on the ground or the ground wasn't there. The trail edged close to one pit and he peered over, then backed quickly away. The edge he stood on seemed solid enough but it was deeply undercut. In fact, the pit opened like a sinkhole and the walls below were actually under the trail. In his brief glance, he'd seen indistinct shapes in the shadows below and an opening, he could swear, into the pit on the other side of the trail. He could tell from the tracks that they'd brought heavily laden wagons along the trail, but he still imagined the land dropping away in great chunks from beneath his feet.

He hurried on. The land sloped down, and the trail cut off to the left in a deepening rut. There were bugs, singletons, here and there. He wondered what the PAC did about them when they brought their wagons through. The trail ended at the bottom of another pit, not nearly as deep as the others. Looking at its shape, Kimble realized it was once a huge tank, a hundred feet across, completely below ground. The very bottom of the tank, about two feet, was still intact, but that was because it was full of dark, still water, reflecting the collapsed opening above. It seemed to have been steel-lined concrete. The bugs had eaten all the above-water metal, but the concrete around it, though cracked, was mostly intact.

They'd built a ramp of rock and dirt on into the bottom of the tank to roll the wagons past the drop.

He took a step forward and his eyes watered. He bent down at the edge. Rainbows sheened the surface of the water. The fumes were strong but not overwhelming. He held a bandanna over his mouth and waded out into it.

The missing wagons were all there. There were the two Conestoga freighters from the Texas boys, the FlyWeight buggies and U-Haul heavy hauler from the doctors' party, and the peddlers' wagons, all standing hub-deep in the water. There were others, too: several two-wheeled carts like Kimble's, some brightly painted with the colors typical of northern Chihuahua, a heavy dirt hauler with bottom dump doors, and something that looked like a gypsy caravan.

He checked the Conestogas first. They were empty. Burlap sacking was tied down over the sides of the driver boxes, but when Kimble untied a corner he saw the Rocking Sunrise brand that Hodges had described.

His head spun and he saw spots before his eyes. He staggered back to the opening and went a few steps up the slope, out of the fumes. His eyes cleared and he breathed deeply. Before going back into the tank, he hyperventilated and held his breath.

Some of the medical supplies were still in the U-Haul's covered bed, but it was the cases of gyro rifles and ammo that were in the dirt hauler that really got Kimble's attention.

His heart was pounding in his ears when he ran back out of the tank. After catching his breath, he went back up to the surface.

There was dust near the cedars when he cleared the rise. He looked around. There was a slight wind from the west, but it wasn't kicking up any dust elsewhere. *Horses, lotsa horses.* He squinted, watching the cedars. Two figures walked out and stood. One of them waved a greeting at some approaching host.

Not the Rangers, then.

He waited for the incoming riders to resolve themselves. Sixteen mounted men came over the far hill, then two more, ropes stretched between them to a horse with an empty saddle. No, it was a mule, he could tell by the ears. An uncooperative mule, who was alternately kicking and balking.

His stomach, already tense, felt like he'd swallowed a stone. They had Mrs. Perdicaris. They probably knew he was here. He considered running for the grass, but they were galloping closer, and they'd see him before he could clear the bug-infested area around the Pits.

He dropped back down the trail and ran, quickly but carefully, looking for bugs. The walls of the trail rose up and he couldn't see anyplace to go but forward.

He hyperventilated again and tried not to splash as he went back into the shallow water where the wagons sat. He didn't want ripples to betray him. A quarter of the way around the tank's edge, he saw a hole. It had been an outlet, perhaps, running through the ground, but the bugs had eaten the pipe and the ground above had collapsed. Still, water had run between the concrete shell and the earth and he could worm his way back behind the concrete.

It's going to collapse on you.

He kept going. He was remembering being whipped

in the stocks when he was caught by the Elders of the People of the Book and, in comparison, the possibility of a cave-in didn't worry him so much.

At first, the fumes were as bad as before, but he found that as he got farther behind the tank wall, there was cleaner air in his face. He was groping now, testing the footing below carefully before putting his weight on each section. While the possibility of a cave-in was worrying, the thought of stepping on a bug in this confined space was terrifying.

A splash of light shown ahead and above. He edged forward. There was a triangular hole, a hand's span wide, above. He found a foothold and shimmied up until he could look through it.

He was looking back into the tank nearer the ramp, perhaps ten feet above the water. The fumes weren't quite as bad as before. He saw the first men come down. They carried gyro rifles held at the ready. They spread across the opening, eight strong. They crouched, rifles still trained forward, and one of them turned his head and Kimble saw white hair and a familiar profile. It was Bickle, who'd been following him back in Pecosito. Bickle shouted back up the trail, "No sign of him, Deacon!"

More footsteps and then a heavier man, white-haired, came into view. He was wearing tan fatigues—not camo like the Rangers, but plain. There was a shoulder patch facing Kimble—it had a Christian cross with a lightning bolt superimposed over it. The man stepped back from the edge and said, "Safety your rifles. Any of you think what would happen if you fired a gyro in here?"

Kimble saw more than one of the men turn white.

"The bugs must've eaten through another stretch of pipeline or something. It was just water before." He took a handkerchief out and pressed it to his mouth while he took a couple of breaths, then dropped it to say, "Fix bayonets. I want every one of those wagons searched. Bickle, Moorecock—chem lights. Check under the wagons. Double-check the rifle crates—see if anyone has been messing with them. *Remember, rifle butts and bayonets.* Hell. Bickle, confirm those safeties."

"Yes, Deacon Rappaport."

Kimble watched them fix bayonets. The blades were composite with a triangular cross section. Kimble had handled one back at Ranger headquarters. Communications Sergeant Chinn kept one on his desk. "They're only really sharp at the end but if you were poked with one— well, a flat blade makes a wound that closes back up, slowing the bleeding. The hole these bad boys punch bleeds you out quick."

The men splashed into the water, moving in pairs out to the wagons.

Rappaport turned and yelled up the trail, "Bring that fellow down here, Ronson!"

A man, dressed in fatigues like Rappaport, came down the trail to the edge of the tank. He was pushing Pierce in front of him. Pierce's hands were bound behind his back.

Crap.

"So," Rappaport asked, "where is this super spy?"

Pierce looked around, caught a gust of the fumes from

the tank, and coughed. "How should I know? You found his mule, right? I told you he was probably coming out here. You didn't have to tie me up. We had a deal, remember? What about my reward?"

"*A man's life consisteth not in the abundance of the things which he possesseth,*" Rappaport said.

Ronson slapped Pierce on the back so hard he stumbled. "That's *Luke*, chapter twelve."

Rappaport nodded. "Patience. *The Lord is good unto them who wait for him, to the soul that seeketh him.* That's *Lamentations*."

They stood there until the men splashed back out of the tank. Two of them supported one of their number, half-dragging him out of the tank. Bickle reported, "Still no sign, Deacon. The fumes are fierce. Doubt he could stay in there. The rifles look all right—they're all there. Ditto for the ammo."

"Right. That means he's somewhere out there in the grass. Bickle, take your squad and sweep around the perimeter of the Pits on foot. Moorecock, mount your squad up and sweep further out."

"Bugs are thick in the grass, Deacon," Bickle said. "How close to the perimeter should we get?"

"*A faithful man shall abound with blessings,* son. You've got good light out there. Don't be timid and don't be stupid. If there's too many bugs to sweep, there's too many bugs for him, too." His expression hardened. "I find any of you shirking your duty, though, and you'll be envying Job his sores—got it?"

"Sir!"

"Moorecock, when you mount up, send one of the horse boys over the hill for the draft animals."

The men moved out, leaving just Ronson and Pierce with Rappaport.

Ronson said, "You've decided to move the rifles?"

"Yes. Whether we get the little sneak or not, we don't know who else he told. Our man at the barracks hasn't seen any unusual activity, but he'll give us plenty of warning if *they* mobilize. And we've been watching the heliograph office ever since Bickle saw him there, but a coded message could be sent by anyone. We'll need those rifles. *The harvest is plentiful but the workers are few, therefore ask the Lord of the harvest to send out workers to his harvest.* The men are promised—trained men, ex-military, ex-police. Righteous men whose faith is strong, who hunger for a land ruled by the Word."

"The promised land," said Ronson.

"Damn straight." Rappaport turned to Pierce. "Have you accepted Jesus into your life, son? Have you drunk the water that gives eternal life?"

"Amen!" said Pierce. The white was showing around his eyes. "I believe!"

"Good. Wouldn't want you ending up in the wrong place." He tilted his head up the trail.

Ronson took Pierce's arm. "With the others?"

"Yes."

Pierce went white. "Thou shall not kill!"

Ronson raised his eyebrows. "Shalt. Thou *shalt* not kill. Exodus chapter? . . ."

Pierce opened his mouth and shut it.

Rappaport said, "Come on, now, chapter twenty. And the verse?"

Pierce said, "It doesn't change it. Are you Christians or aren't you?"

"Verse thirteen," said Rappaport. "*The LORD is my strength and song, and he is become my salvation: he is my God, and I will prepare him an habitation; my father's God, and I will exalt him. The LORD is a man of war: the LORD is his name.*"

And Ronson turned him around, also quoting, "*To every thing there is a season, and a time to every purpose under the heaven: A time to be born, and a time to die; a time to plant, and a time to pluck up that which is planted; A time to kill . . .*"

Pierce began to struggle and Rappaport took his other arm and the two men started dragging Pierce up the path.

Kimble was desperate. It had taken him almost twenty minutes to worm back into the crevice. *If I'd taken one of the rifles I could shoot the bastards through this hole.* But he hadn't, and even if he had the rocket exhaust would probably ignite the damn petroleum fumes, anyway.

Which would destroy the gyro rifles and ammo before they could move them. It might *distract them from killing Pierce, too.* He felt for the waterproof matches in his pocket.

What's the worst that could happen?

He took half of the matches, perhaps a dozen, and bundled them together between his thumb and fingers, adjusting them until the heads were all together. He took three quick breaths, stuck his arm through the hole, and scraped the heads across the concrete. The flare of heat burned his fingers and he jerked his hand back, scattering the burning matches.

His hand was just inside the wall again when the matches reached the fumes below.

swimming in the dark

It was dark, but Kimble wasn't sure whether it was dark because he was asleep or it was dark around him. His ears were ringing and he felt like his nose was running. Sick? The last time he'd felt like this he'd had a temperature of a hundred and three. He touched his tongue to his upper lip. It wasn't mucus—blood.

He tried to sit up and couldn't. Memory returned suddenly, the flash and roar and shifting earth.

So, that's *the worst that could happen.* Well, no. He wasn't dead. Not yet, anyway.

There was a brick-sized piece of concrete lying across his cheek and dirt and gravel covered his ears. He lifted his right hand to clear his face, but he couldn't move it, which confused him more than anything. Then he realized he couldn't even feel his right hand. It was pitch dark but he felt a slight breeze on his cheek, and though the air was cleaner than where the wagons had been hidden, he could smell smoke and the celery smell of burnt hair. Though his ears were still ringing, he thought he heard running water.

He *could* move his left hand, so he pulled the rock off his face and shoved it to the side. He reached over to his right arm, expecting to find it ending in a jagged stump or something, but he ran into dirt and rock instead. His right arm was buried. He pulled, twisting his entire body, and the arm came free, but dirt and gravel showered down and he froze, afraid he'd triggered a cave-in.

Almost immediately the pins and needles of returning circulation let him know, in excruciating detail, that his right arm was intact, just asleep. He took a few more deep breaths. The fumes were definitely gone. He found one of his remaining matches and lit it.

He was at the bottom of a narrow crevice, somewhere below the tank. He could see a tilted section of the concrete tank shell almost twenty feet above him. His feet were covered in gravel and sand, but they moved freely when he tried. He saw water running at the far end of his little pocket, coming down from above, then the match reached his fingers and he dropped it.

He didn't light another match until he'd stood carefully and stretched, moving his hands over his head and body. Besides the bloody nose, a large swath of his hair in front had been burned short and there was a tear on the upper edge of his left ear that went clean into the cartilage. When his fingers touched it the pain was so intense he nearly fell down again. There were a few stinging scrapes on his left side and he had a bruise over his right hip that felt bigger than his hand, but the ear seemed the worst.

The water sounded like it was running harder now, and he wondered if it would fill his little pocket, drowning him, but it was still dry around him so the water had to be draining away as quickly as it was coming in. *Maybe I'm just hearing it better.*

He lit another match and moved carefully down to the wet end of the crevice. The water was not only running away, it was cutting through large sections of gravel and sand. A gaping hole went down at a forty-five-degree angle. What's more, when his match burnt out, he could see the rough outline of the hole and a shelf of rock where the water stopped descending and ran off to the left, horizontally. He looked directly at his hand but couldn't see anything, so the light was coming in from the side, down there.

Kimble lit another match and studied the crevice above. From what little he could see, it was closed in by the tank wall except for a network of cracks at the far end where the water ran down.

Down it is.

He dropped about eight feet, aiming for the flat shelf of rock, and sank to a crouch, absorbing the shock. He couldn't see above, but he imagined his jump disturbing the rock above, causing it to fall on him like a mallet onto a peg. He crabbed quickly downstream where the light was brighter, reflected onto the jagged rock above by the rippling water. The passage curved to the right and Kimble blinked his eyes rapidly, shielding the glare with an outstretched hand. There was sunlight ahead, and his eyes watered, unable to adjust quickly. It seemed an eternity before he could focus, but there was a rock surface in direct sunlight at the far end of the irregular passage. The reflected light was the source of the illumination he'd been following.

By the time he neared the opening he was also hearing better: the scuffing of his feet on rocks, the running water, and, as he crouched a few yards from the opening, thousands of airborne bugs.

It was the huge pit, the one he'd looked down into, the one with the eroded passage under the road into the adjoining pit. It had been mostly in shadow before, but now the sun was higher and he could see more than the suggestions of shadows. Even from back in his passage he could see that the trail into the tank no longer bridged the tunnel between the two pits—it had collapsed, mostly intact. The far side, leading back toward the cedar grove, tilted down, not quite a cliff, but a very steep climb.

The swarm of bugs was the largest he'd ever seen, but it was oddly unfocused. Usually, when bugs swarmed, they made a beeline for the site of their crushed fellow, rising up in the air initially, and then cutting through anything in their path. This was more like confusion. The vast cloud was spinning counterclockwise, and it brought to mind the swirling funnel of bugs descending into the hole made by the not-steer.

Kimble edged forward again. With that many bugs in the air, he thought there couldn't be any left on the ground, but he was wrong. The bottom of the pit glittered like the thieves' cave in *The Arabian Nights*, like piles of coins—copper and silver, bronze and iron—only the coins in Ali Baba's cave didn't shift and crawl.

The very bottom of the pit, just downslope from Kimble, was a dark pool of water, silty gray, with only the lightest sheen of oil. It was being fed by the icy water rushing around his ankles. Before, when he'd looked down into the pit, he hadn't seen any water and, even though his glimpse had been brief, he should have—it was reflecting the sky clearly.

So maybe it wasn't there before.

Which certainly would account for some of the swarm, displaced by water. Kimble felt sure, though, that some bugs had to have been crushed when the trail collapsed.

Every experience he'd ever had with flying bugs told him to find a hole and hide in it, but he wanted to know what happened to Pierce and his captors. The bugs that were flying were at least ten feet above the ground. Kimble cautiously stood, ready to drop and spin the minute a bug headed his way.

The collapsed trail overlapped the edge of the pool near its far end and Kimble could follow his own little cataract down to where it dropped over a ledge and splashed a few feet into the water below. Looking at the shore, Kimble could see lines of calcium marking where the water level had been in previous times: up from rains, down with drought. He was very cautious as he stepped into the greater pool. He didn't want to find some piece of metal eaten jagged sharp by the blind mouths of bugs.

The water was not as cold as the stream had been, but cold enough. Near the shore the bottom was very irregular, but as he walked out it became smoother—rubble, gravel, and silty sand forming a slightly bumpy aggregate. It deepened as he went, so he skirted the edge, far enough out to avoid the ragged rubble, but still no more than waist deep.

His lips were dry and he was thirsty, but he would have to be severely parched before he tried the water he was wading through; at least it gave him a bug-free path. He felt better in the water. If the swarm above dropped, he would, too, lowering himself into the water.

A few bugs had settled on the collapsed trail, but the fissured earth and grass stretched over whole sections of intact limestone substrata, dropped in situ. The collapsed dirt and rock leading up to the trail was a challenge, sliding down a foot for every two gained. Kimble made it halfway up before a seemingly solid ledge dropped out from underfoot and he slid all the way back down to the water's edge and then fell over backward. The water hit his torn ear and he made an inarticulate roar, deep in his throat, without opening his mouth.

"What was that?"

Kimble, about to splash forward to attempt the ascent again, lowered himself slowly back into the water, and crouched until he was neck deep. He wasn't sure whether to go completely under, hiding, or stay up and keep his sight. The thought of putting the cut underwater again was enough to tip the balance.

It was Deacon Rappaport and Ronson. They still had Pierce, too, hands still tied behind his back. Ronson was bleeding from his mouth—a pulped lip, it looked like. Rappaport's pristine uniform was disarrayed, but he was otherwise intact. Ronson had one of the gyro rifles and he was holding it against Pierce's back. They came closer to the edge. Pierce and Ronson both walked hunched over and, at first, Kimble thought they'd been injured, perhaps their backs or hips, but then he realized that the bugs were buzzing overhead and the men were closer to them than Kimble was. Rappaport walked upright, smiling, as if the bugs were a million miles away.

"And see what I said? *Behold, I will deliver thine enemy into thine hand, that thou mayest do to him as it shall seem good unto thee.*" He frowned at Ronson and tapped his arm. "Straighten up, man. This isn't *our* plague. *In righteousness shalt thou be established: thou shalt be far from oppression; for thou shalt not fear: and from terror; for it shall not come near thee.*"

Kimble shuddered. *The man's insane.*

"He's the bastard who blew up the rifles! That didn't happen by accident!" Ronson did straighten up, but Kimble had the feeling that it was more about anger than faith. Ronson raised the rifle and shifted his aim from Pierce to Kimble's head. "Which eye, Deacon?"

Deacon Rappaport stepped over to him and faced away from Kimble. He must've imagined he was speaking privately, but the curved wall of the pit beyond focused the sound. It was as if he was whispering in Kimble's ear. "No! We have questions for him. We must know who he works for and what he has told them." He turned around, crooked his finger in a come-hither motion at Kimble, and said in a loud voice, "Come on up, young man. I assure you, Brother Ronson could hit a fly at this range. And you wouldn't want us to hurt your friend, here, would you?"

Kimble didn't trust himself to speak, but he tried anyway. "*Thou shalt*"—he emphasized the "t," almost making it a second syllable—"*not bear false witness.*"

Rappaport dismissed this with a wave of his hand. "And when the devil tempted our Lord in the wilderness he *also* quoted scripture."

Kimble's fear faded under a wave of anger. "I'm not the murderer. I'll believe you when you let him go."

Rappaport looked offended. "*You* dare to judge *me*?"

"Think you're the chosen one, do you? I can't quote the Bible as well as you, but I do recall something about false prophets. You really think this is your promised land?"

"Soon, yes." He gestured overhead at the bugs buzzing through the open space and covering the walls. "*And there came a grievous swarm of flies into the house of Pharaoh, and into his servants' houses, and into all the land of Egypt: the land was corrupted by reason of the swarm of flies.*"

"I read Exodus, once. Your people are in bondage? I'm not seeing that. Ask the guys in the shantytown who the local pharaoh is."

Rappaport's smile faded. "Ronson, if he doesn't start moving, shoot him."

Kimble shifted back. "That will answer your questions, won't it? *Who do I work for? What did I tell them?*"

Rappaport took a sudden step back, his eyes widening.

Kimble added, "Maybe you're not the only one God speaks to."

"Deacon?" Ronson lowered his rifle and looked over at Rappaport.

Rappaport drew a ceramic knife from his belt and took a long step over to Pierce. He grabbed Pierce's hair and kicked him in the back of his knee, dropping him into a kneeling position, and pressed the edge to Pierce's throat. "You want me to let him go? How about I release him to *his maker*. Get up here!"

Kimble's stomach churned. Pierce *had* betrayed him but . . .

"Do you want his death on *your* conscience?" asked Rappaport. He pointed the knife at Kimble as he said this and Pierce, desperate, threw himself to the side, wrenching his hair out of Rappaport's grip and falling to the ground. He rolled away and Rappaport took a step after him. Pierce reversed direction, suddenly, trapping Rappaport's foot and locking his knee. Rappaport squawked and fell backward, sitting down hard. He raised the knife and slammed it, hilt down, two emphatic thuds.

Rappaport pointed back down toward the lake. "That way, dammit."

Ronson turned back to Kimble and raised the rifle again. He twitched the barrel slightly to the side and fired.

Water fountained beside Kimble's shoulder. "That was a deliberate miss," Ronson said. He slid the fore stock, chambering another round. "Next one goes into your body."

Kimble sank straight down. He heard the splash as a gyro went into the water and the bubbling hiss of its rocket exhaust for a few seconds more. He'd taken in a large breath of air, but now he blew it out, making his body negatively buoyant. He turned and pulled himself across the bottom toward deeper water.

He twisted around to his left, the way he'd come. *Maybe I can make it to the tunnel.* He ran out of breath and, rifle or not, he had to come up. He drew a deep breath and ducked. Two gyros in quick succession hit the water as he went under, one of them tugging at his shirt collar.

He didn't see any way he could make it from the shore's edge up to the passage. He didn't exhale this time, keeping all the air, but he had to keep from floating up by actively paddling with his hands. He felt around for something to grab, something to anchor him to the bottom. He went closer to the shore, remembering the tangle of material he'd waded through, his hands reaching out in front. He felt something cut the back of his wrist and he felt around carefully. It was a chunk of rebar sticking out of the silt, its end coming to the jagged point that had cut him. He grabbed it farther down, to anchor himself, and it shifted, then pulled completely free of the muck.

Damn. The recoil brought him to the surface. A gyro went through his left bicep, spinning him around. He saw the blood in the water but it didn't hurt as much as he thought it should, like someone had hit his arm with a club.

"Next one goes through your head!" Rappaport yelled.

Kimble froze. In his effort to find something to hold on to, he'd swum closer to the fallen trail, and Ronson and Rappaport had just run sideways fifty feet to close with him again. They were only thirty feet away, looking down over a ten-foot drop.

Kimble stood up, waist deep in the water, arms hanging at his sides, his hands trailing beneath the water. The entire left side of his shirt was stained red and he felt faint looking down at it. If he hadn't known where the wound was, he would've thought he'd been shot in a lung.

Ronson lowered the rifle, apparently convinced he wouldn't have to fire again. He gestured with the barrel back toward the slope where Kimble had tried to climb up onto the trail. "Come on, before you pass out from blood loss and drown. 'Cause I'm not going in after you if you do."

The cloud of bugs overhead buzzed louder and Kimble wondered if he was passing out. It seemed as if his vision was darkening, but it could've been that the cloud was thickening.

Ronson glanced up and ducked. "What's got into them?"

Rappaport still stood upright. "Faith, Brother. *The Lord shall fight for you, and ye shall hold your peace.*"

Kimble lifted his right hand out of the water and threw the rebar as hard as he could, flinging himself forward, full length, to splash down in the water. Rappaport jumped to the side and the jagged point of the rebar struck Ronson instead, stabbing into his uniform blouse under his left armpit, where it hung, tangled in the cloth.

"Hah! Missed," Ronson said, ripping the rebar out of his shirt and holding it up triumphantly.

The bugs fell on him like hail, *like locusts*, and the screaming began.

Even at the water's surface, the bugs whirled through the air, and Kimble stayed down, despite the searing pain he felt from the submerged gyro wound. He pressed his right hand against the torn flesh and lay back in the water, only his face above the surface. He took shallow breaths and tried not to pass out.

Using his feet, Kimble scooted across the shallow water, pushing himself out from under the concentrated cloud of bugs. He floated parallel to the collapsed trail back to where they'd left Pierce. There, at the base of the slope, he crouched in the water for another twenty minutes, waiting for the air around him to clear of bugs. Then it took him a good ten minutes to get up the slope without sliding back down. His head was spinning as he dropped to his knees by Pierce. The man was still unconscious but he was alive, two massive bumps on his forehead.

"Proud of yourself?"

Kimble spun around. Rappaport was climbing up the far side of the collapsed ridge, bleeding nearly everywhere, hundreds of bug cuts, and his uniform was in tatters, but he still had his ceramic knife clenched in his left hand.

He reached the top and stood, then walked forward slowly, but steadily.

"Looks like the Plague of Boils," Kimble said. "Are you sure you're the chosen one and all that? I mean, if you are, I'd seriously consider asking the Lord to go choose someone else for a while." He stepped toward the middle of the trail, putting some distance between himself and Pierce.

Rappaport kept walking. "He tests me," he said, his voice hoarse from screaming. "But my faith is strong. It's my time in the wilderness, but I will cast Satan down." He turned slightly, tracking Kimble.

Kimble shook his head. "I'm not Satan. And you're no prophet. But bring it on, Deacon. Let's see if the Lord is with you."

The Lord, apparently, was not.

With only one functioning arm, Kimble couldn't afford to be gentle and Rappaport had no idea about how to fall safely.

Rappaport thrust the blade forward, going for the gut, and Kimble spun out of the way, taking the wrist. He swept it up by his cheek, twisting and then reversed his hips in the other direction.

Kimble kept the knife. Rappaport tumbled down the scree to the edge of the pond where he huddled in on himself, cradling his dislocated elbow and keening.

Kimble cut Pierce's bonds with the knife and looked over where the bugs still swarmed near the rebar. Ronson was down and unmoving. *Guess the Lord wasn't with him, either.*

Pierce groaned and Kimble shook his shoulder, trying to revive him. He tried slapping his cheeks lightly, but the big man remained unresponsive.

Kimble eyed the steep slope up to ground level. He doubted if he could make it up, with his one arm out of commission, much less carry Pierce out. *Or Rappaport?*

He walked back to the edge and looked down the slope to Rappaport.

Rappaport looked back up at Kimble, struggled to his feet, and backed away, splashing through the shallows. When he'd gone a few yards, he turned and ran, following the shore to the far side where he disappeared into the dark shadow cast by the overhanging rim.

Let Rappaport's God help him.

He wasn't sure he wanted to climb the slope. Rappaport's men were probably still up there. They might even come down, looking for their leader. Kimble considered hiding, but it took all his remaining strength to bind up his bicep with strips of his shirt. If he hadn't had Rappaport's knife, he doubted he could've done it.

He heard movement over the buzzing, from down in the far pit, the one without a pond. Rappaport's men? Maybe someone else dropped down into the Pits by the explosion?

Whoever it was wore a broad straw hat, tattered and torn, and a long coat. Kimble didn't think he was one of Rappaport's men. He didn't have a rifle, at least, and those men had been dressed for the warmth above. Seeing the long coat made Kimble realize how cold he was, a combination of his time in the water and the blood loss. He eyed the coat covetously and a shiver that began in his shoulders traveled up his neck and his teeth chattered until he clenched them together.

And then he realized the man was strolling across the bottom of the pit as casually as one would walk down a boulevard . . . and the pit was covered in bugs.

Hallucinations? From the blood loss?

The man came on and when he reached the broken slope leading up to the collapsed trail he looked up at Kimble without eyes.

Oh.

Not-dog. Not-steer. Not-mule. Not-man.

One moment the not-man stood below and the next instant he was standing on the trail looking down at Kimble. Kimble didn't think he'd blacked out, but admitted to himself it was possible.

The not-man took off its coat—not like a human would, but by withdrawing its oily black arms up into the sleeves; then the hands came forward, past the lapels and the shoulders, one, two, and it walked forward out of the coat, which fell to the ground behind. It was wearing pants and a t-shirt. It tilted its head to one side, then ripped the shirt off and wrapped it over its upper left arm. It walked once around Kimble and then dropped to its knees in front of him and cradled its left arm with its right. It hunched in, rounding its shoulders.

Kimble's shivering increased.

The not-man began shaking, too.

"No. You don't have to do that."

The not-man made a humming sound. It wasn't words, but the tone and rhythm were like Kimble's sentence.

Kimble's teeth chattered. He reached over and took the thing's coat where it lay on the ground. It smelled faintly of dried blood and there were stains on it but, when he pulled it one-handed across his shoulders, it helped.

The not-man tilted its head again and stretched out its hand and picked up the trailing end of the coat. Kimble expected it to pull its coat back, but instead, it shifted sideways, coming up under the coat right next to Kimble.

The not-man was warm. Hot, even. Like pavement in early evening after a hot cloudless day, and it was all Kimble could do not to hug it to him. He wasn't sure that he wanted to be hugged back. He wasn't sure he would survive being hugged back.

He dozed, and when he woke up, his legs were going to sleep but his pants were dry and the shivering had stopped. The not-man stirred when he did. Kimble carefully slid out from under the coat. It took him multiple tries to get to his feet, unwilling, as he was, to steady himself on the not-man's shoulder.

He bent down and grabbed Pierce's collar and dragged him a few feet toward the steep slope. He sat down suddenly, dizzy. He waited for the world to stop spinning, then pulled again, without standing, scooting with his legs and dragging with his good arm.

The not-man reached down and grabbed the collar. Kimble tried to ignore him but promptly fell over when the not-man dragged Pierce three yards in three seconds.

"Okay, then."

Kimble didn't really pull Pierce, but by keeping a hand on his elbow and struggling to get himself up the slope, the not-man kept pace with him, doing the real work, sometimes moving Kimble as well. It took over a half hour, but finally Kimble and Pierce lay on the edge of the prairie above.

The not-man lay beside them, looking up into the sky as if it, too, was exhausted and couldn't move another inch, but it lifted its head just like Kimble when four aircraft circled high overhead and dozens of parachutes blossomed.

"THE fireball and the smoke was imaged from orbit. I mean, they were looking, since Colonel Anson passed on your report, but when it went off and all those horses scattered, they scrambled the standby squads from both Texas and Eastern Colorado."

The not-man had disappeared down into the pit before the first of the Rapid Response Force arrived.

Rappaport was found, semiconscious and raving, at the far end of the pond in the "wet" pit. The Rangers brought him out strapped to a fiberglass rescue stretcher. When they reached the top and he saw Kimble, Rappaport began thrashing back and forth so violently that the medtech sedated him.

They airlifted Pierce and Rappaport out, snatching

them off the ground with a cable lofted into the air by hot-air balloon and snagged by aircraft high above. After watching this operation, they offered the same ride to Kimble.

"Do you think I'm *insane*?"

The lieutenant in charge raised his eyebrows and said mildly, "I've done it dozens of times. It's certainly a lot safer than igniting petroleum fumes in an underground tank."

The medtech stitched him up with a plastic needle under local anesthetic. Before the drugs wore off she put him in a sling, and then strapped the arm, sling and all, to his chest. "Lie down and sleep while you can. When that local wears off it won't be so easy."

The RRF captured almost half of the PAC. They were all on foot, their mounts spooked by the explosion. The members who had not been separated from their horses had ridden for Pecosito.

"Where they're going to run into Colonel Anson's men," the lieutenant said. "Funny thing about radio. Speed of light *still* faster than horses."

Mrs. Perdicaris followed one of the squads back to the stand of cedars where they'd set up temporary camp. The Rangers had been warned by Kimble not to try catching her.

"Weird thing," one of them said. "When we first saw her, I could swear there were *two* mules."

Kimble fed her some of the PAC's stored oats. He found his tack and saddlebags stacked with the PAC's equipment, but the medic wouldn't clear him to ride, so he ended up traveling back to the Pecosito Ranger barracks in one of their wagons, part of a cargo that included the burnt and twisted remains of the smuggled gyro rifles.

They wanted to put him in the barracks dispensary, but Kimble talked to the colonel and the colonel radioed the major and the upshot of it was that he was released to *Thây* Hahn and, in his own cart, pulled by Mrs. P, traveled back to the Zen Center, where they put him in a bed in the hospice.

THREE afternoons later, he woke to find Ruth sitting at his bedside. "You're not dying, are you?" she asked.

"No, Sensei!"

"Everyone else here is."

"Yes, Sensei. But not me. Not *yet*." He rubbed his eyes. "Uh, you're really here?"

Ruth nodded. "Why do you ask?"

He gestured at his bedside table, where a plastic bottle of pills sat. "Pain medication. I've, uh, actually talked to you before this."

"What did I say?"

Kimble blushed. "You shouted at me for getting injured. For not being careful enough. For playing with matches and explosive fumes. And for not feeding the chickens and dusting the *kamiza*."

There were footsteps in the hall and a familiar voice said, "I heard that!"

Thayet came to the door, gesturing to someone behind her. "In here."

Major Bentham rounded the doorway. "And did you

have a similar conversation with me? About your general stupidity?"

Thayet echoed brightly, "Stupidity!"

Kimble glared at her and she said, "Uh, things to do, people to annoy." She left.

Kimble sank down in the bed and said to Bentham, "Similar, yes. More, uh, intense, though."

Major Bentham exchanged looks with Ruth and both seemed to exhale slowly.

Ruth said, "Then I guess just repeating it all would be redundant."

Major Bentham opened his mouth, but then closed it again. He rubbed his chin. "Really? What about the *satisfaction*? I mean, I've rehearsed it and refined it every damn mile between here and the capital. Just coming up the hallway I added two more scathing phrases."

Ruth smiled. "Well, I enjoyed your last few variations, and while it was getting more flowery, clever words, I think your first version held more passion."

Kimble's eyebrows raised. "You traveled together?"

"Jeremy stopped in Perro Frio to brief me. He invited me to travel on with him."

"Yes." Bentham nodded agreement. "After last time . . . well, I just thought it would be better."

Kimble sat up and Ruth shifted the pillow so he could lean against the headboard. "You just wanted her to vent on *me* instead of you! Lujan said you were scared of her. Heck, *you* said you were scared of her."

Bentham looked sideways at Ruth and smiled. "Oh, yes. Terrified."

Kimble watched Ruth to see her reaction and was shocked to see her smile back at Bentham.

How old is Bentham? He thought back to the times Bentham had dropped by the dojo "just passing through." He pinched the bridge of his nose. *And you call yourself a spy.*

Ruth leaned forward. "Are you all right? They told me about your arm, but is your head bothering you?"

"No, no. I'm okay. When did you get in?"

"We got in this morning, just before lunch. Jeremy went off to the barracks and I had a nice talk with *Thây* Hahn."

"Yes. I just spent an hour with the colonel," said Bentham.

"Oh, good. Any news?"

"Let's see. Your friend Pierce is conscious. Good thing they lifted him out. They had to go in and surgically reduce a subdermal hematoma."

"I'm glad he's all right. He's not exactly a friend, though."

"Friend or not, he's contrite. He's confessed to trying to rob you twice and betraying you to the Public Action Committee. Not to mention embezzlement of a client's funds back in Oregon."

"I guessed about the embezzlement. In fact, that's probably why he betrayed me to Rappaport. What about the PAC? There were still some missing when I last talked to the colonel."

"A few, but we got all the officers. The whole thing is a mess. The paramilitary, the PAC—we've got them cold. Murder, arms smuggling, sedition, conspiracy. Figuring out what other members of the Church of the New Prosperity are involved is more problematic. The church is screaming religious persecution, and outside, the conservative press is publishing their talking points.

"Fortunately there are members of the PAC who are singing like birds. Did you know it was Ronson that shot Lujan?"

"Which Ronson? The one the bugs—"

Bentham nodded. "Yes. Stories are also surfacing in the community about racism and strong-arm tactics. Hell, even your friend Deacon Rappaport is talking but the man—" Bentham sighed heavily. "Between hearing voices from God above and seeing demons down in the underground portions of the refinery, he's got a pretty good shot at an insanity plea." Bentham laughed. "So, how long have you been consorting with demons? The Deacon says it's the only explanation for his downfall. Well, that and a momentary failure of faith."

Kimble tried to smile, but it must've looked odd because Ruth said, "I knew you were lying!"

"What do you mean?" Kimble said.

"It's your head, isn't it? We've worn you out with all our chatter." She stood up. "You need to sleep, I can tell."

Kimble slumped down in the bed and shrugged weakly.

"Come on, Jeremy." She took his arm in a distinctly proprietary way.

Bentham eyed Kimble with narrowed eyes as he allowed Ruth to pull him toward the door, but he paused just inside the room.

"That lecture, the one where I shout about explosive fumes and getting too close and acting instead of just observing?"

Kimble nodded. "Yes. Invisible like a ghost? *That* lecture?"

"Yeah. Well, consider it given."

Kimble exhaled.

"Also," Bentham added just before he was physically hauled out the door, "good job."

It took most of a year and several pounds of sugar but Mrs. Perdicaris finally allowed Ruth to approach, groom, and even ride her, but, for *this* trip, Kimble still sat on her back. Ruth rode a mare borrowed from the Kenneys. The horse's name was Susan, after her late mother, Suze.

For the first leg, to the capital, it was just the two of them. They stayed overnight with *Thây* Hahn and Thayet. As they were getting ready to leave, *Thây* Hahn asked Kimble, "Where is the Buddha nature?"

"Where is the cup?" said Kimble.

Thây Hahn smiled, bowed, and said, "Travel safely."

Thayet hugged him fiercely and whispered, "I'm not going to wait for you."

He squeezed her back. "I love you, too, kid. Run away from the boys until you catch them. Oh, and try staying awake through meditation."

She cried on his shirt before running into the house.

Bentham joined them at Northgate and they left the city.

"Sushi. You've got to try sushi."

"Milk shakes," said Major Bentham.

"Raspberry sorbet," said Ruth.

"Café latte."

"*Caramel* café latte."

Kimble let it wash over him. Those were the things they missed from outside. No doubt he'd find his own. "I've had ice cream and sorbet."

"Sure," said Ruth. "In the *winter.*"

Bentham chimed in. "Try it when it's hot outside."

"Try it when your clothes are drenched in sweat and the sidewalks are like griddles."

It was late August, but they traveled through one pass at nine thousand feet. Snow dusted the ground. They slept at lower altitudes but were grateful for extra blankets and warm fires. They rode at an easy pace. Kimble's flight wouldn't leave Denver for another week, and it was only a couple of hours from the barrier to the airport by the train.

There were bugs. This part of the territory was rich with old mines. Besides copper and iron bugs, there were occasional flashes of gold and silver—bugs like jewels, their glittering silicon wings flashing like sapphires.

Ruth's mount was well trained but still young and full

of energy, so she would gallop ahead and back again, to get the edge off her. During one of these exercise periods, Kimble turned to Major Bentham and said, "Tell me about the outliers, Major."

Bentham's face didn't react, but his body must've tensed, for his mount broke stride, half-turning, and Bentham took a moment to get the gelding collected again. "Classified," he finally said.

"You remember the not-dog?"

"Not-dog? You mean the dog-shaped outlier with the feral dog pack?"

"Yes, that was *one* of them. I've had other encounters."

Bentham turned his head sharply. "With the dog-shaped one?"

"No. Other shapes."

"Where? When?"

Kimble turned his head back to the road. "Sorry. Classified."

"Oh, very funny."

"When did the outliers start showing up? Are there lots of them?"

"You were making it up about the other outliers, weren't you?"

"Hell, no," said Kimble. "One of them helped me pull Pierce out of that damn pit when I had the hole in my left arm. It shared its clothes with me."

"Clothes? *What shape was it?*"

"That was the not-man."

"Man-shaped? Are you sure?"

"Well, I was losing blood. I'm pretty sure that Rappaport saw it, too, though. 'Consorting with demons.' Come on. I've more data for you. It's a two-way street."

Bentham sighed heavily. "Do you know what's different about you, Kimble? The reason I kept coming back to you with jobs?"

"'Cause I got them done?"

Bentham shook his head. "That was important, but it was because you didn't shoot your mouth off. The real wake-up for me was when Ruth didn't know about the bandits, back when I first met you. Over the years you've kept things close to your chest. For someone your age, that's unusual and valuable."

Kimble thought he could see where this was going, but he kept quiet, letting Bentham talk himself into it.

"If I tell you any of this, can you keep it a secret? Not tell *anyone*?"

Kimble was slightly annoyed. He thought he had other virtues. "Never mind. I don't really want to know. At college, of course, I'll talk about my own experiences. The various kinds of outliers I've encountered and so on. I'm sure I can give out some interviews, do a few HD appearances. Turn it into some cash."

"This is serious, Kimble. I'm not saying this for my sake but for yours. You open your mouth about the outliers, you'll end up in a DHS detainment facility so fast you'll think you've been hit by a train." He stared hard into Kimble's eyes. Then he looked away and said in a milder voice, "Besides, you already have cash. The scholarship is full boat—you even get a clothing allowance! When I was in college . . . grump, grump, you kids today, et cetera, et cetera. You going to tell me about it?"

Kimble raised his eyebrows, then licked his lips. After another few steps he said, "A Dineh told me about a not-crow. It flew but when it landed on tree branches, they bent down as if it was much heavier than a bird. Personally, I've seen a not-steer whose horns seemed to be antennae, sensing metal deeper than the little bugs could. Its feces excavated holes deep in the earth so the regular bugs could get down to deep metal. The not-mule was a duplicate of Mrs. Perdicaris, right down to the bug holes in her right ear. I saw it the same day I saw the not-man." He looked out of the corner of his eye to Bentham. "These things are not man-made, are they?"

Bentham stared ahead for a time, then said, "No. They don't seem to be."

"I heard from an ex-soldier, one who was there during the first days of the infestation, that it started near Socorro. But not at the mining school."

Bentham looked like he was sucking on a lemon. "West of there, up on the plains of St. Augustin. Did you ever hear of the VLA?"

Kimble shook his head.

"The Very Large Array. A radio telescope made up of twenty-seven dish antennas. That's where it started. The first bugs started eating them."

"No spaceship? No meteor crashing to the earth?"

"Nothing observed. But take something the size of a bug—hell, something the size of a hundred bugs—we wouldn't detect it."

"Why the secret, then? Seems like everyone thinks it was a robotics experiment gone wild. Doesn't seem like the authorities are correcting this impression."

"As far as the world is concerned, America shot itself in the foot, sending a sizeable portion of its land mass back into the Stone Age. We keep other countries away for 'safety reasons' but we're really trying to understand this before somebody else discovers how to use the technology as a weapon. Imagine a bug infestation in the middle of New York or San Francisco."

Kimble blinked. "Or Shanghai or Tehran. If the U.S. learns enough, they can use it as a weapon, too."

"The U.S. has been a victim of this technology already. We are *not* going to repeat the experience." Bentham shrugged. "Besides, the world mostly has it right. We *are* the victims of this industrial accident. It's just not *human* industry."

"So where are the scientists studying the bugs?"

"I'm relieved. If *you* haven't sniffed them out perhaps we still have some time left." His voice sharpened. "So you saw the not-mule and the not-man around the old PeCo Refinery. Where did you see the not-longhorn?"

"Albuquerque. South Valley."

"When you ran into Pritts?"

"Yeah. You see a lot of these outliers?"

Major Bentham shook his head. "Very few and only in the last five years. Maybe they were here before and we didn't see them. Your not-man is the only human-shaped one I've heard about."

"Are they studying the bugs outside the territory?"

"Bugs have been transported out in containers too tough to eat through quickly, but they self-destruct when they get beyond a certain range. This is bad since you can't bring sophisticated spectrum analyzers and other equipment *in* and you can't take the bugs *out* to the equipment. Fortunately, this applies to foreign intelligence operatives, too.

"Closest thing is a kind of radio astronomy. There are massive antennae pointed into the territory, listening to the bugs, trying to figure out how they communicate. It's sure not dancing, like bees. And now I've *really* said too much." He looked at Kimble again. "I really mean it—you talk about this and it's completely out of my hands."

"But maybe I could help! From what you say, my experience is not exactly common."

"No. You're a bit of an outlier yourself. A not-boy if ever I saw one. But do you really want to spend the next several years confined to an ultrasecret research project instead of going to college?"

Kimble reached forward and absently scratched Mrs. Perdicaris' neck. "No."

"I'll anonymize the data. I can let them know about these other forms without letting them know about you."

"Won't they push for my identity?"

"Don't teach your grandfather to suck eggs. Testimony gathered from a dying bug victim."

Ruth returned from her gallop and they dropped the subject.

For the rest of the day Kimble was quiet, only responding to direct questions. Ruth was remembering her college days, anecdotes sprinkled with bits of advice, but most of it just flowed in one ear and out the other.

Ruth finally noticed and said, "Where are you, boy? I swear you haven't heard a word I've said in the last ten minutes."

"Sorry, Sensei."

"Thinking about Martha?"

Kimble blushed. Martha was in school at UC Berkeley, not that far from Stanford. She'd written to say she'd escort him to Takahashi Sensei's dojo. "I was thinking about what my major should be."

Ruth nodded. "Ah. Are you coming back into the territory? I mean, there are certain fields that don't mix with bugs. Computer science. Electrical engineering. Metallurgy. Robotics."

"Though those technologies may not mix with bugs," said Bentham, "each of those topics applies to the *study* of bugs."

Kimble looked at Bentham, face still, looking back intently.

"Are you coming back to the territory?" said Ruth. "I mean, besides to visit?" There was an uncharacteristic uncertainty in her voice, but Kimble didn't notice. He was staring into the distance, seeing nothing, seeing everything.

Oh, yeah, I'm coming back. Just try and stop me. He blinked then and noticed the oddly intent way both Ruth and Bentham were watching him, waiting for his answer.

"Yes, Sensei. I'm coming home."

Ruth nodded and then galloped the mare. The wind

must've been sharp in her face, for when she returned she was still rubbing at her eyes.

"Study hard. And I don't just mean aikido, right?"

"Yes, Sensei."